Anonymous Sender

Anonymous Sender

MICHAEL S. McDOWELL

A Scholarly Resources Inc. Imprint
Wilmington, Delaware

Scholarly Resources Inc.
104 Greenhill Avenue
Wilmington, DE 19805-1897

Library of Congress Cataloging-in-Publication Data

McDowell, Michael S., 1966–
  Anonymous sender / Michael S. McDowell.
      p.   cm.
  ISBN 0-8420-2589-8
  I. Title.
PS3563.C35937A82   1996
813'.54—dc20   96-3535
                                                        CIP

For my mother, my father, and Nene

-1-

MICHAEL O'CONNEL APPROACHED his office building at 7 A.M. Grasping his empty briefcase tightly in his left hand, he walked briskly, gazing ahead with an affectation of purpose. His shoes clicked on the sidewalk with a steady meter as he arrived early for another day in his self-imposed cover as an executive with weighty matters on his mind and important things to do. Wearing a specially tailored suit to encompass his broad shoulders, at fifty-eight he was still an impressive figure. Pale, beefy hands poked out from his jacket. His face was big, solid, and square-jawed. Below his brown eyes a flattened and crooked nose revealed a man for whom life had been a contact sport. He looked like a heavyweight prize-fighter long past his prime but not gone entirely to seed.

He glanced at the seven-story grayish-white concrete building as he considered his commute from Alexandria and wondered what ordinary civilians imagined the headquarters of the Central Intelligence Agency looked like. He thought about the placid Potomac, progressing lazily toward the bay nearby, and supposed that at this hour there would be at least one single scull still sweeping downriver. He often watched the oarsmen from a landing in Georgetown on Sunday mornings while drinking a cup of Starbuck's café mocha and reading the *Washington Times*. He reached across his chest instinctively with his right hand as he approached the statue to feel for the plastic-coated photo ID and building pass that were clipped to his left breast pocket.

The timing of this check, if subconscious, was not accidental. The statue bothered O'Connel. Bronze had been cleverly cast into a likeness of our nation's first spy, Nathan Hale. Despite the manacles binding his hands behind his back for all eternity, Nate's burnished alloy face gazed serenely at the burly man as he passed. O'Connel strode by, inwardly shamefaced, pondering once more against his will what storms might have been brewing in the spy's mind as the rope was placed around his neck. Did he seethe with hatred for the loyalist cousin who had delivered him up to his enemies? Did he know or wonder about his personal Judas? Did the fibers of the rope chafe his throat? How did he feel about broken faith? Or betrayal?

Entering the lobby, O'Connel relaxed into the routine of access. The morning watch officer set down a stained coffee mug to accept the ID card. He verified the photo on the front against O'Connel's face and scanned the bar code on the reverse, logging him into the building. Taking another sip of coffee, he consulted the computer screen over the rim of the mug to see that there were no holds on the big man and then waved him through. Proceeding to his suite in the back of the building, O'Connel reflected again on the statue. He could not see it from his office window, for which he was grateful, because Nate reminded him of someone from his past.

O'Connel considered his job to be infinitely interesting but essentially unimportant. He managed what amounted to the CIA's library and museum, known as the Historical Intelligence Collection. It contained thousands of books about espionage, fiction and nonfiction, in all languages, which he cataloged meticulously to pass the time. He had even set up several glass cases that displayed memorabilia of his profession including secret inks, codebooks, wires, bugs, Minox cameras, and "sterile" or untraceable weapons. He enjoyed the library and had made the most of it, even though he realized that his assignment was meant to be a punishment.

O'Connel had been "exiled to the Collection," as he referred to the incident in his mind, in November 1986 shortly before Ronald Reagan acknowledged covert arms sales to Iran. The two events were not unrelated. During October of that year, he had been running four Special Operations Division contract men, former Green Berets, out of a base near Danlí, Honduras, in support of the Contras. His superior, Robert Littlejohn, had gotten a whiff of the upcoming scandal and opted for preemptive damage control. His terse message for O'Connel over satellite link-secure KYX scrambler was only ten words: "Blackout. Drop in-country assets. Clean house. Return in twenty-four hours." Roughly translated, what Littlejohn meant was, "Leave your contract men in the field. Cut communications. Cut supplies. Clear out and return with remaining operational funds to Langley. Destroy all records. Every man for himself. Return in twenty-four hours."

O'Connel had considered his orders for ten minutes before deciding to disobey. Alone in his base camp, he radioed for the contract men to return immediately and began to sanitize the compound. He burned the records in a discarded oil drum, dousing and stirring the soggy ashes into the ground to ensure destruction. He stacked the Chinese AK-47s neatly in an outlying shed along with forty thousand rounds of ammunition and left them for the rebels to find when they returned. He counted thirty-nine paces directly northeast from the northwest corner of the shed and dug six feet into the ground to uncache a Ziploc bag containing his passport and operational-fund cash reserves. Then he waited. It was three days before the last man marched into the camp.

Langley's Central American section was in an uproar, but O'Connel didn't know that because he was maintaining his blackout. He had hacked his communications gear into pieces and buried each section separately six feet deep in the moist jungle soil. When the last contractor arrived, the five men piled into an aging Toyota Land Cruiser and began the trip to Tegucigalpa. O'Connel gave them their unauthorized outbrief during the fourteen-hour trek.

Once in the capital, they made their way to the Honduras Maya Hotel, where O'Connel secured five luxury rooms with cash from his operational fund. The men cleaned themselves up, bought new sets of clothes, and visited the Casino Royale downstairs while their controller made reservations. The next morning, at Toncontín International Airport, O'Connel watched the four contractors board the Taca International Boeing 737 bound for Los Angeles. Each had in his pocket a severance check for $30,000 drawn on O'Connel's personal account. Two hours after his men had departed, the charter flight was ready.

The plane was a decrepit de Havilland DHC-2 Beaver. The green and white float/wheel combination on the amphibious utility aircraft was worn to bare metal in many points from the all-terrain landings that it routinely made on its northern cannabis run. The pilot was a sullen mestizo who never asked questions, or even spoke to his passengers, as long as the destination was clear and the fee was up front. After two landings en route for refueling, the Beaver touched down on the tarmac at Georgetown, Grand Cayman Island. It was then ninety-six hours that O'Connel had been off the Agency's radar screen.

O'Connel took a taxi from the airport to the Bank of Credit and Commerce International. Presenting his identification to the manager and signing left handed as he had when he originally laundered the money into BCCI from First American Bank, he wired $120,000 to his personal account at Chase Manhattan. With the unauthorized severance checks covered, he returned to the airport, where he directed the pilot to fly to Cayman Brac.

On Cayman Brac, O'Connel spent the rest of his operational fund securing a luxury room at the Divi Tiara Beach

Resort. He spent the next three days drunk in the private Jacuzzi, eating room-service meals and considering what he was going to do after the Agency fired him. On the sixth day after he had gone missing, a clerk in the Office of Finance discovered the wire transfer. On the eighth day, they found him and whisked him back to northern Virginia.

The inquisitors who came to interrogate him at Camp Peary were at a loss. After administering three polygraph examinations in the course of five days of questioning and conducting a four-hour psychiatric evaluation, they could detect no evasion or deception. He had done exactly what he told them he had done. They understood the what, when, who, and how. The missing element was the *why*. He was unhelpful on this point. It infuriated them. O'Connel heard them outside his door discussing his aberration.

"There's no indication in his file," a husky, grating voice that O'Connel identified as the lead interrogator said, "of any tendency in this man toward this kind of action. Not a word. Twenty-five years in the field"—there was an exaggerated exhalation—"and not one fucking hint that he could be a loose cannon."

"Perhaps the stress was just too much?" The voice of the psychiatrist faltered, ending the sentence as a question.

"Totally unrepentant. Steals 120 Gs." The lead man's voice fell into hoarse mumbling.

The psychiatrist answered, "Uhm . . . so, what do you want on his file?"

"Littlejohn wants you to recommend retention with transfer to a nonoperational post. He is going to stick him down a hole, but one of *our* holes. He doesn't want this guy writing any books about money laundering and life on the run just now. He thinks that Congress is about a gnat's ass from sticking a probe up our collective derrieres again."

O'Connel smiled faintly at his reflection on the glass of his code-and-cipher display. Almost a decade later, the memory of the escapade that landed him in the Collection seemed mildly amusing. The *why* which they had sought so vehemently lay hidden in plain sight behind the glass. He looked at it and felt a twinge, like touching a now familiar wound and gaining a warm masochistic pleasure from it. That sheaf of combustible cellulose represented his only enduring regret and shame. Like the statue, it symbolized heroism on one side and betrayal on the other.

It was nothing extraordinary. Known as a "one-time pad" in the vernacular of the trade, the grid of random numbers and letters printed on the fragile paper represented a truly nonrepetitive key for the enciphering of text. This simple device provided an essentially unbreakable cipher. Each page in the tablet was used for the transmission of one message and then destroyed. The pad in the display case was half used. There was only one other like it in the world. It was presumably destroyed on Cuba in January 1963.

-2-

August 8, 1963, Key West, Florida

HE SAW LAND IN THE LATE AFTERNOON and adjusted the sail. It wasn't much of a sail. Hastily rigged, the stolen bedsheet was folded to form a triangle and tacked clumsily upon a makeshift broom-handle boom and short 4x4 mast. The mast was held unsteadily in his dinghy by a confused tangle of cotton rope nailed to the bow and stern and tied to oarlocks on the port and starboard sides. A primal howl rang out across the water. It took him a moment to realize that the howl was coming from him. He had been under way in his unlikely craft for three weeks. He was home.

Martin Gore turned his gaze skyward. His eyes were such a distinct shade of blue that they seemed otherworldly. Slightly under six feet tall, wiry, with sinewy arms and legs visible through his now ragged clothing, he seemed to be nothing special, perhaps a refugee. Dressed properly and standing on a street corner, he would attract no notice. One had to see him in another environment to understand what he was. One had to see his head cocked sideways for a millisecond, like a startled deer, noting the sound of a bolt being driven home half a mile away or observe his nostrils flare at the faint smell of cordite to understand his hypersensitive wariness. Then one had to see him disappear into the jungle like a wraith to realize that he was not like most other men.

Martin noted that only insignificant wisps of clouds, like stretched cotton, separated the sea from outer space. He wasn't thinking about the heavens, however; he was considering what he had decided was his last operational posting. It had ended ignominiously and had not begun with much promise, either.

He pictured the unlikely guerrilla, Dr. José Artime, holding the .45 against the temple of the luckless nurse. Tears had streamed down her cheeks as Martin and his men ransacked the medical station. They had left her tied to her chair, otherwise unharmed, and absconded with the bed-sheet sailcloth, cotton rope, a broom, gauze, and penicillin. Dr. Artime was a practical man. Penicillin and gauze could come in handy for the struggle. Gore smiled at the sky. No, this had not been like the movies. Not at all.

His posting had begun in September 1960. Special Operations Division pulled him out of a rebel camp on Sumatra where he was an adviser. He had been dubbed with the career-enhancing label "experienced in denied areas." He had a good suntan. Conversational Spanish was in his file, and Gore had done well in the otherwise abortive effort to overthrow Indonesian President Sukarno. His greatest notoriety had come from a night when he had stolen the guidance system for a SAM-2 from a warehouse in Jakarta. Gore had planned the raid, which involved hijacking a boat and scaling an electric fence over a pyramid of empty beer cans with Dwight Tower, another Agency adviser. Their prank was still saving the lives of B-52 crews as late as 1972 over the jungles of Vietnam. The Air Force had designed countermeasures into the aircraft based on the missile parts Gore had stolen.

He was flown out of Indonesia on a Civil Air Transport B-26. The pilot told jokes and stories throughout the flight to hide his nervousness. The aviator's best friend was halfway through a four-year prison term on the island of Java. His friend had been shot down in an identical aircraft in May 1958, much to the embarrassment of the Eisenhower administration, which strove mightily to deny everything. Out of courtesy, Gore did not tell the pilot that they would likely be executed if caught with the missile guidance system he had helped the loadmaster strap into the rear cargo area.

Back in the Western Hemisphere, Gore attended a three-week briefing and training refresher at "The Farm" near Williamsburg, Virginia. Then he was off again on a Caramar-owned C-46 buzzing to Guatemala. In Guatemala, he had schooled Cuban exiles in conventional and unconventional warfare, just as he had been trained at "The Farm," at the heavy-weapons school in North Carolina, and the Intermountain Aviation School in Arizona. Silencer-equipped machine guns, homemade explosives, soapbox napalm, demolition, evasion, and escape techniques were demonstrated, displayed, and taught by Gore, one of Special Operations Division's best up-and-coming "animals." That was what the East Coast establishment desk jockeys were pleased to call the unconventional warriors.

Gore was landed on the beach twenty miles south of Jagüey Grande, Cuba, at 2 A.M. on April 3, 1961. As the 1930 vintage cigarette boat's twin 450-horsepower engines coughed on low idle to nose the craft away from the beach, the SOD man was already making his way inland. His mission was to assess possible guerrilla potential and the likelihood of an uprising after the invasion by the exiles. He was disappointed to find the

Cubans weary and without spirit. A majority were even satisfied with the Castro regime, inasmuch as it didn't affect them one way or the other. Gore doubted that a revolt would materialize unless the invasion secured a beachhead and subsequently enjoyed military success. He relayed this information in compressed transmissions to the ships offshore, moving and reporting. Prior to the invasion, he had assumed that he would be instructed to mine the three roads and railway bed that led to the Bay of Pigs. He had also assumed that they would connect him with the underground so that he would have the men to accomplish this task. He was wrong. Still, Gore moved and reported. On April 13, transmitting from a position near Cienga de Zapata, Gore suggested that SOD send in a few more operatives. With explosives and a few trained men, the Cuban security forces' trek down the roads to the bay could be slowed considerably. No reply was sent, and the invasion went ahead as planned. Well, not quite as planned.

Gore cared little for politics. He knew, nevertheless, that John F. Kennedy had been elected and inaugurated in his absence. Ike had been content, more or less, to allow the CIA to take whatever actions, including covert ones, it deemed necessary in the fight against world communism. It occurred to Gore that Kennedy might feel that the State Department, not Allen Dulles, should make and execute foreign policy. This invasion had been planned and, for all practical purposes, executed under Eisenhower's administration, and the fact that a different man was now the commander-in-chief disturbed him. On the ground, however, misgivings are liabilities, so he did his job. Moved. Reported. Established a rapport with the natives. Asked to be connected to the underground.

His nebulous suspicions were realized. Just after midnight, on the morning of April 17, Gore watched five Liberty ships disgorge fifteen hundred exiles into the bay. At dawn, paratroopers dropped from C-46 and C-54 Agency-owned aircraft. Air support failed to materialize, with the exception of a few hopelessly outgunned B-26s and ancient P-51s. He watched Soviet-made JS-2 and T-34 tanks rumble down the roads he had wanted to cut. He saw the invaders halted and crushed before they had made it twenty miles inland. Two days later Gore sent his last transmission, buried the radio, burned his one-time pad, and, using only a compass, swam into the sea to meet a converted minesweeper dispatched to pluck him and a SEAL team out of the water.

Six months later, after filling an administrative post at the old naval air station at Opalocka, Florida, he was recalled to Langley and briefed on the Presidential Memorandum of November 30, 1961, by his new controller, a young man named Michael O'Connel. President Kennedy had decided that he wanted Dulles out of the CIA and Castro out of Cuba. General Lansdale took charge of the special working committee and by April 1962, Martin Gore, armed with a new code name, Beowulf, was back in Cuba. He was one of eleven agents put on the beach to raise and train a new guerrilla army on the island nation.

By July, Martin had raised an army of about 250, if it could be called an army, in the Pinar del Río area of western Cuba. He had firmly established his replenishment routes from sea and gone to work. In December, he heard the government broadcast about the trade of the Bay of Pigs prisoners for $53 million in supplies from America. This broadcast was particularly annoying to him because he had bombed that radio station four days before. He had hoped not to hear it back on the air so quickly. Martin did not know that General Lansdale had put it in writing that there were no "U.S.-sponsored acts of sabotage." His orders were to maintain a low profile, make everything deniable, and stay within his "visibility parameters." They said nothing about "studying the possibility" of sabotage. They said to sabotage.

In January, with no explanation, he received the order from his controller to destroy his communications equipment and make a coastal rendezvous. His inquiries received no replies. At the appointed hour, he scanned the beach from an outcropping of rock in the surrounding foothills. The boat that drove its hull into the sand was not the custom-designed, high-speed General Dynamics craft that O'Connel had told him to expect. It was a Cuban patrol boat. Several security troops in uniform and two men in civilian clothes stepped onto the beach. "DGI," Gore muttered to himself. He replaced the binoculars in his satchel and returned to the hills.

It had not occurred to him that he might have been betrayed. He simply chalked up a tiny victory to the KGB-trained Dirección General de Intelligencia officers, who had almost captured him. They were talented, trained, and dedicated. They were just like him. He had mentally tipped his hat to them from the hills. From that time forward, however, his guerrilla band seemed to attract more than its fair share of attention from the security forces. His every move was dogged as his band fought a running, retreating skirmish that forced him inland. His supply lines from the sea were cut. His force was disintegrating as the peasants decided to lay down their arms and go back to their villages. It seemed as though the Cubans knew his operational area, his supply routes, and the number in his band. He was tracked as though his hunters possessed a dossier detailing his training and likely tactics. The enemy seemed to be one step ahead of him everywhere he went.

Martin had been ordered to leave. He began to work on finding his own way off Cuba. His top priority was to protect the remnants of the organization he had created. Before he had been inserted, he had memorized the identity of several suspected members of the provincial executive council of the People's Revolutionary Movement, or MRP. From the list in his mind, he chose Dr. José Artime. A little after midnight, on a cool February evening, he slipped quietly through a sugarcane field into the outskirts of Santo Espindato, a tiny town located five miles inland from Viñales in western Cuba.

Gore scaled the wall of the doctor's villa and hurried across the compound. He climbed the archway above the wrought-iron gate that opened into the central courtyard. Like a cat, Gore crawled onto the roof and crept along the perimeter of the courtyard, looking into every window until he located the bedroom. Dropping noiselessly onto the ground and stealthily moving into the house, the SOD man walked softly toward the doctor's room. Entering, he unsnapped the top of his sheath and withdrew the dark, ten-inch blade of his K-bar knife. The physician awoke with that blade against his Adam's apple.

Gore put a finger to his lips and motioned to the sleeping figure next to Artime. The doctor's wife had not awakened. Artime nodded his understanding and carefully extracted himself from the covers. Martin allowed him to rise, deftly stepping to the side, keeping the knife at the man's throat and a hand locked on his shoulder. They walked together like that to the kitchen. The SOD man sat Artime in a wooden upright chair before the table and took a seat opposite. The doctor, in boxer shorts and an undershirt, looked at Gore curiously through dark brown eyes.

"I am Beowulf," Gore said simply. He was watching the doctor carefully. He saw no hint of recognition cross the man's face. The doctor did not reply. Gore continued, "I understand that you are part of the underground, the MRP." Again, the doctor showed no recognition. Gore rubbed his hand on his forehead and ran it down his face to his beard, sighing. "I trained some of your people at Opalocka and in Guatemala," he said with exasperation. Still no recognition. Gore stood and ran his knife into the sheath forcefully. "Damn!" he said in a loud whisper and turned his back. He heard the ripping of tape, and when he turned around a .38-caliber revolver was on the table in front of the doctor. Gore realized that it must have been taped under the table, probably pointing at him the whole time. Artime did not lift it or train it on Gore. He just let it sit there on the table in front of him, a nonverbal indication that the two were now on a level playing field.

"I keep them at various points around the house." The doctor shrugged, tugging at his mustache and motioning for Martin to take a seat. "Certain avocations require that a man take precautions."

Martin sat. "I have a force. I need to turn it over to someone."

"I know who you are, Mr. Beowulf. Did you think that we believed a fairy was blowing up bridges and radio stations? Our mole said that you were dead." The doctor said this quietly, simply, as if it were their secret.

"Dead?" Martin repeated. He dropped his eyes for a moment and then met Artime's gaze. "Why am I supposed to be dead?"

Artime's eyes softened. He almost appeared sympathetic. "It is like this, Mr. Beowulf. The Cuban secret police have a mole in our exile organization in Miami. The KGB has a mole in the CIA. He is low level, insignificant. But he can see and hear things. Between the two, the DGI knows many things about you and the other ten operatives. We have a mole in the DGI. He is high level, so we hear and see it all." The doctor paused for a moment, giving Martin a chance to make the connection. "It seems that your successes were becoming an embarrassment to someone in your capital. The mole talked of 'exceeding visibility parameters,' something of that nature. A deal was struck. Your controller was directed to lead you into the hands of the DGI. In return, the DGI would not parade you before the television cameras of the world. They would just shoot you. Castro gets to sleep at night and not dream about your bombs. Kennedy gets to sleep at night and not dream of the international embarrassment."

Martin remembered the patrol boat and the soldiers. He had assumed that the rendezvous boat had broken off after seeing them. Now he realized that he had missed the meeting that had been planned for him. His eyes fell, and he felt a chilling numbness. He didn't know what to say. When he spoke, he attempted to smile nonchalantly, but his voice was the cracked whisper of a bereaved man. "Well, I'm not dead. Will you take my force and help me get out?" That was how he ended up in a makeshift sailboat off the coast of Florida in August 1963.

His boat capsized in the surf. He left it and swam the rest of the way to the beach. The sun was setting in the west as he crawled on hands and knees onto the warm sand and kissed it. His body was burned and dehydrated. His buttocks and feet were covered with salt-water sores. His hair was long and disorderly, and his beard was rampant. He lay on the beach for several hours deciding what he was going to do next as the sky got darker and the stars became visible. No one had seen him. No one had asked him for a passport. No one had asked him who he was and what he was doing there. That was when it occurred to him. Now he could start over and be whoever he wanted to be.

July 30, 1969, Delta Flight 223, Hawaii to Oakland

CORPORAL OSCAR PARKS felt sorry for himself. Only thirty minutes ago, before he had boarded the aircraft, everything seemed right with the world. Overall, he had every reason to be happy on his flight home. Drafted out of a steel mill in Bethlehem, Pennsylvania, in 1967, he had spent the last two years in a whirlwind of training and combat. He had survived twelve months "in-country" lugging around his squad's M–60, shooting, being shot at, and generally cursing what to him was a totally inexplicable situation. Vietnam was behind him now, however. His girlfriend, Mary, had even waited for him. Loyalty such as this, while popular in the movies, was sufficiently rare in real life to be notable in its absence among the rest of the men in his platoon. Every last one had eventually received a "Dear John" letter or had been killed, or both. In one week, Oscar would be out of the Army. In two, he would be wed. Now he just had to put up with the guy in the next seat for six hours, for Oscar found himself in a dilemma understood by travelers the world over: being trapped for a period of time with a talkative, insufferable ass.

As the plane began to taxi, the man next to him turned and tapped on the black patch over his right eye. "Name's Dan. Green Beret, man." He shook his head in the affirmative as if expecting some disagreement. "Fuckers are processing me out. Got one little frag, man, right in the middle of my eye. Had to come out, see?" He lifted the patch to show the empty socket. "I still got one good eye." The man clenched a fist in his lap and continued. "Hell, Admiral Nelson only had one eye . . . or was it one leg? Anyway, he was good enough to kick some Frenchie butt and save the British's ass from de Gaulle . . ., no it wasn't him, but it was some frog. This is bullshit, man. Bullshit."

Oscar was listening with only half of his mind. He was uncomfortable with the man's disfigurement, feeling the guilt of the unscathed. He answered, "Yeah, man. That ain't right."

"Hold out your hand." Oscar stretched out his hand. He had no idea why he had obeyed. The man reached into his left pants pocket and placed something carefully into the corporal's palm. "Look at that, man. Got it in the hospital in the Philippines."

Oscar didn't realize what it was at first. It was round and smooth like a large marble, but a little lighter than a marble of its size would be. There were some letters etched in the glass, but they didn't mean anything to him. It wasn't English. He turned it over in his hand, started in shock, and almost dropped it when a brown pupil stared back at him. He quickly handed it back to the Green Beret, who was laughing.

"Yeah, man!" he howled. "It's my new eye! Cool, huh?"

"Yeah, it's cool." Oscar hoped that the man in the next seat would drop the conversation.

"Did you notice the writing on the back? I had it done special by a guy in the machine shop at the air base." He seemed overly enthusiastic to the corporal.

"Yeah, I saw it. Just couldn't read it. Ain't English, is it?" Oscar really just wanted to forget the glass eye.

"Alea iacta est."

"Huh?"

"It says, 'alea iacta est.' Means 'the die is cast.' "

"Oh," Oscar said.

"You know, Caesar said it when he crossed the Rhine or . . . uh . . . well, some fuckin' river before he kicked some butt and became emperor. It's like, inspiration, you know. I just remembered it from high school when I was lyin' in my bed and decided to get it on my new eye. Took Latin."

"Great," the corporal said noncommittally, thinking that they were finally at the end of their conversation. There was a momentary silence. Oscar began to pat his pockets in search of a diversionary tactic. He found his pack of Marlboros, tapped a cigarette out, and lit it. Exhaling, he felt comfortable behind the wall he had thrown up.

"Yeah," the Green Beret said excitedly, failing to notice the wall. "They got this new thing where they can attach your fake eyeball to the muscles in your head, so it moves with the other eye. You know what I said to that?"

"No." Oscar blew smoke in the man's face. The act was unintentional, a subconscious expression of his desire to be left alone.

"I said, 'No fuckin' way, man.' I want to be able to take this bad boy out and admire it."

"Great," Oscar said again and looked at his watch with an exaggerated gesture. He had only five hours and fifty minutes to go.

4

FOR THE PREVIOUS TWELVE MONTHS, Clarence Dubose and his buddies had talked of little else but returning to "the world." Their conversations had centered around fancy dinners, reunions with wives and girlfriends, or nights out on the town. They had dreamed of loved ones waiting at airport terminals to welcome back their heroes. It wasn't until Clarence boarded the airplane in Hawaii that he realized that there wasn't going to be anybody waiting for him on his return. He was going to walk off the flight and cross the tarmac at the Oakland airport and then. . . . Well, he had not considered that yet. Back in the jungle, just getting back to "the world" was enough. That single goal was sufficient when you were sweating in a foxhole, being bombed by your own Air Force and mortared by the enemy in what was once French Indochina.

Now, standing alone in the terminal, like a toy soldier with two Purple Hearts, he was suddenly at a loss. It wasn't a bad experience. Spoiled, cowardly college students who understood rights but not responsibilities had not spat on him. No one in the concourse had shouted "Baby killer!" What struck him was the simple indifference with which he was regarded as he made his way to pick up his seabag. He was a United States Marine. He was a combat veteran. He had survived two tours in Vietnam. He wanted to shout to the entire terminal, "Look at me! I'm home! Look at me, damn you!"

His family was poor and it was too far for them to come to greet him. This he understood. But there were people here who could at least smile or nod, if not at him, at the uniform and all that those in uniform had done.

Clarence was an intelligent man. He knew that the war was not popular. In fact, he agreed that the war was wrong. He had seen the South Vietnamese, content to let someone else fight their battles, having to be pushed out of helicopters in LZs during "joint" operations. The South Vietnamese had disgusted him and the war had sickened him. That was not the point. The point was that his country had asked him to serve. He had been taught in a Southern Baptist church in rural South Carolina that "if a man compels you to go with him one mile, go with him twain." He had.

It was unusual, now that he was back in the Lower Forty-Eight, that he suddenly missed the camaraderie of his little unit in its daily life-and-death struggle. He remembered severed arms and legs, sucking chest wounds, and watching the corpsman crumple and fall, shot in the back as he dragged a dead man out of the fray. He remembered smoking Lucky Strikes over bad coffee and the smell of the jungle. He remembered the heat, the sweat, and the stench of death. Vignettes played in fast forward as he stood there.

He blinked his eyes to drop the memories. As he picked up his bag and headed to the taxi stand, Clarence realized that he didn't know where he was going, either that afternoon or for the rest of his life. Opening the rear door of the taxi, he told the driver, "Sir, please drive me to a quiet beach." Clarence reached back to his wallet to see how much money he had with him. "Can you get me to someplace like that for five bucks?"

The driver draped his right arm across the top of the front seat and turned, looking over his shoulder at the young black Marine corporal. He smiled broadly, revealing a missing front tooth. "This one's free, sonny. I was in the Corps myself. Corporal. Inchon."

Clarence looked at the man, who seemed too old to have ever been like him. He really didn't know how to respond. "Well." He was lost.

"It was a hell of a mess over there, too, and nobody gave us no ticker tape when we came home, neither. How's the shoreline over at Alameda?"

Clarence smiled back. "Never been there."

5-

"WE DON'T HAVE ENOUGH FUEL to make it to Mexico," the flight attendant told the man.

He sat back in his seat, regarding her through sunglasses. She could not see his eyes. His hair was brown and thinning but neatly cut and parted on the left. His suit was also brown. He wore a white shirt and a blue tie. In his lap was a briefcase. In the aisle next to him lay a twenty-one-pound laundry sack filled with twenty-dollar bills and two sport parachutes, which the FBI had kindly provided him at the Seattle-Tacoma Airport. He rubbed his chin with his left hand as if thinking. Then he spoke quietly, mildly. "Well, then, tell the captain to fly south toward Portland and then fly west toward Reno. Maintain altitude less than ten thousand feet, keep the flaps down, and fly less than two hundred miles per hour. Have you got that?"

"Yes," the flight attendant replied.

"Repeat it," he said. She did.

The man then got up and grasped her arm, gently pushing her down the aisle toward the cockpit. Outside the door he motioned her inside. "Do not come back out. I have no further instructions. Keep the door shut."

The flight attendant nodded her assent calmly and went into the cockpit, closing the partition behind her. Satisfied, the skyjacker walked back to the rear of the plane. Picking up one of the two sport parachutes, he inspected it and placed it on his back. Securing the straps and checking himself over, he walked to the rear of the Boeing 727 and unlatched the rear boarding ramp. It took it several minutes to lower completely, and he used the time to finalize preparations for the jump.

He set the briefcase on the seat next to him and opened it up. First he removed the hijack note that he had given to the flight attendant five hours before. After she had read it, he had taken it back. No reason to give the FBI a handwriting sample or any fingerprints. Extracting a silver Zippo lighter from his pocket, he lit the corner of the note. When it had burned half-way to his fingers, he walked to the rear entry ramp and threw it out. He returned to the briefcase.

The two red cylinders that he had shown the flight attendant were a bluff, not a bomb. They were Eveready 9-volt batteries painted candy-apple red with a can of model paint. They would power the personally modified electric under-wear that he had put on under the brown suit. He lifted his trouser legs one at a time and strapped the batteries into pouches sewn onto the long underwear. He screwed the connection wires onto the battery terminals and felt the heat from the underwear, which caused him to sweat immediately. He was no fool. He was not going to jump into a subzero, two-hundred-mile-an-hour wind and die of exposure before he hit the ground.

He began packing the money into the now empty brief-case. It all fit, except for one packet. He tossed it back in the laundry bag and flung them both out of the back of the plane. That $5,800 packet would be found by hikers in 1980. The wind howled as the door came completely open. The three-engine 727 was bouncing, and the pilot was obviously having problems with the rear ramp open and the flaps down. He looked outside. Below him was the wilderness of the Cascade Mountains. The government had trained him how to survive in the wilderness, how to live like an animal, kill with no con-science, and, significantly, how to jump out of airplanes. It had sent him off to do its bidding and then, when he took that "one little frag," the government had retired him on a pittance of a pension and left his health in the care of the indifferent savages who called themselves the Veterans Administration. He had been entitled to come out of it all with a stake; and since they hadn't given him one, he felt compelled to take it. Ten thousand twenty-dollar bills would set him up satisfactorily in life. He took off his sunglasses and tossed them out the back of the plane. They whirled into the darkness.

If anybody had been there to look at him, they would have noticed that his right eye wasn't exactly the same shade of brown as his left and that whereas the left eye moved back and forth examining his surroundings as the iris twisted shut in response to the removal of the sunglasses, the right eye didn't move at all. At ten minutes after eight in the evening, he leapt into criminal history, holding his briefcase close like a businessman on a crowded train.

November 24, 1971, Portland, Oregon

WHILE THE FRONT PAGE of the Portland *Standard* covered the successful skyjacking perpetrated by D. B. Cooper, the third page carried a short article:

> Associated Press, Woodland, Washington State—Andrew Lloyd Oliver was released from custody today after an investigation ruled that the death of his brother was accidental. Oliver had been held overnight by authorities in connection with the shooting of his brother, Todd Scott Oliver. The two brothers had been on a hunting trip near Lake Merwin when Todd Oliver's firearm, a twelve-gauge Remington pump-action shotgun carelessly left against a tree, fell and accidentally discharged. Andrew Oliver carried his brother almost five miles from the scene in an attempt to get medical treatment. Sheriff's deputies investigated the scene, corroborating Andrew Oliver's account. He was released this morning. The Cowlitz County sheriff was not available for comment. He is involved in liaison with the Federal Bureau of Investigation and a U.S. Army detachment from Fort Lewis in organizing the manhunt for D. B. Cooper. Todd Oliver is survived only by his brother.

November 12, 1985, Washington, DC

"JACOB, ARE YOU CERTAIN?" a large ebony-skinned man with a massive face and sagging jowls asked quietly in a bass voice. It was the voice of a man well used to authority. There was a touch of fatherly sadness in it.

"Yes, sir. I had a lot of time to think while I was in the hospital." The younger man's skin was pale from the hospital stay. He had dark brown hair, which bordered on black, cut short, and gray-blue eyes. He was pudgy and unhealthy looking.

"Jacob, I think that I understand what you are going through. God knows that was quite a mess, but, well, frankly," he frowned and allowed his dark eyes to bore into the man on the other side of his desk, "you are one of the best. This is a noble profession, Jacob."

"Thank you, sir. There was a time when I thought that what I did made a difference. I don't think so anymore. It doesn't have any meaning for me anymore." The pale young man looked at his feet.

"Would you be willing to take some leave and reconsider? No one expects you back so soon, anyway."

"No. Thank you, sir, I have made my decision. I doubt that you will have very much trouble replacing me."

"We will not be able to replace you." The older man stood and offered his hand. "Good luck, Jacob."

Jake took the hand and shook it formally. "Thank you, sir."

December 19, 1985, Landover, Maryland

IT WAS JUST AFTER MIDNIGHT on Thursday evening when Aaron Rosen approached the office park on foot. His own mother would not have recognized him. Dressed in a filthy green Army-surplus field coat, torn blue jeans, and scuffed black combat boots, Rosen swung a limp canvas duffel over his shoulder and stumbled on the pavement. His short black hair was covered with a wig of shoulder-length greasy blond locks. He had affixed a scruffy blond mustache to his upper lip and rubbed a charcoal-and-Thunderbird solution into his face and hands to achieve the desired odor and appearance. Gargling the wine and dousing his jacket with it, Aaron became just another forgotten homeless veteran for a night.

Approaching the eastern face of his building, he could see that the parking lot appeared to be empty, except for the green Ford conversion van parked directly in front of the two-story brick structure. The van was his, so it seemed to pose no threat. Aaron lurched drunkenly along the sidewalk, surveying the lot and building entrance. He reached a tree at the corner of the property, sat down heavily, and pretended to arrange himself for sleep. This act was for the benefit of the yet undetected watchers he felt should be there. For the next thirty minutes he scrutinized the building and was beginning to disbelieve his luck. No guards had been posted. Just as he was deciding to move on the front door, he saw a flash in the mirror of the van. It dimmed into a little red circle as the lighter went out and the watcher in the front passenger seat puffed on his cigarette. *The bastards put someone in my van!* Aaron thought bitterly. *Sometimes those guys are pretty good.*

He lay very still for another half hour, playing possum, cautiously scanning the surroundings and considering the events that had led him there. Fifteen hours ago he had driven his equipment-laden van into the lot and parked it in front of the building containing his suite. That morning the other tenants had watched the short, thin, dark-haired version of Aaron in a blue sports coat and tan trousers retreat into his office. They had secretly wondered how he stayed afloat in his computer analysis business without keeping anything like normal office hours. Often, he would come into the building to begin his day as they were leaving for the evening. Many days he would not appear at all. When he was in the office, he spoke to no one and would spend the day behind a locked door. Occasionally they had heard the rhythmic whine of a dot matrix printer, the mechanical tones of a modem, or the metallic clank of a file drawer closing. They had noted that Aaron never left, even to go to the bathroom down the hall, without locking his door behind him. Rumors had abounded. The night janitor mentioned that he had seen the analyst carrying a stack of well-thumbed locksmithing manuals into his office one evening. A real estate agent down the hall, who spent most of his spare time reading true crime books, had suggested that Aaron was in the Witness Protection Program and that the office and computer job were all an elaborate make-work front set up by the U.S. Marshal's Office. Many agreed that the little man looked like Mafia to them.

On that Thursday morning, the gossiping floor had been treated to an unexpected show. Five big, clean-cut men strode in at 9:30 and flashed golden Treasury Department badges as they walked around examining the placards on the suite doors. Two of the men knocked and were admitted into Aaron's office. Muffled shouting was heard behind the systems analyst's door. The other three Treasury agents went upstairs to talk with the owner of the building. Fifteen minutes later, Aaron was escorted out between two of the men. At 3 P.M., two uniformed "locksmiths" appeared in a compact car that should have raised some skeptical eyebrows and replaced the locks on Aaron's suite and the front door of the building. The owner reprogrammed the touchpad alarm for the ground floor under their supervision and they departed. He informed the other tenants confidentially that the Treasury Department had taken the systems analyst away for questioning about a counterfeiting operation and would be back at 6:30 the next morning to impound his records without disturbing the office routine. Tongues had wagged for the rest of the day.

Aaron had known that they weren't Treasury agents. The agents had known that he wasn't a systems analyst. What the building owner hadn't known was either of these facts or that real Treasury agents would have handed him a warrant for the search-and-seizure and taken Aaron's files immediately or placed them under guard until such a time that they could do so. The owner thought of himself as a good citizen and fell easily for the ruse of the lock and code changes. The fact of the matter was that the need to "shut the analyst down" had arisen only at 7:30 that morning. With only an hour's notice, in times of increasing belt tightening, oversight, and budget scrutiny, the CIA's domestic black-bag section didn't have a truck available Thursday morning to take away the files. One would be available on Friday morning.

Aaron had spent the rest of Thursday in a safe house in Oxon Hill, Maryland. He was asked questions for several hours about jobs he had undertaken in the last two months before they got to the point.

"GSA found a bug on the phone in Senator Allen's conference room this morning," the stately gray-haired questioner, who identified himself only as Robert, said.

"Ah," Aaron acknowledged, finally understanding the hasty abduction.

"Did we authorize that, Mr. Rosen?"

"Well," Aaron swallowed nervously. "Not directly."

Robert breathed deeply, as if controlling his temper. "Mr. Rosen, bugs are bad. They are bad for us. We are not the FBI. We have no charter for that. Bugs lead somewhere. I trust that this one will not lead back to us." He frowned. "Tell us about the bug, Mr. Rosen."

"Well, first off, I just want to point out that it was you guys who wanted to know what was going on in that subcommittee. . . ."

Robert cut him off. "Dammit, I know that! You were supposed to burgle his aide's house, not wire the senator for sound!

I need to be able to tap-dance on this and I don't want the Agency to be the only one without a chair when the music stops!" he finished, agitated to the point of mixing his metaphors.

"There wasn't anything at the aide's house," Aaron said.

"The bug, Mr. Rosen."

"Well, it's more of a tap than a bug."

"Describe it!" Robert ordered.

"Direct crosswire keep-alive on the spare line. It's one of those phones with a hold and five lines." Aaron paused for a moment to think. "The spare line is wired to the handset, bypassing the hook switch and keeping the installed microphone live at all times. The transmitter is a Mitsumi K-series and it is located in the baseboard behind the phone jack. It transmits at 161 MHz, police band." Rosen smiled coyly. "I, uh, 'appropriated' that particular piece of gear from the offices of Gawain, Robertson, and Anderson, a law firm that works with several PACs funded by Japanese interests. I think you might find other similar equipment there."

"Blame it on the Nips' lobbyists," Robert said quietly to himself as he rose to leave the room, apparently happier than he had entered it.

When the gray-haired man had gone, two other agents informed Aaron that his contract was terminated and told him: "Since you will no longer be needing your files, we will take care of the destruction. We'll have a man drop off your van on Monday after we have gone over it." By the time they had left him on King Street, near the water, in Alexandria that evening, Aaron was already formulating a plan. He needed some of those files. They were his portfolio and the tools of his trade. He had spent his entire adult life as an investigator and burglar, in and out of prison, compiling the contents of those folders. They were full of contacts in cities all over the country, names of trusted sources, floor plans, blueprints, confidential circuit diagrams for security systems, the latest in lock design, telephone trunk cable layouts, phone numbers for underground suppliers, and innumerable other essential items that only time in the trade could generate. What was in those buff folders couldn't be replaced by any amount of time in a library. He would never become Allan Pinkerton's twentieth-century rival without them. He had decided right there on the sidewalk that if the Agency had not already acted, he would have his files back.

The homeless version of Aaron Rosen rose from the ground drunkenly and began to shuffle down the sidewalk, continuing past the target building. He took a left at the first intersection and proceeded around the block to the opposite side. He could see the western face of the two-story brick complex behind a Hardee's. The premises were separated by a six-foot hurricane fence. He sidled up behind the menu sign for the drive-through and examined the back of the building. He had memorized the layout long ago and was merely checking for any surveillance in the rear. Patience is a virtue that no burglar remains at large without, so once again he waited for thirty minutes, until he felt confident that the only watcher was located in his van.

The sole window which opened on the ground floor was located in the bathroom at the north end of the building. The rest of the windows at ground level were solid and permanently set. They were not alarmed, but breaking one in order to enter would be alarm enough for the man out front. Cutting one of those windows, while relatively quiet, was also unsatisfactory. He wanted to leave the premises as he had found them. It would not do to have the Agency hounding him because it knew that he had been back in the building. Aaron began to check his pockets to verify his tool inventory while mentally rehearsing the first step. With this completed, he flew into action. He was over the fence in one fluid motion and around to the north side of the building in under fifteen seconds.

The bathroom window was a three-by-four-foot single-piece unit with the hinges at the top. It swung outward at its base and was contact alarmed, like the front door, at the bottom of the frame. Aaron took from his pocket a paper-thin, semirigid plastic strip with a notch cut in the end and a piece of eight-pound-test clear fishing line heat-welded smoothly inside the notch. He slid it between the frame and the window, urging it gently through the ninety-degree turn at the inside lip, pulling it to the right and pushing until the end appeared on the other side of the glass. He moved it toward the center of the frame to the latch. Gently tugging in the line, he curled the plastic hook upward until it landed on the latch. With a quick jerk, the window was unlatched. He released the line and removed his tool, replacing it in his pocket.

A bead of sweat dripped from his nose onto the windowsill as he began the next phase. The alarm on the window was the inexpensive but effective contact-break variety. Aaron was thankful that the system was not a more sophisticated version that would detect a change in impedance. He would have needed some of the gear in his van for that problem. From another pocket he produced a plastic bag, from which he removed another tool. It consisted of two malleable copper-foil plates, four inches long with a three-foot light-gauge insulated copper wire soldered securely to one end of each plate. He placed the plates together and slid them between the frame and the window. Holding his breath, he carefully nudged the plates between the existing contacts. No alarm sounded. He exhaled slowly and released the tool, freeing his hands momentarily. From the breast pocket of the jacket he removed a piece of waxed paper, on which were affixed four strips of silver duct tape. Aaron placed this in his mouth and grasped it between his teeth as he began slowly to open the window outward, holding the copper contacts firmly in place to keep the alarm circuit whole. With the window open three inches, he placed his right hand between the two copper plates, holding them in place with splayed fingers. The left hand removed the tape strips from the paper in his mouth and secured the plates to the contacts.

Releasing both hands, he took a deep breath. No alarm. He opened the window the rest of the way outward, until the connecting line had no slack in it, and pulled himself over the sill and into the bathroom. He sat there for a moment adjusting to the darkness inside before opening the door and walking softly down the hallway toward his office. Pausing near the foyer in the center of the building and looking around the corner through the front doors into the parking lot, he could see the watcher's cigarette burning in his van. He dropped to his belly and snaked across the carpet to the other side to reach the door of his suite.

He inserted his key into the lock. It would not enter the face plug. *Changed it already, huh?* he thought. He dropped the key back into his trouser pocket and extracted a small leather case. It contained four instruments which looked like dentist's tools. Aaron selected two. The first was an L-shaped piece of wire with a finger grip on one end, a tension tool. The second was a straight length of hard wire with a triangular-shaped tip, a diamond-head pick.

The burglar dropped to his knees, bringing the lock to eye level. He ran the pick into the lock and pulled it out slowly, determining that the lock contained five pins. He inserted the tension tool and applied slight pressure to the core in a clockwise direction. Reinserting the pick and feeling his way to the last pin, he began the process of gently lifting each pin up to its shear point. Aaron grunted in satisfaction as the last pin fell into place and the tension tool turned the cam. He opened his door and entered the room.

Four hours later, the homeless vet did not exist any more. The formerly limp duffel bag was now stuffed with most of the burglar's important files and lay in the center of his living-room floor. The wig, mustache, and clothes were piled haphazardly in a corner. Aaron, freshly showered, lay dozing on the couch. He had left the building exactly as he had found it, minus, of course, his files. The rest of the folders, filling four large filing cabinets, were left behind for the Agency. They belonged to it anyway, the terms of a two-year contract.

Aaron had always made a habit of recording his work notes in a unique symbolic shorthand. There was nothing of value, really, in the coded raw notes detailing who was sleeping with whom and who was really working for whom in the Washington power structure. The Agency had the real product already and wouldn't be able to make head or tail of his elaborate notations. The *Washington Post* would not be able to decipher them either, and he expected that that was what actually concerned them. To him, the night had been nothing extraordinary, just another few hours spent perfecting his skills in a profession that he loved.

9

January 1986, Oakland, California

CLARENCE SURVEYED THE SCENE with disgust. In the almost sixteen years since his return from Southeast Asia, he had not changed substantially in appearance. He had obtained a college degree in criminology, courtesy of the GI Bill, and had joined the Oakland Police Department. He was a big man, standing over six feet, with broad shoulders, strong arms, and meaty hands. Tonight he looked tired. His bloodshot brown eyes were watery. His broad nose and ebony cheeks glistened with sweat. This was his third scene of the day.

There were three young black men lying on the floor. Their red and black Chicago Bulls jackets were riddled with holes. Their blood pooled together along the scuffed floorboard and soaked into the dingy carpet. He noticed a gold chain around the neck of one of the men. He was lying face upward with his arms flung wide, in a pose of crucifixion. On the chain was a tiny golden replica of an Uzi submachine gun. The bare Sheetrock walls were peppered with holes. Two of the young men had drawn handguns to defend themselves, and the weapons lay on the floor next to their owners.

Clarence's partner, John Allen, pulled a handkerchief from his pocket and bent toward the floor. His badge swung out like a pendulum from the chain around his neck as he turned one of the guns over. "I thought so."

"Thought what?" Clarence asked, unconsciously fingering the badge on his belt.

Allen pointed. "This one is automatic. They can be modified for that, you know." He was talking about the TEC-9 "ugly gun" at his feet. "Thirty-six rounds. Nine millimeter. Fully automatic when modified. These things are made by Intratec in Miami. Cuban exiles. There ought to be a law." He shook his head. Clarence made no reply. The two detectives moved to the next room.

In the bedroom behind the initial scene was a dead black female. She had apparently been hiding and had taken her wounds through the thin wall. She lay crumpled in a disorderly heap like a rag doll. Her head lolled to one side and the blood was still damp on her temple at the exit wound. On a cheap dresser were stacked three kilo bricks of cocaine hydrochloride. They were wrapped in brown paper marked with red and yellow dots. In a drawer were several Ziploc bags of marijuana, smaller two-by-two Ziploc bags of rock cocaine, and two film canisters containing powdered heroin. Apparently, the three men were dealers and the ill-fated woman was a customer who had chosen an inauspicious time to go shopping at their drug supermarket.

Outside the house, just beyond the perimeters of the yellow police-line tape, two local television stations had set up mobile camera units. Young, neatly dressed reporters cheerfully described the carnage for the viewing pleasure of those citizens at home on their living-room couches. The cameras and lights shifted to follow the coroner's van as it made its way through the police lines and backed up to the front door of the housing-project apartment. Clarence had never understood the press's macabre fascination with the meat wagons.

Inside the house, two police photographers circled around the bodies, cameras flashing. They were capturing the scene, layer by layer, as evidence was removed. Detectives bagged and labeled everything, as if in a hurry, which, in fact, they probably were. Clarence reflected that this scene was likely to be replayed several times over the course of the weekend. Drugs. Guns. Young people. People with the seeds of greatness within them. Fine, strong bodies. Fine, unused minds. Kids. Kids who should be walking down shady college thoroughfares discussing the Socratic method or linear regression, but who instead shot chemicals into their veins and killed one another. Clarence felt the burning in his stomach as his ulcer began to bother him. He walked outside with his partner in tow.

As he reached the police line, the reporters moved toward him, shouting, "Lieutenant Dubose! Lieutenant Dubose! Would you make a statement, sir?"

Clarence turned to face the cameras, his eyes squinting against the harsh lighting, "There are four victims. Three black males and one black female. It appears that automatic weapons were used. Names will be withheld pending notification of the families." He continued to walk toward his unmarked car.

"Lieutenant, is there drug involvement?" shouted a high-pitched nasal voice. Clarence would have recognized Jane Nieman's screech anywhere. She was not the OPD's favorite reporter, repeatedly writing negative articles that seized upon every tiny bungle within the Department and more often than not took officers' quotes out of context in order to grab headlines.

Clarence turned again. He paused, his face circumspect. Then he responded in an official monotone. "Preliminary findings at the scene seem to indicate drug involvement. I am unable to tell you any more until we have completed a thorough investigation." He got into the driver's seat, inserted the key into the ignition, and flipped the lock on the passenger side. As Allen got into the car, Clarence reached over to the glove compartment and withdrew a bottle of Pepto-Bismol. He unscrewed the cap ceremoniously, upended the bottle, drank about half of it in one gulp, replaced the lid, and flipped the box shut. Allen watched without comment.

"You know what I wanted to tell Nieman?" Allen said.

Clarence grunted a wordless reply as he reached into his pocket for his pack of Marlboros and began shaking one out.

"The one that asked about 'drug involvement.' " Allen imitated a nasal voice when he said the last two words.

Clarence lit the cigarette and inhaled. He looked at Allen and exhaled as he turned on the ignition. "No, but I can guess."

"God, Clarence! You know I hate it when you do that," Allen said.

"What?"

"Blow smoke in my face." He coughed for effect. "I wanted to tell her, 'Hmmm. Four people gunned down in cold blood with automatic weapons. Well, what do you fucking think, you dumb bitch?' "

"That's why I do the talking, John," Clarence said. He secretly acknowledged that he had wanted to say that, too.

"Clarence?" Allen asked in a more serious tone.

"Yeah, John."

"Do you ever think that you've had enough of this?"

"Well," Clarence paused, taking another drag from his cigarette, "yes, I suppose. What do you mean?"

John Allen motioned toward the glove box. "Well, what I mean, Clarence, is that this is killing you. It's not worth it. This is taking years off your life."

"Yeah, I know, John," Clarence acknowledged.

"Those years are coming off the middle, Clarence. Not off the end, if you know what I mean."

-10-

January 31, 1986, Fox County, South Carolina

HE HAD BEATEN her again. She sat in a tight ball with her arms wrapped around her knees, rocking on her haunches. The trailer was quiet and dark. A sliver of pale moonlight penetrated the darkness to settle on her. Tears streamed down her face, which was a mass of bruises and cuts. There were bruises all over her body beneath the loose-fitting sweatshirt and blue jeans. Her red hair was damp and disorderly. Strands stuck to her wet cheeks. She didn't bother to brush them away. He had held her head in the toilet and flushed over and over. He had laughed at her gasps for air and then become angry when she would not confess.

"You fucking whore!" he had screamed at her, pulling her head above the porcelain rim by her hair so that she could hear. She had gasped for breath before he plunged her face back beneath the water. "I know that you are sleeping with that son of a bitch! I know it! Ya hear?" The water would swirl down the drain as he flushed again, and she would breathe.

There was no use in denying any accusations that he laid on her. He was drunk. It seemed like he was always drunk. He was always vicious. She would say nothing and endure. There seemed to be no other alternative. She knew that it wasn't supposed to be this way. When she had met him, he had seemed so perfect with his wavy dark-brown hair, cleft chin, and ready smile. He was working at the 7-Eleven, but that was only temporary. No one could see his true worth. He hadn't graduated from high school because he was above formal education. One day he would hit it big just because of who he was, not because of who he knew or some phony degree. That was the way he had seen it. That was the way Diana had seen it, too. He was Mr. Right, but somehow it had all gone wrong.

They had been married in the county courthouse two years ago. Diana had been nineteen and Glen, twenty-four. It had been fine for a few months. They had purchased the trailer and accumulated furniture at rummage sales and flea markets. Then he had lost the job at 7-Eleven for stealing from the till. "They are all just hypocrites and liars," he had said. "They weren't paying me what I was worth, so I took it." At this point, Diana started to have doubts about Glen's worldview. Then he had begun to drink in earnest. He never held a job for more than a few weeks before he was sent packing for theft, absenteeism, or incompetence. He fell back to his standard line: "The bastards are just jealous of me. They don't want me around."

The beatings had begun about a year ago. Somehow, he had gotten the notion that Diana was the one who was undermining his success. She was holding him down. She was sleeping around. None of this was true, of course. She was probably the only other person in the world who still retained any belief in him at all. The rest had written off Glen Wells, and, until two months ago, Diana had stood with him against them all.

That was when she had formed the plan, after another particularly vicious beating. During the day, Glen ordinarily slept off the effects of the previous evening, in lieu of working at whatever job he was temporarily holding down. Diana began using this time to drive into Columbia and read books at the library, ranging from Jack Hill's humorous *The Perfect Murder* to William Tichey's *Poisons, Antidotes, and Anecdotes*, with true crime stories filling in the gaps. She was studying. She needed to accomplish her task properly. There could be no hitch. If he changed, if the beatings stopped, and if he stopped drinking, she would not do it. But Glen had not changed.

It was 3 A.M. He had passed out on the couch. Diana went into action. As she walked outside, she heard the spring creak on the screen door. The door slammed close behind her, but she disregarded the noise. She had read that a loud knock drew less attention from neighbors than a furtive one. It had struck her as true. This crime would all be by the book.

Once outside, she rolled the boat trailer up to the back of Glen's truck, a primer-green 1959 GMC. When she had finished hitching the fifteen-foot aluminum bass boat to the truck, she walked to the rear of the mobile home and began to ferry the iron Weider weights, which she had hidden behind the cinder-block pilings, one by one to the boat. On the last run she noticed the front of the pickup as if for the very first time. With its wide-set round headlights and broad curved bumper, it appeared to be smiling at her.

Diana reentered the house and grabbed Glen by his ankles. She pulled him off the couch, and he landed with a thud on the floor, shaking the trailer. He did not awaken. As she had suspected, he was out cold. That morning, as he had slept off another drunk, she had added a bit of insurance. She had ground up sleeping pills and Valium taken from her mother's medicine cabinet and dropped them in his bottle of Jack Daniel's. He would not wake up. She originally had planned to use knock-out drops or chloral hydrate, like in a James Bond novel, but had found that it was virtually impossible to obtain and difficult to make. She had made do with what she could get.

She dragged him down the wooden plank steps that led to their home. His head bounced against every tier. His body cut a neat swath across the gravel driveway as she dragged him to the truck. She had never realized how heavy he was. After considerable effort, she finally tumbled him into the bilge of the boat and returned to the cab of the truck. She started it up. The engine turned and whined for a full minute before catching. Diana calmed herself by remembering the normality of it. "It is typical, common, regular, usual. People often go fishing at 4 A.M.," she said, as a soothing mantra. It was true. They did.

As she drove, she thought over the calculations that she had made. She had read that it took an anchor equal to the victim's weight plus an additional 150 pounds to keep a body down. Otherwise, it would eventually bloat and rise to the surface. This piece of information had come as a shock to her. In the movies a cinder block or dive weight would do. She had 350 pounds of weights in the bass boat and hoped that this would suffice.

She drove to a private ramp about two miles from their trailer. She backed the truck down until the tailpipe was under water and vigorously latched the emergency brake. With the engine still idling and the tail pipe bubbling, she floated the bass boat with its cargo. She drove the truck back up the ramp and parked it nearby. Returning to the vessel, she stepped carefully into the bow and gingerly made her way to the stern. She started the outboard electric trolling motor and backed the vessel away from the shore. A moment later, turning the motor and shifting it into forward thrust, Diana pointed the bow northward toward deep water.

An hour later the boat was drifting near the dam. She was tying the last knot. All 350 pounds of iron were now fastened to Glen Wells. They were tied to his ankles, wrists, around his neck, and two weights around his waist. Diana looked at his face. It was peaceful in sleep. His brown hair was disorderly and his cleft chin had dropped to open his mouth. He breathed in a slow rhythm. To remind herself of why she was doing this, she raised a hand to her face and touched one of the bruises on her cheek. She winced, set her jaw, and hopped over the side. The shock of the frigid water made her gasp and become suddenly alert. She seized the starboard gunwale and began to rock the boat. In a few moments she had managed to overturn it and he was gone. She had not imagined that he would sink so quickly.

Diana righted the boat and motored back to the cove. Stepping unsteadily onto the concrete ramp, she then pushed the boat back into the lake, to drift where the wind might take it. As she walked home, the enormity of what she had just done struck her like one of Glen's blows. When she arrived at the empty trailer, she collapsed into a sobbing, weeping heap. The tears were not for him, however; they were for her. An anonymous poem that she had memorized in high school came into her mind. She began to recite the portion she remembered like a chant, a prayer to God that He might understand, if not forgive:

> Because tomorrow's ground is too uncertain for plans,
> And futures have a way of falling in midflight.
> And you learn
> That you really can endure . . .
> That you really are strong.
> And you really do have worth.
> And you learn and you learn,
> With every goodbye, you learn.

The following morning she managed to keep her nerve and went to work at her mother's beauty shop as if everything were normal. She wore heavy makeup to cover the bruises. This, too, was normal, as were the hushed conversations about her brutal marriage, which would come to an awkward halt when she entered the shop, the bell on the door dinging behind her.

The next day she reported that her husband had gone fishing and had not returned. Sheriff Branson headed up the search. They found the truck and the boat, but Glen Wells was never seen again.

-11-

February 22, 1986, Interstate 26, South Carolina

JACOB WEICHERT sat behind the wheel of his truck. He had changed since leaving Washington. His dark-brown hair had grown long, and he had taken to tying it back in a ponytail. He kept his face clean shaven. Regarding himself in the rearview mirror, his gray-blue eyes looked back at him clear, content, alert, and well rested. He had also lost weight and, while still slightly hefty, was making progress toward regaining the lithe athletic form of his college days. His stomach was becoming hard and his arms thick and strong.

Since resigning, he had driven roughly twenty thousand miles. He had zigzagged his way across the United States, sleeping under the stars when it was warm and driving south and sleeping in the back of his pickup when it was cooler. This freewheeling travel had been something new to him when he had first left Washington, something that he had only seen in the movies or read about in Kerouac's *On the Road*. He now knew that he would never again hesitate to clear his mind by taking a nomadic walkabout out of some misplaced fear of the unknown. In his travels, he had seen at least a little of every state in the Lower Forty-Eight, but he still hadn't settled on a place that he would like to call home. Also, he hadn't decided at all what he would like to do with the rest of his life. He had left one career behind him and never intended to pick it up again, although there was no reason why he could not. He had a good reputation and good credentials, but he had lost interest in being part of the rat race, with alarms to wake him up and liquor and Johnny Carson to put him to sleep again. It no longer held any meaning for him.

Something had happened to him in that hospital, and he didn't think that it was bad. He had experienced a silent insight, a momentary enlightenment. Being shot had somehow brought everything into focus. In a way, it was probably the best thing that had ever happened to him. He had realized that, like Thoreau had written, he had been leading a life of quiet desperation, working a job which his undergraduate idealism had told him would be satisfying. He had learned that the ideal and the real were often disturbingly different.

He had been different, even at Yale. While his classmates had pursued good grades and were courted by Wall Street and Fortune 500 companies or went on to law or medical school, Jake had rowed crew, graduated, and gone his own way, wooed by no one. Although not an outstanding oarsman, he had nevertheless been an initiate of that ascetic order. It was a cult of the mind and body, and it shaped him forever afterward into a person who was capable of the single-minded pursuit of any goal. It also inculcated him with a certain idealism, which led him to the choice of his former career. Jake's problem now was that he did not have a goal, per se. He wanted to find a place and a goal. And he wanted that place and that goal to be quiet.

One thing that he did know was that he loved the water. He had strayed so far away from his true identity that he had almost forgotten this. While living in Washington, DC, he would occasionally see a single scull on the Potomac and feel his stomach tighten with familiarity and fraternity. He would feel at peace with the oarsman on the water for a fleeting moment. And then he would forget it. Things like that were easily dismissed in the routine of his daily life, until he was shot.

Jake had narrowed down where he might live to San Diego, San Francisco, Puget Sound, the coast of Maine, the Chesapeake Bay, Charleston, Savannah, or the Gulf Coast of Florida. As he headed up Interstate 26 away from Charleston and toward Interstate 40 in North Carolina, he began to think about these places that he had visited. In the back of his mind, he thought that he might look at the mountains in North Carolina and see what was there. Perhaps a secluded mountain lake.

The sun was beginning to set, and it was his habit to find a place to park his truck and cook up some dinner on his propane stove before it got dark. He took the next exit off the freeway, "ROUTE 60 IRMO." Jake had never seen or heard of an "Irmo," so he was content to pass through this oddity. He kept driving and saw a sign which announced the Irmo city limits but never noticed anything in particular about the town. Soon he was passing over a dam on a two-lane road. The dam was about a mile and a half long, and when he looked to his right out the passenger window, there was the most spectacular sunset he had ever witnessed. Orange and red fingers streaked over blue water, and indigo and violet reflections beamed off the clouds. He saw islands outlined in the distance and realized that he had stumbled onto one of the most beautiful places in the world.

He had made a decision before he realized it. He kept driving until he ran into Highway 378, which continued along the southern shore of the lake. A sign told him that he was leaving Lexington County. The next sign was the size of a billboard with three-foot-tall letters: "WELCOME TO FOX COUNTY, BIRTHPLACE OF LEROY JOHNSON!" Jake figured that Leroy Johnson must be some sort of local historical figure.

Another mile down the road he saw a sign which read, "JOE'S BAIT AND TACKLE SHOPPE." A green billboard with gold-painted letters and a silver-inlaid line drawing of a fish struggling on a hook, it looked like a sign for a British pub. He decided to pull into the parking lot. The dirt lot ran down to a concrete boat ramp, and Jake could see from where he parked that the shop straddled a beautiful little cove off the lake.

The shop was a two-story cabin with a front porch that faced the road and a back porch that faced the lake. Jake walked around to the back and found three men sitting there regarding the cove and smoking cigars. It was apparently some sort of ritual. Jake asked, "Is one of you Joe?"

The man in the middle replied, "Well, that depends on who wants to know, young man." He squinted at Jake from underneath a Kenworth baseball cap.

"Well, I do," Jake answered.

The man in the middle replied again, "Well, then. Now it would depend on why you want to know." He puffed out smoke, which temporarily masked his face under the bill of his cap.

"Well, sir, I was wondering if I could be your apprentice. I'll work for free if you'll show me how to run a bait and tackle shop, and give me a place to sleep, like maybe that shed back there." Jake pointed toward a shed next to the boat ramp.

The man's face changed. His eyes opened wide from their squint. He waved smoke out from under the bill of his cap and looked at the men on either side of him with an exaggerated turn of his head from right to left. The other two men were attempting to suppress smiles as if there were some private joke and Jake was the butt. Finally, he replied, "Well, young man. Leave us in peace and come back in the mornin'. I'll talk to you then."

-12-

March 1986, Cauca Valley, Colombia

THE LAB WAS A RARITY. It combined cultivation, paste production, base production, cocaine hydrochloride extraction, and transportation into one site. These processes were more commonly divided and separated among facilities across Peru, Bolivia, Colombia, Panama, Venezuela, and Brazil. All-in-one facilities were vulnerable, but, as luck would have it, the Colombian police had not yet located the dirt airstrip or the fields or the huts for the workers. They had not noticed the dormitories, the dining hall, the office, the storage facilities, the radio antennae, the generators, or the filtering and drying equipment. They had not observed the truckloads of chemicals winding their way into the mountains to service the site. A single-engine Piper Cub screamed down the runway, beating the air to rise into the sky with a load to be dropped near Buenaventura. They seemed to have routinely overlooked that, as well. Perhaps they were too frightened of Santiago Valens to see anything at all.

The most abundant harvest took place after the rains in March, and broad-faced peasants were carrying bushels of leaves up the slope toward a complex of concrete-block buildings. Pale green leaves with rounded apexes shifted in the baskets as the workers dropped them outside one of the buildings. Domingo Valens watched and walked inside.

He was there against his brother's wishes. Santiago always kept himself at a safe distance from his operations and thought that his brother should do the same. Everyone knew that they were traffickers. But the authorities were aware that kingpins came in various stripes, and, while not beyond violence, Santiago Valens was a saint compared to Pablo Escobar. He hadn't killed any judges or blown up any newspaper offices. As a consequence, the local authorities left him alone and sighed in relief that they did not have an Escobar in their backyard. When the police spoke about Santiago and his gang, they were *los caballeros*, the gentlemen. When the police spoke about Escobar and his gang, they were *los hampones*, the hoodlums. Despite his good image in the community, Santiago kept his distance from it all. He moved frequently, keeping his location a secret. The only common thread among any of Santiago's retreats was that every one possessed an outdoor, westward-facing terrace. Santiago was discreet, distant, disinterested.

Domingo was different. He liked to dance until dawn in Cali and take women to his bed. The only reason that he was not imprisoned was the informal goodwill of the police, who assiduously avoided nightclubs he was known to frequent. Domingo was also a student of the business. He liked to get his hands onto the process. He wanted to improve quality, distribution, marketing, and repatriation of profits. He wanted to oversee diversification into other fields such as heroin and synthetic drug production. He planned to usher his organization into the big time but didn't see any way to do that without going out to the facilities.

Inside the building, the leaves were spread out on the floor. Nearby, more leaves were distributed in thin layers on a tarpaulin in direct sunlight to dry. Across the compound, in another building, workers stomped leaves in a *pozo*, or paste pit. There were five men stamping the leaves energetically in the plastic-lined hole in the ground. They were working harder than usual. They knew that Santiago's brother was in the compound looking around. The leaves were awash in a solution of sodium carbonate and water which released the cocaine alkaloid.

The next building over contained another *pozo*. The leaves had already been worked for five hours, and the men were adding kerosene to the mix. Domingo looked in the door curiously. The men reentered the pit and resumed stomping the leaves. The kerosene acted to extract water-insoluble cocaine alkaloids. The peasants didn't know the chemistry, but they knew the process and knew that their wages, although laughable by First World standards, were very generous. In a few hours they would pour out the water and leaves, retaining the cocaine alkaloid and kerosene. The leaves would have completed their journey and would be free to decompose without further molestation.

In the same building, cocaine alkaloids were being extracted from the kerosene into an acid solution. Domingo watched, standing with hands on hips. Sodium carbonate was added to the remaining solution. The acid and the water were drained off, and a precipitate was filtered and dried to produce a light-brown putty, or coca paste. At this point the peasants turned the project over to the more educated men who lived in the air-conditioned dormitory and came from the universities in Bogotá and Cali. Now the chemists stepped in.

The workers carried the dried putty to another building where it was dissolved in sulfuric acid and water. Domingo followed. Potassium permanganate mixed with water was added to the coca paste and acid solution. After this was done, the serious young chemists lowered their rubberized plastic eye protectors and allowed the solution to stand for six hours. In the interim, they toured with Domingo Valens. He asked questions. They showed him aspects of the operation that concerned him, particularly quality control. Domingo had read Deming long before it became fashionable in the United States. Quality was his job one. He did not want satisfied customers. He wanted loyal customers.

Domingo looked on as the solution was filtered to remove impurities and ammonia water was added, causing the cocaine base to precipitate out of the solution. The liquid was discarded and the base was dried under heat lamps. The generators outside ran day and night to provide the electricity.

In the next building over, chemists dissolved the cocaine base in ether and filtered it again. Hydrochloric acid diluted in acetone was added to the solution. The addition of the hydrochloric acid caused the cocaine to crystallize and fall out of the solution as cocaine hydrochloride. Domingo watched wide-eyed through his protective goggles. Coke, toot, blow, snow, or pearl flake—by whatever name, 100 percent Colombian pure. Satisfaction guaranteed.

Domingo knew that it was a complicated process. He had personally arranged for all of the supplies required at the lab. The hydrochloric acid came from a company in New York, the permanganate from New Jersey, the ammonia from North Carolina. The drying lamps were made in Texas. The kerosene originated in California. The sodium carbonate came from Michigan. The portable generators were made by a British company in Pennsylvania. The plastic liners were shipped from Korea. The powder was dried in microwave ovens assembled in Japan. This was just an example of why the Cali cartel was a multinational corporation.

This lab alone produced one hundred kilos of pure cocaine a day. It was only one of Santiago and Domingo Valens's facilities. When all of the transactions were done and the money came back in bales measured by weight, not dollar amount, this lab cleared over $100,000 a day in net profit.

The destruction started long before the drug fed addictions, destroyed lives, and fostered crime all over the globe. Every day, thousands of gallons of water contaminated with hydrochloric acid, kerosene, permanganate, and sodium carbonate flowed down the mountainside into the Cauca River, polluting drinking water and killing vegetation and wildlife. Domingo made notes on this problem and planned to order a chemical reprocessing and recovery unit from Norway when he returned home from his field trip to another facility in Panama.

-13-   *April 1, 1986, Solovetsky Labor Camp, Kazakhstan*

GREGOR VIKTOROVICH HAD ENDURED eighteen months of confinement. He had been compelled to work hard for twelve to sixteen hours a day, but they had fed him adequately and he had managed to bargain in the camp for little things like tobacco. The guards knew that he was a powerful man, even inside the walls and behind the towers. They knew that eventually Gregor would find his way back out into the world, and they did not want to be on his bad side when that happened. Consequently, the guards treated him with a discreet deference, allowing him his creature comforts. These were essentially five: his tobacco, his comb, his hair, his dice, and the goose-feather pillow he convinced a nondetainee plumber to bring him against the promise of future gain.

While Gregor was inside, he was not idle. He was interviewing and recruiting the strong young men who were sent there. He was building his business venture and making connections. Some of the guards privately expected to work for Gregor when he got out and, with utmost delicacy, had expressed their desire to do so. They knew who Gregor was and so did he.

Gregor had spent a lot of time thinking while he was a prisoner. Going over the past. Existing. Waiting for the future. Now, at the end of another day in the camp, he choked on the dry cigarette that he had rolled and stared out at the guard tower. He was a sturdily built man with a broad Slavic face and a thick neck. He smoothed back his unruly gray hair and looked out at his barren world through gunmetal-gray eyes. He remembered the night that the KGB had arrested him. It was all very civilized. He had known immediately that it was not the militia. It was the KGB. If it had been the militia, he might have gotten a trial. Apparently, one of his underlings had attempted to bribe the wrong official.

About 30 to 50 percent of the average Soviet bureaucrat's wages could be accounted for by bribes. It was part of how the apparatchiks lived so well. Brezhnev had realized this in the early eighties and given the tacit go-ahead to the emerging black market as a way to jump start the Soviet economy. People like Gregor were created out of that policy.

But, then again, there were the bureaucrats who still believed in the socialist paradise and could not be bribed. They seemed to have forgotten the Twenty-second Congress of 1961, where the Party had declared that the utopia of True Communism would be reached by 1980 at the latest. They did not remember the old lies but latched onto every new promise like drowning men to a life ring. They were dangerous. They were the ones who put people like Gregor in jail.

He remembered the two black Volgas pulling up outside his apartment in Moscow and the stone-faced young men walking purposefully up the stairs to knock on his door. He knew what was coming next. Gregor had always had a secretive mind. It was his destiny to be either a criminal or a spy. The state had overlooked him, so he chose the former. He had planned against the day that he would be arrested, even instructing his protégé and disciple, Yuri, in every subtle clue that he would leave in that event. Now, he had laid an ace of spades face up underneath the throw rug to indicate KGB. He had chalked a black "X" in the upper-right-hand corner of the door frame to indicate that he was arrested. Then he had answered the door with the certain knowledge that Yuri would eventually find him.

A pale-faced man wearing a long, black leather coat and a fur hat had announced to him, "Comrade Viktorovich, you are under arrest for obscene speculation." That was it. Nothing else, and then he was led down the stairs and into the back of the second black sedan. He was deposited in Moscow's aging Lefortovo Prison and held for twenty days. Then he was moved to the maximum-security Matrosskaya Tishina Prison, where he shared a fifty-square-foot cell with forty to fifty other criminals. The number varied as they were taken away and more were incarcerated, but the single, stained porcelain toilet in the corner was constant. After about three weeks, he was moved again. This time it was to the labor camp. The trial was apparently forgotten.

Gregor recalled being piled into a cattle car with twenty other inmates and hearing the sliding door slam shut and the clank of the latch as it was secured and the pin inserted. For some reason, he had envisioned transportation to labor camps evolving into something different from what it had been in the 1920s. It hadn't. But the trip wasn't too bad. It was early spring, so it wasn't too cold and the car wasn't too crowded. They could empty the chamber pot through a hole in the back of the car and could see the outside world through gaps in the side panels as the train rolled along.

They saw white expanses of snow, hills and mountains covered with pine and birch, lakes and rivers, villages with patches of vegetable gardens, geese pecking aimlessly beside the tracks, fields of grain, and green grass popping up after the brutal Russian winter. Gregor remembered being struck by the natural beauty of his country, which lay there before him in stark contrast to its institutional ugliness.

When he thought of the Soviet institution, he always thought of Beria, the head of the secret police. The man had been dead for thirty years, but to Gregor he represented the summation of sins that the nation had to own up to. Gregor's mother was in the eighth month of her pregnancy, carrying him within her, when Beria ordered his agents to shoot Red Army soldiers retreating under a crushing Nazi onslaught in 1941. Gregor's father had been in that retreat and he had been shot. A nation that had allowed a Beria to exist deserved what Gregor wanted to give it.

Gregor remembered the satisfaction with which he had heard the news of Beria's fall from grace. Only thirteen at the time, he had practically howled with joy when Beria was arrested for being an "imperialist agent." He laughed when he read that Beria had collapsed to his knees and pleaded for mercy at the trial and felt exalted when he heard that Beria had been shot in December 1953. Gregor wondered what that cold little man had thought when he felt the icy end of the pistol barrel on the back of his neck. In that moment did he repent? Did he call out to God, just to hedge his bets against His existence? Gregor wondered. He didn't believe in God either, but that had nothing to do with the Party.

Browsing over his past and remembering his father—or a combination of his mother's stories and the rough-edged, black-and-white photographs of him—Gregor suddenly thought of *The Fate of a Man*. Sergei Bondarchuk's production was the story of a Second World War soldier, like his father. His musings were interrupted by a stout young man who stood before him. His biceps bulged under the camp tunic and he had the close-cropped haircut required on all prisoners except Gregor. The stubble that remained on his head indicated that his hair had been almost black. Gregor had pointed him out to several of his *rebyata*, or "boys," earlier in the day. He was new and Gregor had not yet interviewed him. The young man stood at attention. The boys had apparently impressed him.

Gregor looked up at him and broke the silence. "What do you think of Bondarchuk?"

The bodybuilder looked confused. "I do not know him, sir, but I have only been here one day."

Gregor laughed. "He is not here. He makes movies. You young people don't know about a lot of good things."

"Yes, sir," the young man replied, showing no emotion.

"What is your name?" Gregor asked.

"Sergei Blokov, sir."

"Do you want to be with my boys?" Gregor asked.

"Yes, sir," Blokov answered. He was relieved. The boys had told him all about the man who wanted to talk to him. It was Gregor, the *vory v zakone*. A leader. A full-fledged godfather in the Russian mafia, temporarily inconvenienced by imprisonment.

14   *April 13, 1986, Fox County, South Carolina*

JAKE WAS RETURNING from Columbia, where he had picked up some things for Joe, including Cromer's peanuts, one of the oldster's favorite snacks. He had been glad to get out of the shop because Joe was cussing and muttering about the "damn Gestapo IRS" and how he remembered when there wasn't no income tax and how it was unconstitutional and what was wrong with this country and on and on. As Jake had walked out the door he had heard Joe yelling at Senator Thurmond, who was a thousand miles away. "Strom! We went off together to defeat the Hun and it's come down to this! I'd probably be better off if they had won!" He lowered his voice. "Everything is going down the tubes," he complained.

Before he had left, however, Jake had brightened Joe's day. "Joe, next year you can claim me as a dependent."

"Yes, that I will do, young man." He turned back to his accounts. "You know, I remember my daddy talking about shooting at revenuers."

Jake was thinking over all of this and chuckling inwardly, because for the nearly two months that he had known Joe, this sudden irascibility was apparently reserved for the two or three days prior to tax day. He drove past the sign that said, "WELCOME TO FOX COUNTY, BIRTHPLACE OF LEROY JOHNSON!" He smiled. Jake had learned that Leroy Johnson wasn't a local historical figure, at least not in the conventional sense. He probably would be, but wasn't yet.

The sign wasn't official. It had not been erected by a grateful town, county, or state but by Leroy Johnson himself. The town council didn't like it but could not compel Leroy to take it down. As Mayor Ashfort pointed out to the council, "Well, see'n as how that there sign of Leroy's is on his land, we'll just have to rely on the man's good nature to take the thing down." Mayor Ashfort was dead and buried for ten years before Jake arrived in town. The sign was still there, freshly repainted. So much for Leroy's good nature.

The town council had done what it could to combat Leroy's sign and had erected the billboard that Jake now approached on his left. It was hideous. It displayed a mockingbird, beak lifted as if in song, and underneath it read, "WELCOME TO FOX COUNTY, MOCKINGBIRD CAPITAL OF THE SOUTH." There were hundreds of small bullet holes. It was always open season on the Fox County mockingbird. Some scoundrel, who was apparently a very good shot, had dug a crater of a hole right where the poor creature's eye should have been. Jake figured that it was from a twelve-gauge deer slug. County residents were now petitioning the council to take down their ugly sign.

At that moment an oncoming green Pinto took a left turn directly in front of him. He had to cut sharply to the left to avoid a collision. He briefly saw a woman, her head uplifted and staring intently into the rearview mirror with a lipstick tube in her hand, before he rocketed onto the grass of the opposite road embankment and plowed into the underbrush beneath the mockingbird sign. He heard a grating sound on the top of the cab before he managed to bring the pickup to a halt.

He got out to examine the damage. He had run underneath the sign, scraping paint from the top of his cab but missing both supporting posts. The mockingbird billboard was completely unharmed. He turned to look at the Pinto, preparing to be angry. That was when he saw her. She got out of the car like nothing had happened and walked into the beauty shop, which had been her destination when she made the turn. She was like a red-haired Irish goddess, a Gaelic enchantress in blue jeans and a tank top. He was spellbound. His anger drifted away, and he reversed back onto the road, removing more paint, and drove across to the shop. The sign read "DIANA'S BEAUTY SHOP" in faded blue paint on a white background. The paint was so thin that he could see that the sign underneath had once read "MYRNA'S BEAUTY SHOP." The building was constructed of cinder blocks and painted white. He wondered why he had never noticed it before.

He walked in and saw her again. The bell on the door handle rang as it swung shut on its spring. She was crouching at a floor-level cabinet removing some shampoo and placing it on the counter above. She was alone but did not glance up when she heard the bell. He saw that there were several chairs for waiting and one chair in front of a sink and another one with a big bulbous contraption above it. He didn't know what it was for, but he had seen one before on television, maybe on "The Jetsons."

She stood up and turned to see who had come in. He looked at her. Fair complexioned with large green catlike eyes and red hair that ran halfway down her back. She was beautiful, gorgeous, exotic, and Jake was speechless in her presence. Fortunately, she was not.

"May I help you?"

Jake looked at her. "Ah." He paused, feeling like a teen-ager and looking around the shop as if some helpful words might be written on the walls. What do you say to the woman who just ran you off the road? "Did you notice me back there when you turned?"

Her eyes narrowed a little. "Well, no," she admitted frankly. "Should I have?"

Again, Jake felt speechless. "Uhm . . . well, yes. You sort of ran me off the road." He hesitated and watched her face. Her mouth dropped open. "It looked like you were putting on lipstick or something."

Her face became red with embarrassment, and she exclaimed, "Oh, my God! Are you okay?" She practically leapt across the distance that separated them to grasp his arm and lead him to a chair. "Here. Sit down. I am so sorry. I can't believe that I did that!" Her words came out rapidly, like machine-gun fire. "Are you okay?"

Jake smiled at her. "Yes, I'm fine. The sign is fine. My truck just lost a little paint."

"Sign?" she asked and looked out the glass door at the city council's billboard.

Jake looked at it, too. "Yeah, I ran into it."

He examined her face again as she digested his words. He could discern that she was almost disappointed that the sign had not come down. She laughed the short, broken chortle that people use in awkward situations. "You know, I've been writing a letter once a week for two years to the town council, asking them to take down that sign. Now I know all I've got to do is run somebody off the road." She smiled at Jake. "Are you certain that you're okay?"

"Yeah, I'm fine," Jake admitted, almost wishing that he weren't. Wishing that she would be forced to care for him in some way. He looked around the shop. "Can, well, a *guy* get a haircut in here?"

She laughed again. It was different from the one he had just heard. Less forced. More genuine. This time he turned red. She smiled and said, "Well, I think you are the first male customer I've had in here. This is a beauty shop, after all, but I can cut your hair, I suppose. Just lean back in the chair."

Jake complied. She loosened his ponytail from its elastic band and then ran her fingers through his hair. Her touch set him on fire. He asked, "What's your name?"

She pointed toward the door and said, "Diana. You know, like the sign says." Then she laughed again. He looked at her in the mirror as she picked up the scissors. "How would you like it?" she asked.

"Oh, whatever you think looks good. Nothing off the pony-tail, though," he replied. Then he noticed the diamond band on her left-hand ring finger and asked, "Married?"

"Oh," she glanced offhandedly at her wedding ring, "widowed."

-15-

October 12, 1987, San Francisco, California

ANDREW OLIVER WATCHED Corinne leave for school in her green uniform and noticed that at sixteen she was becoming a lovely young woman. Full figured, with long blonde hair like her mother's and cerulean eyes several shades lighter than his own, she was striking, with a perfect complexion and an aristocratic face and bearing. Odin himself might have mistaken her for the comely Freya. She was becoming a beautiful, well-educated, cultured lady. It was what he had wanted her to become. He wanted her to be part of the elite, the nobility, the aristocrats. He had worked hard his entire adult life to remove her from what he had grown up with. Trailer parks. Violence. Poverty. Alcoholism.

He remembered vividly the day when she was born. He had been unable to pay the hospital bill, having been laid off at the paper mill for being late to work or drunk every day for six months. He and his wife were just getting by on welfare, and little Corinne had been born. It had made life harder in that cramped, single-wide trailer. No money. No job. Bills. They had fought every day until it was almost a ritual. After all, what else is there to do when you are trapped together day and night without even the respite of a job? When Corinne was six months old, her mother, in the throes of yet another four-day alcoholic binge, had taken a bottle of sleeping pills, fallen asleep, and never awakened.

Andrew sobered up a few days after the funeral and stopped drinking for several months. Still, he could not find a job. Now that he was alone in the game, he began to consider the future, Corinne's in particular, with a sense of urgency that he had never felt before. Unable to see any way out of his cycle of poverty, he could not bear the thought of his daughter growing up in that kind of environment. He didn't want her getting drunk and doing drugs by thirteen, an unwed mother by seventeen. That was, more or less, the norm for the trailer park and the only life he had known. He desperately wanted something better for her. Toying with the idea of putting her up for adoption, he had even spent a quarter to call a social service agency but hung up the phone, overwhelmed with feelings of shame and inadequacy. Finally, Andrew asked his mother-in-law to keep Corinne for him while he tried to get back on his feet. He hit the pavement looking for a job, but without a high-school diploma, a GED, or military service behind him, he was at the bottom of the heap. The slippery slope back into the bottle was greased by every rejection, and in short order he began to drink again.

That was when the hunting trip had come along. Todd, Andrew's brother, thought that it would be good for both of them to get away for a few days to the Cascade Mountains and go hunting. He planned to broach the idea of Andrew's coming back to the paper mill. Todd had talked his shift supervisor into giving his brother another chance, but Andrew would be taking a cut in pay, at least at first. In fact, if he did the figures, Andrew was better off financially on welfare, but that would be temporary. If he showed up for work on time and sober, he would eventually get paid more.

The hunting trip had indeed changed Andrew's situation. It had cost Todd his life, but the way Andrew looked at it, it was either Todd or him. It had to be that way. Todd could never keep a secret. He remembered the moment that the necessary course of action became clear. Still warm from the exertion of scraping the shallow grave out of the cold-hardened soil with a folding utility shovel and marching several miles back, they were building a fire at their campsite. Andrew was gathering wood while his brother rummaged in his backpack for matches and lighter fluid to get the fire started before they got cold again.

Andrew had finished stacking the kindling and was laying the larger pieces of wood in a teepee arrangement. Todd brought over the briefcase, popped it open, and removed two twenty-dollar bills. He sprayed the kindling with lighter fluid, struck a match, touched the flame to the currency, and tossed the bills into the kindling. The fluid blazed to life.

"Now, com'on, Todd," Andrew said.

"Lighten up, Andy. We're stinkin' rich. We're gonna be lightin' cigars with hundred-dollar bills for the rest of our lives." Todd smiled mischievously and closed the top of the briefcase.

"There isn't *that* much money in there, Todd. Besides, we can't be flashin' it around. You might as well get in the habit now. We've gotta be smart. It's gotta be gradual, ya know? I mean, somebody's gonna come lookin' for this money."

"What's the matter with you, Andy? We're free and clear. Nobody's gonna find that guy up here." Todd gestured off into the woods with one hand while the other reached into his backpack for the bottle of Jack Daniel's. He unscrewed the cap and took a swig before offering it to Andrew.

"No, thanks." Andrew motioned the bottle away.

"Yahoooooooooooh!" Todd shouted suddenly, shattering the silence of the nighttime forest. He broke into hysterical laughter. "Andy, I'm gonna go in Monday and tell that foreman to kiss my ass." He fell silent for a moment. "No . . . no, first I'm gonna go buy a Cadillac to drive to the mill, and then I'm gonna tell them all to kiss my ass. Brother, we ain't gonna dirty our hands doin' another man's labor again."

Andrew frowned. "Where you gonna tell them you got the money to live the high life?"

Todd looked thoughtful for a moment and then broke into a wide, toothy grin. "Inherited it, didn't we? Somebody died and give it to us."

"Who?"

"Whatcha mean, 'who'? You were there," Todd said angrily.

"I mean, who you gonna tell them died, Todd?"

"Don't matter, does it? Uncle. Weird aunt or something. There is absolutely no reason that we have to wait, Andy. This is cash, man! Cash! Who's gonna say it ain't ours?"

"The cops. IRS. People like that," Andrew replied seriously.

"How are they gonna know? It's cash, for Christ sakes."

"Todd, think for a second. Just think. We need to just sit on it for a couple years, that's all. Be cool. Be slow."

"A couple years!" Todd shouted. "What? You think we ought to go gray and eat shit while we're sittin' on a fortune?"

"Yes," Andrew said.

"I think you need a drink." Todd took a mouthful of the whiskey and swallowed with an exaggerated gulp. "Tell you what, Andy. We'll split it up right now. Fifty-fifty. You sit on your half and be safe and I'll do what I want with my half. Okay?"

Todd opened the briefcase and began to lay out the bundles of cash in two piles. Andrew walked over behind him and picked up the shotgun. He racked a deer slug into the chamber and took aim. They would never have pulled it off if Todd had come out of the woods, so he had to die. He didn't suffer, and Andrew drew a certain solace from this.

Since leaving the woods and spending one night in jail, Andrew had never had another drink. The financial empire that he wanted to build was too important for him to risk losing by taking a drink. Ever. Andrew had started at the produce market, selling vegetables that he grew behind his trailer. After he had accumulated a little money, he bought several acres and expanded his produce business. Within two years he had ten employees working to raise organically grown vegetables on a fifty-five-acre plot north of Portland. Corinne came back to live with him. Within five years he had fifty employees and 150 acres, his trucks running all over Oregon. After that he had branched out and bought a construction company. At this point a thousand dollars here and there could be funneled through his businesses into the banks, transferred, invested, and redeposited. In short, laundered.

Finally, this month, it had all been deposited, and he had made 120 times what he originally had set out to launder. Andrew Oliver was worth a little over $25 million. That was enough to move to San Francisco, send Corinne to private school, and continue to expand that fortune in the volatile Bay Area economy.

He sat at his desk and looked down at his hands. He remembered the soil running through them when he started his little produce business fifteen years ago on that plot behind the trailer. He stared at his left hand, which had become a symbol to him of his rags-to-riches story. It was scarred and smooth, with skin that looked like plastic from being burned with gasoline from a motorcycle fuel tank he was working on when he was fourteen. His father had thrown a cigarette butt at him and set him on fire. The scar tissue covered his whole left arm.

He smiled as he thought about it all. It wasn't truly a rags-to-riches story. He opened his desk drawer and removed a tiny glass sphere and began tossing it up and down. On one side, it read "Alea iacta est." On the other, a brown pupil stared at the surroundings as it rose and fell from the air into his hand. He had been worth $194,160 on the day he emerged from the woods carrying his brother's broken body.

-16-

CLARENCE HAD THE DAY OFF, so he slept in, awakening at almost 1 P.M. He had gone to bed the previous evening at 8:15. He had been having a nightmare but was too tired to wake from it. In his dream two murderers walked because the warrant under which their house was searched was not specific enough. The men were guilty, but they could not be convicted. Vital evidence was not presented because it was not legally obtained. The evidence was barred, so the murderers were not put behind bars. In the dream the defendants were confident and cocky as the jury came out. They had walked out of the courtroom laughing at the justice system. Underneath the dream he heard one of his criminal behavior instructors in college admonishing him, "Mr. Dubose, we do not have a *justice* system. We have a *legal* system."

He rubbed his face and looked through bleary eyes at the digital clock on the bedside table. *Jesus*, he thought, *seventeen hours. You know that something is wrong when you sleep seventeen hours when left alone.* He remembered the dream and realized that it wasn't a dream at all. It had been the events of the previous day.

He rolled stiffly out of bed and stood up. He felt good, better than he had felt in perhaps a month. He had been going day and night as one of the city's leading homicide detectives. As far as murders went, Oakland never slept. He walked to the mirror in the bathroom and looked at his face. Dark bags were visible on the ebony skin under his eyes. *Clarence, you have a problem.* He looked at the bloodshot eyes above the smudges, placed his hands on his cheeks to feel thirty-six hours' worth of stubble, and turned away from the mirror. He walked to the bedside table and picked up a pack of Marlboro Reds, shook one out, put it to his lips, and lit it. Inhaling, he walked to the kitchen. He regarded the pile of unwashed dishes in the sink, opened a cabinet, and extracted a bottle of Pepto-Bismol. He took a deep draught, recapped the bottle, and returned it to the cabinet. He looked again at the dishes and remembered that he didn't have any clean ones left.

The disorderly kitchen made him think of Joyce. She would never have let it get messy. He remembered the night she had left. He had been upset about a case like the one yesterday. He had said things to her that she did not deserve. She had gone, taking nothing, saying nothing. She had never sent around divorce papers, and he had never inquired after them. He knew where she lived now. She was not attached, living in an efficiency apartment on South 114th Street. *I should go there and beg her to come back. No, if she wants to come back, she will. I will not condescend to ask her. I have my stupidass pride, after all.*

At this point, his pride made him decide to go to McDonald's rather than wash any dishes. He walked out the front door, closing and locking it behind him, took his mail from the box, and walked to the car. He sat in the driver's seat and turned on the ignition. The engine caught and began to run. He let it warm up as he flipped through the junk mail and bills that were his daily fare. Then he noticed the typewritten letter from his brother, Clyde. He tore it open:

Clarence,

    Forgive the typewriter, but I picked it up at
a garage sale and enjoy using it. It makes it
easier to read my writing anyway. I got your
letter about employment opportunities back here
in your home town, and as it turns out something
right up your alley has come up. Old Sheriff
Branson, you'll remember him. He was the sheriff
when you left. Anyway, he's ready to retire. I
went in and talked to him about you. He said that
it wouldn't be as interesting to you as the big
city out there, but that if you wanted to come
and be a deputy for awhile and relearn the county
and people, he would set you up to more than
likely be the next sheriff. County council will
have to approve you, and then you have to get
elected, but if Sheriff Branson tells them you're
alright, they'll go along with him. He's a good
and fair man and has always treated us colored
folks just like everybody else as long as I can

remember. Law and order ain't never been too much
of a problem around here, but there are times
when you need a good sheriff. So if you come back
home, you can probably be the new sheriff. Look
forward to hearing from you.

Clyde

Clarence considered the letter. Clyde was his oldest brother, almost twenty years his senior. He belonged to another generation who still used the word "colored." Clarence remembered what one of the men who had gone free the previous day had said to him after the verdict was read. Turning to Clarence, he had lifted his dark hand, splaying the fingers apart, placing an index finger against the golden ball of his nose ring, and then shot the hand into the air with the fingers still spread wide, the index pointing at Clarence. "Yo! Dis nigger is NOT going to da big house!" He had turned and walked away. It all seemed so wrong.

-17-

March 1987, Fox County, South Carolina

"MY GOD, JAKE, you are a hunk!" Diana exclaimed.

"What makes you say that?" Jake asked. He was climbing out of the water and onto the dock, peeling off his wet suit. The air was warm, but it would be another month before the water caught up.

Diana smiled seductively. "I just hadn't noticed until now how much you've changed. You were a little pudgy when I first met you, you know."

"Was not."

"Were too."

"Okay, I guess you're right. I have lost a little weight." He patted his stomach.

"Your arms and chest have gotten a little bigger too, I think," Diana added.

Jake flexed like Arnold Schwarzenegger in the muscle maga-
zines. "Ja, I am pumped up," he said. "Look at dat!" He pointed to
a flexed biceps.

Diana laughed and sat up on the dock, sweeping her long red
hair with her right hand around her head and draping it over her
right shoulder where it came down and covered her bikini-clad
breast. "Come here, Arnold."

Jake approached and lay on the boards next to her. They kissed.
"I've got a surprise."

Diana pulled back from the embrace. "A surprise? What's your
surprise?"

Jake sat up and crossed his arms. He looked down at her seriously and, imitating a bad actor's southern accent in a deep bass,
said, "Now, if'n I wuz to tell ya, Di-ana, then it wouldn't be a
soo-prise now, would it?"

"Oh, come on, Jake. Tell me what it is!"

"Okay," Jake relented. "Joe is going to sell me the place."

"Really, Jake? That's great!" She hugged him. "When?"

"Next December. He wants to build himself a little house
down on the water, over there." Jake pointed out into the cove
toward the woods-covered eastern bank. "I just have to help him
build it and another dock to go with it, and when it's ready, he
says that I can have the place for one dollar."

"One dollar?" Diana asked, genuinely mystified. "This cove is
probably worth at least half a million dollars, Jake."

Jake switched to his best imitation of the old man. "Here's
how I figure it, young man. If I sell it for what it's worth, the
damn revenuers are gonna make a mint. For what? Because I
bought it when nobody thought this lake was worth bein' 'round.
I ain't got no sons. If I was to wait 'til I die and will it to ya, the
damn estate taxes will be 'stonomical. Agin, the damn Gestapo
revenuers will make out like bandits. If'n I sell it to ya fair and
square for a dollar, the state makes a nickel for its trouble of processing the deed. There ya go. Take it or leave it. You have to keep
the name on the shop as 'Joe's.' Whatcha think?" Jake completed

the soliloquy with a gesture of Joe blowing cigar smoke up under his Kenworth cap and squinting his eyes.

"That's great, Jake!"

"You know, he told me something else." Diana looked at him expectantly, so he continued. "Remember how I told you about the night that I showed up in town here?" Diana nodded. "Well, remember me telling you that I felt like those three had some kind of joke between them and I was it, but how could I be it? They didn't know who I was." He paused, as if trying to recall something or find the correct word.

"Yeah, Jake, I remember you telling me that," Diana prompted him.

"Well, Joe told me that the reason they looked at me so funny that night was that they had just been talking over what Joe was going to do with the place. He doesn't have any kids and John had just told him not to worry, that maybe someone would show up to learn Joe's trade. Like an apprentice. Joe had told him that he was crazy. Nobody nowadays wanted to live way out here and grub worms and that some slick real estate developer was going to get hold of this cove and build an ugly condominium block. I walked up as Joe was saying the word 'block.' Or so he says. I just thought that was pretty neat. Prophetic or something like that."

-18-

August 12, 1986, Cauca Valley, Colombia

THE BOMB was a parallel circuit construction. The first circuit was a simple dried-seed timer. A thin round metal plate rested upon dried beans soaking in a jar of water. The beans would increase in volume about 50 percent per hour, pushing the plate closer toward making contact with the connecting wires bolted to the plastic lid and firing the circuit. This fiendishly clever timer gave the bomb squad a sense of urgency. It was readily visible through the gaps in the wooden sides of the crate which housed the device.

Equally devilish was the second trigger, a simple clothespin. When allowed to close, it would complete the parallel circuit. Wedged between the contacts in the jaws of the clothespin was a tiny splinter of wood attached with string to two adjacent sides of the box and tied to a nail in the pavement beneath. The rest of the mechanism was composed of two batteries, a blasting cap, and fifty pounds of TNT. It was a classic no-win scenario for the bomb squad. There it was on the pavement in front of the police station.

If they moved it, it would detonate. If they didn't move it, it would detonate. Although all of its components were visible, it could not be defused. Opening the crate would cause it to detonate. The bomb squad decided that the best solution was to attempt to tamp the blast, throwing the expanding gases into the least destructive path possible. Sandbags were filled and brought to the front of the station. As the squad placed the first three sandbags around the base of the device it went off. The entire Nencoona bomb squad was blown to pieces. No recognizable portion of their bodies was recovered during the cleanup. The rescue workers found fragments of clothing, a distorted watch, and two wedding bands which were presumed to belong to the victims and would later accompany the sealed caskets at the burial.

In addition to the casualties, the police station was damaged so severely that it had to be torn down. The blast ruptured the pavement and severed a sanitation pipe, spilling raw sewage into the main thoroughfare of the town of Nencoona. Every window within a five-hundred-yard arc in front of the station was shattered by the shock wave.

Two days later the police had relocated to an office building three blocks away. The telephone rang and Captain Luis Fernandina answered. The connection was poor, but the message was clear. "This is the Revolutionary Armed Forces of Colombia. We are calling you to claim responsibility for destroying your station.

Release Emilio Sampar or we will destroy your new office." The line went dead. The captain held his head in his hands for a moment. He was thinking. He knew these terrorists. The Revolutionary Armed Forces of Colombia had its own agenda, but it also performed contract work for the Cali cartel to fund its political aims. Santiago Valens must want Sampar out of jail. Captain Fernandina had captured Sampar while he was stacking coca paste packages in the back of a single-engine airplane in a field just outside of town. The paste had apparently been dropped there by truck for transport to more advanced processing facilities. Sampar had not fled or resisted. He simply looked surprised. When Fernandina tied his hands to transport him to the police station, Sampar had looked at him as though he were crazy.

Finally, the pilot spoke. "You really don't want to do this."

"Do what?" Fernandina asked.

"Save yourself a lot of trouble. Untie me and let me go now. This can lead to no good." He shook his head mournfully and smiled at the captain as if explaining to a toddler the connection between actions and consequences.

Fernandina had not listened. He also had not paid attention to the lawyer whom Santiago Valens had dispatched to the town to secure Sampar's release. He had not heard the second lawyer or the third. He intended to try Sampar for trafficking and possession of narcotics with intent to distribute. The fourth lawyer had come. He had not been as civil as the previous three. "Why don't you just release this man, yes?" Fernandina had not heeded his request. Now three of his men were dead and his station was rubble. He heard and understood that. He began to type the order.

Just past midnight, Fernandina drove to the outskirts of the town. He pulled up outside the prison gates and showed his identification to the guard. He also showed him the transportation order for Emilio Sampar. "I will transport this prisoner from here to Cali, where he will stand trial. I will take him tonight." The guard nodded, careful to keep his face clear of emotion, and waved the car through. He dialed into the cell block on the telephone and instructed the guard to bring Sampar out. This had been the prisoner's second visitor of the evening. The first had been an Anglo with shoulder-length wavy black hair and a mustache. He had offered the guard thirty thousand pesos for the opportunity to speak with Sampar. The guard had given him an hour.

Twenty minutes later, Fernandina pulled the official black Renault 9 sedan to the side of the road and told Sampar to get out. He untied his hands. "You have escaped while being transported. Go!"

Sampar smiled and walked away slowly and confidently, a man who controls all that he surveys.

-19-

May 1, 1991, Solovetsky Labor Camp, Kazakhstan

"MR. VIKTOROVICH?" A guard was gently pushing Gregor's arm and hoarsely whispering. "Mr. Viktorovich, wake up."

"What? What?" Gregor said groggily.

"Mr. Viktorovich, the new commandant wishes to see you."

"The who?" Gregor sat up, rubbing his eyes and looking around. "What time is it? It is very dark." He paused long enough to recognize the guard. "What time is it, Vasily?"

"It is 5 A.M., Mr. Viktorovich, but it is the new commandant. He has just arrived. Perhaps it is good news!" Vasily said this excitedly and smiled like a child who knows that he is about to receive a gift. "Come on. Let's go." He handed Gregor his boots from beneath the cot. Nothing else was necessary. Gregor slept in his clothes like all the rest of the prisoners, but his head rested on a goose-feather pillow. The rest had sacks of straw.

Five minutes later, Gregor was marched by Vasily, observing the proper form, to the residence of the commandant. It was as if they were in a play. Both knew their roles on the stage, but both were aware that the roles were different when the curtain came down. Gregor had little problem in behaving like a proper prisoner as long as he felt that the guards understood that they too were only playing a part, and a bit part at that.

Vasily knocked three times on the door. He waited for a moment and then opened it enough to announce, "Prisoner Viktorovich to see the commandant as ordered!"

A voice boomed back. "Very well. Send him in."

Vasily assumed his most military voice. "Prisoner, remove your hat!" Gregor removed his hat. "Prisoner, five steps forward, march!" Gregor ascended the stairs and entered the office of the commandant, standing at attention.

The commandant was small but heavyset. He looked more Mongol than Russian, with coarse black hair, a thin mustache, and the pasty-faced complexion of a man who was engineered for the outdoors but worked inside. His insignia indicated that he was a colonel, but he was not KGB. It confused Gregor a little, but he was not here to ask questions.

The colonel looked at Gregor cautiously, noting that he stood at attention as was proper for a prisoner and held his hat folded in his left hand at his side. He spoke out the door first. "Guard! You are dismissed. Come back in twenty minutes." Then, turning to Gregor, "Mr. Viktorovich. Stand at ease, and kindly shut my door." Gregor relaxed long enough to close the door and then returned to attention in front of the colonel's desk.

The commandant looked pleased. The prisoner took no liberties. He liked that. "Mr. Viktorovich, you have probably noted that I am not KGB."

Gregor nodded.

"The Sixth Directorate and local authorities have assumed many of the responsibilities of the KGB during these troubled times. I am a militia colonel and a native of Kazakhstan." He paused, letting Gregor grasp his words. He opened a file on his desk. Looking down at it, he spoke again. "Mr. Viktorovich, I understand that you came here without a trial. Is that true?"

Gregor nodded.

The colonel continued. "I also understand that you have been here for seven years. Is that true?"

Gregor nodded again.

"Mr. Viktorovich, my first act as commandant of this camp is to commute your sentence to time served and release you. The guard will escort you directly from my office to the front gate when he returns. You have a companion waiting for you there."

Gregor was dumbfounded. He was confident that Yuri had been working for his release, but he had heard nothing. He had sent every one of the *rebyata* who had been released to find Yuri and tell him that they were now part of the organization and, more important, tell Yuri where he was. He knew that someday he would be free again, but he was Russian and fatalistic. "Only crows fly in a straight line," his mother was fond of saying. It was a statement on the futility of setting goals and systematically achieving them. To Russians, the way to the end was never straight. It was convoluted. A race repeatedly overrun by enemies from east and west, starved by famine caused by erratic weather, and ruled by nothing but totalitarian governments could hardly help but foster a fatalistic outlook. If nothing else, Gregor was Russian.

Vasily escorted Gregor to the gate. Two guards unchained the wood-framed wire-mesh structure and opened it enough for him to walk out. Vasily motioned for him to leave. Gregor turned and grasped Vasily by the shoulders and placed his mouth to the guard's ear. He whispered quickly and urgently, "You know who has been kind to me here, Vasily. You and those you know can come to me when you too are free. Come to Moscow. Get in any taxi cab. Ask them where you might find a Japanese tape player. All the taxis know the black market. When you arrive, watch your wallet and your back until you find someone who can bring you to me. I am *vory* of the Dark Path. Do not forget it. Dark Path."

He walked out of the gate and heard it shut behind him. Headlights came on in front of him and he saw the outline of a bear-shaped man standing in front of the light. He would have known Yuri anywhere. He walked forward and the two men embraced.

Yuri pushed him an arm's length away and looked him over. "You have lost weight, Gregor. We will have to feed you for a month."

Gregor poked him in the belly through his long coat. "You have gained weight, Yuri. You look very solid."

Both men laughed. Yuri spoke first. "You sent good men. They told us where you were. The boy Sergei. He is strong. He is one of my personal guards." Then he grasped Gregor by the arm and walked him out of the headlights and around to the passenger seat of the Lada. He closed the door and walked around to get into the driver's seat. "It's just a Lada, but times are changing, Gregor. Soon, we will be able to buy Mercedes and Ford and Chrysler. I have always wanted a Ford Bronco. Good truck. American."

"I knew that you would get me out, Yuri," Gregor said.

Yuri looked down at his hands on the steering wheel. He seemed to be staring at the weathered eight-pointed star tattooed on the flesh between his thumb and index finger. It identified him as a member of the guild of robbers. He sighed deeply. "I am sorry that it took so long, Gregor. I have been trying for several years. As soon as I knew where you were, I bribe a man here to talk to a man there. Then, I bribe the man there to talk to a man somewhere else. Somehow no one seemed to talk to the right man. Then I put out feelers. Gorbachev made the Sixth Directorate. I found that the colonel in there was coming here and so, finally, I bribed the correct man."

"You did well, Yuri. You would have everything to gain if I had not come back out. You are next in line, but there is a reason that you are next in line, Yuri. There is a reason. Do you know what that reason is?"

"No, Gregor."

"You are second only to me because you are clever and will do well when you succeed me. Other men are more clever than you, Yuri. You know that there must be another reason, yes?"

"Yes, Gregor."

"It is because I love you like a son, Yuri, and I can trust you. I can trust you not to forget about me after seven years. I can trust you to come and get me. Trust is everything, Yuri." Gregor took a deep breath. He had resumed his former station in life without missing a beat. "Okay, Yuri, drive. Tell me what has happened and how the business is doing."

On the drive to Alma-Ata, where they would buy Gregor new clothes and board a train steaming northwest to Moscow, Yuri told Gregor about the business. The growth of the Dark Path under his stewardship. The new government. *Perestroika. Glasnost.* Since 1985, when Gregor had been imprisoned, the organization's profits had shot from one million to one hundred million rubles a year. He described Premier Valentin Pavlov's scheme to remove all 50- and 100-ruble notes from circulation in an effort to crush the flight of laundered rubles. He described the meeting he had attended with other leaders in the underworld to overcome this and other problems. He told him about Gorbachev's five-hundred-day transition program for moving to an open economy.

Yuri smiled broadly, revealing two silver incisors. "The country is up for sale! We are in line to take over privatization of over one hundred enterprises. Gregor, there are no limits!"

-20-

May 17, 1991, Seattle, Washington

MAYNARD JOHNSON was a rich man. He wasn't fabulously rich, but he had a couple of million dollars tucked away and he owned a shipping company consisting of an assortment of old freighters and container ships. He had purchased them at rock-bottom prices in dry-docks around Southeast Asia toward the end of their service lives. He would run them literally until they sank or suffered a costly engine failure, transporting anything and everything across the Pacific and then selling them for scrap. All of the ships had been reflagged as Liberian and he had set up a shell company offshore in the Caribbean to avoid troublesome interactions with the Internal Revenue Service. Maynard had started the shipping company to increase his profit margin on goods which he manufactured in sweatshop factories that he owned in the Philippines and Taiwan. Social unrest in the Philippines had made that operation unprofitable. Government meddling and regulations in Taiwan had ruined another profitable venture. He had shut it all down, sold the machinery, and torn down the buildings. That left only the ramshackle shipping company. He thought, *I need another company.* He was tired of shipping other people's goods and making other people's fortunes.

Maynard picked up the newspaper and started to read. On the third page of the Business Section, he noticed a small article:

"Lead under Fire"—The Environmental Protection Agency is investigating the effect of lead on the waterfowl population. A spokesperson has said that she expects at least a partial ban of all lead-containing fishing tackle by the end of 1994. This ban would affect shotgun shell pellets used in hunting marine fowl and a variety of fishing tackle.

That will kill a lot of companies, he thought. *They will have to retool and change their supply and marketing strategy.* He flipped a couple of pages further into the indexes. Lead was running about twenty-four cents a pound. He began thinking about metals, specifically, dense metals which could serve as a lead substitute. He thought back over various bills of lading he had signed over the years and remembered that tin was heavy. Not as dense as lead, but dense. He scanned the page again and noted that tin was running at $2.23 per pound.

I need to find it cheaper. Maynard's mind was whirring. He knew that something significant was going to boil over at any moment. It was all in there. It was going to happen. Then he remembered the slick brochure in which he had read about business opportunities in the new Russia. He recalled the key words:

"Government-subsidized access to natural resources to encourage foreign capital and joint ventures."

He sat back in his chair and reveled in his sheer genius. He hadn't even picked up the phone to set anything in motion, but he could already picture the corporate headquarters of his new company outside of Vladivostok. He would call it Maynard Johnson Tackle and Toys, MJTT. For an entrepreneur like Johnson, the project is 90 percent complete when he envisions it. He realized that the former Soviet Union, with no effective courts, an unstable government, and weak currency, was an accident waiting to happen. He snapped his fingers, sealing the deal, and spoke to the wall as if it were a shareholder. "It is time for us to take advantage of another free market."

-21-

December 25, 1991, Fox County, South Carolina

JAKE AND DIANA sat in the back of Joe's Bait and Tackle Shoppe, having a Christmas dinner of roast beef, green beans, carrots, and potatoes. Joe had procrastinated almost four years on his promise, but the shop was now Jake's. They had moved Joe down to his new house and dock the previous week. Joe had made them a present of the roast as a housewarming gift. Dinner being more or less over, Diana reached down and lifted an enormous package from underneath the table and handed it to Jake.

"Open it," she smiled.

"Okay," Jake replied, reaching for the box with one hand. He thought that a box this size would contain a sweater or overalls, so he was not prepared for the weight. He shot a second hand underneath it to keep it from falling on the remains of the meal, and brought it over to his lap. He carefully untied the string around the box and lifted the lid. "Wow!" he exclaimed. He looked at Diana. She was beaming. "Diana, this is too much!" Inside the box was a Pentax K-1000 camera with a 50-mm lens, a 29-mm wide-angle lens, a 130-mm zoom lens, and a 300-mm zoom lens, all with bayonet mounts for rapid exchange on the camera.

Diana pointed to the wall behind Jake. There he had posted photographs that he had taken around the lake of everything from sunsets to garfish. "I saw all of the beautiful pictures that you took with your old Kodak and thought that you should have some really good equipment."

"But Diana, this is really too much. And I'll be afraid to use it. What if I drop it in the water?"

"Nonsense. The stuff is made to be used. Make me some big sunset-over-the-islands photos, okay? I need something like that for the shop anyhow."

Jake looked intensely into her deep green eyes. He could easily lose himself in them. "I will, Diana. I'll take you some beautiful pictures." Then he reached under his chair and brought forth a small package and handed it to her. "Here, I got this for you."

She took the package and unwrapped it carefully, removing the paper in a way that would allow it to be reused. It was a long, thin box, hinged at the back. She lifted the lid and gasped. "Jake! It's gorgeous!"

"Put it on."

Diana lifted the thick white-gold necklace out of the box and put it around her neck. Jake thought that it was perfect. White gold accented her red hair and green eyes.

·22·

July 10, 1991, San Francisco, California

"DADDY, I'M SORRY that you're not home. I'm having a great time here in Washington. Being a Senate aide is a fantastic summer job. Senator Dawson says that I show tremendous potential, and he even took me to the Mall to see the Washington Monument and the Smithsonian. I'll call back later. Love ya." The machine beeped, indicating that the message was complete. Andrew hit a button on his keyboard, and the sound card, which had just recorded the communication, directed his computer to play it back over the speakers on his desk. He looked at the jagged lines on the screen which represented the frequency and intonation of his beloved daughter's voice. "Fucking amazing," he said offhandedly to no one.

He clicked his way back out of the sound program and exited to DOS. He scrolled the directories until he found the file he had just recorded. He had named it 910710co, which was his shorthand to indicate the person and the date in the allotted eight spaces. Next, he encrypted the file. When prompted, he typed in his twelve-letter pass phrase, and it was done. Nobody would ever hear that file again except for him.

Andrew had seen the potential for computers later than many people, but the personal computer had only recently become powerful enough to satisfy him fully. In 1987 he had purchased a 286 machine and lost patience with its slow speed and limited memory. In 1990 he had bought a 386, which had been an improvement but still did not give him all that he wanted. When the 486 machine had come out, he finally had the platform he needed. Software and accessories had finally developed to the point that they would change his life. He purchased the best civilian encryption that money could buy, a sound card, and a full-page color scanner. He had a 14,400-baud modem and was a regular lurker on the Internet and CompuServe Information Service. He learned how to download, send E-mail, gopher, use remailers for anonymity, and FTP. What he learned most of all, however, was that his computer was the most securely locked file cabinet that he could ever buy. It was safer than Fort Knox.

He password protected his computer from the menu and password protected his programs behind the menu. If an intruder got beyond that, all of his files were encrypted. His twelve-letter pass phrase gave him a sixty-two-bit key with which to encrypt the files. That meant that 2^{62} possible combinations would be legal for his key, but only one would decrypt the files. Even if someone developed a chip that could try a billion keys per second and put together a billion such chips, it would still take about a trillion years to come up with Andrew Oliver's pass phrase. He had read all about it on the Internet. He felt that his files were safe.

There was almost no paper of any kind in Andrew's office. All letters were scanned. If they were typed, he ran character recognition software and converted them to a text file before encrypting. If they were handwritten, they were saved as a graphics file and encrypted. When he had finished converting paper into magnetism, he burned it all in the fireplace. There was never more than one day's worth of paper correspondence in his possession. Photographs, letters, and even telephone messages fell onto magnetic media to be protected and saved in a way that had never before been possible.

In his office he had a file cabinet, where he kept hundreds of 3 1/2" high-density disks. He kept most of his files on these disks rather than clutter his hard drive. Andrew walked over to the cabinet and pulled open the top drawer, flipping through roughly three hundred disks until he located one called Corinne 1991–2. He took it back to his desk, put it in the slot, moved file 910710co from the hard drive to the floppy, and popped the disk back out. On his way back to the cabinet, Andrew stopped in midstride, taken by the impulse to look through the disk. It contained all of his daughter's recent correspondence, messages, and telephone conversations. He returned to the computer and began viewing files. He had become so adept at typing his pass phrase that he hardly even noticed he was doing it. He stared at the screen, looking at her fine handwriting on the University of Virginia stationery and her latest note on a letterhead that read "United States Senate." Yes, Corinne was going to be much more than her parents could have ever dreamed. He wasn't sure whether he wanted her to be a lawyer or a doctor, but her grades at Thomas Jefferson University would certainly pave her way down the road to a profession with status. He had money. She was going to be the first generation to give the Oliver family class.

The phone rang and Oliver exited the file. He looked at the incoming phone number ID and opened the desk drawer. Inside was a touchpad. He selected the button labeled 12 and pressed it. This activated the recording machine for Itasco Construction. He picked up the phone on the third ring, secure that, as with all correspondence, this call would be recorded on the correct tape to be filed later.

"Oliver," Andrew said officially.

"Andy, this is Buster." Andrew could tell by the quality of the connection that Buster was on a cellular phone.

"Yes, Buster."

"Andy, just letting you know that I'm heading down with the two weeks of transaction summaries and a pile of payroll checks for you to sign. I think that I'll be there at about five, if that's okay."

"That's good, Buster. I'll see you then." He hung up.

Andrew thought to himself, *Yes, Buster is a good man.* Loyal, and never asked questions. He collected money and kept the books for the construction company and printed out the paychecks. He was the first man whom Andrew had hired almost twenty years ago for his produce business. He had never questioned handing in his blue balance books or the red ledgers which returned with $20 received in cash payment here and $100 in cash payment there. The practice had ended four years ago with the final deposit of the money. Buster had been with him the whole time. He was the only man whom Andrew Oliver could trust completely. But even Buster did not know the whole story. No one would ever know.

-23-

August 12, 1992, Placid Vista, California

Associated Press, Washington, DC—The offices of Senator Ronald Dawson (D–CA) announced today that the Senator will not seek reelection in November. No explanation was given, and Senator Dawson could not be reached for comment. Sources within the Democratic presidential campaign have suggested that the Senator is in line for a Cabinet-level post or senior adviser position in what the party hopes will finally become a Democratic White House. It has also been suggested that the Senator has a significant health problem. His staff has often implied as much when answering for his frequent absenteeism during the current term.

RONALD DAWSON READ the second-page story and snorted. "It's my fucking wife, you imbeciles," he muttered. He was sitting on the back porch of what appeared to be a lovely Victorian-style mansion precariously balanced on the cliffs overlooking the Pacific in northern California. Out in front of the house was a well-manicured lawn, and beyond the grass lay twenty acres of woodland with walking trails throughout. Beyond the woodland, and out of sight from any of the trails, was a ten-foot chain-link fence with old-fashioned barbed wire strung along its top. The fence enclosed the house and grounds, with the only entrance or exit being from the cliff or through the main gate, which was manned around the clock by concerned professional guards. The sign outside read, "PLACID VISTA."

Dawson reflected on what had led him here. His wife had made him come. She had sworn that she would divorce him and reveal his secret unless he submitted to the regimen. "She probably read it in *Cosmopolitan*," he grumbled. "Twenty Ways to Ruin Your Husband's Career that He Can Do Absolutely Nothing About. The fucking bitch." He threw the paper violently onto the porch.

So here he was, locked up for four weeks in a comfortable, twelve-thousand-dollar-a-week drug rehabilitation prison that dealt exclusively with the rich and famous. He remembered the interview with the resident manager. "Discretion and confidentiality are our watchwords," she had said silkily in an overly cultured voice. The accent had sounded upper-class Virginian, but she was his image in the flesh of a tubby German prison matron. She just had the wrong silly accent. "You can rest easy here, sir," she had said.

He picked up the paper and threw it down again. It was his only outlet. "It's difficult to be on the campaign trail when all I get to see are fucking nature trails for the next month."

·24·   *September 12, 1992, Fox County, South Carolina*

CLARENCE PULLED HIS PATROL CAR into the parking lot of Joe's Bait and Tackle Shoppe. He stepped out of the car to watch Jake alongside the road. With a wheelbarrow full of cement and a pile of cinder blocks, he was positioning the blocks one on top of another to form a little fortification where his mailbox had been. Clarence knew what this was all about. He had seen a few of the mailboxes on his way over.

"Whatcha doin', Jake?" he asked innocently.

Jake looked up from his crouch and wiped sweat off his brow with his right forearm as the trowel in his hand dripped mortar on his ponytail. He said, "Building a new mailbox." Then he laid another layer of cement and placed another block on top.

"Why are you buildin' it like that?" Clarence outlined the blockhouse shape with his hands.

"Kids have been blowing up my old mailbox with M-80s. This ought to stop that."

Clarence shook his head. He had been a police officer for a long time. "Jake, did it occur to you that this will only be a challenge to them?"

"Nope. I think that they'll go and blow up somebody else's mailbox, Clarence. It's not a perfect solution, but it's my solution." He scraped the trowel across another block.

"You ought to go talk to Geery. They used to blow his box up, and he built a contraption that hauls the box up into a tree on a big lever. The mailman has to pull a rope to bring it down."

"Why don't the kids pull the rope down?" Jake asked. He was growing perturbed.

"Jake, you know those kids are at least half liquored up on Friday night. Out of sight, out of mind," Clarence laughed. "You might as well paint a bull's-eye on that thing."

"Com'on, Clarence. Give me a little moral support here."

"Okay, Jake. I'm sure those kids will leave a big strong thing like that alone," he grinned smugly.

·25·   *December 1, 1992, Dupont Circle, Washington, DC*

"RONALD! YOU PROMISED ME that you were going to divorce her! I am tired of having to come to this apartment!" She was screaming. Tears were rolling down her cheeks, smearing her mascara. "What do you call it? Oh, our 'safe house.' What the fuck is that, Ronald!" she said sarcastically and turned away from him quickly, sending a mass of blonde hair flying behind her. She took a deep breath and spoke more calmly. Her voice was sad. "I want to go to your house. I want you to come to mine. I don't want to be some dirty little secret that you have tucked away in this apartment."

"I'm going to leave her, baby. It's just a little more complicated than all of that. I am a presidential adviser. You know, one of the knights of the round table. I have to wait a little while. The timing has to be right." He said this quietly, solemnly.

"You bastard!" she screamed in another emotional swing. "You are lying. I can't keep on fucking you unless we're going to get married." She said this with genuine venom. It cut him to the quick.

He replied with genuine venom. "What? You got too much class to be a mistress?"

"What do you mean by that?" Suddenly her tone was mystified.

"I mean that you can take the girl out of the trailer park, but you can never take the trailer park out of the girl."

"Fuck you!" she screamed.

"Fuck me? Fuck me? You act like you are some kind of aristocrat, when all you are is white trash with some cash. You think that your daddy's little rags-to-riches story impresses me?" He was yelling now.

"You really are a bastard," Corinne said meekly and sat down as if defeated. She knew that he had other things she needed besides a wedding ring.

Suddenly, inexplicably, Ronald Dawson felt guilty. He didn't say things like that when he wasn't using or withdrawing. He felt wicked, corrupt, base, evil. What he was about to say was a bald-faced lie, but he said it anyway. "Corinne, honey, I love you. I'm sorry about what I just said. I'll leave my wife, I promise you. Just give me a little time." She didn't respond.

He reached behind her to the liquor cabinet and withdrew a throat lozenge can. He placed it on the table and opened the lid, revealing white powder. A tiny spoon rested on top. She turned and looked at him with renewed interest. He touched a pinkie finger to the powder and put it in a nostril, inhaling. "We're just a little uptight right now." He pushed the container toward her. "This will help, and we can kiss and make up like we always do."

-26-

December 11, 1992, San Francisco, California

ANDREW OLIVER WAS WATCHING the NBC news, as was his custom every evening at six, followed by one hour of CNN. He kept his videocassette machine on at all times to capture important items for review at a later date. The headline story concerned DEA raids in cooperation with the governments of Bolivia, Peru, Panama, and Colombia.

"This is Sally Kim, sitting in for Tom Brokaw, who is on assignment. A stunning series of raids across Central and South America have struck at the heart of the Cali cartel." As she continued to narrate, video footage of running armed men and helicopters flashed across the screen. A dead peasant was shown briefly as he lay at the feet of Bolivian soldiers. Close-ups of laboratory equipment and brown wrappers, presumably containing cocaine, followed. The footage abruptly changed to courthouse steps, where a man was briskly led to a car between two men dressed in suits. "Panamanian Federal Judge Heriberto Enríquez ruled within an hour to allow the extradition of Domingo Valens to the United States to stand trial for drug trafficking and money laundering. Domingo Valens is suspected of being a leading member of the Cali cartel."

The footage switched again to the picture of a DEA press conference. The man at the podium was saying, "Today we have struck a tremendous blow in the war on drugs. We have shown the cartels that the United States and our South American neighbors will not stand idly by, but will work together to stamp out this modern plague."

None of the news this night seemed to bear on Andrew Oliver's life, but he always enjoyed learning about the world.

·27·

December 1992, Fox County, South Carolina

JAKE STOOD REGARDING the rubble morosely. The explosion had been deafening. Flying pieces of concrete and cinder block had broken a window on the front of his house, fifty feet away. The spot upon which he stood had been ground zero the previous evening. Debris was strewn in a wide radius around the blackened base of concrete blocks. Across the road he noticed a glint of metal. He walked over and retrieved a small threaded metal cap, about two inches in diameter. The cap was deformed and the threads were stripped. He recognized the remnants of a pipe bomb when he saw them. *Clarence was right,* he muttered to himself. That was when he noticed the sheriff's patrol car approaching from the west. *Time to eat some crow.*

The cruiser pulled into the parking lot, and a fit young white man got out of the driver's seat, in his gray striped sheriff's patrol uniform. As he stood, he carefully placed the broad-brimmed hat on his head and closed the door. Jake breathed a sigh of relief. He was not ready to face Clarence, the Nostradamus of crime, who had predicted the demise of his concrete mailbox.

"Howdy, Jake. What happened?" the deputy asked.

"Well, Bud," Jake shrugged his shoulders and put his hands in the front pockets of his overalls. "Looks like they blew up my mailbox again." He flipped him the metal piece, which Bud caught in midair.

The deputy looked at the piece and turned it over in his hand. Then he looked at the rubble at Jake's feet. "Pipe bomb, huh? I used to make stuff like this when I was a young hoodlum. Used to fill them with match heads. I'm lucky to be alive."

"It did the job," Jake lamented.

"Sure did. Somebody has been blowing up mailboxes around here pretty regular, but they usually use M-80s. Looks like they did you special," the deputy commented wryly. "I could fill out a report or somethin'. Don't think it would do you much good."

"I'm just going to build a better mailbox." Jake set his jaw.

"You know, you ought. . . ."

Jake cut him off. "I know, I ought to go see Geery. He's really smart. I know, I know."

-28-

March 1993, Vladivostok, Russia

A BURLY MAN in a tailored double-breasted silk suit walked into Thomas Johnson's office and dropped a clipboard on the desk. "Here is the manifest for the shipment going out this evening, sir.

Also, the bill of lading for the shipment which came in last evening in your absence. It requires your signature." Two men who looked like Olympic weight lifters stood behind the man in the suit. In all likelihood, they had been part of the mammoth Soviet sports machine, but now that there was no Soviet Union, there was no Soviet sports apparatus. Well-built young men didn't have much trouble finding employment these days in Russia. It seemed like everyone had some muscle working for him.

Thomas pretended to look over the manifest carefully. It didn't matter, he knew. They would have their percentage of the shipment for their own goods. All the same, he wanted the manifest to at least appear legitimate. He was always afraid of what they might be bold enough to list. He was not as brazen as his partners in this joint venture in the new Russia. There were forty-three containers to be shipped, and each was identified by a six-digit number as holding an assortment of toys and fishing tackle that was turned out by MJTT, designed and manufactured to exacting standards in Vladivostok. Contains no lead.

The man in the suit began to tap his foot. "Sir, we must take this through certain official channels to get the ship under way this evening. I assure you that the manifest is complete."

Thomas signed the bottom of five sheets of paper and handed back the clipboard without comment. The three Russians left, the last one closing the office door. With the Russians gone, he turned his eyes to the bill of lading they had left him. Everything listed was a perishable, nonluxury item and therefore subject to the lowest tariffs. Thomas had seen the actual cargo from his office window: forty Japanese used cars of various makes. On average a Japanese used automobile could be purchased for $1,000 in Niigata and sold for over $3,000 in Vladivostok. MJTT imported several hundred annually, although the transactions never appeared on any ledgers that Thomas was privy to.

This whole business set up by his father made him nervous. That it was making money hand over fist could not be denied, but the arrangement was not totally aboveboard. Thomas had been doing a little snooping around the docks and knew very well that all of the containers did not contain his products.

He had been faced with a simple choice shortly after the factory had been completed. It had been put to him succinctly by Gregor, who had come in as an insurance agent. Gregor had arrived with two muscle-bound young men in tow, just like his underling had today. He had told Thomas, "You have a choice. You can sign me on and I will protect your company and take care of the issues of tariffs and have my men run your docks, or you can go home, because if you do not, I assure you that you and your business are very likely to suffer many industrial accidents and losses." Gregor had said this with such sincerity that it could not have been taken as a threat, only a prediction. Thomas had taken them on. Their fee was 40 percent of the gross profits and use of the line for small "personal" shipments to Gregor in Oakland. This normally amounted to about 20 percent of the container space. The manifests always indicated that the containers were filled entirely with MJTT products. Thomas knew that this was not accurate. The space was used to smuggle out nickel, copper, and cobalt that had been purchased at subsidized prices for internal use. He had also seen religious icons, books, portable military hardware, and what he dimly suspected were synthetic drugs being boxed into the containers and shipped.

He was not concerned with prosecution, however, because he had taken out a little insurance on the American side as well. He was what the CIA referred to as a HUMINT, or human intelligence source. He simply provided a weekly report of any small arms he suspected had gone out in a dead-letter box near the terminus of the Trans-Siberian Railway. His controller left him $200 in cash in another drop monthly for his troubles and guaranteed immunity should the long arm of the law reach toward MJTT. Langley didn't give a tinker's damn if Russian assets, art, and national treasures were wandering offshore. It wanted to know about military hardware. That was all. It also didn't give a damn about Thomas; if U.S. Customs or Russian export control found him out, it would vanish, leaving the entrepreneur's son to their tender mercies.

Gregor's organization took care of MJTT, and Thomas had few complaints. The Russian provided guards on the premises around the clock, workers on the docks, and dealt with all the local bureaucrats on matters of taxes, duties, and tariffs. MJTT had never suffered a break-in, and there was virtually no theft by the workers. Gregor's hoods kept the employees in line to the point that over half were showing up to work sober, no small accomplishment in Russia. Tariffs were another matter. They were remarkably low. Gregor's men had bribery down to a science. A $10,000 tariff could magically drop to $800 if a $600 bribe was inserted at the proper juncture of the procedure. Thomas had an MBA from Stanford, but he could have done the math without it.

Gregor's accountants also handled the federal and local taxes. For this, Thomas was grateful, since Russian tax laws were cumbersome, badly formulated, and constantly changing, often retroactively. There were taxes for things that seemed absolutely lunatic, such as an additional tax on gross intake if one used the word "Russia" in the company name. Investment capital was subject to value-added tax, and corporate profit taxes ran as high as 40 percent. Many deductions that Western businesses took for granted did not apply when calculating profit, so the percentage was often greater than 40 percent. For example, portions of employee salaries that exceeded six times minimum wages were not deductible. The average minimum wage was about ten dollars a month. Any amount paid to employees over sixty dollars a month counted in the Russian business's bottom line as profit. Of course, this was all last week. It was maddening, and Thomas was happy to have Gregor's men handle the accounts. He knew that they doctored the books, but this was not business conducted in America or Western Europe. This was business in the new Russia.

-29-

March 12, 1993, San Francisco, California

ANDREW OLIVER was once again watching the news. He had seen the NBC nightly news and had switched channels by remote control to watch CNN.

A bright-eyed reporter appeared, with the photo of a silhouetted terrorist projected over her left shoulder. "This afternoon we received in the CNN newsroom a videocassette. Broadcast of the contents was delayed while CNN allowed the Federal Bureau of Investigation to examine the tape and packaging. The accompanying letter states that the tape was delivered from the Revolutionary Armed Forces of Colombia, or FARC, a terrorist organization. Sources inside Colombia have told CNN that FARC is closely linked to the Cali cartel. Although no members of this group have made themselves available for comment, we have no reason to doubt the authenticity of the tape."

The image of the young reporter at her desk disappeared and was replaced by the video. A man was sitting at a desk reading a statement. Behind him was a white concrete wall which made the black hood he wore over his head stand out. The Latin rhythm of the Spanish, accentuated with his gesturing hands, mesmerized Andrew. He read the translation which scrolled across the bottom of the screen: "We of the People's Army will not allow our rights to be trampled upon by the might of northern aggressors. Prominent persons in the United States and the puppet state of Panama will die every week until Domingo Valens is released."

-30-

THE CREDITS SCROLLED DOWN Diana's television screen. The room was dark except for the light emanating from the set. The couple sat together on the couch, Diana leaning into Jake with her legs curled up underneath her and her head resting upon his chest. His arm was draped lazily around her.

"Do they *really* think that the South is that way, Jake?" Diana asked drowsily, without moving.

"Oh, I guess some people do, honey," Jake replied, resting his chin on the top of her head.

"I think that it's kind of insulting."

"Well, it's that or *Deliverance* for a lot of folks."

"Jake!"

"I was just joking, honey. Didn't you think the movie was funny?"

"Sure," she said softly.

"Besides, what comes to your mind when I say 'New Jersey'?"

"Toxic waste dumps. Pavement. Highway exit numbers."

"What if I told you that most of the state is green and beautiful?"

"I'd have to see it, I guess," she said as she sighed and snuggled into him.

"See, everybody gets nailed with some image or another," Jake whispered into her hair.

"Okay, Jake," Diana said sleepily, apparently bringing the conversation to an end.

The screen turned blue as the tape ended, and Jake heard the VCR begin to rewind *My Cousin Vinny* automatically. Diana's video machine had reintroduced him to a great pleasure which he had almost forgotten: feature films. They now rented movies twice a week and watched them entwined on her couch. Jake was meticulous in the selection. He would study his video guide and pick out nothing but five-star classics, Academy Award winners, or movies neglected by the critics but noted for being particularly poignant. Tonight had been the regularly scheduled exception to the rule. Diana preferred light entertainment, new releases, and comedy. She appeared to dislike murder mysteries, although she never expressed it in so many words. For the most part, Jake sought to be edified in some way by a film. Diana only wanted to be entertained.

Revelatory or not, however, there were three stars whose movies Jake would not miss: Arnold Schwarzenegger, Sylvester Stallone, and Harrison Ford. Action heroes for action movies, they were larger than life and he loved them.

He remembered when his fascination with movies had begun. He had found the great escape into the silver screen quite by accident, during final examinations in the first semester of freshman year. Feeling tired, nervous, overworked, and unhopeful about his chances of passing an impending calculus final, he had gone for a walk in the rain. An hour later, he had found himself standing outside a rundown theater which was still playing *The Godfather.* "Why not?" he had said to himself, and paid the dollar for admission. Pacino and Brando had whisked him away from his world for over two hours, and the haunting theme music echoed in his head for days. For the next four years he had vanished into Hollywood's world every time he felt depressed, stressed, or bored. From those years he still remembered how he felt leaving *The Sting, The Way We Were, Chinatown, One Flew over the Cuckoo's Nest, Taxi Driver,* and a hundred other films.

Nineteen seventy-six was a banner year. He had never seen a film that moved him as viscerally as *Rocky.* When he later found out that Stallone had written the story, he became a lifetime fan. That year also introduced to the big screen someone little known outside of the tightly knit body-building community. The movie was *Stay Hungry,* the actor, Arnold Schwarzenegger. The next year, Jake's first out of college, he wandered into *Star Wars* and noticed for the first time an actor named Harrison Ford. After that, the routine of his life crowded out the nonessentials, and he gradually fell out of the habit of visiting the theater, with the exception of keeping up with his Big Three. Now he attended movies twice a week at the house of the woman he loved. He wondered how he could have forgotten how much he loved them as the VCR clicked and ejected the rewound videocassette.

The noise made Diana stir. She shifted and nestled her chin more tightly into his chest. "Did you think she was pretty?" she asked, yawning.

"Who?" Jake said.

"The girl in the movie, silly."

"Yeah, sure."

"I thought she was trashy," she murmured.

"I'm sure that she's perfectly nice in real life, honey."

Diana sat up slowly and stretched her arms above her head before draping them over Jake's shoulders and touching her nose to his. Her green eyes twinkled mischievously as she stared into his and purred seductively. "Nicer than me?"

He answered her by lifting her gently off the couch and carrying her to her bed. The love they made was an unchoreographed pas de deux, an unhurried ballet of tender familiarity, perfectly free of any affectation or embarrassment. Theirs was a composure and confidence born of intimacy, each content to become both master and servant, each approaching the task of pleasuring with the attention of the novice and the assurance of the virtuoso. When their exquisite pantomime was finished, each had told the other once again a wordless story of love.

Jake rolled over in the bed and propped himself up on an elbow, looking at Diana's face. She had drawn the sheets up over her breasts and her face was moist and flushed. Her red hair lay in a disorganized jumble on the pillow. Jake swept a few loose strands tenderly off her brow. He could see that once again, in the wake of lovemaking, she had gone. She often did this. Her lips smiled contentedly as she tried to keep her personal demons from rising to the surface of the languorous facade, but her eyes told another tale. If he didn't know better, he would assume that she was thinking of a lover she had betrayed only moments ago.

It occurred to Jake that, perhaps, after all of this time together, Diana wanted more. Perhaps she wanted some sort of commitment. It puzzled him. She seemed to love him but always evaded talk of marriage as if the topic were leprous. She seemed to want things just as they were. No more, no less.

"Diana?" Jake asked.

"Uh-huh," she said distantly.

"You okay, honey?"

"Yeah, I'm fine, Jake."

"Well, I was just thinking . . ." He paused to shift his elbow to a more comfortable position. "I was just thinking . . . well, why don't you come down and live with me?"

Diana was silent for a long moment. Then she said gently, "We can't do that, hon. People don't 'live together' down here. It's just not done. It's not acceptable."

"But I thought, well, you know. People seem to accept us as a couple, you know?" Jake stumbled over his words.

"Oh, yes, Jake. We're a fine couple as long as we don't actually live in the same house. They're willing to overlook us as long as we don't openly flout their values." A stillness settled in the room. Jake could hear a lone cricket outside the window. Diana looked up at him thoughtfully. The expression on her face reflected the confusion and resolution that were wrestling in her mind. "We'd have to be married for them to think so well of us if we lived together," she said flatly. Abruptly, she motioned for him to lie down. "Now, you just go to sleep." She turned away from him to face the wall.

Jake rolled over and stared out the bedroom window for over an hour before he fell into fitful slumber. He was thinking about Diana. The way that she had said, "We'd have to be married," did not sound like a woman who wanted to be asked. The look in her eyes gave him no invitation for the question. He was afraid that if he did not understand now, after all this time, what demons Diana struggled to keep at bay, then he would never understand.

-31-

December 4, 1993, Interstate 95, Virginia

THE GENERIC GRAY CHRYSLER hummed smoothly down the freeway as the four men within it kept their thoughts to themselves. They were all lawyers who worked for the Federal Bureau of Investigation, returning from a meeting in Quantico with their counterparts from the Central Intelligence Agency. The purpose of their meeting had been to hammer out an agreement between the agencies for the sharing of intelligence in the new post-Cold War political arena. On the previous evening the talks had reached an impasse, and this morning the negotiations had been called off. No compromise had been reached.

The youngest man, who sat in the back on the right-hand side, was the first to speak. "What are the spooks afraid of?"

The driver, an older man with silver hair and a dark suit, replied in an official monotone with the phrase that the CIA's lawyer had hammered into him repeatedly in his subcommittee. "It is unacceptable for an outside agency to endanger our human intelligence assets."

"What?" the young lawyer asked. He had been in another meeting.

The older man sighed. He understood the CIA's reluctance. He had seen good men get killed working undercover for the Bureau because some bureaucrat pushed too hard and the long arm of the law got some bad guys before they could extract the good guy from the fray. Criminal organizations become very introspective when they start taking losses, and that was when agents died. The older man endeavored to explain what he was thinking.

"The spooks don't want us to go and indiscriminately arrest bad guys without letting them know in advance so that they can protect their agents. It's really pretty simple at the core."

"Come on. We know that they have someone inside the Cali cartel. High up, from what I hear. Do you realize what we and the DEA could probably accomplish if we had access to that intelligence?"

"Quite frankly, we'd probably get their man killed. They know that." The car became silent again, and the four men listened to the whine of the tires on the highway.

·32·

December 13, 1993, Alexandria, Virginia

"UNIT 42, we have a 10-54, 10-49. 4012 King Street. Code 3," the dispatcher's voice crackled over the car radio.

"This is Unit 42. 10-4. Proceeding." Sergeant Paul Stevens flipped on his lights and siren and took the next right turn to head toward King Street. His partner, Sergeant Harry Wistner, looked over at him and watched the blue lights flash off the buildings around them. Sergeant Stevens concentrated on driving and honked his horn at a car which was slow to give way. "Ten-fifty-four. Possible dead body. I've always wondered about that one. Is it dead or alive? Possible?" He took the next right onto King Street.

Sergeant Wistner was looking out the window and reading off street numbers. "We're in the three thousand block. Even numbers are on this side. There's the first four thousand. Pull over here. There's the address."

Stevens pulled over and lifted the radio mike. "This is Unit 42. 10-97."

An old lady ran out to the car. "Officers, you must help me! I think the young woman who lives downstairs is dead." The policemen approached the house, a blue two-story that had been modified into a duplex. The old woman led them to the lower apartment in back as she continued to talk. "I'm the owner of the house, but not the manager. I don't have any keys. I haven't seen Miss Oliver in two days, where I ordinarily see her almost every morning. She hasn't picked up her mail, so I got it out of her box and walked around to the back here to give it to her in case she was sick or something. I knocked." She paused and took a deep breath. She opened a small white wooden gate that led to the tiny yard behind the building and motioned them through. "I knocked and knocked and when I looked in the window, I could see her in there lying on the bed and not moving. I knocked very loudly and she still has not moved, so I called you."

Wistner banged heavily on the door. There was no response. "Ma'am, I'm going to have to break it down."

"That's why I called you," the old woman replied.

"Okay." He backed away a step and kicked the door at the handle with his right foot. Wood splintered and the door flew inward. The two cops entered and walked toward the bedroom. The smell in the apartment was horrid. They looked at one another. There was no doubt that something was dead in the place. They went into the bedroom and saw what had been a beautiful young woman with long blonde hair lying naked on the bed. Her skin was pale and translucent, azure shaded. Darker blue discoloration was visible on her otherwise flawless right cheek, breasts, stomach, and thighs. She was dead. The two men backed out of the bedroom, careful not to disturb anything that might be evidence.

Stevens turned to Wistner at the door of the apartment. "Call in and tell them it's a coroner's case and possible homicide."

Stevens remained in the doorway, to prevent any further entry. Wistner walked out of the front door and saw the old lady. "Ma'am, could you please return to your apartment? We're going to have to set up a police line here. I'll come around and speak with you in a few minutes."

The old woman sat down on the ground as if unable to stand any longer. She had a distant, bewildered look on her face. She seemed to have aged ten years before the policeman's eyes until she didn't even resemble the scrappy woman who had met them on the street. A single tear coursed down each cheek as she began to weep. "Such a sweet young girl, that little Corinne. Such a sweet young girl!"

Wistner walked to the car and pulled out the microphone. "This is Unit 42. 10-55 possible 187."

"Ten-four Unit 42. Dispatching homicide."

She must have been beautiful, Wistner thought wryly. He reached into his uniform pocket, extracted a packet of Camel Filters, and pulled one out. He lit it and inhaled to get the smell of death out of his nostrils.

·33·

December 13, 1993, Panama City, Panama

HERIBERTO ENRÍQUEZ OBSERVED the motorcade in front of him as the BMW motorcycles roared onto Davila Avenue. He was seated in the back of an armored limousine and had been provided additional protection by the police department. This was necessary because he had been placed in the unfortunate position of being the judge called to rule on the extradition case of Domingo Valens. His life had been threatened repeatedly in the months since the ruling, but Heriberto was an extraordinarily brave man. He had also taken precautions. He had even ordered a fine leather jacket from Miguel Caballero and John Murphy's shop in Bogotá. The jacket was your garden-variety Kevlar- and Spectra-lined bulletproof designer wear that was in style all over South America.

American diplomats could not see from their ivory towers that "taking a stand against the drug lords" was not a harmless political sound bite down here, as it was in Washington. It was a suicidal act in the hard cold reality of Central and South America. Heriberto was a believer, however, and had concluded long ago that narcotics could well be the downfall of civilization based on the rule of law. He took his stand out of moral conviction, not public opinion polls, and he was willing to accept the consequences. What he did not and could not know was that the consequences lay in wait at the next intersection.

Among the many things that he did not know was that the twelve-year-old son of Captain Horacio Rodríguez was the un-willing guest of Santiago Valens on his estate in neighboring Co-lombia. Captain Rodríguez was the officer in charge of the honorable judge's security detail. The only thing that Captain Rodríguez had to do in order to secure the safe return of his boy was to halt the motorcade for thirty seconds at the intersection with Bolivar Street. Santiago had even made this easy for the cap-tain, providing a bevy of peasant children to cross the intersection as the motorcade approached.

Heriberto observed the children scramble into the intersec-tion and saw the motorcade halt as the motorcycle escort in front ordered the children to the sidewalks. He noticed that the side-walks were vacant as the column started to move. Even the chil-dren, sensing danger, ran away as fast as their legs would carry them. He didn't like it. A vacant street in the late afternoon hours, long after siesta, was ominous. The people were aware that this was not a place to be. Consequently, they were not here. The judge hunched down slightly in his seat remembering the safety specifications of the American-made limousine. "It is bulletproof," he muttered to himself.

Just then the limo passed over a manhole cover. A figure on the roof of a nearby building overlooking the scene had been waiting for this moment. As soon as the slow-moving vehicle had completely covered the metal disc, he hit the gray button of the remote he held in his hand. The modified model-car controller triggered a TOW antitank missile to fire through the hole in the cover. Its projectile plowed into the underbelly of the vehicle.

There was the soft thud of the impact, followed by a muffled explosion. The vehicle came to a halt.

Heriberto heard and felt the explosion from underneath the vehicle. The hardened limousine rose a few inches into the air and settled. A credit to its engineers, it protected its charge, but it could no longer convey him. The drivetrain was shattered. Police officers swarmed around the motorcar, and the judge recognized Captain Rodríguez as he approached the passenger side door and motioned for him to get out and keep low. The judge exited the vehicle, his head coming up for just a fraction of a second above the line of the roof. It was enough. The man on the roof sighted him in the cross hairs of his telescopic lens and pulled the trigger once. Judge Enríquez wasn't wearing a Kevlar hat, and his head jerked violently to the left with the impact of the bullet. The police instantly surrounded the fallen judge and returned fire at the roof, but they were now defending a corpse.

Two weeks later, the police inquiry found that Captain Rodríguez should have kept Judge Heriberto Enríquez in the safety of his vehicle and awaited reinforcements but that, under the circumstances, his action had not been criminally negligent, merely incorrect. He was allowed to retain his commission in the service of the city. More important to the captain, and apparently unnoticed by the police department, his son was returned unharmed from his vacation.

·34·

December 14, 1993, Fox County, South Carolina

JAKE DROVE SLOWLY DOWN the two-lane macadamized road. He was looking carefully for the spot which Joe had described cryptically to him. "Drive down Old Mill Road until you come to a fork and take the left one. 'Bout a mile farther on down you'll see a red barn with white trim. As you keep driving down the road toward the barn, you'll start to see a white sign coming out from behind the barn, like, due to the curve in the road and all. When you can see all of that sign, stop right there and get out. You'll be within a hundred yards more or less of the path that leads up to Geery's place."

Nobody knew anything about Geery. Rumor was that he had worked on the Manhattan Project but had rejected the life of a research scientist due to the corrupting influence of the military. Nobody really knew anything, however, and in the rural South, it was still true that if a man wanted to keep to himself, he was more than welcome to do so. He had to accept that what people didn't know, they would make up, and then gossip about that. But, if he really kept to himself, he wouldn't know about that, either. Geery wasn't a hermit, in the strictest sense of the word, but was apparently almost totally self-sufficient back in the woods of his fifty-acre stretch. He came out about once a year and purchased a few things at the seed and feed store, mostly .22-caliber ammunition. Thomas, the postman, however, said that he received packages almost every other day from scientific, chemical, computer, and modeling companies. He received no personal correspondence and his only other mail was monthly statements from Bell South, South Carolina Electric and Gas, CompuServe Information Services, and, a recent addition, America Online. He had a telephone line, presumably for his computer, but no telephone. A lot of the men down on the lake agreed that having no phone, in itself, would extend one's life several years. If polled, most would confess that they wouldn't have one except for their wives.

All anyone really knew was that Geery had appeared in Fox County sometime in the fall of 1964, had purchased fifty acres of woodland, and had disappeared into it. During the first few years he would come out about once a month to buy nails, rope, seeds, cat food, and various other consumable items. By 1968 he was apparently well settled in and came out less frequently. He had no "NO TRESPASSING" signs on fences, but people generally respected his property lines. Over the previous thirty years, there had been repeated encounters by children who had wandered into the woods by accident or to see the hermit with their own eyes. All of these children came back from their adventure with rock candy in their pockets and nothing but stories of wonder at the man with aquamarine blue eyes and what he had built back in the woods. He was apparently a thoroughly decent man, one of the very few who could be content with his own company for long periods of time.

Even knowing all of this, Jake approached the path with a certain amount of trepidation. *Lions and tigers and bears, oh, my!* He started to feel better. At the foot of the path, where it ran into the road, he saw a rope hanging from the trees. Its use was not apparent, so he pulled it and backed onto the road to watch. Jake heard a click back in the woods and saw a pole hewn from a pine tree, about forty feet long, descend in a long arc toward where he stood. When the end of the pole reached him, he saw that it was topped with a large mailbox, its mouth opening toward him. He walked forward and pulled the rope again. The mailbox slowly swung itself back into the leaves, forty feet above the floor of the forest.

"Wow," Jake said to himself, and started walking up the path. He halted at the catapultlike contraption that lowered and raised the mailbox. The descent of the pole was slowed by a tape spring, which it wound tightly on the way down. The pole was raised again by a rope wound around a wheel which was turned by the tape spring. There was a crank on the spring to wind it tighter.

It was ingenious. Jake knew that he had come to the right place. He continued to walk up the path. After covering a thousand yards in the woods, treading over brown leaves and pine needles, the woods thinned and he saw before him a log cabin. As he continued to walk, he realized that it was not one cabin but a series of log cabins connected by halls that ran from one to the other. The buildings were joined together by walkways to form a rough circle. There was a porch on the building that faced him. Somehow he had expected to find Geery sitting on the porch, smoking a pipe and reminiscing about a life spent in the woods, a bearded, contemplative modern-day Thoreau. The porch was empty, but he noticed smoke rising from the chimney of the cabin. That was when he heard the explosion.

-35-

December 14, 1993, Alexandria, Virginia

DOCTOR ARUN KRISHNADAMA WALKED AWAY from the examining table and stripped his gloves carefully off his left and then his right hand, tossing them into the biological waste container. He sighed for at least the three-thousandth time in the last three years and wondered why he had chosen this field. He reconciled himself to it for the three-thousandth time in the same breath. "The money is good. I get to stay in the best country in the world. The work is necessary." This was the mantra he recited to bring himself into death every morning and move from corpse to corpse throughout the day. After medical school at Georgetown, one of his instructors had secured him a job as an assistant medical examiner through a long-standing friendship with the coroner. Arun walked slowly to the door to converse with the detective who awaited him.

Detective Stuart McDermit looked inquisitively at the medical examiner. "Well?" he asked.

Arun inhaled the fresh air of the hallway to clear the smell of disinfectant from his nostrils. Exhaling completely, he replied, "It is very sad, Detective. Such a beautiful young woman."

The detective noticed that a decade of schooling had not removed the singsong Indian rhythm from the doctor's speech. He nodded. "Yes, I know. It is certainly sad."

Arun continued. "Well, there is no doubt that the cause of death is respiratory and cardiac failure due to an overdose of cocaine. There are massive amounts of the drug present in her system. The ulcerations in the nasal cavity indicate that she was a frequent user."

"So, it is not a murder?"

"That is not exactly what I would conclude, Detective." McDermit found himself losing the doctor's reply in the Indian rhythm. He focused on the words. "Your report indicated that she was found lying on her back. Lividity suggests that she did not die on her back; rather, she died lying on her stomach and remained in that position for a number of hours before being placed on her back."

"So, it was a murder?"

"That is not what I said either, Detective. It simply appears that she was moved at some time after her death but before she was found. Either turned over in her bed, or moved from another location."

"Somebody knew that she was dead. Is that what you are saying?"

"Well, yes. Somebody moved her. I place the time of death at approximately 7 P.M. on the twelfth. This was done by core temperature loss. It is fairly accurate for a body found indoors." The Indian paused as if he were considering a more delicate way to phrase the rest of his report. "Additionally, I located semen in her vagina. It indicates she had intercourse shortly before or after her death. I have sent a sample to the laboratory for blood-type determination."

"Anything else that I can go with before I get your written report?"

"The only other unusual thing is that it appears that she was washed after she died, with some sort of grease-cutting agent like Fantastick or Windex. Strange. I have no ideas about that."

"Maybe the perp thought he'd get fingerprints off her body!" the detective laughed.

"Oh, you should not laugh. It is difficult, but it can be done. Iodine fumes or a solution of Benzedrine, alcohol, and hydrogen peroxide." The doctor's brown face lit up and the whites of his eyes gleamed as he grinned in satisfaction. "I found no prints, Detective. They won't usually last two days on a body anyway."

"Oh," the detective said. "Learn something new every day."

-36-

"IVAN, WE CAN MAKE THIS in bathtubs and become millionaires!" Gregor exclaimed, and threw an arm around the younger man's shoulder. "And I mean dollar millionaires, not ruble millionaires. One is big time, one is little time." Ivan grinned back at his mentor as Gregor led him away from the covered swimming pool and back toward the house. Gregor's bathtub millions was a reference to his underground laboratories that were producing synthetic drugs for the Western market. He already had facilities manufacturing Krokodil, Chert, methamphetamines, and methyl-fentanyl, all of which were thousands of times stronger and less expensive to make than organic drugs. Now he wanted to branch out into "synthetic cocaine," or methcathinone. Called Cat by its users, it was not cocaine but a modified formulation of the over-the-counter drug pseudoephedrine.

Ivan looked at Gregor with unconcealed admiration. Gregor was now going international. Branching out from Moscow, he had successfully put his men in business in St. Petersburg, Vladivostok, and Alma-Ata in Kazakhstan. He had left Yuri in charge of the three cities in the western part of the former Soviet Union and had moved himself to Vladivostok, taking Ivan, who had been promoted to Yuri's right hand while Gregor was in prison. Gregor would repay Yuri's loyalty by giving each a continent to run.

Some of Gregor's men had made the leap across the Pacific as early as 1991. They ran a slick boilerplate Medicare scam out of run-down offices in Los Angeles and managed to bilk close to a billion dollars out of the U.S. government before being run to ground by the FBI. Shortly thereafter, in the confusion following the collapse of the Soviet Union, Gregor managed to get himself a visa to the United States. A billion-ruble "donation" had accompanied his application at the Russian end, and his criminal record was overlooked. A tearful description of the indignities suffered by Russian Baptists and a sponsor in Brighton Beach had secured his lawful immigration through the American Embassy.

He was approved, and now he intended to stay. Ivan had come over illegally, as a crew member of the *Pegasus*, a 70,000-ton Maynard Johnson-line freighter out of Vladivostok. He had jumped ship when the *Pegasus* tied up at the Oakland terminal, and Gregor had picked him up at the pier in his new Mercedes.

Gregor's mind held an end in sight. Despite the convoluted tunnels in his Russian psyche, he had an overall vision and was progressing toward it. His long-term plan was to have Ivan running the business in the United States and Yuri running it in Russia. Gregor would reside in the middle of this 12,000-mile-wide web and give his men what advice they might require. The business "line" of his organization would be complete when he had found a connection to the cocaine highway. Then, he would have synthetic drugs to offer to the West from Russia and cocaine to offer the fledgling Russian market from the West. His vision was large. That was why he was the *vory v zakone*.

·37·   *December 14, 1993, Fox County, South Carolina*

JAKE BROKE INTO A RUN toward the back of the circle of buildings where the explosion had occurred. As he got there, he saw a man with goggles and a thick smock expending a fire extinguisher into the door of one of the cabins. Flames were leaping from the gap. Before he could speak, the man had reentered the door, and Jake could hear the sound of compressed carbon dioxide hissing sporadically. Finally, it stopped. Jake walked around to the door and peered inside. A single light bulb, hanging from a wire on the ceiling, lit the interior. Below it, he could see a workbench with a series of fire-blackened test tubes, a Bunsen burner, and an aluminum tub that had apparently been full of ice but now appeared bent and distorted. The roof above the Formica-covered bench was blackened from the fire. The fire was out, and the man was looking dejectedly at the bench. He slowly removed his safety goggles.

"Mr. Geery?" Jake asked quietly.

The man turned. His head was clean shaven and his eyes shone keenly. They were the oddest shade of blue that Jake had ever seen. They made him seem luminous, alien. He was lean and athletic looking, with sinewy arms and thin, slightly bowed legs. He struck quite a figure with his blackened smock, the safety goggles around his neck, and the red fire extinguisher hanging from his left hand. "Yes, I'm Gary Geery." He extended his right hand to Jake.

Jake took it and noticed the strong grip. "I'm Jake. I run Joe's Bait and Tackle Shoppe, down by the lake."

"Oh, yes, Joe left me a note some time ago that I might expect you to come around." Geery's eyes twinkled.

"He did? He just told me how to get here yesterday."

"It was a few months back. He mentioned that you were having some problems with mailbox banditos."

"Yeah," Jake said, looking at his feet. "I can't seem to build anything that they can't run over or blow up or knock down with a baseball bat. I'm at a loss."

"Well, in any event, I have been expecting you. I have taken the liberty of drawing up a few designs in anticipation of your arrival."

"What?"

"Come with me. I'll show you around the place before we go to my library and chat."

Jake stared at the charred room. "What were you doing here?"

"I was making some nitroglycerin. Got above thirty degrees. Blew up," Geery said matter-of-factly.

"Oh," Jake muttered as he surveyed the mess.

"Anyway, let me take you through my humble abode." They walked past the bench and Geery opened another door which led to the next building in the ring. As they entered, Jake saw models of engines and turbines lining the walls. "This is my power room. I have models of engines and turbines. Gas, diesel, hydrogen." He pointed to another model. "This is a boiling-water reactor, like Chernobyl." Geery then opened another door. Inside were computer components. Memory chips, processors, modems, monitors, and mother boards lay strewn about on workbenches with oscilloscopes and a few instruments that Jake did not recognize. "This is my computer room," Geery continued. "I was constructing a parallel 286 system to mimic the performance of a supercomputer, but I gave it up. I have a 486 in another room whose full potential I can't touch. I found that these components are still interesting to play with."

They exited that room and entered another. In this one Jake saw hundreds of squirrel hides tacked to the wall and squirrel tails hung from a line that ran across the center of the room. On the wall were several different varieties of .22-caliber rifles: Winchester, Glenfield, Remington. Jake noticed several foot-long canisters hanging on the wall next to the rifles and a pair of goggles with long protruding lenses extending from the eyepieces. As promised, a Hewlett-Packard 486 computer was displaying a starfield screen saver on the desk. Geery explained, "This is my squirrel room. I have hides from every variety of squirrel in North America, including all ground squirrels, arboreal squirrels, and flying squirrels."

"What are those?" Jake pointed to the foot-long cylinders and the goggles.

"Those are silencers for the .22s and night-vision goggles. That way I didn't scare the little rascals and could see them at night. It made it too easy for me, so I don't use them any more. Fun to build, though." Geery motioned Jake through the next door.

This room was a greenhouse on one side and another laboratory on the other. "Here is where I grow organic vegetables and analyze them according to soil and natural fertilizer content. I'm hoping to patent a multivitamin and roughage supplement." Geery opened still another door and Jake walked in.

It was a library with thousands of books about everything from engineering to astrophysics to philosophy. Looking at the man, Jake realized that he had read them all. He was standing in the middle of the woods staring at a genius, a thoroughly nice person who had come to the forest to learn about everything. Jake was awed. Geery waved at a leather chair. "Have a seat, Jake."

"Thank you, Mr. Geery."

"Call me Gary."

"Yes, sir."

Geery walked around behind the desk and sat in his own chair, a large leather one, well cushioned and set on a rocking-chair frame. It was large enough for Geery to cross his legs and sit like a Western Buddha. When he sat that way, he reminded Jake of Yoda, the Jedi master. Geery spoke again. "Now, Jake. You have to ask yourself a question about your banditos."

"What's that, sir?"

"Do you wish simply to thwart them, or do you wish to punish them?"

 December 14, 1993, Dupont Circle, Washington, DC

"THANK GOD FOR RENT CONTROL," Ronald Dawson muttered to himself. He was wearing forearm-length yellow rubber gloves designed to prevent dishpan hands but also useful for the task at hand. Ronald was well educated, if not terribly intelligent, and he knew about DNA tests and identification by hair. There was going to be no trace of Corinne left in this apartment when he was through stripping and cleaning it.

It had started so normally. He had awakened shortly before twelve o'clock two nights before to go to the bathroom. She had been so beautiful lying there on her stomach, naked. He had decided to wake her for a little midnight fun, but she did not respond to the little nudges and whispers in her ear. He noticed as he sucked on her earlobe that it was cold, unusually cold. He touched her back. It, too, was cold. He turned her over. She was not breathing. Her cerulean eyes stared at the ceiling, seeing nothing. His heart raced as he recalled the scene.

He had jumped out of the bed and begun pacing around the perimeter of the room like a rabid animal, eyes wide, pupils dilated, hyperventilating, and staring at the rumpled sheets and her naked body. "Shit," he cursed. "Fuck." He could think of nothing else to say. It isn't fashionable or career enhancing for a senator to be caught sleeping with a young woman not his wife. It is beyond embarrassing if she kills herself. It is disastrous if she does so with cocaine that he has given her.

For a few minutes, overwhelmed by the whirl of conflicting thoughts in his head, Ronald Dawson went insane. He laughed and cried and sat on the floor rocking on his buttocks, hands wrapped around his knees. He didn't care particularly that Corinne was dead. He could replace her, but if this came out, he could be barred from the halls of power for the rest of his life. Nobody votes for an adulterous drug-using murderer. It must be covered up. He must think. He had to *do* something.

It was midnight. He realized that if he acted quickly, he would have a chance of getting Corinne back to her place unseen. He scrambled around the apartment, throwing open drawers and cabinets, tossing out their contents. He found a pair of Isotoner gloves left by the real occupant and roughly forced them onto his shaking hands. They were tight and painful. He found Corinne's purse and took it down to his car. He wrapped her body in his bathrobe and hefted her over his shoulder. She was in the twilight state of the recently dead. Her skin was waxy. Her lips were blue and her unpainted fingernails were pale on the tiny hands that stuck out of his robe. Rigor mortis had only begun to lock her jaw and neck. Having been dead only a few hours, she was otherwise limp as she lay over his shoulder.

If he ran into anybody, he would attempt to play it off. He rehearsed rolling his eyes and motioning with his head to the body over his shoulder. He winked and smiled at the mirrored liquor cabinet as he passed it, pretending that it was a curious pedestrian. "She just can't hold her liquor. Got to take her home."

As Sherlock Holmes once commented, the commonplace crimes are often the most difficult to solve. Perhaps it was beginner's luck, but Dawson encountered no one as he carried Corinne out of their safe house to his car. He encountered no one as he carried her lifeless body from the car to her apartment, laid her on her bed, and stripped his bathrobe from her body. He turned on all of the lights in her apartment and went through every drawer and cabinet with his clumsy, ill-fitting gloves. He removed address books and journals and notes. He spent three hours there. Corinne had been good to her word about keeping their relationship a secret. Nothing would be left to connect him to the dead girl. No one noticed the lights on in her apartment from 3 A.M. until 6 A.M.

As an afterthought, he even washed Corinne's body. It occurred to him that perhaps fingerprints could somehow be lifted off the corpse. He went through her kitchen and found a bottle of Windex. Pulling several paper towels off the dispenser, he went back to the bedroom and wiped down her entire body. *I am a truly brilliant criminal.*

-39-

January 12, 1994, District Court, Miami, Florida

MARIA ALVAREZ COMPOSED HERSELF on the bench. She was a plump, middle-aged Hispanic woman with large brown eyes and black shoulder-length hair peppered with gray. One wide white streak gave her hair a skunk-like stripe. She smoothed down her judge's gown. Even though it was freshly pressed, she felt that she exuded disorder. She felt rumpled. Her office was disorganized, her car contained a confused mishmash of legal decisions and Big Mac cartons, and her house could qualify for federal disaster assistance. Beneath the disorder, however, lay one of the sharpest legal minds in the United States. That was why she sat on the bench and would soon sit higher.

She looked closely at the defendant who was seated calmly beside his lawyer across the room. She saw no remorse in the man. She had seen not a flicker of regret. No contrition. She did not love this part of her job, as many suspected that she did, but she did not feel bad about it, either. It had to be done.

"The defendant will rise," the clerk ordered.

James Walter Clue rose in his orange, state-provided jumpsuit, with his hands manacled before him. His hair had been cut short and his beard shaved off, so that he hardly resembled his arrest photos. His lawyer had insisted.

"Does the defendant have anything to say prior to sentence being pronounced?" Judge Alvarez asked.

The defense attorney stood up beside his client and spoke for his charge. "No, Your Honor."

"Very well," Judge Alvarez continued. "Considering the viciousness and premeditation with which this crime was perpetrated, the sentence of the court upon James Walter Clue is for the crime for which he has been convicted. You are hereby sentenced to the punishment of death. You are remanded into the custody of the state until which time that the execution may be carried out in accordance with the law." She rapped her gavel on the desk and rose to leave.

"All rise," the clerk ordered.

Judge Alvarez heard a scuffle and a shout behind her as she walked into her chambers. The convict was shouting to her back, "You fucking bitch! You are going to die for this! I have friends! I have friends!"

Then she heard the young defense attorney telling his client to quiet down. "Shut up! Shut up! You aren't going to gain any points on appeal for this, James. Shut up," he urged in a hoarse whisper. This was all that the judge heard before closing the door.

She sat behind her desk, examining the docket. This was her last case as a state judge. An auspicious ending to a brilliant career on the state bench, where she had earned the nickname of "Judge 2500" for the twenty-five-hundred-volt potential used to carry out the death sentences she routinely handed down. She had been appointed to the federal bench in Miami. She was happy because she was likely to try fewer capital cases there, but it worried her. Her next case was *United States v. Domingo Valens*. One hundred thirteen counts for conspiracy, trafficking in narcotics, and money laundering. She knew that Domingo Valens really did have friends who were likely to kill her.

-40-

January 15, 1994, San Francisco, California

"Yes, I would like to speak with Detective McDermit." Andrew Oliver held the phone close to his ear. His face was tense with concentration. His short white-blond hair was unkempt. He had not smiled for over a month. He didn't know if he would ever smile again. His life had ended with a phone call one month before. All that he could think about was exacting revenge on whoever was responsible. He wanted to know what else the police might have found.

"McDermit." A harried-sounding voice came on the line.

"Yes, Detective McDermit. My name is Andrew Oliver. You may recall that we spoke on the phone about a week ago regarding the death of my daughter."

"Yes, sir, I recall."

"Well, Detective, I am calling to ask if you have made any progress with regard to catching the murderer."

Andrew heard the detective sigh before answering. "Mr. Oliver, as I explained to you several weeks ago, there is no murderer. Your daughter was not murdered."

Andrew spoke forcefully into the phone. "Not murdered? Some son of a bitch gave my baby drugs," he stammered with controlled rage, "cocaine and filth. He killed her just as surely as if he had put a gun in her mouth and blown the back of her head off."

"Mr. Oliver. Sir, the case is still open with regard to the person in question."

"Still open? That son . . ."

McDermit cut him off. "Sir, we know that someone moved your daughter's body after she died. We are still searching for that person or persons, but to be honest with you, sir, it is unlikely that we will find them. We have exhausted all of our leads."

"Exhausted all of your leads? What kind of Keystone Cops are . . ."

McDermit interrupted him again. He would not allow the man on the other side of the telephone to insult him. "As I told you, the case is open. The best that we can hope for at this point is for a witness to come forward. We have a DNA sample and blood type. We even have some foreign fibers. None of that is of any use without a suspect. No fingerprints. We need a witness."

"Goddammit! This is unacceptable. . . ."

The detective reached the end of his patience and cut the man off again. "Now, you listen to me, Mr. Oliver. This department is doing the very best job possible. Remember this. Your 'baby' was a girl with a serious habit. The medical examiner reports that she was probably a daily drug user and had been for a number of years. She wasn't killed by someone else. She did it herself. Good day, sir." Andrew heard the click of the phone as the detective hung up on him.

"So, you aren't going to catch the son of a bitch," he said to himself. "Well, if you aren't, I am. I'm going to catch him and hit him where it hurts and kill him." He walked over to his file cabinet and extracted all of the disks titled "Corinne." He took them to his desk and began to go through them, file by file. If she had ever mentioned the man in her correspondence, he would find him. He would find some clue. The screen flickered as he reviewed letters and academic reports. He scribbled notes. He examined the photos she had sent him and struggled to identify every person, cross-referencing faces and names with comments in letters. He listened to the audio files and scrawled his square, blocked handwriting on page after page.

The next morning found Oliver still at his desk, where he had been the previous evening. He had a list of names and places and dates. He had narrowed his suspects to three. He picked up the phone and dialed Memory #1. The phone rang.

"Itasco Construction, this is Buster."

"Buster, this is Andrew. I need you to find me a good private investigator. I mean the best. Money is no object. Call over to Microsystems. They hired some guy from DC to find out who was leaking source codes to Toshiba. John Peters said that he was expensive but that he had results within five days. Got that?"

"Yeah. John Peters over at Microsystems. On it, boss."

"Good. I'm going to take a nap. Find him and call me this afternoon."

"Okay, boss." Buster's voice became low and sad on the line. "Oh, and Andy . . . I just wanted to say how sorry we all are up here about Corinne."

"Thanks, Buster," Andrew said, and hung up.

-41-

January 18, 1994, Fox County, South Carolina

JAKE REGARDED THE SCENE with a great deal of pleasure. His mailbox was blown apart on its 4x4 post, but it did not dampen his spirits because forty yards down the road was an early 1970s sky-blue Chevy Nova with four flat tires. He had called Clarence and asked him to bring Geery with him to inspect the results.

A few minutes later, Clarence's cruiser pulled up and he stepped out of it in civilian clothes. Geery hopped out of the passenger seat with a briefcase in one hand and a duffel bag in the other.

"Capital! Capital! It seems to have worked as I designed it," Geery beamed.

Clarence looked down the road at the Nova. "Looks like Josh Bryant is gonna have some explaining to do to his dad, huh, Jake?"

Geery peered down the road. "So your bandito is young Josh."

"I reckon so," Jake replied. "There's a bunch of empty beer cans in the back seat, and I found this," he proffered a red M–80 firecracker for Clarence and Geery to inspect, "in the glove box."

"Seems to settle things," Clarence observed. "Do you want to press charges, Jake?"

"Naw, but if you could go by and talk to Doc Bryant and get him to make his boy come and build me a new box, I'd be much obliged." Jake noticed that he was beginning to pick up the local accent and dialect. He was amused with his own speech.

Clarence laughed. "Like community service."

Geery had removed a fold-up shovel from his duffel bag and was digging in the earth in front of Jake's mailbox. He struck metal and reached his hand into the hole he had dug and pulled. What emerged was a ten-foot 2x6 board with half-inch diameter holes drilled through at two-inch intervals. Beneath the board were spikes, spring loaded, with the springs resting on a 2x4 board bolted with spacing blocks at one-foot intervals parallel to and one inch from the 2x6.

Clarence observed the contraption being disinterred and re-marked, "Wow, that's quite a device you built there, Gary."

"Yes, yes, thank you. I was happy to oblige. Contact switches here, see. That is what released the spikes. As soon as the bandito opened the mailbox door to insert his incendiary, his fate was sealed." He reset a spike until it clicked, and released it with his finger, allowing it to shoot through its hole with a twang, for emphasis. "Yes, yes, works well."

At that moment, Geery's attention was taken by something over in the woods. Clarence and Jake watched as he ran to the cruiser and opened the briefcase that he had left there. He withdrew a long thin cylinder, inserted something in the top, and stalked toward the trees. A few moments later, he placed one end of the cylinder to his lips and blew. A dart exited the other end and he flew into the woods after it. A few moments later, he emerged carrying a limp gray squirrel. He carried it over to the cruiser and set it on the warm hood as Jake and Clarence came to look. He took out a measuring tape and checked its body length and tail length, recording his findings in a notebook. He opened the squirrel's mouth and looked at its teeth. Then, he examined its feet.

Clarence and Jake looked at each other quizzically. Geery explained, "I'm working on figuring out the demographics of these little rascals. I don't kill them any more. Got the idea from Marlin Perkins. Tranquilize the little buggers and take a look." He lifted the rodent's hind foot to reveal a tiny green band. "I caught this one before, about eighteen months ago. Nice specimen."

Geery got into the cruiser with the squirrel in his lap. He spoke again. "Jake, just bring my bandito catcher over to the house at your convenience."

"Yeah, okay. Thanks, Gary."

Clarence walked over to the driver's side, and Geery closed his door. Before he opened his door, Clarence whispered to Jake. "There is truly a fine line between genius and madness."

42

February 1, 1994, San Francisco, California

"HELLO?" ANDREW OLIVER ANSWERED the phone and started taping the conversation.

"Mr. Oliver?" the voice on the other side of the line inquired. Andrew saw from the caller ID system that the phone call was from area code 202—Washington, DC.

"Yes," Andrew replied.

"This is your private investigator. We spoke about two weeks ago." The sound of traffic in the background suggested that the PI was using a public phone.

"Yes. Do you have any results?"

"Yes, sir, but first I just wanted to make sure that the payment arrangements are understood. I ran into many expenses in the course of my inquiries. I know that the fee is high, but I don't always have work, and jobs like this require equipment."

Andrew chafed at troubling over a few dollars, but he remembered when he, himself, had been a poor man. He replied, "Sir, if you have answered my questions, I will pay you double what I promised and also reimburse you for any expenses you have incurred on my behalf."

The PI sounded excited when he replied. He had been promised $500 a day plus expenses. This revision meant that he was going to pull down $10,000 for two weeks' work. "Yes, sir! It is more than a pleasure doing business with you."

"What have you found out?" Andrew inquired.

The detective paused, and his tone became more professional. "Sir, I investigated the three persons whom you indicated. I subcontracted two of the tailing jobs but conducted hardware installation and, uh, 'premise inspections' myself."

Andrew didn't want to know about the so-called premise inspections but was curious about the equipment. "Hardware?" he asked.

"Radio-direction-finding for the target cars and my tails. Bugs for offices. Taps for phones. All of the equipment has been recovered, except one RDF unit, which was damaged. Guy had a fender bender. It will be on the bill," Aaron stated matter-of-factly.

Andrew was beginning to understand why this man had a quiet reputation for results. "Okay, what have you got for me?"

Aaron began to give his report. "Only one of the three, during the two-week period, approached a dealer and obtained the product in question. He keeps an apartment over on Dupont Circle, where he changes into a disguise and proceeds in another vehicle

to northeast DC to interact with the dealers up there. His disguise
is amateur, but it seems to be effective. I took the liberty of searching
the apartment. He has a substantial stash up there. An interview
with the property manager revealed that the apartment is a rent-
control unit and belongs to a Miss Annette Buca, a popular novel-
ist, who is currently overseas on a project. He therefore has no
legal connection with the dwelling."

"Good. Good."

"There is more, sir. And this is where I ran into a few more
expenses. He has three times been a resident at Placid Vista, a
swank drug rehab joint, with strict confidentiality."

"Confidentiality? How . . ."

"Well, being aware of his habit, I did some checking. I have
some contacts in the airlines who looked into his travel arrangements over the last three years. I checked the newspaper morgue
to see if he fell off the reporters' radar screen during any of those
journeys. He did. Three times, for two weeks a pop. I followed
the trail to Sacramento where my contacts found a charter flight
from Sacramento to Crescent City on each of those three occa-
sions. I have a good friend in the trade up in Eureka, so I rang him
up. He snooped around, for a fee naturally, and found PlacidVista.
The sow who runs that joint was in his clippings file. She has a
record in Arizona for fraud and embezzlement. He leaned on her
a little and she gave your man up."

"Okay, I want the address and his times of coming and
going." Andrew listened carefully and took detailed notes which
he would check against the tape before embarking on his journey.
Of the three men he had identified from Corinne's correspondence, this had been the one he suspected least. After the PI had
finished giving him the facts that he desired, he sat at his desk for
several hours mulling over what he had learned. He could simply
kill the man, once he felt certain that he was the right one. He
thought, however, that he wanted to attack the overall problem
more directly. Dollars and cents. He understood money and what
it could give and what it could take away. Money could provide

opportunities, but it also could be responsible for taking lives. Andrew wanted to use it to take. The only question was how.

He thought ruefully of the joke about the bitter old miser on his deathbed. His children had been surprised to see him praying. All of his life he had been a violently antireligious man. When asked what he was praying for, the old man replied, "I asked God to give me ten more years so that I can get revenge on all the people I haven't gotten around to yet."

Suddenly, Andrew sat up in his chair. He was struck full force by inspiration. Enlightenment. He was Buddha under the *bodhi* tree. He started an idea tree program on his computer to hash out his plan. The next morning he expressed mailed the resourceful detective four times the agreed-upon fee. Included in the mailer was a short note describing several other people whom he wanted Aaron to find and a substantial advance toward those jobs.

-43-

February 14, 1994, Orlando, Florida

HE WAS A TALL MAN, a classic ectomorph, birdlike in appearance and demeanor. He had a long thin nose and bushy eyebrows underneath his hat. His lack of a suntan would have made him stand out on the beach. He was dressed in a navy-stripe London Square suit which fit him poorly and tended to accentuate his bony knees and elbows as he walked and moved. On his wrist was a gold-plated Seiko watch. His appearance told you that he was a man who had not yet "arrived" but was on his way. His name was Eddie, but his acquaintances called him Chamber.

As he sauntered away from the bank, he was thinking. It was shocking. "What a bunch of criminals. The guys I work for are more honest than them," he muttered to himself. Eddie was upset because he had just opened a business account in accordance with his instructions. He had found that the bank was going to charge him four cents a check and another fee for every deposit. He couldn't believe it. It was highway robbery! The bureaucracy was amazing to him as well. That dumb bitch asking, "May I see your corporate resolutions?" He had no idea what that was, but his employer had provided him with a bunch of papers so he presented them all. He had indulged himself in yet another identity. He was now calling himself Miles Jalopi, an immigrant from Great Britain. That was who his newest driver's license and Social Security card, courtesy of a fine street artist in Miami, said he was.

With the signing of the bank paperwork, Jalopi Enterprises was formed. He had rented a small office on the south side of town, about half a mile from an orange grove, and set up Jalopi Enterprises in modest style. The barren little office housed only a desk, a chair, and a file cabinet. It was interesting to note that there was not one stamp or coin on the premises, with the exception of the small change in Eddie's pocket, although Jalopi Enterprises's corporate resolutions identified it as a fine stamp-and-coin dealership.

There was a phone as well. Another story in corporate larceny. The phone company takes the liberty of charging a business customer almost ten times the residential rate, simply because the phone is in an office. Eddie didn't understand all of this but suddenly developed an appreciation for the small businessman and entrepreneur in this country. He remembered explaining to the phone company in his best imitation British accent, "No, no, my dear lady, I do not wish to have a Yellow Pages listing. Our customers are by referral only. We will not have just any riffraff off the street on the premises." At least that had been fun.

He had only a few more trivialities to attend to. His employer, who had identified himself only as Cassius, had insisted that a telephone answering machine be placed in the office, so he had to go to Sears and buy one. As soon as the answering machine was hooked up, Eddie was heading to Miami to do the rest of the job. After that was completed, he was to return to the office, file all of the mail, deposit any checks in the new corporate bank account, and report the completion of the assignment to Cassius by mail to a post office box in Walnut Creek, California. His employer had paid him $25,000 cash in advance and promised $50,000 on completion of the job.

This was quite a coup for Eddie "Chamber" Smith because, prior to this job, he was only a small-time $500-a-hit killer. He thought his friends called him Chamber after "chambering" a round of ammunition. This was incorrect. His friends just thought that he wasn't very smart and would end up taking a deep breath in the gas chamber.

44

February 18, 1994, Cali, Colombia

SANTIAGO SAT ON THE DECK cautiously sipping his first glass of wine for the evening. He was accustomed to taking quiet time for himself at sunset. This time was inviolate to him, and everyone in his organization knew it. The wine was Chilean, widely regarded as the best in South America. His servant had taken away the bottle, so he couldn't read the vineyard or vintage, but his first taste suggested to him that it was Concha y Toro Don Melchor. He was dressed casually in a cotton denim sports shirt and oyster chino pants, sitting in an oak-framed chair with his feet on a matching ottoman. Santiago was obviously a man who took care of his body but did not obsess over it. He was lean and rangy with black hair and dark brown eyes that now surveyed the sun setting in the west. He felt serene.

Emilio Sampar tread lightly as he walked onto the deck. He was dressed casually, like Santiago, but, in contrast to his boss, his face looked grave. Emilio had assumed most of Domingo's duties since his arrest in Panama. December 11, 1992, had been a dark day in Santiago's house. Domingo, in direct disobedience to his brother's wishes, had been inspecting a paste-processing facility outside of El Real, Panama, where he had been swept up in the American-inspired raids. The consequence of this was that Emilio had become Santiago's new right hand. He spoke respectfully, careful not to destroy his employer's tranquillity with unnecessary abruptness. "Santiago," he said.

"Yes, Emilio. I heard you creep up on me," Santiago said quietly.

"Santiago, we have a small problem."

"Yes. I assumed that you would disturb me at this time only for a problem."

"Yes, sir. I know that you wish to be left in peace at this hour, but this is important," Emilio said apologetically.

"Okay, Emilio. Spit it out."

"Sir, the *Toro* has gone down with all hands."

"All hands," Santiago stated to himself. "Cargo?" he asked.

Emilio swallowed. "Three thousand kilos."

Santiago whistled loudly. This was an unmistakable sign that he was angry or shocked. Emilio felt a shiver go up his spine. There was a long silence. Three thousand kilos was a lot of cocaine, three tons in English measure. Its repatriated monetary value would exceed ten million U.S. dollars. The *Toro* was one of ten operational narcosubs that the Cali cartel possessed. It had a round-trip range of seventy-five nautical miles, sophisticated communications gear, a crew of two, and a cargo capacity of just over three tons. The submarine had paid off its construction cost in just two runs off Barranquilla. It had made hundreds of such runs to mother ships offshore in the past three years. Santiago could not be upset by the balance sheet. He did not care about the men, and ten million dollars was tipping money. Yet he was obviously upset.

Santiago finally broke the silence. "How did it happen?"

Emilio was relieved to be spoken to. He relaxed. "It was apparently a malfunction in the ballasting."

Santiago digested this explanation. "You know that she sank? Tell me this. You know that she is at the bottom of the ocean?"

"Well, yes," Emilio answered, not certain where the questions were heading.

"You are *certain*, Emilio? You have seen this with your own eyes? Do you *personally* know that she did not off-load to the mother ship first? Did you see this with your own eyes?"

"Well," Emilio gulped, "not with my own eyes, Santiago. The captain of the meeting vessel radioed and said that the *Toro* had surfaced and approached, then signaled trouble, and had sunk almost immediately. That was the report that I got."

"I am asking you this for a very simple reason, Emilio. Three thousand kilos could very well set up a man or three men or ten men for life. It could make their fortune."

"Yes," Emilio answered numbly.

"This is what I want, Emilio. You take care of it. I want ten men to meet the mother ship at her next port of call. They are to search the ship. If they find nothing, just label me a paranoid Latin bastard, and we are even. But, *if* they find *something*, ah," Santiago paused and took a sip of the crimson liquid, "yes, if they find something, bring them back here. They will watch their wives and children die. Then we will kill them. No one will steal from me, Emilio. No one." He turned away and looked at the sunset as he took another sip of his wine.

Emilio started to leave. He had his orders. Then he heard Santiago speak again. "And Emilio, pull out one sub at Barranquilla and one at Santa Marta. Have them put in dry dock and checked over for ballasting problems."

-45-   *February 18, 1994, Dupont Circle, Washington, DC*

ANDREW CLIMBED THE STEPS slowly until he could read the apartment number from the hall light. He put his ear to the door and listened intently. No light peeked out from underneath. No noise emanated from within. Aaron had told him not to expect Dawson for another hour, but he was a cautious man. He removed the lock-picking instruments from his coat pocket. The investigator had instructed him in the use of the implements and allowed him to practice on his own door. Swiftly he unlocked the door and went inside. Locking it again behind him, he turned on the lights and began to look around. He searched the liquor cabinet first and found what he was looking for. It was in a throat lozenge can. White powder. Toot. Blow. Snow. Intelligent people said that it was the true Montezuma's revenge. A genuine curse on the white invaders. He placed the can on the coffee table and began to inspect the apartment carefully.

It was tastefully furnished in the preference of the writer who was its usual occupant. A velvet overstuffed sofa rested against the farthest wall. In front of it was an eight-posted brass cocktail table with a glass top that as good as screamed, "No feet on me!" In the far corner sat an upright, cherry-finished curio cabinet with adjustable glass shelves. An assortment of liquor bottles was positioned on the top shelf, and the lower shelves displayed silverware and a vase. A comfortable-looking wing chair, hidden in the shadows of the corner nearest the foyer, rounded out the room. The kitchen was small, efficient, and clean with gas appliances and neatly organized cupboards. The bedroom had a king-sized, four-poster bed flanked by two neat wooden nighttables. The bathroom was immaculate. His inspection complete, Andrew turned off the lights and retreated to the wing chair. Once seated, he withdrew a snub-nosed .38 revolver from its shoulder holster and waited for his quarry.

He waited for almost exactly thirty minutes. Then he heard a key in the lock and saw light coming from the hallway as the door opened. The apartment became dark again as the door shut, and he heard heavy footsteps approaching the room where he sat. Suddenly, the room was illuminated as Dawson entered and turned on the table lamp.

"Good evening, Mr. Dawson," Andrew said quietly.

Dawson started, noticing for the first time the man with the gun sitting in the wing chair. He kept quiet, however, seeing the gun trained on him. "You have me at a disadvantage, sir," he said nonchalantly.

"Yes, I do," Andrew replied coldly and pointed at the can on the coffee table. "Would you like some? I don't mind if you kill yourself."

"What? What do you want? Who are you?" Dawson asked. He was used to being deferred to as a presidential adviser. He didn't like this situation.

"Well, that's a long story, Ronald. May I call you Ronald?"

"No."

"Well, Ronald, it's like this. I'm a friend of Corinne's." Andrew paused significantly on this last word to watch Dawson's reaction.

Dawson did an admirable job of covering his emotions but was not entirely successful. His face mirrored a brief instant of panic before he reined himself in and became expressionless. "Corinne? I don't know any Corinnes," he said. Then he pretended to think carefully. "Oh, yes," his face brightened, as if just recalling something he didn't expect to remember. "I did have an aide several years ago. From UVA or GWU. I think she was named Corinne. Seemed like a nice girl."

In less than fifteen seconds, Dawson had convicted himself. The transparency of his lie was embarrassing. He was an actor well out of his depth. Andrew had been willing to think twice about Dawson's guilt until that moment. Now, he wanted to shoot him, but his plan was more involved. He wanted this bastard to suffer. "I'm glad that you remember her, but I think that you saw her more recently."

"No, I don't believe so," Dawson replied.

"Well, I do, Ronald. I figure that you slept with her eight weeks ago and gave her cocaine and she died. It could have been right here."

"That is ridiculous."

"It is pretty ridiculous that you are here right now, isn't it, Ronald?" Andrew added particular emphasis to the name. "Why, pray tell, aren't you at home with your loving wife? Oh, I forgot." Andrew pointed to the can on the table. "I suppose that all of those weeks at Placid Vista didn't really help you kick the habit, huh, Ronald?"

Dawson's eyes widened in surprise before he attempted to take the offensive. "You, sir, are insulting. I insist that you get the fuck out of here. Now."

Andrew didn't budge and kept the gun pointed at his victim. "What's your blood type, Ronald? Oh, no. Let me guess." He put his hand to his forehead as if waiting for a vision. "A-positive, isn't it? Funny thing, Ronald. The man who slept with Corinne on the night she died was A-positive. Did you know that? Oh, of course, you knew that," he sighed. "Did you know that the police have a DNA sample, Ronald?" Andrew threw his hands apart in mock despair and then retrained the gun on Dawson. "It's a hell of a thing, Ronald." He paused again to give the senator a chance to assimilate what he had already told him. "You know, if I was to drop a dime, or a quarter nowadays," Andrew continued sadly, "I bet that your DNA would match that sample they have at the station. What do you think, Ronald?"

Dawson started to shake and sat awkwardly down on the sofa across from Andrew. He started to breathe heavily. "I don't know . . . what you want."

"Well, Ronald, what I want is up to you. I can shoot you. Well, naturally, I'll have to take you somewhere private first. Have you got any good strong duct tape around here? I'll shoot you a few times and watch you suffer for a few hours and then I may shoot you in the head. Maybe I'll cut you up some, too. Whatever occurs to me. I really liked Corinne." Andrew said all of this with such a quiet candor that Dawson's eyes dilated with terror. "Or, you can give me a phone card. You have one of those, don't you, Ronald? Sprint or MCI? Also, you can write me a check and then continue to write checks for four months."

"You intend to blackmail me?" Dawson asked.

"Well, it's that or kill you. I told you that you could choose. I'm a fair man," Andrew said with feigned calmness. Maintaining a cool facade was becoming increasingly difficult. The despoiler and murderer of his baby was mere feet away. He desperately wanted to kill him. Inside, he was seething with anger. His mind was a whirlwind of hatred, anguish, and revulsion. *Remember the plan. Delay gratification*, he was screaming over the internal tumult.

Dawson sat back on the sofa. He realized that there was now a good chance that he would walk out of this alive. His spirits improved. He reached into his coat pocket to retrieve his checkbook.

"Uh-uh, Ronald! Hands! Let me see your hands. What are you doing?"

"I'm reaching for my checkbook."

"Okay, slowly, or you'll get what's behind door number one, if you know what I mean." Andrew trained the gun at Dawson's chest.

Dawson carefully pulled out his checkbook. "Who do I make it out to?"

"You can make it out later and mail it. Four payments of $5,000. Write this down. Jalopi Enterprises. Twelve hundred Orange Grove, Suite 102, Orlando, Florida. Look up the zip code. If I don't get it, I'll be dropping an anonymous tip. Got it? Now the card. Slow with the hands."

Dawson reached into his back pocket and withdrew his wallet. He selected a silver Sprint card and tossed it over to Andrew, who returned it, ordering, "Write the code on the back, in the signature block."

An hour later, Andrew was walking down King Street in Alexandria. He felt numb from the encounter with Dawson. He picked up a pay phone and called a number in Orlando using Dawson's phone card. He waited for the answering machine to pick up and stayed on the line for five minutes, saying nothing.

40·

CHAMBER WATCHED THE SCENE unfold below him. As he viewed the spectacle, his hands disassembled the weapon, automatically placing each component in a foam-lined Samsonite briefcase. The Harris bipod slipped into a pocket in the upper half. He slid the 6-20X Leupold scope off the barrel and placed it in its nook. Next, he broke the synthetic stock from the barrel. He broke the stock again into two smaller sections and inserted them. He unscrewed the homemade silencer and dropped it into the case. Then he laid the Remington Model 700 "bull" barrel and bolt assembly diagonally into the case and closed the lid.

He felt exultant. He had never "whacked" anyone who was prominent before. He had never killed a public official. Most of the people he had assassinated were deeply in debt to a shark or a dealer or had in some significant way annoyed the type of person who would possess both $500 and Eddie's number. As of forty-five seconds ago, he had moved into the big time. He had hit a federal judge.

In his mind he relived the scene as he had seen it through the telescopic sight. Alvarez had been walking down the steps of the federal courthouse. She was wearing a gray business suit. As she had walked, she had continually smoothed down her skirt and clumsily flipped the pages in a stack of papers that she was reviewing. Somehow, that was not how he had envisioned her before the job. He had pictured her in long flowing black robes, a graying Hispanic witch floating down the steps. He had recognized the telltale white streak in her hair and had taken aim at her face. He had enjoyed the pleasure of seeing her head jerk violently backward before she crumpled onto the steps. The silencer had done a marvelous job, and pedestrians were looking wildly in all directions as people raced toward the fallen judge. Two security guards were rushing out of the courthouse building as he dropped the fatal cartridge on the rooftop and left.

Chamber remembered the note, turned, and bent his long frame down to tuck an envelope underneath the cartridge that he was leaving on the roof. On the outside it read, "To the Government of the United States." He placed one gloved hand in his pocket, picked up his briefcase, and headed toward the elevator. Ten minutes later he was driving north to Orlando. Half of his job was completed.

-47-

February 24, 1994, San Francisco, California

GREGOR EXAMINED HIS HANDS as he left the manicure salon on Union Street. The calluses from the labor camp were long gone and his palms were soft and doughy. He did not know what had possessed him to go in there. Then he noticed the white panel van parked down the steep incline and on the other side of the one-way street. The van had a rubberized magnetic sign advertising it as "JACK'S PLUMBING. ESTABLISHED 1957. FAMILY OWNED." He had seen a similar van on the previous day. Its magnetic sign had read "ARBORVIEW SIGN COMPANY." Gregor had been filled with a growing suspicion that he was being tailed. That was why he had pulled his cream-colored, 1958 Mercedes-Benz 190SL convertible over to have his hands worked on. He had wanted to irritate whoever was following him.

He turned to walk back to his car. As he faced about, an unshaven man with blond stringy hair ran into him. The man was wearing a filthy tan full-length London Fog. His hands were shoved deep into the pockets, pulling the fabric tight over his shoulders. Beneath the jacket, he was wearing worn black PRO-Keds and socks that didn't match. Gregor's initial assessment was that the man was homeless, but the icy blue eyes looking back at him suggested something else.

"Sorry, mister," the stranger apologized and lifted his hands in a no-harm-intended gesture.

Gregor stared for a second at the guy's burned left hand and replied, "It's okay."

The blue-eyed man lowered his hands and looked at Gregor thoughtfully. "Thou, comma, too, comma, Brutus, question mark." He paused. "Repeat it to me."

Gregor looked at the man, searching for that spark of insanity that he had seen in some of the prisoners in the camp. It wasn't there.

"Repeat it," the man insisted.

"Thou, comma, too, comma, Brutus, question mark," Gregor said in an exasperated tone.

"Good." The man whirled and strode away purposefully.

Gregor did not reply. He turned and continued to walk toward his car. After he had leaned back in the black leather seat, he thought to check his wallet. It was there. Something in the man's demeanor bothered him. He felt that he had been worked over somehow.

As Gregor drove over the San Francisco Bay Bridge he managed to catch a glimpse of the white van in the rearview mirror. He could see that the sign on the side had been changed again but could not read it. He looked out over the bay and saw a tanker easing its way back out to sea and saw another at anchor near the Oakland terminal, apparently waiting in line to off-load its cargo. He always enjoyed the drive to San Francisco more than the trip away. The view was better on the top half of the split-level bridge.

Pulling into the development south of Oakland where his estate was located, he noticed another van turn off and park where it would be out of view from his house. He drove to his gate and stopped next to the touchpad to type in a four-digit number. The barred, steel-frame gate responded by rolling to the side. Gregor entered and directed the Mercedes up the driveway toward his tan Spanish-style home. He parked in front of the garage underneath an archway and got out of his car.

As he tramped into the entrance foyer, he stripped off his jacket to hang it on the coatrack. A white security envelope, folded in half and taped, fell out of one jacket pocket and landed with a clatter on the inlaid brickwork floor. Gregor picked it up and examined it. He walked straight ahead, which took him outdoors again into the central courtyard. Turning the envelope over in his hands, he crossed the courtyard and entered a large room which was an open living, dining, and kitchen area. He stepped off the white carpet of the living room and onto the white tiles of the kitchen. In one of the drawers he found a steak knife. He sliced open the envelope and extracted a 3 1/2-inch diskette. The disk was unlabeled but a yellow Post-it note was wrapped around it. The note contained instructions written in small primitive block letters:

> If the correct person is still in possession of this disk, I told you the password and made you repeat it. If you do not have a personal computer, buy one. Purchase a modem as well. DO NOT run this disk on a computer that you do not control personally. The file INSTRUCT will tell you everything you need to know to communicate with me. It will also tell you why you should.— Cassius

Gregor read the note twice. He did not own a computer. He walked over to the telephone and dialed a number from memory. He listened for a moment. The voice at the other end of the line answered, "Yes."

Gregor replied, "Ivan, are you ready to go over?"

"Yes," Ivan replied.

Gregor hit a red button on the box that lay on the floor. It was installed between his telephone and the wall jack. Now his voice was scrambled. Four of those boxes had been stolen from a Russian Army depot near Gorky. They were the Soviet answer to the American Data Encryption Standard (DES). In 1979 a female GRU agent had shamed the entire Washington KGB residency by single-handedly obtaining the algorithm from a disgruntled NSA employee. It added insult to injury that it had not cost the Soviet people one ruble. She had simply given her attentions to a lonely mathematician.

Soviet scientists tore into their latest technical acquisition. Their engineers doubled the key length and removed part of the algorithm. They could not discern its function and, with paranoia characteristic of their nation, suspected that it was a secret "trap door" designed by the National Security Agency. One of the final products was an unwieldy, ugly, ten-pound Army-green box. It displayed the legendary durability for which Soviet products were not very well known, with the notable exception of the Kalashnikov AK-47. Despite its hardiness, it was not widely used in the field. There were a number of problems. Its jack was not compatible with the standard issue radio. Units had to exchange keys prior to communicating. After keys were transferred, lengthy programming procedures were required before units could confer. Unit after unit quietly shuffled the boxes off to storage yards and depots or just lost them. There was even an unconfirmed report of a captain abruptly drawing his pistol, putting a bullet in his company's box, and instructing the radioman to run back to the position he was attempting to communicate with.

What the Red Army had disposed of as worthless was, in fact, an incredibly sophisticated tool. Lack of centralized key control impeded its use on the battlefield, but the flexibility built into the unit for key changes made it ideal for an organization such as Gregor's. He had hired work-starved engineers from the crumbling Russian military-industrial complex to set the keys of his four machines. After that, he was in the business of no-brainer secure communication. He had an added advantage in the United States. His gear was nonstandard. It didn't use a 56-digit key like DES or a 128-digit key like other standard algorithms. It was neither. It was Russian.

The history of the green box was transparent and unimportant to Gregor. What that red button meant to him was that when he said, "Ivan, I want you to buy me the best personal computer you can find and bring it to the house tomorrow," nobody else in the world understood what he said. All of the vans that Gregor had noticed were innocent. He was not under surveillance, but if he had been, the agent minding the tap would have been throwing his headphones to the ground and cursing the high-pitched whine that came from Gregor's green box.

-48-

February 24, 1994, FBI Headquarters, Washington, DC

"WHAT THE FUCK IS THIS? This is crazy!" Charles Briar complained. He was the Director of the Federal Bureau of Investigation. He adjusted the bifocal reading glasses on his nose and looked at the paper. His brown hair was disorderly from his tendency to rub the top of his head when perplexed. He was regarding a fax from the Miami Field Office. It was a copy of the note found with a .308-caliber Remington cartridge on top of the building opposite the Miami federal courthouse. "They haven't even begun pretrial motions and they decide to kill the judge? What? Do they think that the United States of America is going to release this two-bit hood because they kill a judge? Do they think that they are dealing with some banana republic here?" All of these questions were, of course, rhetorical. He was blowing off steam.

Mason Giles took the question literally. He took everything literally. That was the kind of man he was. "Sir, as is often the case, and I believe the recent Gulf War was an example, within the framework of their perspective, they actually have no conception of the power of this country, military or otherwise." Giles pushed his own spectacles up a notch. "They think of the United States as merely a slightly larger version of what they see at hand, which is largely ineffectual, at best. Put simply, sir, they have no idea what they are confronting."

The Director thought for a moment how consoling Giles's erudite manner was during tense moments. It was probably the only reason that he didn't fire the pompous prick. He returned to studying the note. It was handwritten in Spanish, with another handwritten translation underneath, presumably from one of the agents in charge down in Miami: "As you can see, our reach is long. Domingo Valens must be released, or we will bring your government to its knees before us."

"Who is it?" the Director asked.

Giles was prepared for the question. He had been gathering files for the previous two hours in preparation for this moment. He shone when attacking problems that required only the accumulation of information. Leaps of intuition were beyond him. For this reason, he had made a poor field agent. This was why the Bureau had seen to it that Mason had been promoted to a position—an analyst—where he was unlikely to get anyone killed. He took a deep breath and opened the first file. This would be a lengthy report. "My analysis points to three possible groups, sir. They are by no means the only possibilities, but given the present situation. . . ."

Briar cut him off. "I know that you don't know, Mason," he said gruffly. "Just fucking tell me what you *do* know, okay?"

"Yes, sir," Giles said quietly. He licked a pointed index finger and flipped over a sheet in his file. He quickly slipped into his nonchalant, I'm-just-one-of-the-boys mode of speech in hopes of keeping the Director's outbursts to a minimum. "Three possibles are the Ricardo Franco Front, or RFF; the Revolutionary Armed Forces of Colombia, or FARC; and the Nineteenth of April Movement, or M-19." He licked his middle finger as if to even the wear and used it to turn to the next page. "Ricardo Franco Front. RFF. Formed as a faction in March 1984. Thought to be no more than one hundred strong, though estimates are difficult. Headquartered in Cauca Department, Colombia." He sighed and continued. "Your basic leftist anti-American group. A splinter group from FARC. Disoriented since the fall of the Soviet Union. Targeted U.S. commercial sites in '84 and '85, but haven't done much since. More a bunch of bandits than a guerrilla movement. Their big moment in the sun was an attack on the U.S. Embassy in Bogotá, September '85."

Briar had anchored his elbows to the table, made a cup of his hands, and lowered his chin into it. He looked up at his analyst. He appeared disinterested but was listening intently. He sincerely hoped that Giles had found something useful. He was going to have to talk with the President in an hour.

Giles licked his index finger and turned another page. "The Revolutionary Armed Forces of Colombia. FARC. They are the granddaddy, formed in 1966. Thought to have a strength of five thousand or greater. FARC is easily the largest, most disciplined, well-armed, and effective guerrilla movement in Colombia, and, with the exception of the Shining Path in Peru, in South America. They are leftists. Pro-Cuban. Anti-American. Also shaken by the fall of communism and the disintegration of the Soviet bloc. The FARC has the closest relationship with Colombian drug traffickers of any group. In return for the FARC's protection of their assets, the cartels give them money for the purchase of weapons and supplies. It is unclear whether the movement is involved in the actual processing of cocaine."

Mason flipped to another page, this time using his ring finger for a change of pace. The Director did not move. He just blinked his eyes wearily, thinking about the President. It was going to be very unpleasant. The analyst continued. "The FARC's rap sheet. In '77, abducted a U.S. Peace Corps volunteer outside Buenaventura. In '80, kidnapped a U.S. citizen from his banana plantation in the Cauca Valley. In '83, snatched a U.S. citizen from her farm in southern Meta Department. Again in '83, kidnapped another U.S. citizen in Meta Department. All were released after ransom payments. In '85, bombed seven businesses in Medellín. IBM. General Telephone and Electronics. Union Carbide. Xerox. Three Colombian interests. Also in '85, kidnapped four engineers and thirty workers from a construction site in Huila Department. Later in '85, abducted four missionaries. In '86, attempted to extort $100 million from Shell Oil. The company shut down operations. Later in '86, bombed a police station in Nencoona. Killed the bomb squad. Also in '86, executed over one hundred men, women, and children in Turbo. No reason given. Another kidnapping in '87. Also, ambushed a Colombian army patrol. At the end of '87, attacked the town of Gaitania, killing two policemen. In '88, hijacked a helicopter."

Giles flipped to another page. "It goes on and on. Kidnappings. Ambushes. Hijackings. They are in business. They are in bed with the cartel. It is a leap. They have carried out no known activity in this country. But we could have said the same for the Sudanese before the World Trade Center. If a terrorist group did this, my money is on these guys."

Briar lifted his head from his hands and scratched his ear. He squinted and looked over Giles's shoulder. He was thinking. Then he said brusquely, "You said that there was another group."

Giles closed the folder that he was holding and moved one from the bottom to the top. He licked his index finger once again and opened it. "Sir, this group proclaims that they are out of the terror business. They are attempting to join the mainstream of Colombian politics. I would not eliminate former or disaffected members, but I doubt the participation of the group. Additionally, their relationship with the narcotics growers and traffickers has been more extortive than symbiotic." Giles smiled in satisfaction, as if he had found just the right word. Briar did not return his smile.

"Anyway," the analyst continued nervously, "M-19, or the 19th of April Movement. Headquarters in Cali, Colombia. It stole the sword of Simón Bolívar from a Bogotá museum in '74. In '80, received an arms shipment from Cuba via Jaime Guillot Lara. It's the only one we know about. In '80, seized the Dominican Republic's Embassy in Bogotá, taking the U.S. Ambassador hostage. In '81 the Movement kidnapped U.S. citizen Chester Bitterman in Bogotá and executed him. In '82 it hijacked an Aerotal 727 commercial jetliner which it exchanged for a plane to fly to Havana. In '83, bombed the Honduran Embassy in Bogotá. In '84 it raided the town of Florencia. In '85 it helped the Ecuadorian terrorist group AVC to capture and hold ransom a banker near

Guayaquil. The banker was killed. In '85 the M-19 occupied Bogotá's Palace of Justice, taking five hundred hostages. Eleven Colombian Supreme Court justices were murdered before government forces reclaimed the building. In '86 it attempted to assassinate Minister of Government Jaime Castro, made off with 1.6 million pesos from a bank in the capital, and even robbed a jewelry store to the tune of 700,000 American dollars. In '87 it seized the offices of the Bogotá newspaper *Diario 5 p.m.* and published its own propaganda edition." He closed the folder. "There're more kidnappings and robberies just like the FARC. All of these guys have gone small time since the Soviet Union fell."

Briar lifted his head from his hands again. He frowned. "So, I gather that you think the FARC did it."

The analyst swallowed. He hated being forced to make judgments without all of the facts. He backpedaled. "Sir, of the three most likely candidates, FARC is the one that stands out. It could very well be a personal job. Someone inside the cartel. Who knows? It could have been Valens's girlfriend." He smiled weakly.

Briar looked back down at his desk. "That's all," he said and motioned for Giles to leave. Then, as an afterthought, he added, "Thank you," but heard the door shut before the words were out of his mouth. He stared at the note and then buzzed his secretary.

"Yes, how may I help you, Director?" Jamie's cheerful voice came back over the speaker.

"Jamie, would you get me the special-agent-in-charge in Miami?"

"Just one moment, sir." The intercom went silent. The Director read the note three more times and began to flip through the files that Giles had left. The intercom came back on. "Sir, Special Agent-in-Charge, Miami, line 3."

"Thank you, Jamie." He picked up the telephone and stabbed the button for line 3 so forcefully that the phone gave an extra ring. "This is the Director. Who am I speaking to?"

"Sir, this is Special Agent Jiménez," the voice replied.

"Good," Briar said, "Well, James, I have a few questions and I hope you people down there have some answers."

"Yes, sir." Jiménez was irritated that the Director had misunderstood his name on the other end of the line but did not correct him.

"Are there any fingerprints?" the Director asked.

"No, sir. Apparently the signer used gloves. The paper is common. It can be purchased at any Wal-Mart. Same with the envelope. It was taped, not licked, so no chance of even tagging saliva."

"The weapon?"

"Probably a Remington 700 series, .308 caliber. The cartridge we found matches the bullet. We did what we could here and sent everything up to Evidence Control. They should get back to me in the morning."

"You are telling me that there is no physical evidence to point to any person or group other than the note?"

"Sir, we did get some fibers from the rooftop. Apparently the shooter aimed from a prone position. Left a little of the elbow of his shirt for us to examine. Unlikely that we can trace the guy with that, but we may be able to link him if we find a suspect."

"I see," said the Director. "When do you expect results?"

"Again, sir, we sent it up to Evidence Control. I expect the Hair and Fiber Unit to get back to me by tomorrow morning with preliminary results."

"Thank you," Briar said and hung up. He was glad that he had something to tell the President.

49 *March 1, 1994, USS Arleigh Burke, South Caribbean Sea*

"EXECUTIVE OFFICER, dial 7111. Executive Officer, dial 7111," the 1MC announced. Commander Paul Wayne heard the announcement and walked across the crew's mess to the nearest telephone. He dialed the number, which was the captain's cabin. Captain Russell Steward picked up before the first ring was complete.

"This is the XO, Captain," the commander said.

"Paul, please come to my cabin immediately," the captain ordered.

"Aye, aye, sir," he replied and proceeded to move up and forward. He wondered what required his presence immediately, but he knew that he would find out soon enough. He approached the cabin door and knocked solidly twice.

"Enter," he heard from within.

He opened the door and went in. The captain was looking carefully at a map of Colombia. There was a message at the upper left-hand corner of the map. The captain pointed to the message and said, "Read it, Paul. It's very interesting."

The XO picked up the message, noting the TOP SECRET typed in the header, and began to read. It only took him a few seconds. He blew out a deep breath and looked at the map. The captain had circled several locations with a red pen.

He spoke again. "Paul, we will receive technical representatives from General Dynamics and the Naval Surface Warfare Center on board in approximately one hour. They will load the TERCOM data required to hit these targets. Tomorrow morning we will launch." He gestured at the red circles. "Welcome to the war on drugs," he added ruefully.

"Yes, sir."

The captain was circumspect for a moment. "You know, Paul, when I joined the Navy, I never thought that my career would culminate with launching Tomahawk missiles at South American villages, but, then again, I never thought that they would let women into the Academy, either."

"Well, sir . . ."

The captain did not allow him to finish. "I guess that we'll have to have faith that those really are drug-processing centers underneath those huts, huh? Go to the bridge and order the Officer of the Deck to make wind across the flight deck to receive the tech-reps' helo. Dismissed."

  March 2, 1994, Cauca Valley, Colombia

JUAN FLORES HAD A SPANISH NAME but a Chibcha heart. As he carried the heavy basket of freshly picked coca leaves up the steep slope to Santiago Valens's processing facility, he spat the remnants of the leaf and wood-ash mixture he had been chewing onto the ground. Juan's ancestors had battled the troops of Gonzalo Jiménez de Quesada on the outskirts of Bogotá when it was still a Chibcha city called Bacatá, nearly two centuries before it would become the capital of New Granada in 1717. They had been defeated and his people nearly exterminated before they fled into the mountains and over to the next valley.

The Chibcha people boasted a tradition that had passed into legend long before the arrival of the conquistadors. They would coat each new chief with sticky tree gum and cover his body with gold dust. The new leader would then leap from a boat into Lake Guatavita and wash off the precious metal as an offering to the gods. The avaricious Spanish conquerors took the folktale to heart and expended countless lives in the search for the wealth of "The Gilded One," El Dorado.

The name El Dorado came to mean not a man, but a place. Some called it Manoa or Omoa, and it lured the likes of Francisco de Orellana, Philipp von Hutten, and Sir Walter Raleigh to the South American continent. Through the years, El Dorado has become synonymous with a mythical place that, when found, will afford the discoverer sudden and fabulous wealth. Juan was approaching the twentieth-century gilded man's compound, re-established where it originated, in Colombia. The precious dust wasn't gold, however, and today it was luring a new conqueror who wanted not to take it, but to destroy it.

The President had made his preliminary decision on February 24, following his briefing from Charles Briar, and ordered the Navy to position a carrier off the coast of Colombia. The scouting had begun on February 26. The order went from the White House directly to the National Reconnaissance Office, rubber-stamped by the U.S. Intelligence Board along the way. The request was posted to the top of the list immediately in the Joint Reconnaissance Schedule, and within an hour the Satellite Control Facility in Thule, Greenland, was feeding instructions to a KH-12 spy satellite occupying a 100-degree near-polar orbit. Three hours later, from an altitude of 137 miles, tiny direct-current motors whined as they swept the satellite's telephoto lenses back and forth, cutting a swath across the Cauca Valley. The images were digitized and relayed to a KH-11 over the Pacific and transmitted to the Satellite Control Facility, Guam. From there, they were dispatched via two relays to Mission Ground Site at Fort Belvoir and relayed to the National Photographic Interpretation Center at the corner of 1st and M Streets in Washington. At NPIC, an Air Force intelligence officer stared at the images through a stereoscope while a representative from both the DEA and the CIA, South American Desk, marked suspected sites on a contour map. By the morning of February 27 the President was able to review the map showing fourteen target locations confirmed by both on-the-ground intelligence and aerial observation. Approved at the Oval Office, the directive was sent to the Pentagon.

At the Pentagon the usual bureaucratic infighting prevailed for the rest of the 27th and the most of the 28th as each service attempted to wheel and deal itself into the lion's share of the operation. At 4 P.M. on the 28th, General Milton Stone (USA) cursed Lieutenant General Moore (USAF) and Vice Admiral Lloyd (USN) and left the joint planning meeting to his staff. The blowup was precipitated by Moore's refusal to waste Military Airlift Command resources transporting Apache helicopters to Panama for the express purpose of allowing them to be "on hand" during the operation. There would be no medals for the Department of the Army in this plan.

Fortunately, this interval was not entirely wasted. Less partisan civilian Department of Defense staff quietly parceled out the targeting requirements to the bespectacled civilian engineers at the Naval Surface Warfare Center and Air Force Systems Command. These scientists were the men without which the precision-standoff modern war would not be possible. When this mission was said and done, they were as crucial to its success and as shamefully unheralded as the code breakers at Bletchley Park who turned the tide of World War II by reading Germany's ULTRA. They wouldn't get any medals, either.

The operation began at 8 A.M. on March 2 as two Big Ugly Fat Fellows, B-52H Stratofortresses, roared off the runway at Barksdale Air Force Base, Louisiana. Eight turbofan engines lofted each plane to forty thousand feet, where they pointed their noses southeast and began the six-hour commute at 405 mph. Slung beneath each BUFF's massive wings were twelve AGM-86C air-launched cruise missiles bearing 1,000-pound conventional blast fragmentation warheads.

At 10 A.M. the USS *Nimitz* steamed to a position fifty miles off Buenaventura after a five-day run at flank speed from the coast of San Diego, where it had been conducting carrier qualifications. The flight deck sprang to life as A-6 Intruders rode the elevators from the hangar bay to the roof. Crews wheeled carts bearing 2,000-pound delayed-fuse Paveway II-equipped laser-guided bombs to the bombers' wing mounts. At noon, a single E-2C Hawkeye fired up its twin turboprops and taxied to the starboard bow catapult. Fifteen minutes later, it was airborne over Panama to serve as the air traffic controller for the converging forces.

Ten F-111 Aardvarks began to take off from a strip outside Panama City at 12:30 P.M., just as the first Intruder was hurled off the port bow catapult of the *Nimitz*. Each Aardvark carried six BLU-109, 2,000-pound earth penetrator Paveway III-equipped laser-guided bombs.

At 12:55 the B–52s lumbered into the Hawkeye's control zone and checked in. At 12:56 the Stratofortresses loosed their twenty-four cruise missiles and banked into a turn northward. At 12:57 the tech-reps stood on the bridge of the USS *Arleigh Burke* and watched as twelve BGM–109C Tomahawk missiles rocketed out of the forward VLS cells. At 1:01 P.M. the Aardvarks and Intruders began to radio in "Feet dry" in rapid succession.

Twenty minutes later, it was done. The F–111s and A–6s radioed "Feet wet" and were vectored by the Hawkeye back home. The strike aircraft had destroyed eight underground processing facilities on the outskirts of Tolima, 1.064-micron laser designators illuminating the way for the Paveway-equipped bombs into the inner sanctum of the cartel. The BUFFs' cruise missiles had sped across the mountains at .65 Mach, accelerating to .8 Mach as GPS provided terminal guidance, allowing them to plow into four of Santiago's sites outside of Popayán. The *Arleigh Burke's* Tomahawks flew up the Cauca Valley at 550 mph on inertial guidance until reaching terminal phase outside of Cali, where they began to compare the terrain below with the digital imagery stored inside. They finished their kamikaze mission, destroying much of the two remaining target sites.

Juan Flores was shocked when he saw the huge white cigar fly over his head and suddenly plow into the chemists' dormitory. He did not see the other four as they exploded around the compound because he had been knocked unconscious by concrete shrapnel. The battle damage assessment held in the Pentagon that evening showed an overall effectiveness of 98 percent, meaning that virtually all of the ordnance ended up on target.

What the BDA did not show was Juan being hauled down to Cali in the back of a pickup truck where he was carried into a hospital. Santiago Valens had built that medical facility from his ill-gotten gains and Juan, along with twenty-three other wounded Chibcha workers, was treated free of charge. Cultivating coca shrubs on the terraced land that had been his family's for over four hundred years was ten times as profitable as coffee or any other crop, but there were other reasons Juan would serve Santiago. In the collective Chibcha memory, there were few descendants of the conquistadors who gave back more than they took away.

·51·

ANDREW STROLLED LAZILY around the boat yard. He examined the boats for sale, running his hand over hull penetrations and marveling at the workmanship of the interiors. Andrew knew very little about boats, so he had read a book about them on the flight down from San Francisco. Upon close inspection, it seemed to him that Southport Yachts manufactured some fine small sailboats. They ranged from thirty to fifty-five feet and were made with heavily ballasted full keels. They were all suitable for open ocean sailing. What was not readily apparent to the naked eye was that these vessels were manufactured to the specifications of drug smugglers, who were also Southport's primary customers.

The full keels were easily hollowed out to transport the product without damaging the stability of the boats. Andrew walked nonchalantly up to the dry dock and looked over a thirty-foot sloop named *Intrepid*. The keel and hull up to the waterline mark were covered with barnacles the color of sand. A small section of the keel had been scraped clean. He noticed that a plug, its outline barely discernible, had been replaced in the metal. A few strokes of the brush with bottom paint and it would be invisible once again.

"Yes, Aaron is very good," he said to himself, thinking about his private investigator. He had asked Aaron to find him a company like this one, and three weeks later the detective had provided what he wanted. A company that was flush with cash from indiscernible sources. A company that was likely to have connections in Colombia. Aaron had uncovered the fact that Southport had manufactured seventy boats the previous year varying in size from thirty-foot sloops to fifty-five-foot ketches. Sixty-five of the boats were sold to a Central American buyer who ran a charter cruise business in the Caribbean. Five were sold to local San Diegan sailing enthusiasts. Aaron had tracked down the charter company. It only ran two of the ketches for charter. That left sixty-three boats unaccounted for. From there the detective's conclusions were obvious.

Aaron had also found that the sixty-five boats were sold at almost double the market value and that their contracts included a ten-year agreement stipulating that Southport would fly representatives to any American port to service the boats, obviating any need for local chandlers and craftsmen. It was tidy. It was dirty. It was what Andrew was looking for.

He entered the office, where a winsome young Hispanic secretary was sitting at the desk inspecting her bright red fingernails and holding an emery board in her left hand. Embarrassed, she lowered her hands to her lap when she saw him. "I have an appointment to see Mr. Rollins."

The woman looked down at her opened appointment calendar. "Mr. Cassius?"

"Yes," Andrew replied.

"You can go right in. He is expecting you."

"Thank you." Andrew walked forward, passing the desk, and turned the handle of the door to the inner office. A brass placard on the door read, "Captain Eric Rollins. Knock and Enter." Andrew neglected to knock but did enter.

Rollins rose behind his desk. He was short, fat, and balding. He assiduously maintained a few strands of hair carefully combed across the bare tanned scalp which topped his head. He wore a white button-down shirt with an open collar. The buttons strained against their bonds around his midsection. He was perspiring, although the office was air-conditioned. He held a damp hand out to Andrew. "Mr. Cassius, I am happy to meet you." He gave Andrew his best salesman's smile and wiped the back of his neck with a handkerchief that he picked up off the desk. "I understand that you are interested in purchasing one of our fine boats. I assure you that the quality cannot be matched."

Andrew closed the door behind him and looked seriously at Rollins. "Well, not exactly."

Rollins looked Andrew over nervously, his eyes quickly surveying him up and down. Andrew thought that he might be looking for a weapon. The captain did business with dangerous people. There was a moment of silence before Rollins spoke. "Well, then," he forced a short laugh, "what can I do for you?"

"It's more what I can do for you. How would you like a connection to the Russian market? No Sicilian middlemen."

Rollins touched his upper lip with his tongue. His eyes flickered with interest. "I'm listening."

"I have a million dollars as up-front capital," Andrew said carelessly.

Rollins reached across his desk and hit the intercom. "Maria, cancel my one o'clock. I'm going to be tied up a while." He released the button, and, with an afterthought, "Maria, also hold any calls."

-52-

June 3, 1994, Kirghiz Republic, Former Soviet Union

THE STRAINED MONGOL FACES of the Kirghiz workers glistened in the sunrise as they hustled above ground. On signal from their foreman they covered their ears and looked away from the shaft. This type of labor did not come naturally to the nomadic people. It was the legacy of Stalin. A muffled thud echoed out of the shaft and the wait began. In twenty minutes, according to their work agreement, the dust would have settled enough for them to return below and continue the extraction of the lead ore that the world needed to fuel its desire for lead acid batteries and other commodities. Oddly, they had waited twenty minutes before returning to the mines even before the work agreement.

Outside of the shaft, it was a beautiful scene. Soaring above them was the Tien Shan mountain range. The Chinese translation, "Celestial Mountains," was not an exaggeration. Below them, flange-wheeled carts on narrow gauge rails pushed by human labor dumped ore onto Russian-made Kamaz trucks, which would haul the ore to the Kazakh Republic to be processed.

The International Miners' Union had come to these humble people about a year before. It hadn't done anything of note to improve their lives. A few work agreements were made. The miners now received imported vacuum-packed meals, which were not as nutritious as the meat and vegetables that they had eaten formerly. The most significant change that the IMU had introduced to the workers was the novel idea of extracting union dues automatically from their pay. A small percentage of this money went to the Dark Path, which enforced union policy when workers suffered under the illusion that the union acted for them.

June 1, 1994, Berkeley, California

ANDREW LOOKED CAREFULLY at the chemist. The man was a Ph.D. candidate in philosophy at Berkeley with his undergraduate degree from Stanford in chemistry. A bush of sand-colored hair covered his face, and a ponytail, gathered at the nape of his neck with a rubber band, slid neatly down his back. His hazel eyes reflected the ardor of a religious zealot. Aaron had informed him that the chemist was "sort of a nihilist." Andrew had pretended that he understood until the detective left, and then he had looked up the word. The definition had struck him as amusing until he'd met the man Aaron had selected. He was perfect, a man who possessed fire in his eyes, intent upon denying all values, questioning all authority, destroying all social institutions. If Andrew had ever seriously doubted that evil did not exist, those doubts had vanished under the chemist's penetrating stare.

The detective had found him through a contact in the Idaho militia who knew Aaron by his fanatically anti-Jewish alias, Johann Werner. The contact had on that occasion provided Aaron with rappelling training and gear for a job that required him to enter a fifteenth-story window on a twenty-story structure. Security had been too tight on the ground floor, so the burglar had waited on the roof until dark and dropped down the side of the building like a spider. The chemist had spent two of his summers away from Stanford manufacturing nitroglycerin and TNT at the militia's compound before deciding, according to Aaron's contact, that the militia "talked the talk, but didn't walk the walk."

The two sat at a sidewalk café on Shadduck Avenue, not far from the Berkeley campus.

"So, John, you can put it into liquid form?" Andrew asked.

"Yes, certainly. It's in the actinide series. It should certainly dissolve in hydrochloric or perchloric acid. No problem." The chemist reached around and absently pulled his ponytail.

His eyes bore straight into Andrew. They made him nervous. Andrew averted his gaze to focus on a point beyond the man's left shoulder. "You can do it at your house?"

"No." The chemist looked at him as though he had suggested that he get a haircut and conform. His pupils dilated slightly as a cloud passed, compelling Andrew to look back at him. "I need a place. I need some special equipment."

"What equipment?"

The chemist began stroking his beard absently. His face moved around eyes that were constant. Unchanging. He carelessly began to list a few items that came to his mind. "HEPAs. You know, high-efficiency particulate air filters. Poly containments. Forced-air breathing for myself. Lead shielding. A few other things. Some poly bottles and some glassware for the acid. If you'll let me know how to contact you, I'll get together a list."

"Would twenty thousand dollars cover those expenses?" Andrew asked.

The anarchist thought carefully. "Yes."

"Can you get hold of all the equipment yourself?"

John thought again. "Yes."

Andrew removed a manila envelope from his pocket and slid it onto the white table top. He leaned close to the chemist's ear and quietly instructed him. "There is twenty thousand dollars in cash in that envelope. Obtain what you need with discretion. I will find you a place to work and contact you within the next week with the location. Have it ready by the end of August. I will contact you again at that time."

The student gave his benefactor a penetrating stare. "Who are you?"

The chemist's yellow-brown mullah's eyes almost compelled Andrew to tell him at least part of the truth, but he caught himself. "Just call me Cassius. That's all you need to know."

"Like Mohammed Ali?" the nihilist asked.

Andrew stared into those insane eyes, momentarily confused. "Yes." He stood and walked away, reflecting on the reality of evil.

54

May 25, 1994, Alma-Ata, Kazakhstan

"GREGOR TELLS YURI. Yuri tells us. We get it. Gregor is *vory v zakone*. He is wise. We get it."

"We have never tried to get anything like this before, Yosef."

The two Russians were engaged in conversation in the bar. The rough-cut wood floor had been smoothed by years of leather soles tramping across it. A modified telegraph-wire spool, which had been left behind when the communication lines traced the railway beds into Kazakhstan, served as their table. Short and stout with a full, thick black beard, one of the men prominently displayed a gold tooth when he smiled. It had replaced one of his incisors knocked out while at the Vorkuta labor camp. Also stocky in build, his companion boasted an elaborately maintained pencil-thin mustache. He was Chechen. Such camaraderie was unusual in a Russian gang, for the Chechen tended to be clannish, nationalist, and profoundly anti-Russian. Yosef and Viktor had met at Vorkuta, however, and prison ties are often thicker than blood ties. They were waiting for a particular Russian officer, the one overseeing the dismantling of the arms cache near Alma-Ata and its repatriation to Greater Russia.

"It is risky, Yosef. We could wind up before a firing squad," Viktor said, twisting one side of his mustache nervously.

"Nonsense, Viktor. It's child's play. The man is hopeless. I have been watching him. He has come back with quite a burden." His right hand made the motion of injecting something into his left elbow, while he tilted his head toward the ceiling with an expression of relief on his face.

Both men fell silent for a moment. Yosef was referring to a problem which had plagued the Russian soldiers returning from Afghanistan: heroin addiction. Yosef could not know, but it had all been Count Alexandre de Marenches's idea. The head of France's Service de Documentation Extérieure et de Contre-Espionnage, or SDECE, Marenches had suggested OPERATION MOS-QUITO to Ronald Reagan in 1981. The President had dismissed it out of hand. The CIA had seen it differently, however, and had released the MOSQUITO that was still driving the Russian bear crazy. Hard drugs, Russian-language Bibles, and pamphlets that instructed soldiers to shoot their officers made their way into Afghanistan and into the Red Army. The MOSQUITO had pricked the officer whom they waited to meet and had allowed Yosef to say to Viktor with confidence, "If we supply him, he will give us what we want."

The young captain of artillery looked haggard and worn. His greatcoat concealed his body, but underneath it he was thin, frail, and pale. The flesh behind his knees, usually concealed by his uniform, was a mass of needle pricks, strawberry fields. His expression was that of a man in shock. His dark-brown eyes looked out of focus. His supply was obviously low. Yosef beckoned him over to the table. "My friend, how are you?" Yosef clapped him on the back of his greatcoat and pulled a chair over for him.

"It goes well with me," the officer lied.

"Good, good," Yosef said. "I think, however, that we can be of assistance to you nevertheless."

"What do you want that a poor officer can provide?" The captain's watery eyes looked desperate.

Yosef passed a package over the table. The officer eyed it carefully, hungrily. Yosef spoke again. "This will help you, I think."

"I cannot pay you. I am destitute." The captain could not take his eyes off the package. His attention could go no further.

Yosef smiled broadly, his gold tooth twinkling in the dim light of the bar. "It is a simple matter. There is a mountain where that came from."

"Yes?" the officer answered warily. Yosef noticed with satisfaction that he had already hidden the package in his coat. He could not resist. "How simple?"

"It is a matter of accounting, really. You make a simple oversight."

June 1, 1994, Fox County, South Carolina

JAKE PUT DOWN A COPY of Viktor Frankl's *Man's Search for Meaning*, leaned back in the rocker, and thought. He enjoyed that part of his business. When no customers were around, he got to sit on the back porch in the white wicker rocking chair that Joe had left him and think. Smells drifted out of the shop as he regarded the cove beyond him. He identified them as they wafted by: the scent of the soft black earth where he kept the night crawlers; the smell of the bait, fish meal, and frogs, along with the rust in their metal tanks. He could hear the violin chirp of crickets in their mesh cages. He pictured the glass case lined with a variety of hooks and sinkers and lures. All of this was now his life. He didn't make much money, but you didn't need much money in Fox County.

He had decided one night years ago that it was not money that would make him happy. It was time. Time to think. At that stage in his life, Jake had not known why he had to leave. He just had to. Somehow he sensed that he was at the end of some personal era and on the brink of another. A bugler deep inside of him had sounded retreat, and he was compelled to obey.

It was not until recently that he had begun to understand. His feelings had something to do with meaning. His former life had no meaning. It was for no one, with no one, by no one. It wasn't even against anyone. That was when he had begun to look in earnest. This search, or the realization that a search was in progress, had happened upstairs.

Jake reflected on the room above the shop. When Joe had moved to his cabin, he had taken the furnishings and left the redecorating to the new owner. The first item that Jake had purchased was a green Naugahyde sleeper-sofa. It had cost him two limp twenty-dollar bills at a garage sale in Lexington. That sofa was the homeliest piece of furniture he had ever seen. It was hideous. Therefore, he had to own it. It was so solidly constructed and heavy that it had taken Jake, Clarence, Bud, and Joe almost two hours of heaving and straining to muscle it up the stairs, one step at a time. They had placed it underneath the back window, and Jake privately suspected that it had found its final resting place in this world. He just didn't think that it could be moved again. The rest of the room was now filled with bookshelves built with plywood and cinder blocks. One step closer to meaning.

The search had begun on those shelves. There were books about everything from hard science to trash fiction. James Fenimore Cooper, Dickens, Cervantes, Dumas, Chaucer, Cicero, Emerson, Marcus Aurelius, Shakespeare, Aesop, Twain, Steinbeck, Asimov . . . anything that he could find in a dog-eared paperback. There was even a ragged set of Funk and Wagnalls encyclopedias that he had purchased at an estate sale in Saluda County. They were well thumbed, as were several dictionaries. When he wasn't reading, he was listening to books on tape from the Richland County Public Library. Borrowing privileges cost him fifty-five dollars a year, since he lived in Fox County, but the expense was well worth it to constantly be feeding his brain. He loved knowledge, but what he was more interested in was less tangible. When he read now, he wasn't attempting to follow the plot as much as he was trying to understand the characters. He read Freud and Jung and Dr. Wayne Dyer. The Book Dispensary, a used bookstore on the other side of the dam, was his mecca. Any topic was of interest. In rereading the books that he had been compelled to study in high school and college, Jake was surprised at what he found. They had meant nothing to him then, just assignments to be completed. They had been meaningless because then he had not been looking.

Somewhere he had read that when the student was ready, the teacher would appear. That was how he felt now when he read. It was how he felt when he paddled his kayak or drove his truck. It was how he felt when he fished. He had changed in such a way as to be open to what was presented to him, to finally learn his lessons. He didn't feel as though he was becoming wise, but rather that somehow he had taken the first step down the road to wisdom. He was beginning to think that meaning lay entirely in the search.

Jake was awakened from his reverie by the bell on the front door. Someone had entered the shop. He stood up lazily from his chair, stretched, and glanced inside.

Joe was walking around looking in the bait tanks and examining the contents of the display case. As Jake entered from the back porch, Joe spoke. "Son, you're runnin' a little low on these surface lures. I may not have told you, but a couple months from now, the bass'll start going for these and ther'l be a demand." He grinned a crooked smile underneath a new Caterpillar cap.

Jake knew that Joe had reviewed seasonal inventory with him a hundred times. He had pointed out those lures hundreds of times, but Jake had missed it. He supposed that he was spending too much time thinking. Jake crossed to a cabinet to see if he had another box. There wasn't one. "Thanks, Joe. I'll order some today."

"No problem, son," the old man said. He turned and left the shop.

Well, Jake thought, *I have a few left and there is no such thing as an emergency in the tackle business.* Taking the East Coast Nautical Wares catalog from the cabinet, he laid it on the counter. He filled out an order for a gross of the surface lures. After adding the tax and postage on his calculator, he wrote a check for $43.95 and slid it into the envelope. Licking a stamp, he placed it on the envelope and walked out to his mailbox to leave it for pickup.

-56-

June 2, 1994, CIA Headquarters, Langley, Virginia

"SIR, SNIFFER SAYS that we are being confused somehow." Lance Jamison handed the Director a single typewritten page from a green folder. TOP SECRET was stamped in red across the top. Jamison stood nervously as his boss read the report. Jamison was Sniffer's recruiter and controller. His shoulder-length, wavy black hair and mustache looked out of place in Langley, but he spent most of his time in Colombia, posing as a trafficker. "My hair is my cover," he had jokingly told a clean-cut acquaintance from "The Farm" while they ate soy burgers in the screened-off SE-CRET portion of the dining hall.

The Agency had generated an elaborate legend to allow Jamison to move tons of narcotics through a Venezuelan army unit, enriching and promoting the career of a corrupt general. Langley, in its convoluted wisdom, had decided that General Salinis was someone whom they wanted in their debt. Jamison did not know why, but it was not necessary or desirable in his job to know all of the whys. He knew that the assignment had led him to Sniffer. That asset had made him a rising star.

Sniffer was one of the Agency's most closely guarded but open secrets. The FBI was aware that the CIA had an asset inside the cartel. The DEA knew. *Newsweek* knew. What none of them knew was who and how high. The Agency viewed the cartel as a hydra. If the one head that they were beginning to know and understand were cut off, then two that they didn't know or understand would emerge. In many respects, they were correct. They felt that if they burrowed deep enough into the enemy that they knew, interdiction could be that much more effective. The DEA's KINGPIN strategy, starting at the top of the organization and bringing it down from there, was the antithesis of the Agency's view. KINGPIN was all about lopping off the head of the hydra.

The Director of the Central Intelligence Agency, James Barrow, looked up dolefully from the report before him. He had the countenance of many in his profession. Between the jousting matches in Congressional oversight committees, emerging crises requiring assessment, and the political infighting typical of any Cabinet-level post, he found little time for the luxury of sleep. His face was lined and pale, his blue eyes bloodshot and accented underneath by dark bags. He looked twenty years older than his actual age. Thinning brown hair, a nervous twitch in his right cheek, and a slight caffeine-induced tremble in his hands rounded out Barrow's appearance. What you saw was what you got, a harried executive with too much responsibility. He was the DCI.

He looked back down and read the report again. It was indeed confusing. The Sniffer code name assigned to their asset inside the cartel was an in-house joke. What Sniffer had related was no joke, however. The Director looked up at Jamison and spoke. "I have read and believe that I understand. Tell me your assessment."

"Sir, what Sniffer is telling us is that the cartel did order the execution of the Panamanian judge and that the FARC did carry out that execution. The FARC did send the videotape to CNN threatening both Colombians and Americans. The cartel, however, reined in the group and has not authorized any action on American soil."

"So they deny killing Judge Alvarez." The DCI's cheek quivered.

"Yes, sir. But they have not denied it publicly. Valens is a wanted man, so it may be difficult getting to the press, but there is a second possibility. They may be having their own in-house investigation to find out if some lone wolf did it. They are nervous and upset, especially since the missile strike. These are not Escobar guys. They are businessmen. America is their biggest market. Just like any multinational corporation, they do not want to blow their biggest market."

"Corporation," the Director said, as if mulling over the use of the word to describe drug lords. He had read in a business magazine that the cartels netted over seven billion dollars a year. This catapulted them past household names like Pepsi, Texaco, and Boeing in profit. The DCI decided that Jamison was not far off target.

"Yes, sir. A corporation. Killing the Panamanian judge," the officer rummaged through a few sheets of paper before finding the name, "Heriberto Enríquez, was good business. They cannot allow people like Enríquez within their own sphere of influence. They have successfully cowed the Colombian courts. Arousing the antipathy of the Western world, however, is not good business. Sniffer has merely confirmed what we should deduce on our own. We are dealing with big business here."

"Big business," the Director murmured half to himself. "The Soviets were easier to work against."

Jamison took a red-eye Avianca flight to Bogotá that same evening. Sniffer Report 42 was placed on a BIGOT list, which restricted its access to about ten CIA senior officials. The FBI was not forwarded this information, as no agreement on sharing intelligence had yet been reached. Earlier that same day, a FBI secretary had misread the routing slip on a photocopy of the assassin's note and had faxed a copy of it to Langley. That evening those two documents lay in the same file folder in the DCI's wall safe, mutual indecipherable clues—one document indicating that the cartel did it, the other suggesting that it did not.

·57·   *June 3, 1994, Twenty Miles outside Alma-Ata, Kazakhstan*

THE TRAIN WAS SLOWING. Sparks rose from steel sliding on steel. Brakes on the cars ground the train to an unplanned halt, its wheels squealing on the wide-gauge rails unique to Russia and Finland. The engineers wondered what the thieves wanted. Many of the cars were full of sheep and cattle, and the three end cars carried a shipment of 180-mm artillery shells being repatriated to the Russian Republic. The last three cars were lightly guarded. In fact, there were only two young soldiers on board to watch over the Army's cargo. Large-caliber artillery shells were not of interest to most criminal organizations, which were after portable items: Kalashnikovs, pistols, mortars, antipersonnel mines, shoulder-launched rockets, plastic explosives, or small-caliber ammunition.

As the train slowed down, the engineers noticed a convoy of Ulyanovsk utility trucks lining the tracks. The vehicles went into gear and followed the slowing cars. The central switching station in Alma-Ata had called and ordered the train stopped. Just two hundred meters more and it would have impacted the bus sitting on the tracks. In front of the bus was a triangular sign bearing the image of an old-fashioned engine belching smoke, complete with cattle scoop. It was the Soviet-era symbol denoting an unguarded railroad crossing.

A stout man with a beard emerged from the lead Ulyanovsk and walked briskly to the third-from-last car. The two guards inside peered out fearfully. The man approached the sliding door, stroking his beard. "Relax, boys. This inspection is merely routine. Please come out with the paperwork."

"Sir, we must stay with the shipment. Those are our orders," an apprehensive young corporal said, staring out of the cargo door. The other guard was a private. Both were barely nineteen and frightened.

The stout man stepped closer. His head was now inside the car. He smiled, revealing a gold incisor to the soldiers. Addressing the corporal, he ordered, "Son, you must come out and talk with me. Otherwise, we will be forced to kill you." He motioned to the convoy of trucks that now surrounded the last three cars of the train. Yosef's men unlimbered an assortment of weapons. AK-47s, Uzi submachine guns, and even an aging .45-caliber Thompson submachine gun were quietly brought into view. At the front of the train the engineers positioned themselves with the aging diesel engine between them and the weaponry on display.

The corporal looked at the private. The private grimaced and shrugged his shoulders. Not wishing to die, the corporal nodded assent and opened the door wider. He jumped to the ground, a cloud of dust rising from the impact of his feet. He walked forward to meet the golden-toothed man. Yosef threw his arm around the young man's shoulder and began heading away from the car. To someone who had missed the preceding scene, it might have appeared that the two were old friends just having a quiet conversation.

Yosef explained the situation to the corporal. "Young man, we have a dilemma here. It is easily solved without bloodshed, or it is easily solved with bloodshed. The choice is yours. I need for you and your friend to walk to the other side of the track and take advantage of this stop to relieve yourselves. When you return, you will take an inventory of your car and you will find that nothing has changed. The alternative is that we can shoot you, and the administrators in Moscow can take several months to decide that nothing has happened. Do you understand?" Yosef squeezed the young man's shoulder affectionately and smiled, revealing his golden tooth again. "Now, go. Talk to your comrade up there."

The corporal returned to the car and spoke to the private. There was some shaking of heads and discussion with repeated motioning toward the armed men outside. Finally, the two shouldered their rifles and hopped out of the car, whistling. They stepped between the cars, crossed the tracks, and faced away from the car, as instructed.

If the transaction had been timed, it would have come out at under one minute. Twenty men in the trucks sprang into action. They pulled a tarp off two artillery shells. Three men per shell heaved them to the ground beside the railway car. Eight men climbed into the car and handed out two artillery shells to men waiting on the ground. Those men placed the shells from the train onto the trucks. The shells from the ground were quickly lifted into the car. The two Ulyanovsk trucks bearing the shells started up and headed across the steppe with two vehicles in tow as escorts.

Two other trucks started and drove up the tracks to pull the bus off the rails. One man jumped out of the lead utility vehicle and instructed the engineer to inform Switching that a farmer was towing the bus off the tracks with his tractor. He handed the engineer $100 in American money while his companions proceeded to move the bus. At the end of the train, Yosef was retrieving the two guards. He handed each of them $1,000 in small bills. He spoke to them as he led them back to the car. "Isn't a market economy grand? You win. I win." He walked over to his truck and turned. "Do not buy a Zhiguli with your money. They are garbage."

As the train began to move again, the young guards completed the inventory of their car. It was all in order. It matched their paper inventory. They had the correct number of shells. What they could not know was that although the number had not changed, the type had. Through a clerical oversight and a little green paint which had covered the red serial number marking a nuclear round, a certain captain of the Russian Army had contrived to allow two nuclear artillery shells ride with their conventional counterparts to the depot at Chelyabinsk.

Those two shells should have been aboard a heavily guarded train bound for Ozersk, also known as Chelyabinsk-65, where they were to be dismantled and processed to make nuclear isotopes for export. Instead, two crude .2 kiloton, 180-mm Soviet copies of the American M–454, 155-mm nuclear artillery shell with W–48 warhead were bouncing in the back of Ulyanovsk utility trucks. Designed to be fired out of the S23, 180-mm towed gun, each contained a 3-kg spherical pit of plutonium 239.

-58-

July 4, 1994, Lake Murray, South Carolina

AT A LITTLE AFTER 9 O'CLOCK, fireworks shot into the sky, exploding in marvelous spheres of green, blue, and red. They were coming from three sides: from over the dam, from the Spence Island chain, and from the vicinity of Billy Dreher Island. Jake and Diana were anchored off the Spence Islands in an O'Day 22 sailboat, which he had borrowed from Clarence.

Clarence was out with Bud and a few other men on a Chris-Craft yacht with a small-block Chevy. Clarence normally didn't approve of powerboats, but he figured that since there was going to be drinking, he was better off on one anyway. You don't get knocked down by a blow from out of Jake's Landing because your friends were stinking drunk and put up all of your sails while you were down below in the head on a Chris-Craft. Anyway, this was going to be a special occasion for Jake.

Jake smiled tenderly at Diana as the rocket's red glare backlit the islands. "Diana, I took you out here on Clarence's sailboat to see the fireworks and all because I didn't want you to forget this night."

Diana looked intently at Jake. Curiously. Warily. She said, "It's a mighty nice night, Jake. I don't think that I'll soon forget it."

Jake seemed confused, but he continued, stumbling over his words. "Well, I guess what I'm trying to say is, well, you know, I'd like to come out here every July Fourth with you."

"Well, I'll certainly come out here every July Fourth with you, Jake. You just have to ask."

Jake was beside himself. Why couldn't he just say it? If you wanted life to have meaning, you have to just do things. He tried again. "What I'm sayin' is, well, I don't really want to have to ask you every year."

"What?" Diana was starting to get the drift of the conversation, but she didn't let on. Wheels started turning in her head. She didn't know what she was going to say.

Jake steeled himself. "Well, we're not getting any younger." *Wrong thing to say*, he thought.

"That's true, Jake."

"Well, I was just thinking, well, I was wondering what you'd think about us gettin' hitched, you know?" He reached into the pocket of his overalls and tentatively withdrew a jeweler's ring box.

Diana took the box and opened it. Her eyes were watery. Jake could see the indecision in her eyes. He felt for her. He remembered a Pirandello play he had read in which some character had said that there was nothing more pathetic for a woman than to see love in a man's eyes. He felt horrible.

She spoke at last. "I just don't know, Jake. It's not that I don't love you . . . but I just don't know." Her eyes were blurry with tears. She looked into the water and thought about Weider weights and overturned bass boats and the beatings. She thought about all of the things that she could bar from her mind while she was awake but could not prevent from creeping in through the unguarded gates of her dreams. Her voice choked. "Jake, honey . . . I love you . . . but there are just some things about me that you don't know." She handed back the ring.

He refused to take it and folded her hands around it. "You keep it," he said. "If you decide that you want me, you just put it on one day, and I'll know. If not, just keep it." He reached behind him and lowered the eight-horsepower outboard into the water, pulled the starter twice to cause it to sputter into life, engaged the propeller, and started backing out of his anchorage. He went forward to pull up the hook, leaving Diana to think. Before he got the anchor on the deck, the fireworks display was over.

-59-

August 9, 1994, Oakland, California

THE FOREMAN LOOKED UP from his desk. Before him stood a thick-necked, sturdily built silver-haired man with a broad Slavic face and flat gray eyes. The man wore a black silk double-breasted suit, a red-striped dress shirt, and a red silk tie. He was flanked by two burly young men dressed in single-breasted black suits that were less expensive but tailored. The foreman, who had once been an Army MP in Italy, knew suits that were cut for guns when he saw them. The tough young men stood like bodyguards, not companions.

Gregor did not ordinarily bring muscle with him everywhere he went. He had brought Constantine and Andrei only because he needed them to drive the truck and unload the box at a warehouse in Sacramento. It was a two-hour drive, but Gregor liked to keep distance between himself and his merchandise. Constantine and Andrei also made Gregor nervous. They had not yet adapted properly to the United States. They had come up through the violent Gopodnik ranks in the streets of Moscow and had grown used to shaking down kiosk owners, beating up taxi drivers, and killing rivals. They had already killed two Los Angeles drug dealers who had attempted to rip Gregor off on a shipment of methcathinone. They had not been caught, and the LAPD didn't care much about a couple of dirtbags who had gotten themselves double tapped. Nevertheless, Gregor felt that he needed to know if they were going to kill people in the States. Los Angeles is not St. Petersburg, after all.

Gregor reached into his suit jacket and removed a sheaf of papers. He spoke nearly flawless English, which he practiced for at least an hour every day, repeating the words of morning talk-show hosts and their guests. "I have come to collect Container 14655. I received a call that it had arrived early. It was on the Liberian freighter *Constance IV* last night." He handed the papers over the desk. "I have brought a truck. If you would please have a forklift place it on the bed, we will take it to our own warehouse."

"Was that the pig out of Vladivostok?" the foreman asked, crossing his own arms and looking hard at the trio in front of him, feigning a bravado he did not feel in the face of Gregor's hired help.

"I don't know or care where it came from. I am here to pick up my container. Here are the papers," Gregor said with a touch of irritation. He did not intend to answer questions.

"That tramp steamer should be scrapped and its crew have their licenses to breathe taken away. That pig came in here yesterday without calling ahead for tugs or telling the harbormaster jackshit. It wasn't on the schedule, and have you ever tried to get union longshoremen to do anything on a Sunday afternoon without giving them some kind of overtime? No? I didn't think so. It scraped one of our pilings. It was bullshit."

The Russian raised a hand to halt the foreman. "It is not my ship. I do not care about the ship, only my container."

Andrei had unbuttoned his suit and brushed the left flap back slightly. The foreman noticed the movement and shut up. "Yeah, right. Sorry. Come with me." He grabbed a wooden clipboard from its hook on the wall behind him. The top page read, "Manifest for *Constance IV,* 10 August 1994." The 10 had been penciled through roughly, tearing the paper, and a 7 written above it in pencil. The foreman turned and walked out of his office and onto the warehouse floor. He headed down a row of containers and looked at the numbers. The group turned the corner and walked down a second row as the foreman referred to his clipboard and compared numbers with those on the containers. At Container 14655, he stopped. Pointing, he said, "Well, there she is. I'll have one of my boys down here in a jiffy with a loader. Where's your truck? Which dock?"

Gregor looked carefully at the container and frowned. "Look. That is Container 14656. The bottom part of the 6 has been scraped during movement. It looks like a 5, but it identifies this as another container."

The foreman squinted curiously at the container and then at his paperwork. He frowned and then flipped a few pages back on the clipboard. Then he said gruffly, "You're right. I guess the midshift foreman made a mistake."

"A mistake?" There was a quaver in Gregor's voice.

"Yeah, a mistake, but fortunately, it's okay. That container was shipped out a few hours ago. *Constance* wasn't supposed to be in here until Wednesday. Early arrival screws up our space allotments. That's why you got a call to come in. We needed to get this shit out of here. A big container ship from Hong Kong is coming in tomorrow." He flipped to another page on the clipboard. "No problem," he said. "Those two containers have the same stuff in them on the manifest. I'll just give you this one."

"Where is the other container?" Gregor knew very well that the two containers did not contain the same thing.

"Let's see here." He flipped back a couple of pages on the clipboard. "Baltimore. East Coast Nautical Wares."

"Was is shipped by truck or rail?"

"It went with an independent carrier. It was supposed to go by rail, but we needed to clear out the space." He paused as he looked back a couple of more pages on the clipboard, and said, "Carlton Fisk and Sons, out of San Jose."

"Thank you." Gregor turned to Andrei. His gunmetal-gray eyes burned with anger. "Take this container to our warehouse and both of you report to me before seven this evening."

-60-

ANDREW TOOK A PLEASANT late-afternoon flight into Bogotá. Avianca Flight 030 had been comfortable and the service good. Although the FAA had criticized the Colombian carrier for poor safety standards, he had felt at home on the 727 as it descended. On the ground he had passed through Immigration with no problems, showing his return ticket and being waved through into the early evening hours in the Colombian capital.

At the terminal he hailed a green and cream-colored tourist taxi. The driver was a dark-complexioned, cheerful, round-faced man who talked during the entire trip, explaining buildings and historical monuments as they passed. Andrew thought that the tour was an incredible bargain at 5,000 pesos per hour, or just slightly above American minimum wage. On 90th Street, he asked the driver to pull over and wait while he stepped into the Telecom office and settled into a phone booth. When he had contacted the international operator, he made a collect call to northern Virginia.

Ronald Dawson answered at the other end of the line. "Hello?"

Andrew could sense the confusion in Dawson's mind as the operator told him that Corinne had placed an international collect call from Bogotá. "Will you accept the charges?" the operator asked.

"Uh . . ." Dawson hesitated, "Yes."

"Go ahead, sir," the operator said to Andrew.

"Well, hello, Ronald!" Andrew said enthusiastically into the mouthpiece. "Remember me?"

"Yes," Dawson answered flatly, then added, "I am hanging up now."

"No, no, no," Andrew scolded. "If you hang up, my next collect call will be to the Alexandria police."

Andrew could hear the static on the international line. Dawson did not answer but had not hung up. Andrew spoke again. "So, Ronald, how are you doing?"

"I'm doing fine," he said in a tired monotone.

"Well, good," Andrew said. "I'm glad to hear that. I want you to get enough sleep and eat your veggies so that you can keep sending those checks, Ronald. Well, I'm gonna go now, Ronald. Give my love to your wife. Toodle-doo." He hung up. He had fulfilled his purpose in coming to Colombia.

The cabby was still waiting for him at the curb. Andrew directed him to show him more of Bogotá, and the driver drove him to the historic district where he pointed out many colonial-era churches and recited fact after fact. Then the cabby took him to the Candelaria neighborhood, near the Plaza Bolívar, and pointed out colonial-era buildings in which people still worked and lived. Andrew sat back in his seat and listened contentedly. He didn't speak, only listened. After about an hour in the cab, he was still feeling expansive. He spoke, interrupting the driver in midsentence. "What is your name?"

The driver smiled at Andrew via the rear-view mirror and told him, "Carlos, sir."

"Well, Carlos. How much money do you think you would make during the rest of your day?"

Carlos thought deeply for a moment. His answer depended heavily upon where the question was leading. He didn't know whether to exaggerate or underestimate. Since he couldn't decide, he exaggerated. "Oh, maybe 30,000 pesos, sir."

Andrew answered immediately, "Well, then, Carlos. How's about I pay you 50,000 pesos and you go to dinner with me?"

Carlos could barely believe his good fortune. He accepted and drove to La Fragata, where Andrew bought them both imported mussels, shrimp, and expensive crab platters. Carlos got drunk on Chilean Concha y Toro Marques de Casa Concha and drove Andrew back to the airport. It had been an evening to remember.

-61-

"CARLTON FISK AND SONS," a deep monotone rumbled into the phone.

"Yes, this is Mr. Gorof from East Coast Nautical Wares. I believe that your line picked up a shipment for my company at the Oakland terminal last night. I was wondering when to expect delivery."

Carlton Fisk was an old-school trucker. His arms were as large as other men's legs from loading and unloading his own trucks and driving the big rigs in the days before power steering or assisted brakes. He was a hard man who had come up through the union ranks. Now that he ran his own company, he was becoming increasingly dissatisfied with the climbing wages, shortened work week, and inflated overtime demanded by the same union which had once protected him. The whining of a driver the previous evening who had wanted more than double overtime because he wasn't previously scheduled for a pickup still had his blood pressure elevated well above a healthy level. "It's in your contract. Page two. I faxed it to your office this morning," Fisk said, attempting to remain civil but sounding irritated.

"Regrettably, my assistant has misplaced the contract. I wish to ensure that our warehouse is open at the right time," Gregor said smoothly.

Carlton pulled open a file drawer and thumbed through a folder. He read into the receiver, "The carrier will deliver the container after noon but before five on Friday the 12th."

"Thank you," Gregor said politely and hung up the phone.

Carlton didn't tell Gregor that the driver was an undependable drunken slob named Ron Bowker who wouldn't have lasted two weeks in the old days. He hoped that he would deliver the container on time but could not be certain. The only thing that he could count on Bowker to do on time was to show up for his paycheck.

-62-   *August 10, 1994, Pittsburgh, Pennsylvania*

ANDREW SAT ACROSS from a clean-cut young man whom Aaron had found—the next link in the chain. Andrew had decided to put the detective on the payroll at Itasco. He wanted Aaron to work only for him. The young man before him was a former electronics technician for the Navy. He had worked extensively in the repair and maintenance of electronic equipment at the Norfolk Ships' Intermediate Maintenance Activity. He had left the Navy because of an alcohol and gambling problem and had managed to gain employment at Westinghouse. Aaron had tracked him down for an Ocean City loan shark two years before. The former Navy man was someone who was likely to need money, knew about electronics, and had access to the kind of equipment required.

"So you can build it?" Andrew asked.

The young man looked arrogantly at Andrew. He blew a bubble from his chewing gum and it burst. He spoke with a Long Island accent. "Yeah, sure, I can build it. No problem. I'll just swipe the tubes from work. The rest," his tongue retrieved a bit of gum from his upper lip, "the rest, I can buy at Radio Shack."

"I want it to be a black box. I just want a green light to indicate that the threshold has been reached. No fancy meters."

"You want the threshold based on alphas or gammas?" The gum popped in his mouth as he chewed.

"Which is more accurate?"

"Depends on what you're measuring. You haven't told me." The technician leaned back in his chair and blew another bubble.

"This is for a plant that I am operating overseas. It manufactures plutonium batteries for pacemakers. I want it to tell if a dangerous level is reached if the plutonium is spilled." Andrew reached in his pocket for a three-by-five card. He had made some notes from his computer E-mail exchanges on the subject. He added, "The probe. It needs to be able to be lowered into a hole for measuring. The hole is two inches in diameter. It will need to extend about a foot."

"Plutonium, huh?" the man dropped his chair back onto four feet with a bang.

"Yes. These are Malays that we are dealing with. Superstitious little runts. I don't want to frighten the workers. I'd be training a whole new factory's worth every couple of months."

"Just need one?" the young man asked.

"The one you are building will be a prototype. If it works well, I will order more," Andrew lied.

"A probe. Two-inch diameter. Extend a foot." The technician was thinking a little behind the conversation. He smacked his gum again. "Yeah, I can do it. I'll build it to trigger off of alphas for the plutonium and gammas for general radiation. If it reaches threshold on one or the other, the light will light. It's just an 'or' logic gate circuit. Can do."

Andrew handed over an envelope. "Mr. Waters, in that envelope is ten thousand dollars to defray the expense of building the item. I will contact you in two weeks and arrange to pick it up, at which time I will pay you another ten thousand dollars. Cash. If I decide that I want more, I will pay you fifteen thousand dollars per detector."

The young man smiled greedily. "Yes, sir."

"Also, Mr. Waters, don't be stupid. Do not buy anything that you cannot afford on your current salary. Do not deposit all of the money at once in a bank. The IRS is informed of every transaction exceeding ten thousand dollars."

-63-

RON BOWKER WAS THINKING. He did a lot of thinking on the transcontinental hauls. He hated listening to the radio, and there wasn't much to hear on the lovely tundra of Wyoming, as one of his buddies from the state called it. It was boring and he didn't even have any new tapes. He had already listened to his entire Joan Jett collection and even the Runaways. Ron loved Joan and was certain that if she met him, the feeling would be mutual.

He pictured the two of them together. He was five feet, ten inches tall and weighed 260 pounds, most of it in his enormous beer gut. Ron considered it to be his workingman's belly and preferred to think that he presented a rough-cut, tough-guy image to the girls. He smiled as he thought of one of his favorite bar lines: "Honey, when you've got a big tool like mine, you need a big shed over it to keep it out of the rain." He rubbed his stomach reflexively. He pictured himself clearing a path through the fans for his wife, Joan Jett Bowker. Basking in this image as his rig rumbled through the tundra, he put "I Love Rock and Roll" into his cassette deck.

He was going to make a drop in Baltimore and a pickup in Wilmington, Delaware. Then he remembered Hammerjacks. What a place! The noise, the smoke, the bar, the beer, the girls, the bands. Ron remembered a delivery to Baltimore a few months back and the flyer posted outside. If he recalled correctly, Joan was going to be playing there on August 11. If he put the pedal to the metal, kept the shiny side up and the greasy side down, and paid attention to his radar detector, he could drop this shipment by Thursday afternoon and see his idol. He accelerated to eighty-five mph and hummed in unison with the music.

-64-

August 11, 1994, Baltimore, Maryland

DAN SEYMOUR SIGNED for the shipment and stepped back onto the forklift to carry it into the warehouse. It had arrived early, but he was glad to have it in. He had several back orders to fill, and although East Coast Nautical Wares put out a slick catalog and did a pretty brisk business, the company consisted of only him and Darlene. That was it. That was the beauty of the mail-order business. He didn't need a lot of employees. The electric lift whirred across the warehouse, and he set down the container in the northeast corner. Driving the forklift to its parking spot next to the office, he waved through the glass to Darlene and grabbed a crowbar.

Walking back to the container, he pried the lid off and grabbed one box off the top in both hands. It was labeled "Surface Lures, Style 1432, 1 Gross (144)." He hefted it out of the container and returned to the office. He dropped it into a larger box and dumped some packing peanuts around it. Before he taped the lid shut, he noticed a small red dot painted on the box. Thinking nothing of it, he strapped the tape over the seam.

Still looking down but reaching out in Darlene's direction, he said, "Darlene, hand me the order we got yesterday for a gross." She handed it to him. He grabbed the order, ripped off the return address section, and taped it to the box. He put the box on a scale, referred to his postal chart, affixed $2.90 in postage, and placed the package outside the door for pickup. "So, spells his shop a 'Shoppe,' huh?" he commented to Darlene as he walked back into the warehouse to get another box.

-65-

August 11, 1994, Cali, Colombia

EMILIO WALKED QUIETLY onto the deck. It was getting close to sunset, and he cringed at the thought of interrupting Santiago's quiet time. He looked quickly toward where Santiago sat, leaning back in his chair, with his feet upon the ottoman, staring toward the western sky. As he got closer, he noticed Teresa, Santiago's wife, hunched on the deck next to his boss's chair speaking with him. He was smiling. She was beautiful. Emilio reflected on how different his marriage was. Emilio's wife had turned into a shrew almost immediately after they had taken their vows. He wanted to divorce her, but, being a devout Catholic, he was considering killing her instead. Teresa laughed, and Santiago turned his head in such a way as to indicate that something he had said was the source of her amusement.

"Santiago," Emilio said quietly.

"Yes, Emilio, I heard you creep up on me," Santiago answered. He did not turn his head but kept looking westward.

"Santiago, it is business."

Teresa stood up. Santiago motioned for her to give him a kiss. She bent and kissed him, and he told her, "Teresa, ask Roberto to bring out my evening wine."

"Yes, my love," she said jokingly. Santiago chuckled. Emilio gathered that it must be a reference to the joke his boss had just told her.

"Santiago," Emilio said respectfully, "we have suffered a small setback in Italy."

Santiago still did not turn toward his underling. He continued to face the setting sun. Roberto came onto the deck wordlessly and handed the drug lord his customary glass of red wine. "Thank you, Roberto," Santiago said to the servant. Then he swirled the wine around the glass and smelled it. He took a sip and inhaled through his mouth, tasting the wine thoughtfully. To Emilio, it seemed that the silence had lasted an hour before his master spoke. "So, Emilio, tell me about our little setback."

"Sir, we lost approximately 4,000 kilos." Emilio waited for his master's characteristic long whistle. It did not come. It was almost as if the magnitude of the loss was beyond the whistle. Santiago's expression remained unchanged. Emilio continued, "Italian carabinieri seized the cocaine in Turin."

Santiago still did not turn or whistle. He sipped his wine again and spoke. "It sounds like it is Palermo's problem. They have paid for it. They lost it. They will take out contracts on a few of their own. That is a bloodthirsty bunch, like Pablo." He took another sip.

Emilio remembered witnessing the execution of twenty-three people over the submarine cargo heist. Santiago had been correct. The cargo had been stolen and the submarine sunk to cover their tracks. Santiago brought in some of the FARC to carry out the slaughter. The drug lord had watched it all, puffing on a Cuban cigar and telling jokes with José Sanchez. The thieves had watched the guerrillas cut the throats of their wives and children. Then the "pirates," as Santiago had labeled them, had been castrated, eviscerated, and given a coup de grace gunshot in the head. If the Sicilians were more bloodthirsty than that, he would take his chances in Colombia. With these thoughts in his head, Emilio continued reluctantly. "Sir, the problem is that they are blaming us."

Santiago waited a moment, as if digesting the new information. "So they blame us. Why do they blame us?"

"The Cosa Nostra says that the leak must be on our end. The ship was tracked from Colombia to the Ligurian coast of Italy. It pulled in at Genoa, truckers hauled the cocaine to Turin. Bang. They got arrested. They say that the problem is at our end." Emilio nervously shoved his hands into the pockets of his trousers.

Santiago let the silence hang in the air for a few moments. He took another sip of wine. Still staring at the red ball descending in the west, he spoke. "Emilio, I am becoming increasingly uninterested in what the Italians think. I think that the old men in Palermo are past their prime." He paused and looked at the wine glass, running his index finger around the rim. "Yes, past their prime. I have found some new blood, Emilio. The Italians have just lost their monopoly."

Emilio did not speak. He waited for his master to continue. He stared at the concrete deck. After a few moments, Santiago continued. "Emilio, there is a Russian gang. Their operation extends from San Francisco to St. Petersburg. They have control of a shipping line. They paid a man who is unknown to me a finder's fee to connect us." He paused again. "Russia is an open gateway to Europe, Emilio. We will give the Continentals what they want from the East. Fuck the Italians."

Two days later, Sniffer Report 51 landed on the DCI's desk at Langley. It described all that Emilio had heard about the new connection between the Cali cartel and the Russian mafia. It mentioned the unknown connect man and described a conference that Santiago had conducted with José Sanchez, leader of the FARC. Sanchez had unequivocally denied any involvement in activity outside of Colombia and Panama. The report was BIGOT listed and filed with the others.

-66-

August 12, 1994, Baltimore, Maryland

"EAST COAST NAUTICAL WARES. This is Darlene." The voice was sing-song secretarial, and the words seemed to tap-dance on the line. Gregor developed a mental picture of a buxom blonde filing bright red fingernails and chewing gum at her desk as she answered the phone. She sounded like she had blue eyes. He didn't know why that was. Maybe, he thought, it was just that middle-aged Russian men like him fancied Germanic women. "Hello? Is anybody there?" the lovely voice asked in the bouncy rhythm.

"Yes, quite," Gregor recovered. "My name is Yuri Denisovich. Good morning."

"Well, good morning, Mr. Denisovich. What may I do for you today?" Gregor's mind raced, but he remembered the issue at hand.

"Well, there has been a mix-up. You have received a shipment of fishing lures, which is mine, and I have received the shipment which is yours. I would like to exchange. May I speak to whomever I need to in order to arrange the exchange?" A clattering diesel engine could be heard in the background.

"Hold one second, Mr. Denisovich. I'll find one of the warehouse supervisors." She hit the hold button on the phone and laughed. She always enjoyed pretending that ECNW was a bustling company. She opened a door out to the warehouse and shouted, "Dan, got some Russian guy on the line. Tell him that you are the swing-shift supervisor, all right?"

Dan walked in and picked up the phone, and Darlene hit the hold button. "Swing-shift supervisor," he said gruffly into the phone, playing along with Darlene's lead.

Gregor answered, "Yes, this is Yuri Denisovich, from San Jose Bait and Tackle, in San Jose, California. There has been a mix-up and you have received my shipment of lures. I would like to arrange an exchange."

"Well, Mr. Denis . . . how do you say that again?"

"Denisovich," Gregor said slowly, but the last syllable was drowned out by a pulse of traffic noise.

"Well, uh, yes," Dan said, "seems like a lot of trouble to cart a bunch of lures back across the country. Why don't you just keep our shipment and we'll call it even."

Gregor had prepared for this eventuality, "Well, the only problem is that mine was a special order from the factory. It has our logo imprinted on the metal. It is a promotional item."

Dan had never heard of such a thing, but he believed it. "Well, there is the matter of the expense. I suppose that you are going to hold the shipper accountable?"

"It is not a problem. I will have a truck drop off your container and pick up mine within the hour." Gregor hung up the receiver of the pay phone and breathed a sigh of relief. He turned and smiled at Andrei and Constantine, who stood behind him. He sniffed the diesel exhaust smell that permeated the air of the truck stop off Interstate 495. "Piece of pie," he said, rubbing his hands together.

Dan walked out to the warehouse floor and nailed the top of Container 16455 back on. As he drove the last nail home, he remembered that he had already filled one order. He shrugged. "They can suck up a gross and that guy can live with a company logo on his lures."

Two hours later, Gregor and his men pulled into an alley in downtown Baltimore, not far from the Inner Harbor. The rear door of the trailer was slid open unceremoniously. Constantine and Andrei nimbly hopped up into the bed with a crowbar to pry the lid off. The tearing of wood and wrenching of nails echoed against the walls of the trailer and the top gave way. Pulling it aside for the older man to inspect, the younger men stepped to each side of the crate and waited.

Gregor looked and cursed. There was one box missing. Without further investigation, he knew that it was the one. There should have been a small red dot painted on its corner. He turned to the men and spoke harshly. "Unload the container, so that I can see all of the boxes."

The young men did as he asked, and thirty minutes later Gregor was certain that there was no box with a red dot on it. They unpacked all of the boxes and found 143 gross of lures. Gregor's face hardened during the process. When they were finished, he spoke again. "I want all of the records out of that company's office. Get them tonight."

-67-

August 12, 1994, San Francisco, California

ANDREW SAT WITH A DARK-COMPLECTED middle-aged man at a public table near Fisherman's Wharf. The other man had just arrived. He had looked around curiously and been motioned over by Andrew, who had studied the photograph provided for him by Aaron.

"Have a seat, Mr. Onasis." Andrew motioned to the concrete bench across the table from him.

Onasis sat, looking peevish. "What do you want? I received a telephone call that someone important wished to discuss a business proposition with me."

"Yes. I am and I do."

"Then you know that I told him that I was not interested."

"Yes, I do."

"He then wanted me to look in my mailbox." Onasis tossed a photograph, face down, across the table. "He called back and asked me if I had reconsidered. This is blackmail."

"Yes. You could say that, if you wish. I prefer to think of it as a business proposition."

"Well, let me hear it, then," Onasis said impatiently and glanced at his watch. "I have to report for swing shift in an hour."

Andrew smiled warmly. "Mr. Onasis, I am the vice president of a large firm, Vitaplex. Perhaps you have heard of it?"

"No," replied Onasis coldly.

"Vitaplex has developed a water-treatment supplement, which can economically give everyone in this city who drinks water 100 percent of all the U.S. recommended daily allowance of vitamins. We have run clinical trials on the supplement and it has FDA approval. In short, Mr. Onasis, it works. It is a tremendous breakthrough."

"What does your 'tremendous breakthrough' have to do with me?"

"It is simple, Mr. Onasis. No city manager has leant an ear to our treatment. We need to run a demonstration. I want to run it out of your treatment plant. I believe that the city will benefit tremendously. We have a study in place to measure the gross effects on the city's population through hospital admission statistics. People who feel better have fewer accidents. People who ingest all their vitamins do not sicken as often or as seriously. This will be a tremendous breakthrough."

"You like the word 'tremendous,' don't you?" Onasis said sarcastically.

"Yes, I do," Andrew said firmly.

"So why the strong-arm tactics?" Onasis asked, pointing toward the photograph.

"It needs to be a double-blind study. My statisticians cannot know when or what section of San Francisco will be affected. It could skew their study. I need someone like you."

"Someone like me," Onasis said sadly. "What are my choices?"

Andrew turned over the photograph. It showed a naked teenage girl on her knees with her head in Onasis's lap. He was sitting in the La-Z-Boy chair in his den, and the photograph was taken through the window of the room by Aaron. "I take it that your wife would not be thrilled with these photographs."

"No," Onasis said again morosely. His eyes were immensely sad.

Andrew turned the photo back over. "Then she will not have to know that you call hookers every Wednesday night while she works the night shift at the hospital." He handed Onasis an envelope. "In that envelope you will find ten thousand dollars in cash. It is the first half of the payment. The second half will come upon the completion of your part of the study."

-08- *August 17, 1994, Route 378, Fox County, South Carolina*

TWO SQUARE-JAWED PALE MEN sat in the rented Ford Mustang, parked on the side of the road, two hundred yards away and across the two-lane road from Joe's Bait and Tackle Shoppe. The man in the passenger seat squinted through a pair of binoculars at Jake's storefront and mailbox. They had a simple plan. They were waiting for Jake's mail to come. If the package they sought arrived, they would wait for the postman to leave and go take it. Simple. Direct. To the point. Very Russian. They had been watching this mailbox for three days and no packages had been delivered. It had been a boring assignment. The man who lived above the shop had left on the first day for a few hours in the morning with his blue pickup truck and returned with a small paper bag and a newspaper. On the second day, it had rained and the light had remained on upstairs all day. The only other event of the second day was that a sheriff's patrol cruiser had passed by their parked vehicle during the height of the storm, but it had not stopped, either not having noticed them or not interested. This morning, the owner had walked out the back of his shop with some sort of canoe and had paddled off onto the lake.

Andrei and Constantine were bored. Andrei was reading a tourist guide for Lake Murray, and Constantine was focusing his binoculars on Jake's house. They almost didn't notice the sheriff's cruiser pull up behind them and come to a halt. Hearing the crunch of gravel, Constantine quickly placed the binoculars between himself and the seat while his partner placed a folded jacket on top of it in a neatly choreographed move.

The officer stepped out of his dark blue and gray cruiser and placed a wide-brimmed hat on his head as he approached the driver's side window. His name tag identified him as Deputy Bud Jones. He removed his hat and placed it in his left hand as he bent to address the driver. "Nice day, ain't it?" he smiled.

The driver responded, "Yes, sir, it is."

"Nice view, ain't it?" the deputy noted, sweeping the hat toward the cove their parking place overlooked.

Again, the driver responded, "Yes, sir, this is a beautiful place."

"Y'all from 'round here?"

"No, sir, we are just tourists."

"That so?" the deputy said with mock shock. He placed his hat on the roof of the Mustang and leaned into the car, taking a look around.

"Yes, sir, we are just tourists," Andrei repeated evenly, showing his Lake Murray guide as evidence.

"Well, I noticed you tourin' around here yesterday in the thunderstorm," the deputy continued, "and I noticed you here again today. Ain't that somethin'?" He smiled.

"Yes, we were here yesterday, but the storm did not offer us the opportunity to appreciate the view," replied the driver, warming to the game the deputy was playing.

The deputy leaned farther into the car and looked straight into Andrei's eyes, an act anyone performed at their peril. Bud held up two fingers for the men to see and said, "Well, I'll tell you what I think, boys. One and one is normally two." He shook both fingers at Constantine for emphasis. "I've seen you two boys twice sittin' here on two different days. It's not like we're not nice to strangers around here. We've got the good ol' Southern hospitality and all, but we don't like strangers creepin' 'round our back doors or," he reached down and uncovered the binoculars, "peepin' in our windows." He withdrew his head from the car and put his hat back on. He held the binoculars in his hand for a moment, examining them. Then he tossed them into the road. There was a sound of cracking glass. "I want you boys to get on down the road. Y'all hear me?" He walked back to the cruiser and got in. The lights started rotating and blinking, and his voice came over the amplifier. "I'm goin' to escort you to the county line. Move."

As they made their way to the Fox County line, Constantine and Andrei spoke fervently. They had to get that box with a less direct approach.

-69-

August 17, 1994, Fox County, South Carolina

JAKE COULD SEE the blinking light from the tower behind the dam as he made his way back across the lake. He had caught two striped bass and was looking forward to cooking them up for dinner with some onions and butter.

He loved his kayak. It was a green Keowee, about nine feet long, and it made a nice straight line in front of him as he paddled to the other side of the lake. He enjoyed fishing on weekdays because there were fewer powerboats out to make troublesome wakes. He enjoyed kayaking also because it was quiet and peaceful. He had time to think and benefited from the relaxation that came from strenuous exertion. The lake was 14 miles at its widest point and 41 miles long. It had 520 miles of coastline, and he had only explored a fraction of that in the eight years that he had paddled on its waters. He was happy. He had found his home, his place of power, as Carlos Castenada would have called it.

On days that he didn't paddle his kayak, Jake would swim in the lake. Ordinarily he would go from his dock to the middle, a point three-quarters of a mile out, and then swim back. He even swam in the winter months, having purchased a surfer's wet suit which fit him marvelously. After the initial shock of the icy water, he was as snug as a bug in a rug in that suit. Form follows function, and Jake had developed a physique that was formidable. The physical results of his exertions were not what interested him, however. He used that time and the mental state he achieved to work on the formulation of his own personal philosophy. He would continually ask himself, "What is the meaning of this act that I am performing? What is the meaning of life?" He would think about Zen Buddhist koans and the Sermon on the Mount and the enigma of Diana. Sometimes he would get a glimpse of some understanding and could hardly wait until he got back to shore to write it down. By the time he had gotten out of the water, the idea was usually gone, leaving only a warm afterglow.

He had once overheard a conversation on the porch between the older men as he returned from his morning swim. It was when he was still relatively new in town. Joe had taken him under his wing but had not yet begun to think of him as the son he had never had.

"It just don't seem natural, y'know," one of the men said. It sounded like old Jim.

"Oh, I don't know," said another voice. It was Joe. "The boy is a good man. I think somethin' from the past is eatin' his lunch, that's all."

"But doncha think it's a bit strange, him doin' all that swimmin' and paddlin' and such? He needs a nice johnboat and an electric trollin' motor, is what he needs."

Jake could smell Joe's cigar from the boat ramp. Joe spoke again. "Well, I don't know 'bout that. He don't cause no trouble with that Eskimo canoe. Keeps the stock up in the shop. Quiet."

Old Jim continued. "Joe, where'd the man come from? What's eatin' his lunch?"

"Well, Jim, I don't see how it matters where he come from. He's been here on nine months now and he ain't never caused a lick of trouble 'round here, except for old gossips like you. I even think he's gonna marry Diana if I don't miss my mark."

"Diana? I didn't know them two was carryin' on."

Joe pursed his lips and blew a smoke ring. "Oh, yeah. He's down at the beauty shop twice a week like clockwork courtin' her. It'll do that woman some good to be married."

"What happened to that boy again?"

"Drownt. Down by the dam."

"Hell's bells. I remember now. Never found him, did they?"

"Nope. Probably hooked one of them forty-foot catfish that live at the base of the dam and didn't wanna let go. Spent most of his time drunker than a hoot owl. No surprise to me that the boy drownt."

"Joe, there ain't no forty-foot catfish at the dam," Jim said doubtfully.

"Sure as hell are! I heard from one of the rangers that they hired divers to go down and clean. Those boys were in an' out of the water like Jaws was down there." Joe paused for emphasis. "They come right back up sayin', 'We ain't fish food!' and that the catfish were keepin' the place clean just fine. Handed back the state check as quick as you please and said 'thank you but no thank you.'"

"Joe, you know that ain't true. He was just talkin'.'"

"Jus' tellin' you what I heard."

At this point Jake had walked in as though he hadn't heard anything. He had felt good from that swim. He felt that good today. The sun was setting in the west as he paddled toward home. It turned bright reddish orange as it backlit the clouds and slid over the horizon, streaking the smooth lake with crimson lines of light. A familiar serenity overtook him. His mind fell silent and still, its surface becoming smooth like water with no ripples. It lasted only a moment before a thought splashed into the placid pool like a stone sending concentric waves of consciousness rolling outward. These fleeting instants of absolute tranquillity always surprised him. They were unearned gifts, like the grace of God. The very act of analyzing or attempting to create them for himself caused them to flash into vapor and dissipate.

He paddled into the cove and made for the boat ramp in the twilight. He released the skirt of the kayak, pulled it over his head, folded it up, and shoved it behind him as the boat glided toward the concrete. He balanced his paddle on the bow and left it to tend to itself as he reached below and stuffed his thermos into the lunch box he had carried with him. Closing the lid, he noticed that it wouldn't shut completely. His knife was wedged in there. He folded the knife and stuck it in its leather sheath on the back of his belt. The bow scraped along the concrete, and he climbed out of the kayak and pulled it onto the land. He noticed that a pontoon boat was tied at his pier but didn't give it any thought. People were always tying up there to walk up to Maurice's Bar. He picked up the fish and his lunch box and walked toward his shop. He never locked the shop so he didn't have any keys. He swung the fish over his left shoulder and opened the door.

He saw a baseball bat arcing toward his head and heard the lunch box crash on the concrete floor. After that, there was nothing.

-70-

"LAST CALL! LAST CALL!" the bartender yelled. Ordinarily, he wouldn't have yelled it, but the bar was filled with "squids," or Navy sailors who had just arrived home from a Western Pacific deployment. The sailors were loud, drunk, and generally obnoxious. Like most Navy towns, Alameda wished that it could get the sailors' money without the sailors tagging along behind it like extremely annoying houseguests. Andrew was in town to meet a sailor, a disbursing clerk. Aaron had found him through a contact in Bank of America. This clerk was hand-over-fist in debt. Nothing spectacular, as far as Aaron could glean, but he couldn't make the payments on his new Honda, Harley-Davidson, and the tiny house that he had purchased for his new wife. Andrew suspected that the sailor had thought a lot more of her when she had cost twenty dollars a night in Olongapo. She was costing him a lot more than that now. She had become Americanized. The clerk was in trouble. Aaron had brokered the deal, and now Andrew was here to be the answer to the petty officer's dreams.

"Last call" was the clerk's signal to proceed slowly down the south side of Webster Street toward the Oakland Tunnel He would be contacted as he walked. Feeling generous as he stood up from the bar, he left a ten-dollar tip and stepped out the door. He turned right and began walking slowly down the sidewalk. As he passed by some bushes beside a bank building, a street person pushing a shopping cart approached him. He continued to push the cart unsteadily until he was beside the petty officer. Then the vagrant said in a steady voice, "Walk around behind the bank. He is waiting for you beside the teller machine." Then the homeless man who was not homeless continued to walk slowly and unsteadily down the sidewalk, pushing his shopping cart. He looked as though he was searching for a good place to go to sleep. Aaron had called upon one of the many disguises in his repertoire.

The clerk did as he was told and stepped into the bushes and exited on the other side into the parking lot of the bank. There, as predicted, a man loitered beside the teller machine. Sighting him, the clerk used his identification phrase: "Man, it's cold tonight."

Then came back the correct reply, "It is colder in August in San Francisco than in January." The man motioned for the clerk to come over beside the building out of sight of the automatic teller's camera. He asked, "Do you have what we need?"

"Yes," the clerk replied. "I was only able to get nineteen of them. They are all logged as destroyed misprints." He handed over an envelope.

Andrew opened the envelope to look at the merchandise. He examined the tan blank checks that read "The Treasury of the United States of America" and pulled out one to look at it through the dim light of the street beside the bank. The watermark was there. They were legitimate. He counted them. Nineteen. "Good," he murmured. He pulled an envelope out of his pocket and handed it to the clerk. "Thank you. Inside is $500 for each check. I was led to understand that there would be twenty, but nineteen is sufficient."

The clerk looked thoughtfully at him. "What are you guys? The Mob, or something like that?"

"Yeah, something like that." Andrew turned and walked out of the light.

-71-
August 17, 1994, Lake Murray, South Carolina

THE PONTOON BOAT approached Lunch Island as moonlight streamed in from the east, silhouetting the Spence Islands. The boat cautiously approached the eastern shore. The men on board were dropping a lead sinker on a line over the side and carefully measuring the depth.

One of the men whispered, "Forty feet." The man at the helm stopped the motor and backed down momentarily to still the boat.

"Now measure it again." There was a splash as the lead weight dropped.

The voice whispered again, "Yeah, forty feet."

"Good," said the first voice. "Jason, drop the anchor." The man at the helm killed the motor. There was complete silence, except for the miniature ocean sounds of small waves making their way onto the tiny island. There was a splash and the sound of chain running over the deck, followed by the sound of the rope feeding itself out and then being made fast to a cleat. Jake, who had just regained consciousness, heard all of this. He was wrapped tightly in a tarp. He could feel that his feet were tied together at the ankles. His hands were not tied, but he could not move about freely due to the tarp, which was tied at intervals on the outside, around his body. He couldn't see anything to be gained from letting them know that he could hear them, so he remained silent and listened.

A voice spoke. "Whatcha doin', Charlie? I thought that we were supposed to deliver this stuff to them guys who come by the station."

"Shut up," said the voice that had commanded the anchor to drop. "Hold this." There was a splash. "Hand me that. Hand me the knife." There was another splash, but not as loud as the first.

Charlie sighed again. "The way that I figure it, boys, is if whatever is in that box is worth ten thousand dollars to them suits, there's no harm in asking twenty." There was the sound of a beer can top popping, "Yes, sir. It's Miller time, boys."

"But ain't that PBR, Charlie?"

"Shut the fuck up, Vince."

"Hey, Charlie, what'r we gonna do with that guy Vince killed?"

"I didn't mean to kill him."

"Well, you sure knocked hell out of him with that bat. He ain't moved since."

"Shut up, Jason. I didn't mean it. He just surprised me."

Charlie laughed. "Well, you sure surprised the shit out of him. Wham!"

"Well, we got to do something with him."

Charlie tossed the beer can over his shoulder. It clanked on the side of the boat and landed in the water. "Boys, I have already come to a resolution for our dilemma." He spoke with the authority of the senior drunk. "You were probably wondering why I loaded up this concrete block at the dock." There was the sound of concrete scraping paint off the aluminum, and Jake felt his ankles being lifted and another rope being tied at his feet. The man tugged twice on his ankles, apparently to ensure that the knot was tight.

"Help me here a little." Jake felt himself being lifted.

"What?" Jake heard one voice say.

"We need to drop him in the big water. It's deeper up there. Besides, I don't wanna think of him dangling down there when we come back for the stuff."

"Yeah, right."

Jake heard the motor start up. He heard the men retrieve the anchor and felt the boat turn and accelerate. He was thinking as quickly as he could. From the movement of the boat, he figured he was on the bow, facing forward. How was he to get out of this? He could barely move. Although his hands weren't tied, he was essentially in a tarpaulin straitjacket. He tried to relax. There had to be a solution. He had to get out of here. Why was this happening to him? It never occurred to him to speak.

The boat motored for about fifteen minutes before he heard the pitch of the motor decrease as it descended to an idle. He was being lifted again. Charlie was telling a joke as they muscled him to the side. "You know, boys, I heard that Martians had landed in south Georgia. That's the bad news." Jake was lifted by three sets of hands. They set him along the aluminum railing.

"So what's the good news?" Vince asked.

"They eat niggers and piss gasoline." Charlie added the punch line as he pushed Jake off the railing. In the split second that it took to traverse the three feet of open air before hitting the water, the tarpaulin tube that confined him like a coin roll gave him a glance at the moon. It seemed to mock him.

Jake struggled as he descended. He heard his sinuses crack and thought his ears were going to explode from the sudden increase in pressure. The water went from warm to frigid as he passed the thermocline. Suddenly he stopped. He had hit the bottom. In a foolish instant he thought about Joe's forty-foot catfish. *Fuck*, he thought. *Fuck, fuck, fuck, fuck, fuck!* He had no time for more noble thoughts as he twisted against his bonds. He knew that it would only be a matter of a few more moments before he had to concede, breathe in the water, and let it end.

As he twisted, he felt the bulge of the knife sheath. Then he knew the answer. He put his index finger under the flap and flipped it up as he reached his other hand around to grasp the knife in a single motion and unfold it. From that awkward position, standing with the knife at his waist, he pushed the point through the tarp and drove the knife upward. It tore the tarp until it hit the upper rope on the outside which bound him. Jake sawed at it desperately and it separated. His upper body was free, but he was still anchored to the floor of the lake by the concrete block. His whole body was burning from oxygen deprivation. He was dying. He bent double and felt the block imbedded in the mud, groping frantically for the rope looped through it which bound him to death. Finding it, he slashed and chopped at the loop with his waning strength until it parted. Dropping the knife, Jake bent his knees and pushed himself away from the muddy bottom.

In the darkness, there was no reference point to tell him that he was rising toward the surface. There was no steadily lightening murk to indicate that he was heading away from the bottom, but he swam in the direction that he had pushed himself. He exhaled strongly as he stroked. His legs were still bound and he dragged the tarp with him. He needed air. He needed air desperately. He stroked and stroked and stroked. In the darkness, it seemed as though he was not making any progress. Jake felt his brain shutting down even as he told his body, "Stroke!" He felt his consciousness waning and darkness descending. Then, he saw the twinkling disk of the moon like a quarter hung in a shadow box.

He realized that he was at the surface. One more stroke and he broke into air and gasped the sweetest breath he had ever tasted. He breathed deeply, over and over. Thinking of nothing but the lovely air, he lay floating on the surface, exhausted, his feet still bound and the tarp floating beside him. A fourteen-inch striped bass floated next to him. It had been killed by the propeller of a retreating pontoon boat 120 seconds before. The lake was all quiet in stark contrast to the roaring in his mind.

After floating and breathing for a while, Jake started fumbling with the knot that tied the tarp to his feet. He would take a deep breath, bend to reach the knot, and sink until he had to relent and swam to the surface. After thirty minutes of fruitless attempts, the knot finally gave and his feet were free. Guided by the moonlight, he made a course for the Spence Islands. He had decided that he would spend the night there, curled up under a pine tree, and think of what to do next.

What do you do when you have been murdered and don't know why? He decided that he would avoid that question until the morning. He would be safe on the islands. Since it was Thursday night, it was unlikely that he would even encounter any campers. It would be quiet and safe. He fell into the familiar rhythm of open-water swimming. Stroke, stroke, stroke, breathe. Stroke, stroke, stroke, breathe. Stroke, stroke, stroke, breathe and look and alter course. Forty-five minutes later he was crawling out onto the banks of the outermost Spence Island. He found a large white pine tree and curled up at the base of its trunk and fell into a dreamless sleep. He wouldn't feel the pain from being hit with a baseball bat until late the next morning, when he awoke with a splitting headache.

72

August 17, 1994, Saluda, South Carolina

ANDREI TURNED TO CONSTANTINE in the car as it rounded the Saluda traffic circle. His travel guide lay open in his lap. "You know, I read here that this traffic circle was the only place in America which was bombed during the Second World War." He spoke in Russian.

Constantine looked at him disinterestedly. "Oh, really?" he replied without emotion.

"Yes. It was bombed by accident during practice by B-25s over the lake."

"Yes, the Americans made many sacrifices during the Great Patriotic War," Constantine said sarcastically. "Andrei, look at the map. We must get back to the interstate. If you have forgotten so soon, may I remind you that we left a mess at that dock."

Andrei sobered considerably and tossed the travel guide to his feet. He extracted a map from the glove compartment and began unfolding it. "Yes, Gregor is going to be very displeased. He has told us not to do that without telling him."

"How could we have foreseen that they would hide it?" Constantine said defensively.

"It is not me that you have to explain it to," Andrei pointed out morosely, knowing that he was in just as much trouble.

Constantine continued as if he had not heard. "We had to shoot at least one of them to make the others talk." He braked as they approached a stop sign. Coming to a halt, he said, "Once we had killed one, we had to kill the other two. They had seen us."

"I know," Andrei said. "At least we know where it is. We need to find a boat." He looked at the map. "I think we can get to the interstate on this Route 391." They drove on in silence toward Prosperity, South Carolina.

73

August 18, 1994, Fox County, South Carolina

THE PHONE RANG at least fifteen times. At first, Clarence's mind dealt with it effectively, incorporating it into the dream that he was enjoying. The phone, however, persisted and woke him at last. He reached for it groggily and knocked it off the night table. Leaning half out of bed, he fumbled for the loose receiver and put it to his face, earpiece to mouth, mouthpiece to ear. He spoke hoarsely, "Hello." Getting no reply, he switched around the phone and tried again.

"Sheriff, this is Bud. I'm sorry to wake you at this hour." Clarence looked over his shoulder and noticed that the clock's glowing face read 3:05. "But we've got a, well, three, it looks like down here at . . ."

Clarence interrupted him. "Three what, Bud?"

"Three dead guys. Down at the marina."

Forty-five minutes later, Clarence killed the flashing lights as he made the left turn onto Merrit Drive. It was a dirt and gravel road that sloped steeply downward toward the water. His tires crunched on the rocks and the vehicle bounced up and down in potholes as he made the descent. He passed by a sign which would have made him chuckle under different circumstances. Only in rural communities would one see a hand-painted sign that said, "TRESPASSERS WILL BE SHOT." He continued his descent as quickly as road conditions allowed. Half a mile down the track, he could see the lake and a forest of sailboat masts off to the left. He drove to the water's edge and came to a halt in front of a concrete boat ramp. Ordinarily, he would not have parked in front of the ramp, but nobody would be putting a sailboat in at 4 A.M. on a weekday.

As he stepped out of the car, he remembered the business that he was about. Murder.

Clarence had been the sheriff of Fox County for almost six years and this was his first murder. He was not new to homicides. In Oakland, they had been a daily affair. It wasn't the murders that bothered him so much. It was the fact that the murders had happened here. Here, in his county. He'd have to look at the county records to see when the last one had occurred. It was probably back in colonial days. He had heard of a man named Black Luke who had been hanged in the 1700s, but he hadn't heard of any more recent cases. Even Black Luke had not been hanged for murder.

As he walked onto the dock, he saw that Bud had already set up some spotlights and put up some of the yellow "police line" tape that he had ordered from the Richland County Sheriff's Department a few months back. The yellow tape surrounded the dock around the slip where the *Baby Cakes II*, a pontoon boat with a seventy-horsepower outboard hanging limply at its rear, was tied. There were three mounds on the boat covered with sheets.

Clarence surveyed the floodlit scene grimly. He wasn't happy. His mind was racing. *Have drugs and all the death that comes with them finally found me again?* He would not allow this to happen in his beautiful county. *My county,* he thought. He liked the sound of these words. If it were drugs, he would make Dirty Harry look like a choir boy. He would stop it in his county. After Oakland, there were no rules in Clarence's book when it came to drugs.

After looking around carefully, he realized that there was something else different about this crime scene. There were no reporters. No whirring video cameras with young sharply dressed women in front of them, smiling, smelling of hair spray, and telling the audience of death. Nobody monitored the police band in Fox County for news. Ordinarily, there was no news.

"Bud, who are they?" Clarence asked his deputy.

Bud looked at his feet. "I don't know, sir. Three white males. No wallets. No identification. Look local, from the way they're dressed, but I don't recognize them. Apparently they'd been drinking. It looks like they were killed with a small-caliber weapon. There are no shell casings. Just seventeen empty Pabst Blue Ribbon cans and one unopened one. Must have lost the rest of the case overboard. There are a couple pieces of nylon rope that have been cut up. That's about it except for the bodies. I called up Dr. Jones and he's heading down with the rest-home station wagon."

Clarence turned to the only other person at the scene. It was James Merrit. He owned the marina and lived aboard a thirty-foot Pearson at the other end of the dock. "James, did you find them?"

"Well, yes. I called Bud at about 2 A.M. That was right after I found them."

"Did you see anything before you found the bodies?"

"Well," he paused, "No, I didn't. It's like this. I'm not as young as I used to be." James self-consciously combed his graying hair with his hand. "Well, I woke up at about five minutes 'til two and I had to go like a racehorse. I got a portable toilet on my boat, but I'd just as soon not use it except when I need to, 'cause it's a man's job emptying that son-of-a-bitch. Anyway, I was walking up to the clubhouse to relieve myself and I seen a car driving up the lane."

"Did you recognize the car?" Clarence asked.

"Nope. I didn't get to see the front or the shape of the lights, 'cause it was driving out of and not into the club, here. And no, I didn't think to look at the plates and I couldn't have seen them through the trees, anyhow. It wasn't a great mystery or anything to me then. I just had to go, you know." James looked into Clarence's hard face and continued. "It was then that I noticed that blue pickup truck." He pointed at the '64 Chevy Sport Wide. "It doesn't belong to any of the members that I can remember, so I figured that I'd take a walk around the docks and make sure everything was okay. That's when I found them." He pointed at the three dead men.

Clarence stepped on board the pontoon boat and pulled aside the sheet from the first man. Single gunshot wound to the back of the head. From the way he had fallen, it looked as though he had been on his knees when he was shot. An execution. He pulled aside the other two sheets. It was the same grim picture. Single gunshot wounds to the head. Neat as you please. The three had been lined up on their knees and shot in the back of the head. Clarence stepped under the canopy and walked to the other side of the boat. He looked around carefully. He could see the cut pieces of nylon rope. On the railing he noticed a few strands of blue plastic fiber, probably from a tarp. He noticed beer cans strewn all over the open bay of the boat, and then something caught his eye. It was a little mound of white powder. He licked his pinkie finger and stuck it on the pile. First he brought the finger to his left nostril and sniffed. No odor. Then he touched it to his tongue. It was salt.

74   *August 18, 1994, Cowlitz County, Washington State*

MARTIN BREWER AND HIS SON Arnold were walking through the woods. Martin had taken a week off to spend with Arnold in the Cascade Mountains. He wanted to teach his son about tracking and woodsmanship and thought that there was no better time than before school began next week. Arnold was walking ten paces ahead of his father, glowing bright orange in his fluorescent hunting vest and cap. His twelve-gauge pump-action Remington shotgun was at port arms, and he walked as he had seen the men in the movie *The Last of the Mohicans* walk, stealthily and with his attention scattered all around him. Martin stomped the ground carelessly, keeping pace.

Something in front of Arnold caught his eye, and he dropped to a crouch and leaned his shotgun against a tree. He began sweeping leaves and twigs away from the spot he was examining. Martin approached and dropped next to his son, who looked over his shoulder at his father. "I think it's some animal bones or something, Dad," he said excitedly. He continued to dig with his fingers.

Martin watched as the rust-colored crown of bone became more visible. Arnold kept digging and a ridge brow came into view. Shortly thereafter two eye orbits showed, and Martin pulled the boy away. "Those aren't animal bones, son." His face was tense. He shifted his shoulders and shrugged off his orange vest. Dropping it on the ground as a marker, he spoke again. "Pick up your gun, son. We have to go get the police."

 August 18, 1994, Fox County, South Carolina

"SHERIFF! SHERIFF! Hey, Clarence! Wake up!" Bud cajoled Clarence. The Fox County sheriff had been sleeping fitfully at his desk with his head resting in his palms. His face was still looking downward at the personal effects of the three dead men, as he attempted to make some headway before nature got the best of him.

"Sheriff, the DMV came back to us with that tag ID. It was registered to Charlie Hicks, over in Newberry County. I called over at his house and his wife said he didn't come home last night, but apparently that's nothin' new on Tuesday night. She says that it's 'boys' night out' for Charlie and we ought to look for the 'good-fer-nuthin' at his service station. The station owner says he didn't come in and neither have the other two who work for him. Newberry County is sending a deputy over to have a look at the bodies."

Clarence blinked his eyes a couple of times to clear the sleep out of them and clipped his fingers on the bridge of his nose, drawing them down slowly. He looked at his enthusiastic deputy. "Good work, Bud. Now you go on over to the funeral home and wait for that deputy."

"Yes, sir," said Bud and headed back out of the door.

Clarence reflected on Bud's enthusiasm. There wasn't much formal training required to become a Fox County deputy. It wasn't a system run by the good ol' boy network or cronyism, per se. Nobody was interested enough in Fox County for the sheriff's office to be hotly contested or corrupt. Law enforcement was something that a resident just fell into, like others fell into working at the garage pumping gas. Bud was different. He loved to protect and serve his county. Every resident was safer because of Bud's presence, because he cared. He studied law enforcement and asked questions of the larger local departments. He even got equipment from neighbors when he thought the county should have it. Clarence had come to love the serious, crew-cut young man like a son and felt certain that Bud would eventually be the best sheriff that Fox County had ever had.

Clarence resumed looking at the evidence on the desk in front of him. There was a plastic bag filled with the salt that they had found. Another bag contained the blue fibers, one quarter, four dimes, eight pennies, a receipt from Wal-Mart, a pack of Marlboros, and a Bic lighter. *Slim pickings*, he thought. He dumped the cigarettes from the pack, and ten fell out. Nothing. He looked at the pile again and picked up the receipt. In the reflection of the morning sunshine flashing in the window, Clarence noticed indentations on the paper, as though it had been behind another sheet that was written upon forcefully, in a primitive hand. He opened his desk drawer and removed a number two pencil. Gently he began to shade over the back of the receipt until he could read "JOE'S 378. BOX."

"Well," he said softly to himself, "it's my only clue." He grabbed his hat and placed it firmly on his close-shaved scalp and walked out of his office to investigate.

August 18, 1994, Los Angeles, California

FEDERICO MARTÍNEZ LOOKED AHEAD of him at the casting line. Almost two thousand men had come out for the part that he wanted. They were all shapes and sizes. Tall and thin. Short and fat. White. Black. Hispanic. Asian. It seemed as though every male actor who didn't have a job today was standing in line. The advertisement said that there were twenty bit parts to fill in an upcoming television movie for Fox, specifying only that auditioners be "Male, twenty to forty years old."

Then Federico noticed a guy walking down the sidewalk beside the line. He seemed to stop and speak for about thirty seconds with every Hispanic he came to in the line. Then he would reach into his pocket and hand that actor a card. A few minutes later the man arrived at Federico. He looked him over for a moment and then asked, "What's your name, young man?"

"Federico Martínez, sir."

"Good. Good. I'm looking for a few men to fill some roles that I have available. Would you be interested?"

"Yes," Federico replied as if the question were rhetorical, which it was to a jobless actor.

"Fine. Here's a number to call. Call it tomorrow. I will take the first five applicants." When he handed Federico a card, the young actor could not help but notice the man's burned left hand. Returning his hand to his pocket, the stranger continued to walk down the casting line until he came to the next Hispanic.

-77- *August 18, 1994, Spence Islands, Lake Murray, South Carolina*

JAKE SAT ON THE GROUND with his back against a pine tree and looked out across the placid waters of Lake Murray toward Pine Island. The sun was setting over Lunch Island, to his left. His clothes were dry now, but he still shivered a little remembering the chill of the previous evening spent in wet, clay-stained clothes.

Jake had been murdered. Why? By whom? The voices had sounded Southern, rural, and white. He hadn't recognized them, however. *Start from the beginning*, he chided himself. The problem was that the whole incident was so singular and short that it really didn't have a beginning. It connected with nothing that had preceded it. There was no motive. He went fishing. He came home. He got hit with a baseball bat. He got tied to a cinder block and dumped in the lake. Simple. Straightforward. But why? They sank something else before they dropped him over the side. His mind started racing. They had dropped something over the side, and they didn't dump him in the same place because they were coming back for it. That something was worth ten thousand dollars, but they were going to ask twenty thousand. His mind raced again. Presumably, that something had been taken from his shop. What? Did he have some rare, first-edition paperback in his collection? He laughed at the thought.

They had abandoned him in the "big water." They had dropped that something over the side in forty feet of water. He pictured the bottom of the lake like a contour map in his head. It had been about fifteen minutes between the time they had dumped "it" and him. During that fifteen minutes they had traveled away from it. Wrapped in his tarp, he hadn't been able to see anything. He only knew where he came up. Then he remembered the moonlight. He had been pointing forward in the tarp, and when they had lifted him, he had seen the moonlight reflected down the tube. So he had been pointing east. They had traveled east, or maybe they hadn't. Maybe the bow of the pontoon boat was merely pointed in that direction as they threw him over. It was forty feet deep at many places around the perimeter of the lake, but it was also forty feet deep around the island he was on and around Lunch Island. *It must be here*, he thought. He had gone over all of these things at least a hundred times during the day.

Jake waited for the sun to set. When darkness came, he would wade to the next island in the chain, walk over it, wade to the next one, and swim to shore. After that, he would hike until he reached Highway 378. It would be about five miles from there to Clarence's house. He had to talk to the sheriff. He didn't understand what was happening. Maybe Clarence would. Jake knew that he had been a big-city cop somewhere—Oakland or Chicago? One of those places that had crimes like this. Maybe he could figure it out. Until then, however, Jake assumed that nobody knew that he was alive.

The sun lumbered off to the west, leaving a beautiful scene of blue water, cresting lightly from a fifteen-knot breeze, streaked with orange. Jake suddenly wished that he had his camera. Diana would love a photograph of this scene. He wondered if anyone had missed him yet. He was known to go fishing without notice, but he rarely stayed overnight. Jake sighed and stood up. "Time to stop thinking and start doing," he told a tree. He walked out into the water to wade to the next landfall.

78

August 18, 1994, San Francisco, California

ANDREW HAD TAKEN Northwest Airlines Flight 1305 from Los Angeles to San Francisco. It was his own private joke. He always flew Northwest on any domestic route. He figured that he owed them the courtesy. Arriving at the San Francisco International Airport, Buster was waiting for him with a company van. Andrew noticed the two-foot-high red letters identifying it as Itasco property, walked to the passenger door, and got in. He didn't have any luggage, since the trip to Los Angeles was only a brief one.

"Thanks, Buster," Andrew said.

"No problemo, boss," Buster replied. "What I'm here for. Aim to please and all that stuff."

Andrew laughed and Buster joined him. Andrew asked, "Say, Buster, did you get that detective on the payroll yet?"

"Yeah, boss, I did." He appeared to think for a moment. Then he turned to face Andrew. "Say, boss, we aren't into anything fishy or nothin,' are we? I mean, well, you know."

Andrew seemed thoughtful. "Why do you ask that, Buster?"

"It's your business, boss. But, you know, all these trips you've been makin' and hiring that detective on permanent and all. I've just been wonderin'. That's all. I guess what I'm tryin' to say, is, well, I'm with ya. No matter what. I might just be able to be with ya more if I knew what was going on."

Andrew sat silent for about a minute. Then he spoke. "Buster, we've been together for almost twenty years now. I've never kept anything from you." That was a lie, but a small one. "All that I can say on this is, trust me, Buster. No harm will come to you. Just trust me."

"Okay, boss. Got it." Buster looked straight ahead into the traffic. He was obviously hurt that he was not being let in on the secret. Then he remembered the envelope. "Say, boss, the detective gave me this to give you when you got off the plane."

Andrew took the envelope and opened it. Inside was a short note that read:

```
Dawson arriving at SFO @ 2 P.M. Touring and talk-
ing to city mayors about concerns for President.
Will remain overnight in SF at Marriott and leave
in a.m. —A.
```

Andrew looked at his watch. It read 4:32. Tonight he would put another nail in Dawson's coffin. He turned to Buster. "Don't be hurt, Buster, you're my closest friend and confidant. I'm gonna ask you to do a few things for me in the next few weeks. It is just better for you if you don't know the big picture, okay?"

"Okay, boss," Buster said. "You wanna go home?"

"Yes."

At 5 P.M. Andrew turned on the television and watched "Hard Copy." He enjoyed the sensational tabloid news on occasion. This particular evening, they ran an old fifteen-minute segment which indicated that a retired mercenary in Texas might be D. B. Cooper. Then they ran a thirty-second item on the recent discovery of human bones in the Cascade Mountains. With typical tabloid flair the announcer began the commercial break by saying, "Could this sylvan grave have been the fate of the famed hijacker?" Andrew chuckled and programmed his VCR to tape the repeat broadcast.

At midnight he hopped into his Jeep Cherokee and drove downtown to the Marriott. Inside the lobby, he pulled a silver Sprint card from his pocket and settled down in a phone booth. He dialed Dawson's home number and waited. A dazed female voice picked up the phone on the eighth ring. He said, "Sorry, honey. Forgot the time difference." He hung up. Next he dialed the number in Orlando for Jalopi Enterprises. He waited for the answering machine to click on, chuckling at Chamber and his lousy imitation of a British voice. Then he remained on the line for five minutes, saying nothing.

-79-

August 18, 1994, Fox County, South Carolina

CLARENCE DROVE HIS CRUISER into the dirt and gravel lot of Jake's place and cut off the engine. A fine, rust-colored dust rose from the tracks that his vehicle had made. He walked to the front door of the shop. It was ajar, and he noticed two striped bass lying on the ground next to Jake's metal lunch box, which was open.

"Jake!" Clarence called out, his voice booming throughout the shop. There was no reply. "Jake! You home?" The screen-door hinge creaked as he opened the door farther and strode into the shop. The "GONE FISHING" sign was hung in the window. Clarence looked back down on the ground at the fish covered with flies. He smelled them in the air, a distinct odor in a tumult of smells. He touched the fish. They were room temperature, which was roughly 90 degrees. He looked at the lunch box again. It appeared to him now as if it had been dropped and had fallen open, and the fish dropped as well. Something strange was going on.

He began to look around the shop in earnest now, treating it as a potential crime scene. Something had happened here. Walking around the shop didn't suggest to him anything beyond the ordinary, so he went back outside. Jake's truck was there. He walked around to the rear of the shop and down to the boat ramp. The kayak was there. So where was Jake? If he was gone, how long had he been gone? He returned to the front of the shop and found himself standing in the parking lot, perplexed. He looked around again. When was the last time he had seen Jake? Saturday or Sunday. Could Jake have been gone since last weekend?

He walked up to the mailbox. Clarence thought over the day Geery had bagged the "mailbox bandito" as he opened the aluminum box that Josh Bryant had erected. There was only one sheet of paper inside, a yellow postal slip. None of the return address information was filled in. On it was written, "The box is out back, T." Thomas, the mailman, was "T." It was dated August 17. Clarence walked back behind the shop and looked around. There was no box. He went into the shop again. There was no box visible there, either. Or upstairs in Jake's room. No box. He pocketed the note and got on the radio to Bud.

The deputy arrived ten minutes later. Parking his cruiser next to Clarence's, he stepped out and strode toward the front of the building. "Clarence, I was thinkin' on the way over here." Bud turned and pointed back across the road. "Yesterday I ran off a couple fellas who were parked over there. Just didn't seem to matter until you called." The deputy looked sheepishly at his feet.

"What'd they look like?"

"White guys. Dressed nice. Kinda pale. Foreign, talked with some kind of accent."

"Would you recognize them if you saw them again?" Clarence asked.

"Yeah."

"What kind of car?"

"Mustang GT."

"Plates?"

"Sorry, Clarence, I was just shooin' them. When it comes down to it, they weren't *doing* anything. I thought that they might just be *thinking* of doing something, so I sent them on down the road. That's all."

Clarence shook his head and said nothing as he fumbled in the left breast pocket of his shirt for a cigarette. Extracting one, he faced away from his deputy toward the front of the shop to light it out of the breeze. With an exaggerated exhalation, he puffed out a cloud of smoke as he turned back around. "Well, you know, Bud, you should really take notes about things like that." Seeing his deputy's crestfallen expression, he added, "Just gotta learn from it, Bud. Probably unrelated anyhow. Now, go on down and talk to Joe about securing this house until we can sort this all out."

Bud arranged for Joe to lock up the shop and not disturb anything inside. No one could be certain, but it seemed more and more like a crime scene. Clarence was determined to preserve any possible evidence, just in case he had to bring in the state crime lab technicians. Joe had balked at the yellow police-line tape, and the issue was finally resolved by leaving the "GONE FISHING" sign in the window and affixing tamper seals on the front and back doors.

The remainder of the day was dedicated to an unofficial search for Jacob Weichert. Clarence had located Thomas on his rural route late in the afternoon. The mailman told him that yesterday he had left a package around back of Jake's house. It was registered, but Jake hadn't been there, so Thomas had just left it behind the shop rather than lug it around for another day. After that, the trail went cold. At 7 P.M., Clarence had ended up at the bait and tackle shop. The tamper seals were still in place. Joe didn't seem to attach any significance to Jake's absence, but Clarence did. It was a hunch, but a strong one. An adult can come and go as he pleases. In a big city, missing persons' reports are not acted on for seventy-two hours. Jake had been gone for only a day, according to Joe. Still, Clarence thought that Jake was involved with what happened at the Merrit Marina late last night. He returned to his patrol car and began the drive home. At 7:15 P.M. Clarence radioed Bud and told him to report to the office at 8 A.M. and to have a good night. Bud had been up for over twenty-four hours, and Clarence wasn't feeling so well himself. He was tired. He had few clues and a headache. His ulcer was acting up. It was Oakland all over again.

These were the thoughts in Clarence's head as he opened the creaky screen door on the gallery of his house and noticed the note tacked to the door:

Clarence,

I'm over at Geery's place. We need to talk. Please come over when you get home.

Jake

Clarence shoved the note into his pocket and ran back to his car.

-80-

August 18, 1994, Miami, Florida

"HOW IS THE PROSECUTOR?" the Miami special-agent-in-charge asked. He was trim, athletic, and dark. The son of Cuban exiles, he had long ago forgotten his parents' dream of recapturing their homeland. Instead, he had turned his attention to law and order in the United States. He had always jokingly called himself the "token equal-opportunity employee." J. Edgar Hoover would not have rolled over in his grave, however, because Special Agent

Eduardo Jiménez was a good agent and, in concert with the DEA and the Dade County Police Department, had been responsible for trashing more narcotics smuggling rings and money-laundering schemes in south Florida than all of his predecessors combined.

"He's gonna be okay, Ed. It's not fun to be shot, but the assassin just winged him," Special Agent Thomas Callahan replied.

"That's fortunate." Jiménez was looking at the three evidence bags in front of him. One contained some blue fibers. One contained a note. One contained a .308-caliber shell casing.

"Yeah, the guy said that he's never been so glad that he dropped his keys in his life. If he hadn't bent down to pick 'em up, he would have taken it right in the face." Callahan smiled briefly. "Still, it's no fun to take one in the shoulder, either."

"Have they swept the parking lot?"

"Still looking for the bullet, but the roof showed the same MO. Same type of weapon—.308. Left us a cartridge and a love note. I wanted you to see them before we send them to Evidence Control."

Jiménez sat back in his chair and exhaled, looking at the tiled ceiling and then at Callahan. "Thomas, do you think the cartel is behind this?"

Callahan rubbed his chin thoughtfully. "Well, he *is* the prosecutor for the Valens gig." He paused. "It could be, you know, but it just doesn't sit right. Do you know what I mean?"

"Yes, I know what you mean. Do you think that Valens would know?"

Callahan rubbed his chin again. "Hard to tell."

Leaning forward in his chair, a mischievous twinkle in his dark brown eyes, Jiménez asked, "What would you say to me sending Goshgarian and O'Malley over to interview Mr. Valens tomorrow morning?"

Callahan tried to keep a straight face but did not succeed. "Mr. Valens hasn't seen men like that yet, has he?"

-81-

ALL MANNER OF THINGS were running through Clarence's head. Was Jake involved in some drug deal gone sour? Why had he disappeared? Why had one of the murdered men written down Jake's address? Where was the box that Thomas had delivered? Clarence pulled over on the section of road that led to Geery's path and followed it into the woods. After a short time, he reached the front porch and saw the lights burning in the library. He knocked on the door and saw Geery motion for him to come in. When he entered, he saw Jake lying on the floor next to a contour map of Lake Murray. Geery lay on the other side of the map with a red pencil.

Geery turned to Clarence. "Sit down, Clarence. I'll need to hear what you know in a moment." Then, turning back to Jake, he said, "So they dumped you here? You could see the tower?"

"Yes."

"And you saw the moon through the end of the tarp as they lifted you?"

"Yes."

"What time was it?"

"I don't know, Gary. It was after I got hit on the head with a Louisville slugger. I don't know how long I was out."

"Unfortunate." Geery paused to run a hand over his bald head and think. "Where was the moon? How far above the dam?"

"I don't know," Jake said hopelessly. "I just saw it through the end of the tarp."

Geery mumbled to himself. "Before that, you say that they measured forty feet in depth before they dropped the 'thing' into the water?"

"Yes."

Geery made several quick notations on the chart in red pencil. He circled where Jake had come up and placed lines around the contours that would indicate forty feet in depth. "Clarence," he said, addressing the sheriff for the second time, "they haven't started lowering the level for the winter yet, have they?"

"No," Clarence replied. He suddenly had a mental image of a Sherlock Holmes mystery.

"Then, Jake, you say it was about fifteen minutes before they dumped you, here." He pointed to the spot where Jake had surfaced. "What did the motor sound like?"

"It sounded like an outboard motor, Gary."

"No. Was it 'wa-wa-wa-wa-wa-wa,' or 'weh-weh-weh-weh-weh,' or 'weeeeeeeee'?" Geery asked, like a child imitating an accelerating motor.

"It was running slow."

"Do you have any idea from the sound what size motor it was?"

"I don't know, Gary. For a pontoon boat like that, it was probably a fifty-five horsepower."

"It was seventy horsepower," Clarence said definitively. Geery and Jake looked up at him with confusion registering on both of their faces. "And I'll put money on the fact that the tarp you were thrown over in was blue and cost $13.95 at Wal-Mart. I'll also bet that there were three guys on that boat."

Jake's jaw dropped. "Yeah, I think that there *were* three guys!" He looked at Clarence with admiration. Maybe there was something to that big-city-cop mystique. Clarence seemed to know what had happened already. After a pause, Jake continued. "It was dark. I don't know what color tarp it was." He turned to look at Geery for a moment and then returned his gaze to the sheriff. "I didn't think anybody knew about any of this. I wanted to let you know that someone tried to kill me and I don't know why."

Clarence looked thoughtfully at Jake. "Well, somebody already killed the three guys who tried to kill you, so I guess that you could call it even there." The sheriff smiled wryly. Then his face turned hard and serious. It was the first time that Jake had ever seen Clarence appear menacing. "What did you have that was worth your life, Jake, and the lives of those other three?"

"I don't know, but I think they hid whatever they took in the lake. Gary is trying to help me find where it might be located."

Geery looked up at the sheriff. "Clarence, is there anything else that you can tell us?"

"Not that I can think of. Just that Thomas dropped a package off for you, Jake. It was the day that all of this happened. The only other thing was that I found granular salt on the boat. Don't know what it means."

"Salt. Hmm. Salt." Geery said. "Very interesting." Then he jotted down a few numbers on the corner of the chart. He walked over to his desk and took out a compass and a ruler. He measured out a distance on the compass and put the needle end onto the spot where Jake had been dropped. He swung the arc across the Spence Islands. He picked up the compass and measured again on the ruler. He spotted the point south of the islands on the arc that he had drawn before and marked the chart. Then he spotted the point on the north end of the islands and drew another arc. He circled two spots off the eastern shore of Lunch Island where the red forty-foot line intersected his penciled arcs. Pointing at the two spots, he spoke again. "Well, given what we know, your 'thing' should be about there." Then Geery's face broke into a big smile. "Of course, it may not be there, too. Just a guess, really."

Jake looked at the sheriff. "Clarence, let's go find it. We'll talk more on your boat. You've got a snorkel and fins, don't you? We've got a couple more hours of daylight."

"Okay." Clarence turned to walk out.

Geery had one more thing to say. "Ah, Clarence, I remember reading sometime that salt was an old smuggler's trick. Just a thought."

"Smuggler's trick?"

"Yes. If the authorities were about to pull over a smuggler's boat, they would drop their merchandise—rum or a crate of guns, let's say," Geery's aquamarine eyes twinkled as he spoke, "into the water, and after it they would drop a buoy weighted with salt. In a few days, the salt would dissolve and the buoy would rise to the surface, allowing them to find their stuff. See?"

"Yes," Clarence said as he and Jake ran out the door.

-82-

August 19, 1994, Route 378, Fox County, South Carolina

"WELL, WELL, WELL," Bud muttered to himself. "Lookee here." His head swiveled to the left as he drove past. What he had seen was a blue Ford Mustang backed down the boat ramp behind Joe's Bait and Tackle Shoppe. It was the same Mustang that he had told to leave Fox County two days before. He drove another two hundred yards down the road and crossed the centerline to make a U-turn. As he backed around and commenced moving forward, he noticed Diana's green Pinto in the rear-view mirror. He pulled down the road and took a right into the parking lot of Joe's. As he got out of his cruiser, he removed the twelve-gauge pump shotgun from the rack behind the driver's seat. Placing his sheriff's patrol hat squarely on his head as he closed the door, he unsnapped the holster for his .38-caliber service revolver and walked down the slope toward the boat ramp.

The two pale men were busy launching a dark green johnboat that they had trailered behind the Mustang. The trailer, the boat, and the motor were obviously new. Bud looked at the two men and they looked at him. The deputy was the first to speak. "Didn't I talk to you two a few days ago? What are you doin' here?"

"We are launching our boat. We are tourists," Constantine said.

"Bullshit," Bud said as he racked a shell into the chamber of his shotgun. "You are under arrest for suspicion of murder."

Constantine said nothing. Andrei merely withdrew a 9-mm Glock Model 17 pistol from a shoulder holster and shot Deputy Sheriff Bud Jones unceremoniously in the face. The second round took his hat off. The shotgun clattered on the concrete of the boat ramp. As Bud crumpled into a heap, Constantine noticed a red-haired woman staring down the slope at them. She had obviously seen everything. Her hands were covering her mouth. Her green eyes were wide with horror. Constantine pointed at her as she turned to run. Andrei sighted down the barrel of his pistol and caught her in the back. She fell forward in headlong flight. He walked up the slope and stood over her. She was still breathing, so he put the pistol to the back of her neck and fired twice to silence her forever.

He grabbed Diana by the feet and dragged her down the slope to lie next to Bud. "It is a shame," Andrei commented, looking down at Diana's lifeless figure. "A beautiful woman."

Constantine was nervous. "We should not have killed them, Andrei. This is not St. Petersburg. We do not own the streets here."

"We had no choice," said Andrei gruffly as he returned the pistol to the holster. He straightened his suit as he climbed up the slope to the parking lot. Constantine saw him drive the police car into the woods, out of sight of the road. Andrei walked back and sat in the Pinto for a moment and then got out. He descended the ramp and looked at the woman's body, rolling her over with his foot and pulling the keys from her pocket. He tramped up the slope again and drove Diana's car into the woods behind the patrol car. Now both were out of sight from the road. He went back down to the water. "Put them in the boat."

The other Russian looked apprehensive. "I hope that our instructions are correct. I fear that now it will not be long until we have hounds upon our trail."

"What trail?" Andrei asked, pointing at the bodies.

-83-

August 18, 1994, Miami, Florida

THE TWO FBI AGENTS walked purposefully into the interrogation room. The Miami special-agent-in-charge had selected them specifically for their record of brutality. Each man had at least four complaints against him. They were extraordinarily effective, however, and the Bureau had dutifully "investigated" each charge and dropped it. The Bureau knows that it needs a certain percentage of neanderthals to offset the touchy-feely sensitive men and women of the nineties if it expects to continue to fight crime. Hence, Special Agents O'Malley and Goshgarian. O'Malley was an Irishman with jet black hair and brown eyes under a thick Cro-Magnon brow. He had the physique of a Bulgarian power lifter with pistons for arms and an enormous round belly. Goshgarian was a black man. His head was clean shaven. At six feet, six inches tall, he packed 245 pounds of solid muscle and looked like Sergio Oliva. The pair loved to work together.

They strolled nonchalantly into the interrogation room and stood in front of Domingo Valens, who eyed them arrogantly. He had gotten used to the American justice system. After learning that torture was not permitted, he had become accustomed to being rude and sarcastic to the officials who came to interview him and to the guards who kept him under lock and key. In fact, he had begun to derive real pleasure from tormenting his jailers. These same jailers, it appeared, had found a malfunction in their closed-circuit television system during that very hour.

Goshgarian started. "How's it going, dirtbag?" He crossed his arms to emphasize the size of his biceps.

"What?" Domingo looked meaningfully toward the lens of the camera.

O'Malley looked at the lens as well. "Gee, it's too bad that camera isn't working today, isn't it, Hal?"

"Yeah, Mike. It's too bad," Goshgarian replied.

They both sat menacingly across the wooden table from Domingo. Goshgarian spoke again. "Well, Domingo, we need a few answers."

O'Malley continued. "Yes, we need to know about your friends who killed Judge Alvarez. Before we leave, we mean to know everything that you know. Got it, douchebag?" Murder gleamed in those dark Irish eyes, and Valens saw it. The only thing more legendary than a Latin temper is an Irish temper.

O'Malley and Goshgarian left mildly disappointed. Valens had crumpled before they had laid a finger on him. All of the trouble of cutting off the video system had been for nothing. Domingo had told them everything he knew. They had it all on tape. He had talked for almost an hour without interruption, sometimes breaking into Spanish in his haste to please them. As Goshgarian drove back to regional headquarters, O'Malley put the cassette into the car's stereo deck. He listened and fast forwarded the cassette several times until he came to the part of Domingo's testimony which he considered to be vital.

They heard Valens's timid English, spoken with a Latin cadence, over the stereo. "Santiago told me, through the lawyer, that they had killed Heriberto Enríquez. It was his just punishment. But we didn't kill any Americans. I am a businessman. We are a big business. My instructions are to go to jail and not to compromise our business. In ten or fifteen years, I will be out of prison and the business will welcome me back. I will be a rich man because I kept faith, see? It is a stupid man who enrages his customers. Santiago did not kill your judge."

O'Malley switched off the machine. "Fuck."

"Well put," Goshgarian said as he craned his head to get a better look at a woman in a bikini top. "Well, if those spic dirtballs didn't do it, who did?"

"Dunno. You know, Hal, I wanted to break that guy's fingers." Callahan was looking at his knuckles thoughtfully.

"Why?" Goshgarian said, looking over his shoulder to change lanes.

"Oh, just 'cause."

August 19, 1994, Federal Bureau of Investigation,
Liaison Office, Moscow

"THEY'RE NOT FUCKING SURE? What do you mean they're not fucking sure? What in the fuck is wrong with you people?" Janice heard the special-agent-in-charge yell over the phone. "Goddammit, Yuri, we are trying to help you people!" He was red in the face, but he was trying to control his temper. He was definitely not succeeding in being diplomatic. "I'm sorry, Yuri, I know that you are doing the best with what you have." There was a pause as he listened. "Yes, yes, I know. Yes." Another pause. "So where did it go? That is, if it went." There was another pause as he listened. "Shit! Shit! Shit! This is shit city, Yuri! I know it's not your fault, but this is shit city. This is what I'm here to prevent and it's happened. Thank you, Yuri. I apologize if I was rude. Please send over a copy of your file. Thank you. Keep up the good work." He hung up the phone quietly, solemnly.

"Janice, get me the San Francisco Office."

-85-   *August 19, 1994, Oakland, California*

GREGOR WAS BESIDE THE POOL in the backyard of his mansion when his telephone rang. He picked up. "Da?"

"We have it, Gregor."

"Good. Take it to the warehouse." He hung up, reviewing the conversation in his mind to ensure that nothing would be useful to a listener. He hadn't gone to encrypted mode, as he usually would have. He had no evidence but was naturally suspicious of telephones, particularly land lines. It might be simple Russian paranoia, or it might not be.

-86-   *August 19, 1994, Lake Murray, South Carolina*

JAKE AND CLARENCE had gotten a late start but had been diving continually since noon. The evening before had proved fruitless. They hadn't found anything. Clarence climbed up the ladder affixed to the port side of the O'Day 22, breathing heavily. He flung the mask and snorkel combination into the cockpit and tossed the flippers after them. "It's your turn, Jake." He wrapped his arms around himself and shivered. "It's a lot colder down there than on the surface. If we don't find anything by sunset, I'm going to Wal-Mart and buy myself a wet suit. We could also use a light. This one doesn't work too well." He motioned to the flashlight tied in plastic wrap to make it waterproof. "I end up just feeling around down there."

Jake put on the mask and adjusted the snorkel. He jumped into the water and Clarence handed him the fins. Bending double in the water, he sank as he put them on. He popped to the surface face down and blew water from the snorkel like a whale. He looked up at Clarence. "I'm going to go in a little closer this time." He pointed to the island.

"Yeah. We haven't looked there yet. I think we've got right under us covered," Clarence observed. Jake swam about twenty yards closer to the island. Clarence heard the rush of air through the tube as Jake took a deep breath and then submerged. Now, Clarence wished that he had been able to get ahold of Bud this morning. The delay in their start was due to the sheriff's telephone and radio search for his deputy. Bud was nowhere to be found. He did not answer the radio and no one had seen him. Clarence had given up after three hours, assuming that the deputy had neglected to turn on his radio. This job would have been easier with three divers.

Jake emerged suddenly, spitting out the snorkel and struggling for breath. He swam rapidly toward the boat. He had something in his left hand. As he reached the ladder, Jake grasped it with his right hand and tossed the object into the boat. It was a buoy with about half a bag of salt tied to it. A rope ran back from the buoy. "Looks like Geery was right," Jake gasped. He climbed awkwardly up the ladder without removing the flippers. "Let's see what that rope is attached to."

He removed the mask and bent to take off the flippers as Clarence began to pull in the line. It was heavy, but it slowly gave way. It tugged and caught along the bottom like an anchor. Clarence motioned for Jake to help. They both began heaving in on the line. It felt as though concrete blocks were tied to the end. The little O'Day listed to port as the line was pulled in over the cockpit bulkhead and tended itself underneath the boat's keel. Finally the line went taut, straight up and down. They heaved in earnest now, pulling it to the surface. When the first object came into view, Clarence's eyes bugged out of his head and Jake said simply, "Shit." They both let go. The line fed back out as it descended to the bottom. They both sat down.

"Shit," Clarence said again, echoing Jake's comment. "Was that what I thought it was?"

Jake was breathing hard, but not from exhaustion. "Clarence, that was a body."

"Well, I guess we had better get it up," Clarence said, and picked up the line again. They pulled together until the body surfaced. It was a man. Face down on the surface, he was naked except for a pair of undershorts. Clarence hooked him by the elastic band with his boat hook and pulled him against the side. He grasped the body under the armpits and heaved it into the cockpit.

A second body emerged when the first had been pulled into the boat. Red hair splayed wildly on the surface around its head. There was a gaping wound in the back of the neck. Jake recognized Diana and leaped into the water. There was, of course, nothing to be done. He turned her lifeless face toward him and screamed. It was feral, the screech of a wounded beast. His howl echoed across the placid water. He held Diana's naked form close to his as if the heat of his body could bring her back to life. Clarence rolled over the corpse in the cockpit and saw that it was Bud. A single tear formed and ran down his ebony cheek. "He was a good boy," he said. It was all that he could think of.

Jake climbed up the ladder with Diana over his shoulder. As he stepped into the boat, three cinder blocks broke the surface on the rope beyond her. Holding it all in the air, like Atlas with the weight of the world on his shoulders, Jake reached down to his ankle and removed his dive knife. With one savage stroke, he severed the line to allow the blocks to drop back to the bottom. He laid Diana gently in the cockpit and looked at Clarence. Down his cheeks ran tears mixed with the lake water that dripped from his hair. His eyes were wild. "Clarence, you had better put me under arrest." He gulped a breath of air to prevent another sob before continuing. "I am going to find who did this and kill them all."

Clarence looked thoughtfully at Jake. His eyes were watery, but no second tear would trace the path of the first. He motioned to the male body. "It's Bud," he said with no apparent emotion.

Jake looked back at Diana. He grasped her hands in his. "Baby, baby, who did it? Why?" He screamed again toward the sky. He was flinging his grief into the heavens at God. He looked at the small hands he held in his own. That was when he saw that Diana was wearing his engagement ring. He collapsed into the cockpit. Clarence went below and returned with a gray woolen blanket. He covered Bud with it and went below again. When he returned, he handed another blanket to Jake, who gently wrapped Diana in it. He felt numb, exhausted. He looked up at Clarence. "There is no meaning, Clarence. It all has no meaning."

August 20, 1994, FBI Regional Office,
San Francisco, California

SPECIAL-AGENT-IN-CHARGE Harry Trasker was combating a raging hangover and blinking through bloodshot eyes at the files that the Moscow Office had faxed to him. He read two pages and left the folder at his desk. He walked to the corridor and got a paper cup full of water. Dropping in two Alka-Seltzer tablets, he watched them fizz. Trasker read two more pages but then put down the folder again and opened a desk drawer, extracting a bottle of Nature's Way B-complex vitamins. He threw three into his mouth and washed them down with the gritty remainder of the Alka-Seltzer. Somewhere he had read that the headaches that accompany hangovers were a result of vitamin B deficiency. The faxed report and the phone call from Moscow didn't help his head, either. "Eager beavers," he complained when he saw the cover page. "Not even open yet and sending reports."

Trasker had spent the previous evening at Tar-n-Feathers listening to a fabulous guitar player belt out the best tunes of the sixties, seventies, and eighties and reminiscing with another agent about their involvement in breaking the Walker case a decade before. He had consumed too many beers and been driven home by the other agent, who did not drink. Ten years earlier, Roy and he had just been starting out. They had only been on the fringe of the investigation that brought down one of the most serious spy rings in American history, but they still liked to talk about it. It had reaffirmed the need for the FBI unlike any other case they had seen since, at least in their office. The next most significant thing he had seen was the Aldrich Ames case in Virginia. If bank robberies and kidnappings were the FBI's bread and butter, then spies were their wine, the elixir of their lives, the glory cases. They were the cases that allowed the G-men to feel like heroes.

The file on Harry Trasker's desk, however, was a totally new ballgame. It lifted the FBI to a new, higher plane. Instead of affecting national security in a roundabout way like most spy cases did, no matter how severe, this file represented a direct threat to the United States. It did more than imply or suggest. It *said* that weapons-grade nuclear material had more than likely already been off-loaded into the continental United States. Six kilograms of plutonium 239 was somewhere in the underworld.

Harry had decided that Roy Dobkins was going to be the case officer and was going to have everything that his agency could provide. He was awaiting Roy now, having summoned him from a northern California bank robbery scene back to the main office. Roy had been instrumental, while at the St. Louis Office, in bringing down an Abu Nidal group in the midwest. He entered about twenty minutes later, his white shirt soaked with sweat underneath a dark suit. He took off his jacket and laid it across the chair on the other side of Harry's desk, revealing a shoulder holster containing a .45-caliber Sig Sauer pistol.

"Okay, Harry, I'm here. Where's the fire?" Roy asked.

Harry motioned at the half-inch pile of thermal fax paper in a file on his desk. "It's there," he said. "Take it to your office and read it. When you are done, come back and we'll discuss what we want to do next."

Three hours later Roy returned to Harry's office looking pale and tired. "So, it's finally happened," he said.

Harry looked haggard himself. "Yes, it has happened. And we aren't dealing with a bunch of ragheads with barrels of fertilizer here. No Beta Cell bullshit. We don't have and won't get any informants. We're dealing with 100 percent dyed-in-the-wool Russian mafia hoods. The Russian police call them the *organizatsiya*, among other things, I'm sure." Harry looked down at the back of his hands as if counting the hairs on the surface. "What did you see when you read it?"

Roy swallowed and started to speak, falling into the senior/ subordinate role-play without missing a beat. "Sir, this is a brief summary of what we know. Captain Kukchinko goes home on leave to Moscow. The Moscow city police pick him up while he is trying to score at a kiosk behind the Lushniki Sportkomplex. Heroin is mentioned in the report. They felt that he may have a guilty conscience about other things. They know that it is difficult to support a heroin habit on a captain's salary. They interrogate him. After a day or two of their tender ministrations, he sings like a jaybird. He tells all. He mentions plutonium, and the city police put their fingers in their ears and turn him over to the Federal Counterintelligence Service."

Trasker interlaced his fingers and allowed his thumbs to wrestle one another. "I asked our guy over there about the Federal Counterintelligence Service. He's not opening the office until November, but he's been trying to network with the right people. He says the name has changed, but the faces are the same. It's basically Yeltsin's version of the KGB. They open mail, head off coup plots, catch spies. They are our counterpart, more or less, although our liaison over there is talking more with the Interior Ministry guys, the regular cops." The right thumb pinned the left.

Roy turned a page and continued. "Once the new and improved KGB gets hold of him, Captain Kukchinko continues to tell his life's story and fingers the two bad guys who compelled him to make the error in the inventory. It takes two weeks, but the Ruskies go and pick up the two thugs. With me so far?"

Harry nodded. "Gotcha."

"Well, the Russians can't make the mafia guys talk. I'm sure that they tortured them, although it is not in the report." Roy flipped through the pages. "Viktor and Yuri, both with long Slavic names . . . they are a lot more afraid of their own organization than they are of the authorities, so they keep quiet. A few days later, they suddenly talk. Again, it is not in the report, but I would assume that they drugged them, in addition to torture. The Russians are savages," Roy grinned. "Wish we could do that sometimes."

Harry nodded again. He wished that they could do that, too.

"Anyway, these guys spill the beans on the plutonium theft. Their boss is a guy named Yuri. He runs Moscow. Yuri's boss is a guy named Gregor. I'll get back to him. These guys have the Russian officer over a barrel because he is torching his insides with heroin. They supply him and he makes an accounting error. Sends two nuke artillery shells out on a conventional shipment. The crooks stop the train. Steal the shells. Simple. Three kilograms of plutonium each."

"Okay," Harry said

Roy continued. "Turns out these guys are big time. Part of an organization called the Dark Path. Mostly ethnic Russian, but an equal-opportunity employer if you have the right credentials. One of the poor slobs they have is Chechen. The Dark Path, it turns out, has 'offices' in St. Petersburg and Moscow, but their strongest branch is in Vladivostok. Gregor, no other known names, is their leader, the thief-in-law. He spent seven years in a prison camp in Kazakhstan. His organization predates the fall of the Soviet Union. They apparently opened for business in '81 or '82 when Brezhnev was still around. This Gregor managed to get himself out of the country during the collapse. His men only know that he is residing in Oakland and that he was the guiding hand in a big Medicare scam in the U. S. of A."

"The one we cracked in '92," Trasker finished the thought.

"Over here, they didn't finger their boss, but we don't have Russian methods of interrogation, either." Roy smiled crookedly and closed the top folder. He pulled a second folder from the pile. Opening it, he said, "Here is where the guessing comes in. This comes from Immigration." He indicated the folder with a nod of his head. "Gregor Viktorovich, 53. Immigrated in December of 1991. On his forms it says that he was a 'victim of religious persecution.' Seems to be a man of means. Lives alone, south of Oakland. Says in his visa application that he is Baptist. I think that he is our man."

"Baptist?" Trasker asked.

"Yes, Baptist. They are actually less than one tenth of one percent of the population and are persecuted by the Orthodox Church."

"Okay," Trasker said, secretly impressed that Roy had already begun the investigation during the three hours he used to assimilate the report.

"So here's the second guess," Roy continued. "If Gregor was going to get the plutonium out of the country as rapidly as possible, which would be prudent, he would not use the route that so much intercepted material has taken. He would not use cutouts and mules in Eastern Europe. He would go a different way." He closed the Immigration folder and opened a third one. "The CIA has this guy in Vladivostok. They don't give us all of his product, but they give us a few scraps, along with the Customs people. Almost all relevant or useful information is blacked out before we see it. I don't think that we, DEA, or Customs has ever used it for an arrest. It just sits on the back burner, waiting to supplement a case, but I've been keeping tabs on what it says. If you read between the lines, it says that a Russian organized-crime group basically controls a company called Maynard Johnson Tackle and Toys. They use their shipping space to smuggle icons, currency, synthetic drugs, and small arms out of Russia. The mob runs their security and the docks. This company is a subsidiary of the Maynard Johnson outfit and has its own shipping line. The guys that the kinder and gentler KGB hold said that Gregor's organization is now centered in Vladivostok. Two and two sometimes equals five, but my bet is on this MJTT. I think it is likely that if the material has left Russian territory, it left on one of those ships."

Trasker looked at Roy with sincere admiration. Seven hours ago he had completed reading the report. He was hung over and dejected. The problem seemed insurmountable. Three hours ago he had given Special Agent Roy Dobkins a vague report out of a chaotic country, and he had already figured out a likely suspect and route. If Trasker had his way, Dobkins would be on the fast track to be the Director. "Well, let's nail the guy," Trasker said.

"I already sent an agent to the courthouse with the phone-tap request. We should be listening to Gregor's 900 calls before he turns into a pumpkin tonight," Dobkins smiled.

 August 21, 1994, Smithsonian Institution, Washington, DC

THE COWLITZ COUNTY CORONER had looked over the bones found in the Cascade Mountains for a solid day, made some notes on soil composition, and drew sketches of the initial arrangement of the skeleton when excavated. The coroner was a bright, well-educated man, a diplomate of the American Board of Forensic Anthropology. He had some suspicions and hunches about the remains, but he knew that it would be better if the men with the best equipment and resources got the bones in as close to an original state as possible. He left remnants of clothing intact and placed a Mason jar containing soil from the site in the crate before he shipped it to the regional FBI office in Portland, Oregon.

From Portland, the crate was shipped to FBI Headquarters in Washington, DC. It was received by Evidence Control and tagged with a Q, indicating a questioned item or an item of unknown origin that may or may not be related to a crime. Evidence Control forwarded the bones to the Hair and Fiber unit, which for obscure reasons receives bones as well as hair and fiber. From there, Special Agent Harvey Ersoy took the crate to the Smithsonian Institution's Anthropology Department, to the waiting desk of Dr. Walter Pruitt, often called the Bonemeister by a worshipful following over in Hair and Fiber.

Special Agent Ersoy heaved the crate onto the desk and breathed a sigh of relief. "Whew, they must have sent some dirt, too. That thing is heavy."

Dr. Pruitt looked out from beneath bushy gray eyebrows and smiled. "Okay, Harvey, let's see what we have here." He opened the crate and started to lay out the disarticulated bones on the table. The anthropologist began to piece them together as they would have been in life. The long bones of the legs and arms were patterned with a crisscrossed grid of greenish stains. As the doctor positioned the ribs and thoracic vertebrae, they too showed green crisscross staining. The cranium and mandible were placed at the top of the table last. The final items in the crate were the soil sample, a ragged piece of stained brown cloth, a cylindrical object with two corroded metal projections on top, a few strands of pitted copper wire, and the leather sole of a single shoe, disinte-grating around the edges.

To Ersoy, this collection said nothing. He knew that it would say volumes to the anthropologist, so he stayed to watch. The initial examination took four hours. Ersoy saw Dr. Pruitt go over every bone with a magnifying glass, sometimes picking one up to inspect it from another angle. Later, he removed the cylindrical object from the box, looked at it carefully, and laid it next to the left tibia. After studying the leather sole, he placed it below the bones of the left foot. Then, checking the cloth, he put it along-side one of the lumbar vertebrae. Finally, he arranged the strands of copper wire over some of the green stains.

At last, the anthropologist spoke. "Well, the skull has recessive cheekbones, narrow nasal aperture, narrow palate. Caucasian. The pelvic girdle and pubis indicate that he was male. I'll section one of these long bones and do an osteon count tonight, but from the teeth, I would say that he was thirty to forty years old. I'd have to do some calculations, but a rough estimate based on this femur would indicate that he stood a little under six feet tall. He has been dead from one to twenty-five years and must have been buried at the time of death. There is little indication of animal activity." He lifted a radius for the FBI man to see. "Larger carnivores will ordinarily gnaw the ends off these big bones. Smaller animals will leave teeth marks in the bones. There are none. He spent some time in the military. His dental work is field-hospital work. He may have lost an eye prior to his death. There is a wound in the rear of the right eye orbit, but the bone has healed itself. It occurred at least a year or more before his death. He was shot to death with twelve-gauge deer slugs. Where was he found again?"

Ersoy looked amazed. The Bonemeister had done it again. "Cascade Mountains, Washington State."

"Hmm." The anthropologist rubbed his chin. "There are a few other things. The green staining," he pointed at some of the lines on the right tibia, "is from prolonged exposure to copper. I think that the victim was wearing electric underwear and that these wires are part of it. A thorough sifting of the area where he was found will reveal more. From the staining on the left tibia, this battery," he lifted the cylindrical object, "was attached in some way to his lower leg. There is also a twelve-gauge deer slug embedded in it from the bottom." The anthropologist lifted a shattered bone from the left foot. "That particular slug passed through the left tarsus and embedded itself in the battery." He lifted the fragmented sole of the shoe. "Can't prove it, but a missing segment of this sole is consistent with the penetration of the slug. When you boys take apart the battery, you may find some bone fragments and a piece of this shoe in there along with the slug. The ribs and backbone have what look like blunt trauma injuries that could have been caused by bullets as well. They don't make nice holes except in the skull."

"How do you get shot in the bottom of the foot?" the agent asked.

"Well, you have to use your imagination, Harvey." The anthropologist's eyes twinkled from beneath his brows. "Say, for example, a man was hanging in a tree from his parachute lines and someone shot him from the ground."

Harvey's eyes lit up with sudden understanding. "Doc, can you do a facial reconstruction?"

"I won't have time to do a manual restoration this week, but if you can give me some computer time across the street, I'll CAT scan the skull into our CAD/CAM computer and put in all the markers. We'll let your computer draw him for us overnight."

"Okay, I can do that."

"Also, Harvey, call the National Personnel Record Center in St. Louis. Get them to fax you copies of the dental charts for all the men who lost their right eye between, oh, let's say, '65 and '72." He appeared to pause for a moment. "That's going to be a lot. Narrow it to white males. Army and Marine Corps only."

August 21, 1994, Lake Murray, South Carolina

JAKE AND CLARENCE were back out on the lake. They were anchored off the northernmost of the Spence Islands. Clarence was working the foot pump to inflate his dinghy, and it was slowly taking shape in the cockpit as Jake stood on the bow tossing out the second anchor and pulling it in, trying to set it. The little Danforth finally dug in and Jake tied it off on the bow cleat. He performed all his functions as a robot. He was still in shock. With the O'Day secured by two anchors, Jake walked back to the cockpit, where Clarence was almost finished inflating the dinghy. The sheriff looked at Jake and realized that he needed something to do to occupy his mind. "Jake, down in the cabin, underneath the starboard quarter berth, are the paddles. Would you get them out and put them together? Then bring my ladder out."

Jake went below. He lifted up the cushion and pulled open the cabinet underneath the berth. He took out the unassembled paddles and tossed them onto the port berth and replaced the cushion. He picked up the folding ladder and carried it back up into the cockpit, leaned over the side, and attached it to its connections, lowering it into the lake. Clarence looped the dinghy's tie rope onto the top of the ladder and flung the smaller craft into the water. Going below again, Jake put the oars together. As he was screwing the paddles into the handles, Clarence brushed past him on his way to the V-berth to pick up a black knapsack. He returned to the cockpit, tossing the rucksack into the inflated craft. Jake climbed back up to the cockpit with his assembled oars and threw them over the side as well.

"Let's go," Clarence said, and lowered himself down the ladder to the dinghy. Jake followed and sat forward as Clarence rowed toward the pebble-strewn beach on the south shore. A large metal frame jutted out from the island, bent and rusting. Clarence pointed at it for the mute Jake. "I'm not sure, but I think that used to be a target holder, for gunnery practice. You know, back when B-25s used to bomb the islands for practice." Jake made no response, so

Clarence continued. "There are supposed to be up to twenty airplanes in the bottom of the lake. Nobody knows. The records burned up in an Army Air Force warehouse. You've seen the models at the airport, haven't you, Jake?"

"No," Jake replied. "Never been to the airport."

Clarence kept talking. "Well, you know that Jimmy Doolittle practiced here before bombing Tokyo, don't you? The Columbia Metropolitan Airport used to be an Army air base. Don't remember the name of it."

Jake had a faraway look in his eyes. It was like the thousand-yard stare that Clarence had seen sometimes in Vietnam. Jake was thinking about the events earlier in the day. He had hidden in the woods and watched them lower Diana into the ground. Clarence had told him that it was best for him to stay missing, but he couldn't keep away. Jake had cried as he watched the service through binoculars. He figured that Diana's mother would be asking where he was. Clarence told her that he was gone on a three-week hunting trip in the North Carolina mountains and could not be reached. Jake had seen the bent figure of the mother crying as they lowered his beautiful red-haired angel into the soft South Carolina earth. Later that day, he had watched Clarence and Bud's parents as they scattered the deputy's ashes onto the surface of the lake.

Clarence had urged Bud to make a will. It had seemed foolish to the young man. He didn't believe that it would ever be needed. Men who are twenty-five and single and in good health do not think about wills. Clarence, who had spent a lifetime in harm's way, insisted. Reluctantly, Bud had written it, turning his will in like a homework assignment to a tyrannical teacher. Cremation was still unusual in the South, but Bud had loved the lake and wanted to rest there. Bud's father had stood at ramrod attention and his mother had wept as Clarence carried out his deputy's wishes from the bow of the *Marie*. Jake had viewed this, also through the lenses of binoculars, keeping well out of sight. He could hardly believe that all this was real.

Clarence hopped out of the dinghy and dragged it up onto the beach. "Help me gather some firewood, Jake."

Forty-five minutes later they both sat on the beach facing the dam, which loomed about a mile off in the distance. Darkness was falling, and the flashing light at the top of the smokestack tower was becoming visible. Light filtered dimly through the trees behind them, and the air took on the chill of impending fall. The fire was good. The water was soothing as it lapped quietly onto the beach. It seemed as though nothing evil could survive the surroundings, they were that peaceful. The two men sat in silence for a long time. It was well past sunset before Clarence turned to Jake and spoke. The firelight reflected off his eyes and the whites were in stark relief against the blackness of the older man's skin. "Jake, I wanted you to come out here so that we could talk."

Jake looked over at Clarence. He picked up a rock from the beach and skipped it across the water. He finally replied, "I know, Clarence, I know. What are we going to do?" The sorrow crept through his words. "Will you be able to catch these people?"

"Jake, I'll be honest with you. I don't think that we'll find them." The sheriff eyed the flames somberly. The wood crackled and popped as it was transformed into smoke. "I think that this has something to do with drugs. I haven't seen anything like it since I worked in Oakland. It was all senseless, Jake, senseless." Clarence shook his head.

Jake skipped another rock across the smooth surface of the lake. It bounced five times into the air before landing with a splash and sinking. "What about the state guys? You said that they had come down and looked at everybody. Bud and Diana and the three guys from Newberry."

Clarence sighed. "Jake, they know as much as you and I know. When a crime has no motive or one that you don't understand, all the labs in the world can't put it together. They know that all of them were killed with the same gun. It's a 9-mm pistol. When they send it to the FBI, those guys will be able to figure out the make of gun and ammunition. It still doesn't help us."

"I thought that the FBI was pretty good."

Clarence tapped a cigarette out of the pack in his pocket and lit it, inhaling. "They're good, Jake, but in a lot of ways they have to run around fighting the bad guys with one hand tied behind their back. Warrants. Probable cause. Half the time when they nail the right guy, the case falls apart because of some clever dick lawyer, or the greaseballs whack the witnesses that the federal marshals were supposed to protect." Clarence noticed that he had slipped back into big-city-cop vernacular. He fell silent.

"So they really won't get them, Clarence? Really?" Jake was staring at the dam. His face was open and innocent, disbelieving.

"That's why I brought you out here, Jake. I want to give you a choice. The state and the feds don't know about you. They don't know that anything happened to you. They don't know about your box or your trip to the bottom of the lake. Only you and I and Geery know about any of that." Clarence exhaled the sweet tobacco smoke.

"I guess that we ought to tell them," Jake said numbly.

Clarence stubbed out his cigarette in the sand and moved closer. Jake noticed something in Clarence that he had never seen before in the man. He had always struck Jake as a black Andy Griffith, a kindly, small-town lawman with little need for or interest in the big, bad, outside world. What Jake saw now was the look of a bounty hunter, a predator. "Do you remember what you told me when you pulled Diana back into the boat?"

"No," Jake said honestly. All he could remember was seeing that red hair scattered on the surface.

"Think, Jake! Remember! I can't put the words back in your mouth for you."

Jake skipped another rock across the water and thought. "I told you to arrest me because I was going to find who did this and kill them."

"Yes." Clarence's eyes were savage.

"Yes, I remember. I just don't know who to kill, Clarence." He looked sad. Defeated. His posture was that of an old man.

"Jake," Clarence said softly, retreating back into his small-town-sheriff demeanor, "Jake, do you know that all the animals in the world are predators or prey at birth? It is their birthright. It is what they are. Mostly, predators have eyes in the front of their heads. Depth perception. Prey usually have eyes on the sides of their heads for a wide range of vision. Humans are the only ones that get to choose whether they are predator or prey. Most of us choose to be prey. It is easier to stay in the herd and hope that someone else will get old or sick and be taken down by the predators. Do you see what I'm saying?"

"No."

Clarence moved closer, so that their noses almost touched. He grabbed the top of Jake's shoulders and pulled him toward him. Their eyes met. In Clarence's eyes Jake saw Joseph Conrad's Kurtz at the heart of darkness. His eyes were apocalyptic. Survival was written in them. They frightened Jake but were hypnotic in their effect. Finally, the sheriff spoke. "One of two things can happen, Jake. We can go back to town, and you can call from my office and tell them what happened to you and about the box." He paused and stepped away, shaking another cigarette out of the wrinkled red package. He placed it in his lips and lit it, inhaling. Exhaling smoke, he told Jake the second option: "Or we can try to find these cockroaches ourselves and step on them. No warrants. No trials. No appeals. No hung juries. We find them and we exterminate them."

Jake sat for a long time attempting to attach meaning to either option and failing. Revenge was the only thing that held meaning for him now, although he knew that it was wrong. *But what made it wrong? Someone came into my life and blindsided me. They have probably forgotten that I ever existed, if they knew in the first place. Wasn't that wrong?* He felt a growing sense of purpose reemerging in him. The empty space left in his soul by recent events was being filled anew. *My cup runneth over*, he thought incongruously. *I will find them.* He looked up at Clarence, his eyes once again ablaze with life. "How do we start?"

 August 21, 1994, San Francisco, California

"MY FELLOW AMERICANS. Tonight, I address the nation on a matter of great importance. As you have seen reported, I have ordered a number of military strikes into the Republic of Colombia. We are not at war with Colombia. The nature and targets of the strikes were by mutual agreement with the leaders of that nation, and we are enjoying the full cooperation of the Colombian armed forces. The entity with which we are at war is the heart of the narcotics traffic and trade. There are others who are responsible for the misery that we see perpetuating itself on our very streets, but our particular target tonight is the assets of the Cali cartel. We have targeted identified processing facilities and airfields. Colombian troops have embarked on a campaign to destroy the coca fields on the hillsides. In order to minimize the loss of life, we carried out pinpoint strikes using Tomahawk missiles and laser-guided smart bombs."

The President lifted a map on a poster from behind his desk and held it up for the cameras. Polls had revealed that the American people identified more with the President if he used "low-tech" aids in presenting any plan. The map could easily have been shown with computer animation on a separate screen, but was not. It showed a rough topography of Colombia with major cities and national boundaries, with red circles around thirty-two locations. The President continued his presentation. "This map, a copy of which has been provided to the press so that you will all be able to examine it in the newspapers tomorrow, shows the thirty-two locations that were targeted this evening. The Pentagon will give a press briefing at 11 P.M., Eastern time, to review the results.

These targets have been identified by satellite reconnaissance as processing laboratories and airstrips used for the manufacture and transportation of illegal narcotics."

He put the poster behind the desk, out of sight of the cameras. "Some of you may be asking, Why? Or why now? What has changed? Or, 'I thought that we were making progress in the war on drugs?' " The President favored the nation with his most ingratiating smile. "My fellow citizens, law enforcement agencies in this nation are continuing to make enormous strides in the war on drugs. Tonight, however, we were retaliating, in kind, for terrorist acts on our own soil." His face sank into a serious expression. He lifted a second poster board from behind his desk and raised it for the cameras.

"The persons you see on this poster are the late Federal Judge Maria Alvarez and Federal Prosecutor James McAdams. Judge Alvarez was assassinated in February by a representative of the terrorist organization in the hire of the Cali cartel. An attempt was made three weeks later on the life of James McAdams. He was fortunate and was only wounded. These two representatives of the United States Government were assaulted in the performance of their duties as servants of the people. Judge Alvarez and Mr. McAdams were both involved in the Domingo Valens case. Mr. Valens was captured last year and was extradited to this country to stand trial. Mr. Valens is a prominent member, if not a leader, of the Cali cartel. It is not acceptable to me, as your President, for public officials to be assassinated. If the cartel wishes to match wills with the United States of America, we have, tonight, given them a sample of the results. As former President Ronald Reagan said so eloquently, 'They counted on America to be passive. They counted wrong.' I regret that I have other pressing obligations and will not be able to remain to answer any questions. I urge the members of the press to attend the Pentagon briefing at eleven. Thank you, and good evening." The President waved, left the podium, and walked down the hall away from the White House briefing room.

Andrew Oliver switched off his television set and put his hands together, interlacing the fingers. He then lifted his arms, placed his hands behind his head, and yawned.

-91-

ROY DOBKINS FELT as if he were sitting at the feet of a guru. He was actually sitting in a chair next to Dewitt Arnold, the San Francisco Office's resident computer expert. Arnold was a slight man, wearing blue jeans and a flannel shirt with pens, pencils, and a stack of Post-it notes jumbled in the pocket. He wore government-issue, black-framed "birth control" glasses but with no safety pins or tape. If Roy had seen him on the street, he would have pegged him in the computer nerd category, but Dewitt was a little out of the ordinary. He held a black belt in Tae Kwon Do and a Ph.D. in ancient history. He had come to computers late in life, but he found that they suited his contemplative nature and had fallen into them like a duck into water. Together, the two men were examining the results of the phone tap on Gregor Viktorovich.

"Well, the long and short of it is that we are more or less fucked," Dewitt said unemotionally. "You need to get a more intrusive warrant. This guy is encrypted up the wazoo. Everything. His phone. His E-mail. Everything. You need a warrant to bug his house and tap his computer."

"Can't you decipher this stuff?" Dobkins motioned around him at all the equipment, including several 486 machines, a Pentium, a Macintosh, and the terminal connecting Arnold to the UNIX which pulsed with power downstairs.

Dewitt sighed. "Well, Roy, it's like this. In the last twenty-four hours, Gregor has made two encrypted telephone calls. He has sent one encrypted E-mail message and received another one. We have several problems."

"Okay," Dobkins said, his eyes focusing on a point about a foot in front of his face, which was a certain indication that he was preparing to listen attentively and assimilate everything he was told.

The computer technician continued. "First, the telephone calls." He hit a button on the machine in front of him and a bunch of gibberish appeared on the screen. "This is what the digital signal looks like. You can't tell anything about it by looking at it, or by listening to it. Most commercial telephone encryption systems are DES, or Data Encryption Standard. The really good ones are triple DES. That's commercial grade. Anyway, IBM developed it and the NSA has impounded their notes. Now, I'm not saying that the NSA built a back door into DES or anything like that," Dewitt winked mischievously, "but I can send DES stuff to those guys and they can usually turn around plaintext in twenty-four hours. On this thing, they couldn't. They said, 'No dice, we'll get back to you.' If they get around to it, they'll break it, but, in the meantime, that doesn't help us in the least. You need to bug his house."

"Okay. Translation: we can't break the code. Right?" Dobkins said.

Arnold apparently had a stray thought and, before he began speaking, whipped a yellow note out of his pocket, scribbled on it, and stuck it to the side of the terminal alongside about twenty similar notes. He turned back to the special agent. "Okay, the E-mail is another problem entirely." He hit a couple of keys, and the note that Gregor had received came up on the screen. It looked like this:

```
From: <an178345@anonet.nz>
Received: by mail04.mail.anonet.nz
(1.38.193.5/16.2)id AA22305; 21 Aug 1994
    10:55:44-0500
Message-Id: <941204105544_5323730@anonet.nz>
To: gvikt@enet.com
Subject: see text
```

—BEGIN ENCRYPT MESSAGE—
Version: 2.6
hEwDGbEsPUkzOgUBAfwMztNaI1uV+vk4ra9ug5PGi3mJMkoGSA5/
ZZbKT9VwAjTSyvRzMqhYM/O2RKiAQWjCygXbN6XXJzawJK5/
vArapgAAAacsf3YJzprrsrf1hp+NM1x5gHZmVtW6R2PGrYa4vVdJqGe
Zuhq3CyaN4er+FuNJdK9wPCO1sDsPhX1dYtvraM2vqiUd+che
OLijGkpzDLBWFk91tQuxJBSXQte3Y+2V6FiJfcXxJ0lCbjDfjtIk
xJeMH5wZxgADt7bNmsuRSk+qp69D2qaAJKI58wZ1QgSQQVE4I5
YigZ6t5+OpTeUPSbL7KjqBWGQSlomUG71F+VktipkHH+15Hjq77
CRd1B3JKIL7CDzyaEoEPtN1KTnsAbLwXSFUIEu0cZh/
6LDuWOLw6qWS9oRWr8X6jAjWwwz5lNjhfXijk1P9hPlcofP5yiWsGuy
6rXRfbj2y5Qh5KVv5maPt0Kk9UHMQn4eBFXi2V+qwP4V0YE
1x28dhepmbrFU3tjqGDWUOUZrJacZvb2s529ADzSiVyhoQ18LG
PvIVcB9WOJjiacnHFNULFu9pajp/BRKdXw4kMb/KDWN+U5G
if+yGnnn0yVYz1+mm7QzJryiIpX+HBISuK6NcsbASppOyx
CSPR8z72ZE3e6KRDMLCrWYzI4N7w/0==2E1Y
—END ENCRYPT MESSAGE—

Arnold shook his head dolefully. "This is a bitch, Roy. Two ways it's a bitch."

All Dobkins saw was that he couldn't read the message. He didn't see the second problem, but he nodded in agreement, knowing that an explanation would follow.

The computer technician pointed at the gibberish between the dotted encrypted message line. "First, the encryption. I've studied this program. It's good. It uses a combination of RSA public key encryption and IDEA conventional encryption. I can tell you the math if you are interested."

The special agent shook his head. "Just give me the layman's version, Dewitt."

Dewitt sighed for a moment, as if deciding where to begin. It is almost impossible to describe modern encryption in layman's terms. "Roy, it's like this. There is plaintext and cyphertext. Plaintext is what you can read. Cyphertext is the plaintext jumbled in a fashion that you cannot read. A key is what determines the relationship between plaintext and cyphertext. It is made up of a certain number of binary digits. In conventional cryptosystems, a single key is used for both encryption and decryption. This means that the guys at both ends have got to have the same key. This can be bad, because you have to have a secure method of exchanging the key. That's normal standard encryption. With me so far?"

Dobkins nodded.

"Okay. Public key encryption is different. In public key cryptosystems, everyone has two related keys, a publicly revealed key and a secret key. They are complementary. Each key unlocks the cipher that the other key makes. If you know a guy's public key, it does not help you in any way to figure out his secret key. Anyone can use a recipient's public key to encrypt a message to that person. The recipient uses his corresponding secret key to decrypt that message. After the sender has encrypted the message, even he cannot decrypt it. He doesn't have the secret key. I know that this sounds like witchcraft, but do you get it?"

Dobkins's brows were furrowed in thought. "So it's like a lock with two special keys. One can only lock it. It can't do anything but lock it. The other can only open it."

"Right," Arnold said encouragingly. He was impressed. The agent had grasped the concept immediately.

Dobkins rubbed his chin and unfurrowed his brow. "Dewitt, it just seems that if you know one, you should be able to figure out the other one. Aren't they related in any way?"

Arnold sighed. He knew that the agent would not understand what he was about to tell him. "Okay, Roy. You are right. When I said that knowing one doesn't help you get the other, that wasn't entirely true. They are related, but it is just not practical to factor them out." He looked at the agent as if waiting for him to cry uncle. Roy didn't blink. Arnold continued. "RSA. The initials stand for three guys at MIT who invented it. When a message is encoded using RSA, the text is converted into a number which is then raised to a certain exponent. From that number, a fixed large number, or modulus, is subtracted repeatedly until the result is smaller than the modulus. The public key is the exponent and the modulus. To figure out the reverse function and decipher the text, you have to know the two prime numbers that when multiplied yield the public key. With a computer, it is simple to generate products of large prime numbers. It is another matter altogether to factor out the products."

"Okay," Roy said. "Basically, it's too big a math problem for your computer. Is that it?"

"Yes," Arnold said.

The agent's brow furrowed again and he looked at the message on the screen with interest. "Dewitt, you said that this message was bad two ways. What's the other one?"

The computer expert pointed at the top of the message. "See that? Where the sender address is 'an178345@anonet.nz'?"

Roy looked. "Yeah. It's just a computer address, isn't it? We'll get a warrant and get the user from the system administrator."

Arnold shook his head. "That address is a remailer. It's also in New Zealand."

"A remailer?" Dobkins repeated.

"It's basically an electronic post office box. It allows people to communicate anonymously with one another. The guy at the other end of Gregor's mail goes through this machine in New Zealand. It strips all identifying marks off the mail and forwards it with a new address. It also may be the last in a whole chain of remailers. We are not going to catch the second half of this dynamic duo with his E-mail account."

"Can't we get at that machine somehow? Talk with the New Zealand cops?"

"Roy, that machine is probably a 486 stuffed in some guy's basement. The cops aren't going to know where it is. There are hundreds of these things. We'll have to get Gregor and make him cough out who the other guy is."

"Okay," the agent said. He was frowning again. "Back to these keys. Can we just steal them?"

"I thought you'd never ask."

It took until noon the next day to get a judge to sign off on the intrusive tap. At 2 P.M., Gregor went for a drive and agents went over the wall of his compound. They bugged his kitchen, installed a remote dialup system inside his computer, and tapped his keyboard. The operation took thirty-one minutes.

-92-

August 22, 1994, Columbia, South Carolina

CLARENCE SAT IN A BOOTH at Burger King in Columbia Mall. Burger wrappers and french-fry holders lay empty on the plastic serving trays before him. Jake had just walked back across the mall's thoroughfare from the public phone booth opposite the restaurant. As he sat down, he returned Clarence's phone card. The sheriff handed it back. "Keep it. You'll need it again."

Jake was wearing blue jeans and a white T-shirt, which, combined with his ponytail, made him look like a hippie who had wandered onto a "Happy Days" set. Clarence was dressed conservatively in a blue-collared shirt, without a tie, and dark slacks.

Jake spoke. "Well, Clarence, it has to be the lures I ordered from East Coast, you know. It's the only item that I mail-ordered. The rest of my stuff is delivered from Star Bait and Tackle. It's the only check that isn't to Star in the last four months."

"Okay," Clarence agreed. "What did they say on the phone?"

"They said that they couldn't be sure. The guy I talked to was the swing-shift supervisor. It must be a pretty big operation. Anyway, the guy said that he remembered filling my order. He remembered 'Shoppe.' It was unusual, you know."

"Why can't they be sure? Don't they have records?"

"Well, that's the part that makes me think it must be them. He said that they had a break-in about a week ago. It was funny, he said, because the burglars didn't take any merchandise. They took all of the company's records. File cabinets. The PC on the desk.

Everything. The guy said that he is pulling his hair out. There's going to be hell to pay getting together tax records."

Clarence ran a large hand across the top of his head, as he often did when thinking. "It's our only lead," he said, as much to himself as to Jake. "What was it that you ordered, Jake? Do you remember? Specifics are what I'm after. What was the brand?"

"No. It was just surface lures. Let me make a call." He stood back up.

Three hours later, Jake and Clarence were at the main branch of the Richland County Public Library. East Coast Nautical Wares had told Jake that the lures he had ordered were in all likelihood the ones that they had advertised from a company called MJTT. East Coast had placed their bulk order through a post office box in San Francisco and didn't know anything else about the company, except that it delivered acceptable products at low prices.

It took thirty minutes at the computerized periodicals desk, but Jake finally found an article about the company in the *Russian Life* Fall/Holiday issue. It was half of a column on page twenty-nine in the "Business News from Russia" section. Next to it was an article about Ulyanovsk trucks and a plan to export them to America:

> "Russian Engineering to Tackle American Market"—Maynard Johnson, a prominent American industrialist, has announced his intention to construct a toy and fishing tackle manufacturing facility in Vladivostok. In a press conference held in that city on October 12, he said, "I feel confident that with the combination of resources available for the plant, the ready accessibility of the port, and the expertise of Russian engineers, we will have a very successful enterprise." The company is scheduled to begin production in November and will turn out an entire line of lead-free fishing tackle. Additionally, it will manufacture inexpensive wind-up toys. Named Maynard Johnson Tackle and Toys, we look forward to MJTT on the skyline of Vladivostok as an example of American-Russian economic cooperation.

After they had both read the article, Jake glanced up and said, "Looks like the next stop is Vladivostok."

93

THE ATMOSPHERE was tense. Roy Dobkins was watching Dewitt Arnold practice computer sorcery. The surveillance team had radioed into headquarters that the tap and remote dialup were installed and Gregor was out. The mobile unit which was tailing Gregor reported that he was returning over the Bay Bridge, southbound. If he drove straight home, his ETA was twenty-five minutes. Dewitt was feeling the pressure. He felt a single bead of sweat roll down the center of his back. The surveillance team hit the switch which turned on Gregor's machine and put in host mode. They radioed that it was on. Dewitt dialed, and Gregor's machine answered.

He started with a cursory examination of the root directory. The machine had all of the usual software that comes prepackaged in new machines. He skipped it. He found the encryption directory and downloaded all of the encrypted messages that were stored there to be examined. When he located the key rings, he downloaded all of the keys on Gregor's public and private key rings. Nothing else was visible.

The mobile unit radioed that Gregor's ETA was now five minutes. "Let's hope that he never read the manual," Arnold said to Dobkins as he started a disk recovery program and began probing the hard drive. He downloaded several more files that were invisible to the usual directory command.

"He is approaching the entrance in his vehicle," the surveillance team reported.

"Okay. You can turn it off," Arnold instructed.

"Turn it off," Dobkins relayed.

Arnold's monitor read, "NO CARRIER." "It's off," the computer expert acknowledged.

"Did you get the keys?" Roy inquired.

"Yes, Roy, I got the keys." Dobkins began to dance around the room with his hands in the air. "But it won't help us just yet," Arnold finished.

Dobkins stopped dancing and looked at him. "Why not?"

"They are password protected. That's why we installed the keyboard tap. The next time Gregor reads his mail, we will have the password to his secret key. We can read the mail he receives."

"What about the mail he sends? You can't pin a crime on a guy because someone else sends him mail. We need to read what he sends."

"Roy, remember when we talked last night? Remember the two keys?"

"Yes."

"Each guy has two keys. We are dealing with four keys here. Two public, two secret. In the very near future we will know three out of the four." Arnold turned his attention back to the screen. He began tapping away at the keyboard. "Oh, how now? Look at this, Roy! Ha! He didn't read the manual!" Arnold was pointing at the screen.

Dobkins looked but didn't understand. It was a directory. "Okay, Dewitt. What's the big secret?"

Arnold didn't reply. He tapped away at the keyboard some more. He was examining two files in a text editor. They were gibberish. "These guys fuckin' blew it," he was saying to himself. "This is like turning a rubber inside out to use it again."

"What do you mean, Dewitt?" Roy said.

"Roy, there is a big difference between the command 'wipe' and the command 'delete.' Do you know what that is?"

"Not exactly."

"Well, when you 'delete' something, it isn't gone. Just the title is gone. It would be like Oliver North shredding the title page but leaving the rest of his papers in the file cabinet. It can be recovered. That's what I've done to Mr. Gregor here. If you 'wipe' something, it gets overwritten. He should have wiped." Arnold chuckled at his own joke. He brought up a file in the text editor which was titled INSTRUCT. They both began to read.

Roy's jaw dropped. Arnold felt queasy. It was only one page long. The first half of the page gave the simplified commands for sending, receiving, encrypting, and decrypting mail. Wiping was included in the command lines, so there would be no mistakes. The only mistake had been with the first file. It was the second half of the message that alarmed them:

```
Welcome to the information superhighway, Gregor.
Here's my proposition. I want 3 to 6 kilograms of
plutonium 239 for my own personal use. I propose
to exchange 100 kilos of uncut Colombian cocaine
for this merchandise. After the initial exchange,
you will be afforded access to the cocaine super-
highway. My E-mail address is an178123@anonet.nz.
Welcome aboard. —Cassius
```

"If there ever was an unholy marriage, this is it," Roy said.

"The cartel and the Russian mob. Plutonium for drugs. Sounds like a thriller novel," Arnold said.

-94-

August 23, 1994, San Francisco, California

"GOOD MORNING, gentlemen. My name is Special Agent Cassius." Andrew smiled warmly. He was dressed in a dark suit and a long-sleeved white shirt with a blue tie. He had removed his jacket, revealing a shoulder-holstered snubnosed .38-caliber service revolver. He was standing in front of a dry-erase board on an easel with a blue pen in his hand. Seated in chairs before him were five young Hispanic men.

Aaron had worked overtime for the five previous days. Thursday, while Andrew was in Los Angeles walking the tryout line, he had spent hours creating Andrew's FBI identification, forging signatures, cropping and heat-sealing the photograph into the folder, scrubbing the plastic and leather to simulate wear. The badge wasn't a perfect counterfeit but would stand up to cursory examination. As a test run, he dispatched Andrew to rent the office space Friday morning under the new alias while he waited by the phone. From the phone interviews, he selected fourteen of the actors who had no family in California, were single, had no live-in girlfriends or roommates to restrict their movements, and did not know one another. Late Friday afternoon he subcontracted intensive background searches to several private investigators in the Los Angeles area who had contacts in the LAPD or Transcom Credit Service. By Monday afternoon, the results were in. Eight of the men were clean. Six came up dirty, vulnerable. One was a closet homosexual. One had a girlfriend who was an illegal alien. All of them were in financial difficulties significant enough for money alone to motivate them. Tuesday morning, after deciding not to lean on the one with the illegal girlfriend, he called the five men and told them about the money. They all agreed to pick up their tickets and come to the job in San Francisco.

All of the time that the detective was not on the phone giving instructions or taking notes from his PIs, he was planning with Andrew. He explained, as he had every step of the way thus far, what the millionaire needed to know to pull off the deception. He worked all day Tuesday obtaining post office boxes and cellular phone accounts that led to those boxes and all that night generating the individualized handouts for the actors. Aaron had begun to develop a number of theories about his boss's overall plan, but he never inquired beyond the immediate requirements. He was the nuts-and-bolts man, the finder, the front-line grunt. Andrew was the general, and the detective was beginning to think that he didn't want to know the bigger picture. For the first time in his life, he was afraid that he might have gotten into something well over his head.

The office that they were in had been rented on a six-month lease at $3,000 a month, but it was the best. Located in the Alcoa Building, 1 Maritime Plaza, it exuded class, power, prestige, and legitimacy. Andrew continued, "First things first. The matter of compensation. You are all being paid the per diem rate for a GS-15, which is $110 a day. Your additional travel allowance is $500. Each of you will receive a Treasury check for $1,270 before you leave today. This will cover the first week of your service and travel to and from this training session and any travel necessary during your service. Are there any questions?"

Federico Martínez raised his hand. The agent nodded for him to ask his question. "What if this lasts more than one week?"

The agent replied, "We expect this operation to be completed in three weeks' time, maximum. You will have a Treasury check to cover the balance of your service mailed to you three weeks from today. Any more questions regarding compensation?"

There were no raised hands.

"Good, then we will get started. Gentlemen, you have been selected to take part in a Bureau sting operation. It is unusual for us to recruit civilians for this type of operation, but, in this case, the Bureau decided that it was the best way to approach the problem. We needed fresh faces. So, here you are.

"If you will turn to page one of your handout, you will see a brief profile of our target. His name is Gregor. He has been illegally importing Russian artifacts and icons into the United States. I urge you to read and digest the material provided on this man during the study period this afternoon. Please turn to the next page.

"The next three pages detail the operation. You are expected to memorize each code name, cutout, route, and cellular phone number. You may not take your handouts or any notes with you out of the building. A synopsis of what you will read is as follows. We have tagged an illegal shipment of Gregor's with a radio beacon. You are to negotiate and effect the trade of this shipment for another container of merchandise which will be provided to you. Each of you has been given a legend, or background story, in your handout. You are all representatives of the Revolutionary Armed Forces of Colombia, or FARC. Many believe that in the post–Cold War era, the FARC is little more than the political and military arm of the Cali cartel. When the trade is completed, the leader, who by random selection is Alberto," the agent pointed to Federico, "will make contact with this office in the manner detailed in Appendix A of his handout. When we have retrieved the marked merchandise, your job is complete, and the target will be arrested.

"All contact between the five of you is to be only by the cellular phones which will be provided to you with the use of the assigned code names in the handout. Each handout is personalized in this regard. Do not exchange handouts. Do not exchange your real names, addresses, or phone numbers. Do not plan a ten-year reunion." Andrew smiled at his little joke. "This is all for your own protection. We are dealing with ruthless men, and if by unlucky coincidence one of you should slip and identify himself or others to the target, retribution would be certain. Do I make myself clear?"

"You mean that this is dangerous?" one of the men asked, and looked nervously around at his comrades.

"Not at all," Andrew said evenly. "You will be under constant surveillance. We will end any situation that appears to be, shall we say, going down the wrong path. The danger lies in retribution after the fact. We are dealing with a large criminal organization that pays its debts. The objective of the operation is to allow the Russians to think that you are Colombian terrorists. After the sting is over, you go back to being actors. Gregor goes to jail. The Russian mafia has antipathy toward sloppy cartel terrorists. You drop totally out of the picture, so long as you maintain your cover until the end. If the cover breaks down, it is essential that you have remained compartmentalized, for the safety of the others. I can arrange for witness protection. I do not wish to arrange it for five." He grinned.

"You now have five hours to study the contents of your handouts. Lunch and dinner will be brought to you in this room. A bathroom is located across the hall. At the end of the study period, I will take each of you aside individually and orally examine you on the material you need to memorize. Assuming that you all pass, you will return to your homes this evening. Your leader will contact you in three days' time to commence the operation. Keep your calendars clear and stay near the phones we will provide you. Are there any questions before I leave you to study?"

Federico raised his hand. The agent nodded again. "What happened to your hand, Mr. Cassius?"

Andrew lifted the burned left hand and examined it as though it didn't really belong to him. "Well," he said, "that's a long story, but it was in the line of duty."

 August 24, 1994, Vladivostok, Russia

JAKE STARED OUT THE WINDOW of the trans-Pacific flight. He couldn't see anything but mist-covered ocean rollers stretching in all directions. It wasn't like Lake Murray. It was impersonal. Lake Murray was *his* lake. This would never be anyone's ocean. Jake was sitting alone in the back of the airliner, in the section that used to be reserved for smokers. He was glad that the plane was not full. Sitting cheek to jowl, surrounded by howling children or talkative salesmen, had never appealed to him. He liked to have space. He liked to be left alone. He looked at the credentials that Clarence had given him and recalled their last conversation in the concourse of the Columbia Metropolitan Airport. The sheriff had made him look at the model airplanes in the main lobby.

"This is history, Jake. History isn't dusty old books. It's real live people and stories and airplanes at the bottom of the lake." Clarence had beamed like a proud schoolteacher who has just introduced a student to a new world.

Jake had dutifully examined the models. Then he had inadvertently found himself imagining what it would be like to be sitting in the cockpit staring through those tiny windows. He pictured looking to the right and seeing one propeller feathered and the engine on fire. He could see the surface of the lake approaching and feel the knowledge dawning that he was really going to crash into those cold waters. He shook off the memory and looked down at the two items of identification.

"I used to work in Narcotics and then Homicide for the Oakland PD. I thought that you might be able to use this," Clarence had said. He had flipped open a wallet to reveal an FBI shield. They had stood in the corner of the departure lounge. "It's real. This agent was killed in a kidnapping investigation and the perps took it. We nailed them on a narcotics bust and this shield went into evidence. It was in the evidence locker, along with his driver's license. A friend of mine sent them to me. The trial is already over. Nobody will miss them. Geery put your picture in them." Clarence rubbed a beefy finger over the plastic-covered photos. "Did a good job. They won't get you into anywhere official, but they might let you bluff your way around with civilians. Don't use them unless you have to." Clarence had shoved them into Jake's pocket and patted him on the shoulder as he filed into the boarding ramp.

Jake then focused his attention on the travel magazine stuffed in the pouch on the seat in front of him. He glanced at the table of contents and turned to the article about Vladivostok. The article was upbeat. It portrayed the city as the Russian version of San Francisco, with rocky hills and trolley cars, the romantic last stop on the Trans-Siberian Express. It showed a glossy color photo of a classic railway station. Jake honestly didn't know what to expect, but he remembered an article that he had read in *Newsweek* while researching the city the day before his departure. It had described a Chernobyl-scale accident that had occurred thirty miles north of Vladivostok. A submarine reactor had blown off the top of its vessel and contaminated the entire surrounding area. It had happened in 1985 and had been covered up until 1994. It was difficult to reconcile the dark and the light sides without seeing the city firsthand.

Jake stepped off the Alaska Airlines flight and walked across the tarmac. Vladivostok International Airport had not yet come up to world standards of direct embarkation and debarkation into a comfortable terminal, but it was August and the temperature was mild. He entered the building and went through the Customs line. The Russian official looked him over. "Purpose of visit?" he asked.

"Tourist," Jake replied.

The official inspected the clean passport. "Never traveled abroad?"

"No," Jake answered, "except to Canada."

"How long do you intend to stay?"

"One day."

"Short visit," the official commented.

"It's all I've got. I was just out for three days on business in Seattle. Saw the airline fare and decided 'why not?' since I was already across the U.S. on business."

"The nature of your business?"

"Back home?"

"Yes."

"Fishing tackle."

The official stamped the passport and handed it back to Jake. "Enjoy your visit to Vladivostok, Mr. Weichert."

Jake walked to the front of the terminal, looking for a cab. He had no baggage. He intended to return to Seattle by the evening flight. Seattle was, by agreement, the "sister city" of the sprawling industrial port of Vladivostok. As Jake exited the terminal, he was struck by the pungency of the air. He could smell diesel bus exhaust and marine fuel. The air even felt oily. He knew that he was still twenty-five miles from the city. A rickety Zhiguli cab driven by a pasty-faced Russian pulled up to the curb. The driver motioned for him to get in. Jake sat in the back.

The cabby looked over his shoulder. "American?" he asked.

Jake stared at the man with a perplexed expression. He hadn't said a word. "How did you know?"

"I used drive cab in Moscow. I always tell American. In your eyes. You know? American see world differently than other people. Also you have good teeth and look well fed." He flashed a smile of crooked brown teeth at Jake in the rear-view mirror. While he was delivering this speech, he had pulled away from the curb and was going around the circle to exit the airport and head toward the city. "I can really tell whether people are American after I drop them. Big tippers. Where to?"

"Maynard Johnson Tackle and Toys, please."

"Ah. New. Big building. South by docks. You sure you want go there? I know good restaurant."

"Yes, that is where I want to go. Why?"

"Just curious." The cabby looked at Jake again in the rearview mirror. Concern showed in his eyes. "You not go to cause trouble, no?"

"No, I'm just a businessman. I buy their products. Why do you look at me that way?"

The cabby motioned for Jake to lean forward over the seat. He turned and whispered to him in a hoarse, thickly accented voice, "It is mafia. Mafia." Jake could smell the disinfectant odor of cheap vodka on his breath.

"Oh," Jake said as he leaned back away from the driver. "It's okay. I'm just going to talk with them about products. The mafia has no interest in a simple businessman like me." His mind was now racing. Mafia? Did the Russians have a mafia, too? He quieted his mind. "Oh, how much is this ride?"

"Dollars or rubles?" the driver asked.

"Which do you want?"

The cabby snorted and then laughed. "Which do you think? Who want rubles? Huh? Thirty dollar. It is forty-five kilometers. For you, twenty-five dollar, okay?"

"Okay, and can you pick me up about an hour after you drop me off?"

"One hour?"

"Yes."

"I'll be there, sir."

Five minutes later, the driver was forcing his cab through the gray concrete metropolis of Vladivostok. The streets were choked with old Japanese cars. The sidewalks were littered with trash and dead rats. The air smelled of decay and rust. Part of the harbor, filled with rusting ships, was visible as the cab approached MJTT. The cab driver stopped a block away and pointed. Jake got out and walked to the front gate of the facility. There were two body-builder-type young men in blue jeans and collared shirts just outside the front gate, as if standing guard. Jake went up to the one on the left. "Do you speak English?"

The man shook his head and Jake turned to the other tough. "Do you speak English?"

"Da. Nimnoga. I mean, yes, but little."

Jake spoke slowly for the young man, after the fashion worldwide of foreigners attempting to make themselves understood. He said, "My name is John Wren. I work at East Coast Nautical Wares, in Baltimore. USA. We recently ordered a large consignment. My boss wanted me to swing by here to speak with Mr. Johnson about some problems."

"Problems?" the Russian had obviously understood that word.

"Technical problems. The surface lures don't stay on the surface unless moved at too great a speed through the water."

"Ah. Problems. Come with me." The huge man turned and beckoned Jake to follow him. They crossed a dirt yard stacked with crates and into a double door. Machine noises and the hum of electric motors could be heard in the distance. Jake figured that the hallway must exit somewhere onto a shop floor. He was led through another double door and it became quieter as the doors swung shut behind them. The burly young man walked purposefully up to a large wooden door in a metal frame and knocked twice. From inside, Jake heard "Enter" in English.

They entered and the guard pointed at Jake. "Sir, an English customer with problem. Technical problem."

"Thank you, Alexis," the man behind the desk said. "That will be all. I will escort our visitor out."

As the Russian exited, Jake looked at the desk before him. The man behind it was short and thin, with sparse hair and a long nose on a round face. He looked like a gnome. The placard on the desk read "Thomas Johnson" and below it was, presumably, the same name in Cyrillic script. Jake spoke. "American, actually. From East Coast Nautical Wares."

"Yes, I assumed so. You don't look British, and I don't, as yet, export anything to the UK. Please sit down." Thomas motioned to a plush leather armchair across from him at his desk.

Jake sat. "We received something rather unexpected in our shipment several weeks ago."

Thomas put his fingers to his lips and then pointed to the walls, indicating that they had ears. "So you say that you have discovered a technical problem," he said smoothly.

"Yes," Jake answered, and began to spin the same yarn he had given the men outside. "Our customers have complained that they have to reel in your surface lures too fast to prevent them from sinking."

"Ah, well, let's take a trip down to the shop, then."

Thomas stood and Jake followed him out. They passed through both sets of double doors and once outside, the little man turned and led his guest past the side of the shop building. The noise inside was loud, loud enough to drown out their conversation. Walking alongside the building, Thomas spoke again. "So, Mr. Wren, who are you? East Coast has never complained, much less sent us a man."

Jake handed over the wallet that Clarence had given him. Geery had done a marvelous job placing Jake's photograph in the wallet. He hadn't disturbed the subtle eagle-crest seal on the clear laminate that covered the photograph. Looking at the ID, Jake believed himself that he was John Wren, FBI agent-at-large. The little executive handed the FBI shield back. He said, "I don't suppose that you have a second form of identification, Mr. Wren?"

Jake replied, "Yes, I do." He didn't offer to present it, however.

Thomas seemed to accept the answer. There was a moment of silence as a grinding machine on the other side of the corrugated wall fell silent. The crunch of the coarse soil under their shoes sounded loud and echoing until the grinding noise started again. "So, what do you want?" the executive inquired.

"I want a little piece of information, Mr. Johnson. That is all. After that, you will never have to see me again." He stopped walking to face Thomas for a moment.

The executive halted. "Everybody wants information, Mr. Wren. It is the only gold standard," he said dryly.

"Mr. Johnson, this is what I have to say. I have no authority or jurisdiction here. I am out of bounds. In fact, I am on leave. It was the only way that I could come over here and try to get at the source. Something that came out of your company was worth killing for stateside. I want to know who the connect is over there."

"I'm not sure I know what you mean."

Jake looked menacingly at the little man. "Mr. Johnson, I saw the beef you've got around here. It's not safe for you to talk in your office. Someone has their claws in you. All I want to know is who is getting the stuff at the other end. If you give me somewhere else to go, I'll go there."

Thomas looked at Jake and began walking again. The machine had stopped. He waited to speak until the whine of the machine started. "His name is Gregor. You people should have a file on him. He lives in Oakland." Then he turned as though nothing had happened and said, "Let's go down to the shop floor and you can show me what you think is wrong with the surface lures."

On the shop floor the two men handled several of the lures. Jake pointed at a few parts and made some motions with his hands about curves and lines at several points. Thomas nodded, and, after fifteen minutes of essentially saying nothing at all, they left the floor. Jake headed toward the gate and was met by the taxi driver. Thomas returned to his desk and waited for the workday to end. That evening he wrote out a coded message detailing the visit by the FBI agent. On the way to work the next morning he dropped it in a dead-letter box not far from the classic train station Jake had looked at in the magazine.

96

SPECIAL AGENT DOBKINS was once again watching the master at his screen. The cursor was blinking insistently beside the word "PASS-WORD:." Dobkins was holding the telephone to his ear. The surveillance team had reported that Gregor had turned on his computer and was dialing out. If he retrieved E-mail, the team would get his password via the keyboard tap. They would also record another message as its digital signals passed through the telephone wire.

"Okay. He has downloaded his mail and he is going off line," Dobkins heard through the earpiece. "The keyboard tap is on and broadcasting," the surveillance team leader reported.

"Come on, come on," Dobkins said to the telephone and to Arnold.

"Here it is!" The team leader's voice crackled as the radio distorted. "Tango cap, hotel, oscar, uniform, comma, tango, oscar, oscar, comma, bravo cap, romeo, uniform, tango, uniform, sierra, symbol-question mark." The team leader read the variation of radio spelling transmission that they had formulated for this case.

Dobkins read it back. "I copy Tango cap, hotel, oscar, uniform, comma, tango, oscar, oscar, comma, bravo cap, romeo, uniform, tango, uniform, sierra, symbol-question mark."

"That's correct."

"That's it!" Arnold said. Then he spun himself around in his chair, arms and legs flying. Dobkins began to dance, just as he had the night that they had stolen the keys. Arnold returned to the keyboard. "Tell them to wait one minute while I set up to receive." His fingers raced across the keyboard. "And then to send that last message. We're going to look at all of them."

Dobkins relayed the instructions and hung up the telephone. A few moments later a string of ASCII characters began to fill Arnold's screen. When the transfer was complete, the computer technician gave a few more commands and the screen went blank, except for the prompt and a list of files.

"See these extensions? Where it says '.enc' after the filename?"

"Yes," Dobkins said.

"Well, chances are that we are going to be able to read half of them. The half that Gregor received. The other ones that I down-loaded will be the ones that he sent. We won't be able to read those. We have to try to decrypt each of them to be able to tell the difference. From the outside looking in, we cannot tell." He smiled at Dobkins.

Dobkins began describing a small circle with his hand, mo-tioning Arnold to get on with it. "Come on, Dewitt, let's start reading the guy's mail."

Arnold was already typing in the commands. The computer asked, "PASSWORD:." He typed it in. The computer responded, "THE PASSWORD IS INCORRECT." Arnold typed it in again. The computer printed on the screen, "THE PASSWORD IS INCORRECT. EXITING PROGRAM." The prompt appeared.

"Shit!" Dobkins exclaimed.

Arnold turned around in his chair to face him. He was smil-ing broadly. "This isn't bad, Roy. What it means is that we have a chance to read both sets of messages. It would have said, 'NO KEY' if the second secret key was not on the ring." He started laughing and tapping his feet on the tiled floor. "Yes! Yes! Yes!"

"I don't get it," the special agent said.

"It's like this, Roy. This Cassius apparently gave Gregor the program and the keys. Remember the instructions that we read? Cassius set it all up. He left all four keys on Gregor's disk. It didn't matter to him, because he knew that Gregor would only try to use his key. It was the only password that he was given. What it means to us is that we don't have to figure out Cassius's secret key. We only have to break his password. Unless he is very, very clever, we can do that."

"Why is that easier than trying to back out the secret key? Can't the password be anything?"

"It's easier, usually, because people don't use truly random passwords in real life. They use something that they can remember. Words, proper names, places, quotations. Things like that." Arnold turned back to the screen and typed in Gregor's password at the prompt. He pointed at it. "See that? It's not random. It is a famous quotation from history."

"THOU, TOO, BRUTUS?" stared back at the two men from the screen.

"After we read the messages that Gregor has received, I'll set up to break Cassius's password." Arnold turned back to the screen and began to decrypt the messages. In less than five minutes the laser printer was spitting out the plaintext versions of the messages that Gregor had received. They were cryptic but revealed much about the crime that had been committed.

```
3 Mar 94

Glad to hear from you, Gregor. Inform soonest on
date of expected shipment.
                              Cassius


12 Apr 94

FARC informs me desires shipment by latest
30 August.
                              Cassius


1 Jun 94

Your shipment is secured. One hundred kilos.
Wholesale value one million US dollars.
                              Cassius


14 Jul 94

FARC desires details of arrival schedule.
                              Cassius


19 Aug 94

FARC desires to send representatives to negotiate
exchange.
                              Cassius
```

```
25 Aug 94

FARC will send two representatives to your house
tomorrow, 26 Aug 94, to negotiate exchange. Send
backup communication schedule soonest, in event
that contact is broken off.
```

Cassius

"I can't believe that this is really happening," Dobkins said.

 -97-   *August 26, 1994, Oakland, California*

ON THE OUTSKIRTS of Oakland, to the south of the sprawling metropolis amid the hills that ring the San Francisco Bay area, there
is a large Spanish-style villa with a red tile roof, a ten-foot high,
solid white wall surrounding the complex, and a swimming pool
located at the rear of the main house. The pool reflected light
back as pale blue from its crystal-clear water. Jake could see it all
from his vantage point at the top of the hill. The desertlike area
where he sat seemed a stark contrast to the greenery around the
bay. The villa was the home of Gregor.

He had found the villa by calling Clarence, who had told him
to contact Lt. John Allen of the Oakland PD. Lieutenant Allen
had called Jake back at his motel in less than ten minutes with the
address. Clarence had told Allen everything, so he was in. Clarence
said that he would help with anything. Allen was close to retirement, and unlike many who follow the path of extreme caution
when nearing the end, he wanted to pull out all the stops. Arrests
were up in narcotics, as were car seizures. Allen was going to go
out with a bang, and he was more than willing to help Clarence
with some justice on the side.

Jake had his camera out and was photographing the compound
from his view with the 300-mm lens. The camera always made
him think of Diana. She had given it to him. Now he was going

to use it to track down her killers. As he was shooting several aspects of the compound, he saw a car drive up and two Hispanic men, in blue jeans and T-shirts, step out. He photographed both of them and, as an afterthought, photographed the man at the wheel as he made a three-point turn and drove away. The two men that had been dropped off walked up to the gate of the compound, and Jake saw the gate roll open in front of them. Two burly men fell into step with them as the four strolled up to the main building. The front gate, apparently motorized, rolled shut automatically. That was when he saw two dozen men pour onto the street from two inconspicuous cars, a telephone repair van, and a plumbing van parked about half a mile down the road in the opposite direction from which the car had just left. He focused his lens on them for a better look and noticed that they were all wearing blue windbreakers with "FBI" in large yellow letters printed on the back. They were storming the compound.

-98-

August 26, 1994, Oakland, California

SPECIAL AGENT ROY DOBKINS sat in the back of the surveillance van wearing a set of headphones. He was listening to the various surveillance posts set up around the front gate and perimeter of Gregor's house. A technician at the front of the van could switch his earphones to hear any telephone calls from the tap. Dobkins heard the crackle of the radios disappear as the tech switched him to the tap. Gregor was talking without encryption. The agent looked back and saw the reels turning, recording what he was hearing live.

"Da," he heard a gruff Russian voice answer the phone.

"This is Alberto. I have dropped two," a man's voice said. Dobkins guessed that it was on a cellular phone. He heard engine hum in the background.

"Pick them up at 3:42," the Russian voice ordered.

"Got it," the other voice said, and hung up.

The technician switched Roy's headphones back to the radio circuit. The post outside the gate called in. "Sir, I have two Hispanic males entering the compound now. They were admitted and now are being escorted up the main drive to the house."

Roy reached for his radio and keyed it. "Okay, that's it. Contact has been made. Let's go in." That was the point when two dozen agents piled out of four vehicles and began scaling the walls of Gregor's compound. Twenty minutes later, Gregor, two Hispanics, and two Russians were escorted in handcuffs out the front gate to FBI vehicles.

-99-

August 26, 1994, Langley, Virginia

JONATHAN WENTZ BEGAN to black out the information that the FBI would not need. He was a conscientious man and always attempted to keep Customs and the Bureau apprised of information that might be of value to them but not damage the cover of his source in Vladivostok. It was a full-page, double-spaced typewritten rendition of the information contained in the handwritten report. Thomas Johnson had left the report in the dead drop a few days previously. After he was done, the only portion of the report that remained for the Bureau said, "Special Agent John Wren, FBI, visited ▬▬▬▬▬▬▬▬ in an unofficial capacity. He conducted an interview with ▬▬▬▬▬ in regard to a shipment ▬▬ organized crime ▬▬▬▬."

He put the report in a manila routing folder and addressed it to the Federal Bureau of Investigation, Records.

-100-

ROY DOBKINS WALKED into Harry Trasker's office. He was not a man to become frustrated easily. He did not anger easily, either. But the things which had come to light in the previous twenty-four hours were beyond him. He had never seen anything like it in all his years at the FBI. This situation was a new one, and he had to tell the boss that it was all a dead end.

"Yes, Roy," Harry said. His eyes were bloodshot. He was obviously nursing another hangover.

"Well, sir, this is very unusual."

"Lay it on me. I've got to hear it sometime," Harry grimaced.

"The Hispanic men that we picked up, they aren't terrorists. They aren't even foreigners. They are true-blue red-blooded Chicanos. They are actors who say that they were hired and trained by an FBI agent for a sting. They are posing as FARC terrorists and carrying out a switch for some illegal merchandise with Gregor. They do not know what the merchandise is. After the switch is made, the FBI comes in and arrests Gregor. They were interrogated separately and gave us the same story. They say that there are three more, but that they were rigorously compartmentalized so that they could not identify one another, even if they wanted to."

"Actors?" the Director repeated in disbelief.

"Yes, actors. There is one who is in charge. His code name is Alberto. That's the guy we heard on the phone tap. They say that if any of them were taken, Alberto was to contact the remainder of the squad and instruct them to change their cellular phones to another account number. Alberto is the only one who knows the numbers."

"What the fuck?" Harry said slowly. "Where were they trained?"

"They were trained in a small office suite in the Alcoa Building downtown. We checked it out. It is an empty suite. It was rented for cash for six months. The building manager said that it was an FBI agent, named Cassius. I have a copy of the lease in the file. No prints. Block handwriting. Analysts are going to take a look at it, but I don't expect anything from that. Manager didn't check it out because he says, 'I'm a patriot. If my country wants something that I can give it, I do.' Anyway, he didn't check up on the guy. Cash in advance always makes people more patriotic. We sent a sketch artist out, but the manager wasn't much help."

"Phone accounts?" Harry asked.

"Nothing there. The numbers that these guys had were all to individuals with apartment numbers. You know, like '1235 Broad Street, Apartment 398.' If you check the street addresses, they are post offices. They are post office boxes. We have already traced all of the numbers that these guys know. They lead to boxes, and the boxes aren't even really in the names listed. Again, each cellular account was opened with a large advance-credit balance. No leads. This Cassius is fucking amazing. We could use him."

"How is he paying these guys?"

"That's another kicker. Treasury checks. One of the guys we got even had his folded in his back pocket. The checks are legit. Watermark and everything. We gave it to Treasury to hunt down where it came from. Somebody's ass is going to be in a sling."

"So what are we going to do with them?"

"Send them back out with surveillance and hope Mr. Cassius reestablishes contact."

"What about Gregor?"

"Team went in last night with their warrant. Haven't found much. They found the disk that contained the E-mail encryption program. Got a clean thumbprint off it. It's not Gregor's. It may be Cassius, if Arnold is right about how the encryption went down. The print has been run through AFIS. No comeback. Doesn't mean that he's never been booked. Just means that he wasn't in the military and isn't on the national net or Interpol. The match could be in some detective's filing cabinet in Warner Robins, Georgia, for all we know.

"The house is clean. He has an encryption system for his phone, but there is nothing illegal about that in and of itself. NSA is going to want to take it apart. It's some kind of Russian thing. We are charging him with trafficking in illegal goods based on the testimony of the phoney FARC men and the messages that we have been able to read, but it won't stick. We can't get an indictment with no plutonium and no proof that he responded to those messages. It will keep him locked up for a day or two, that's it. We'll have to drop it after that. We just went in too soon."

"So, Gregor thinks that he is in bed with the cartel. He may be, for all we know. This Cassius has arranged for him to think so. Presumably, Cassius is the recipient of the nuclear material, but is he getting it for a terrorist group? Is he a terrorist group? Why does he want to make it very clear to Gregor that the FARC is receiving the material?"

"I don't know," Roy said somberly.

"Put Gregor under the lights. Let's see if we can't get something out of him."

-101- *August 27, 1994, Smithsonian Institution, Washington, DC*

SPECIAL AGENT HARVEY ERSOY and Dr. Walter Pruitt were staring at the computer-generated facial reconstruction of the skull found in the Cascade Mountains.

"Put dark glasses on him, like in that drawing there," Dr. Pruitt instructed the computer technician. A few seconds later the face appeared with dark sunglasses.

Ersoy whistled, "Man, that is good. That is him. No doubt."

"There is always doubt," the Bonemeister cautioned. "This is half art, half science. The composite sketch wasn't necessarily very close to begin with. Nobody really remembered him at all." Then, with his cautioning statement made, the anthropologist smiled broadly. "All things being equal, though, I think that after twenty-three years, the FBI has found its man."

"I still can't get over how close they are," Ersoy said. He reached up and pulled down the composite sketch of D. B. Cooper that was tacked to the bulletin board and brought it next to the computer screen. The two images were startlingly similar. "We still don't know who he is. We've got him there in a crate, the Robin Hood of hijacking, but we don't know who he is."

"St. Louis may still come through," Dr. Pruitt said encouragingly.

"They say that they have gone through it all. They don't have any more that meet your criteria. They say that a lot went up in the fire of '73. It's the National Personnel Record Center's generic excuse for everything," Ersoy complained.

"Well, I'm certain that they are doing the best they can."

Ersoy laughed. "Doc, I called those guys once about a former Marine corporal who got his throat cut in North Carolina. He had been in the Corps from 1983 until 1988. They couldn't find his record. You know what they told me when I called back?"

"No," Dr. Pruitt said.

"They told me that the record probably went up in the fire of '73."

-102-

August 28, 1994, Alameda, California

JAKE EXITED OFF I-580 onto High Street on the island of Alameda. He drove down to Park Street and took a left, heading toward the ocean. Along the way, he pulled into the South Shore Mall, where he found an Hour Photo shop and dropped off his film to be processed. After leaving the store, he walked through the parking lot and then jaywalked across Shoreline Drive to the beach. For an hour he sat on the beach watching the tiny rollers come in from the bay. Off to the south he could see the San Mateo Bridge. Nightfall was approaching, and a fog was beginning to descend.

The headlights of the cars on the distant bridge were becoming faint.

He reviewed what he had learned so far. Someone had hired three guys from Newberry to get a box that had arrived at his place. They had "killed" him. Someone had killed the three guys from Newberry, probably the same men who had hired them. The people who had hired them had expected them to have the cargo. Jake had heard the conversation about the cargo. They had outsmarted their employers and dropped it into the lake. Okay, it played so far. The people who hired the three guys from Newberry must have made them talk before they killed them, because they had gone back and retrieved the box. Okay, why did they kill Bud and Diana? What did they have to do with anything? Maybe Bud tried to arrest them? He didn't know why Bud would have tried to arrest them, but it could be. That left Diana. Why Diana? He couldn't get past that point.

He had to believe that the box was the shipment of lures that he had ordered from East Coast. It was the only thing that he had ordered in the past few months that didn't come from the company in Orangeburg. East Coast had been burgled and their files taken. That would be how the crooks had found his address. Okay, it played. East Coast had ordered what they had delivered to him from a post office box in San Francisco. That box belonged to MJTT. Okay, MJTT had been the origin of the shipment. Thomas Johnson had told him that Gregor used his company to send things out of Russia. Then it made sense that something that was Gregor's had gone astray and he would be behind the efforts to retrieve it. Therefore, Gregor was responsible for the deaths of the three guys from Newberry, Bud, and Diana. But today, Gregor had been arrested by the FBI, along with the two Hispanic men who had visited the compound. This, Jake had seen and photographed. Where did he go from here? Maybe the FBI was going to catch him.

His thoughts were interrupted as a wave lapped against his shoes. The tide was rising. He looked at his watch and realized that the hour had passed. He would go and get his photographs. He jaywalked back across the street and passed the post office, crossed the parking lot, and returned to the photo lab. He paid $16.38 for double prints of the twenty-three photographs and started flipping through them as he wandered back to his car. He studied the photographs of the Hispanic men, the driver, and the two that had been dropped off. Then he studied the ones of the compound and the FBI windbreakers as they scaled the walls. The photographs told him nothing. He dropped thirty-five cents into a newspaper vending box and purchased the daily edition of the *Oakland Tribune*. Turning to section D, he looked at the movie listings. *True Lies* was playing in forty-five minutes in Hayward. Arnold Schwarzenegger was one of his must-see three, and Jake was feeling depressed, so he decided to drive down and take in a movie while he continued to think.

Forty minutes later he paid seven dollars for a ticket and two dollars and fifty cents for a Diet Pepsi. "Highway robbery," he muttered to himself as he walked in and sat in the back row. It was a weeknight, but there were several groups of teenagers in the theater throwing popcorn and ice at one another and making noise. They laughed loudly and tried to strut coolly as they exited to the bathrooms during the show. Jake hardly noticed them. He was mesmerized by the picture. Arnold, as always, was larger than life. Toward the end of the movie, in the group of terrorists surrounding the nuclear device, Jake suddenly saw the man. He took out his photographs and flipped to the one of the driver. He looked back at the screen and watched. A few minutes later he saw the same man get shot by Jamie Lee Curtis. It was the driver. He ran out to the lobby and got a pen from the girl at the concession stand. Fifteen minutes later he furiously scanned the credits and wrote a name on his ticket stub.

He walked out of the theater and scurried unnoticed to the other theater that was playing the movie. He watched the end of it again and reviewed the credits. Certain that he had picked the correct name, he ran back to the concession stand and gave the girl back her pen. "Thank you," he called as he ran headlong out of the theater.

He drove to the McDonald's down the street and stood at the pay phone. "Hello, Lieutenant Allen? This is Jake Weichert. Yes, Clarence's friend. I need an address for Federico Martínez. And anything else you can give me on him. I'll be at the Days Inn, Room 209." He gave him the number and hung up.

-103- *August 28, 1994, San Francisco, California*

Roy was watching the interrogation through the one-way mirror. He was nursing a cup of coffee and wishing that they had found something at Gregor's house. They had been questioning the Russian for five hours. He hadn't told them anything.

He was impressed with the team conducting the interview. Special Agent Anne Price was in charge. Special Agent John Pollard was her assistant. It was a textbook interrogation, combining an easygoing building of intimacy by the female agent and the hard-nosed questioning by the male agent. It was good cop/bad cop with a twist. In real life, Pollard was the easygoing one, Price the meticulous one.

Other aspects of the questioning were also well orchestrated. The room contained no pictures or other distractions. Gregor's chair was lower than Price's, and Pollard always stood. Gregor was not allowed to stand. The interview had begun with generalities and small talk. It had started out nonthreatening, with Price attempting to establish rapport. The rules of proxemics had been observed perfectly. The interviewers had begun the questioning at a comfortable distance, well out of Gregor's personal space. As the interrogation progressed, Pollard began to draw nearer to the Russian. For a psychologically normal person, it becomes increasingly more difficult to lie when an interviewer invades his space. It was all by the book, but Gregor was not psychologically normal. He was Russian, a prisoner in a labor camp, sentenced without trial. He never blinked an eye at the FBI's "psychological pressure." He might have blinked if they had beaten him—but only blinked.

Roy observed it all with growing anger. Gregor was not telling them anything, verbally or nonverbally. He gave them not the slightest clue as to whether he was telling the truth or lying. He didn't drum his fingers or cross his arms or blink his eyes too much. Nothing. He even feigned a lack of knowledge of English during the interview. It slowed the pace. Roy knew that Gregor's English was perfect. He had heard him talking with his lawyer.

The team's only restriction during the interview was that they were not, under any circumstances, to reveal the existence of the bugs or the computer surveillance. They could let Gregor know about the tap, but only in the context of the single nonencrypted conversation that they had on tape. If they had to release him, which it appeared that they would, it was important not to lose the surveillance tools that they had in place. Time was of the essence, and they could not afford to start over. Not with three to six kilograms of plutonium somewhere in the underworld. It was almost comic. *He is like Al Capone*, Roy thought. *Well, maybe we can nail the bastard on tax evasion, if nothing else.*

"Mr. Viktorovich, can you explain why those men came to your house?"

"Oh, I do not know. I think to do yard work. Isn't that what most of them do in your country?" Gregor gave the interrogator a toothy smile. "Da, that is what most do, eh?" He laughed.

Pollard did not smile. He was finally ready to drop his bombshell. "Mr. Viktorovich, would it surprise you to learn that the men who came to visit you yesterday were emissaries of a Colombian terrorist organization and that their stated intention was to arrange an exchange of goods with you?" Roy nodded behind his mirror. The interrogator was good. Gregor was better, however.

"That would surprise me much!" Gregor exclaimed. "Ha! You cannot get good help, eh?" He laughed heartily.

"I am glad to see that you find this so amusing, Mr. Viktorovich. The men who came to your house have stated that they are members of a Colombian terrorist organization," Pollard said sharply. He was having a hard time staying calm.

"Oh, I am not amusing," Gregor said seriously. "This is great country. I, an innocent man, cannot be made to say things that are not true here. You do not hook me up to wall socket or beat me to make me confess. This is great country." He smiled a toothy smile again.

Pollard took a deep breath, looked at Price, and continued. "Mr. Viktorovich, what does 'pick them up at 3:42' mean?"

"I do not understand." Gregor shrugged his shoulders.

"Mr. Viktorovich, we have you on the phone saying 'pick them up at 3:42.' What does it mean?"

"Oh, yes. Their boss called me and asked when to pick them up. I said, 'Pick them up at three forty-two.' " Gregor smiled at Special Agent Price, who was saying nothing and throwing a disapproving look at her "heavy-handed" partner. She would play the good cop until the end.

"There is a problem with that, Mr. Viktorovich. He never returned. Did you manage to warn him off in any way?" Pollard asked.

"Well, you pick us all up earlier, eh?" Gregor laughed and looked at Roy through the one-way mirror. The Russian winked, pursed his lips, and kissed toward the mirror.

"He's making fun of us," Roy said to himself as his face turned red with anger.

104

August 28, 1994, Los Angeles, California

JAKE WAS AMAZED at Los Angeles. It seemed as though the town was wall-to-wall automobiles. Interstate 5 was bumper to bumper. He took the exit off the freeway and drove across the concrete jungle until he reached the Long Beach area. Finally, he located the cheap apartment complex, pulled into the parking lot, and settled in to watch. He was waiting to see when Federico Martínez, former juvenile offender gone straight except for several speeding tickets in the previous twelve months, would arrive home. He just wanted to see what he was up against. You can never tell from the silver screen, and he had only seen the man sitting in the car when he had photographed him. He had the license plate number and the make of the car, a 1974 Plymouth Fury four-door model with an Earl Scheib $129 special making it candy-apple red. He didn't think that he could miss it.

Two hours later the Fury pulled into the lot and parked across from Jake's rented Ford Escort. A small, well-built Hispanic man got out of the driver's seat. Jake recognized him. He had his man. Martínez was the last link in the chain to tie him back to whoever had murdered Diana. The actor was about five feet, six inches tall, but muscular. He obviously lifted weights. He bent and opened the rear door, taking out two brown paper bags of groceries. Wrapping his arms around the two bags, he backed up and shut the door with his foot and headed up the stairs to his apartment. On the second floor concrete walkway he paused, balancing his groceries with one arm and leaning against the bricks, extracted the keys from his pocket, unlocked the door, and entered. Thirty seconds later, Jake saw an overhead light go on through the open curtains.

"If it comes to it, I can take him," Jake said to himself as he started the car and drove out of the parking lot. He turned onto the street and drove to a BP gas station. The green aura of a BP station at night always left him feeling as though he were standing on an alien world. He pulled up to a public phone booth and got out of the car. He took out Clarence's phone card and dialed a number in the 510 area code.

"Hello," a man's voice answered.

"John, this is Jake. I've got my man in LA."

"Great. Have you approached him yet?"

"No. That's why I'm calling you, John. Can you take the day off and be the San Francisco regional FBI office for me?"

"Jake, San Francisco has a different area code."

"Oh." Jake thought that it was the same. "What about the Oakland Office? Have they got one?"

"They've got a satellite office," Allen replied.

"Can you be that for me?" Jake asked, concerned.

"Yeah, I suppose so, Jake," Allen said with mild amusement.

-105-

August 28, 1994, San Francisco, California

SAMUEL ROSS was a bundle of nerves. Some who knew him might have said that he was paranoid, which accounted for his bad case of the jitters. He would have told them that he wasn't paranoid at all—half the world really was out to get him. In reality, Samuel had a lot to be nervous about. He was Gregor Viktorovich's chief legal counsel. He had been kicking himself for years for accepting the job. He had few illusions about his fate if he couldn't get Gregor out of jail and back to business as usual at his compound. He would have an accident. Paranoia doesn't help you when a guy like Gregor is out to get you.

The guards led him through a series of steel doors, with wire mesh-inlaid windows, that slammed shut behind him. The sounds seemed to echo as he approached the prisoner interview room, where he would be allowed to consult with his client over the speaker through the window. As he was brought into the room he saw Gregor seated in his prison jumpsuit on the other side of the partition. He looked calm and collected, more like a confident Wild West gambler than an inmate waiting for his legal wizard.

Samuel took his seat with a trembling hand and put a file on the desk in front of him. "How are you doing, Gregor?"

Gregor smiled broadly and lifted his hands in a shrug. "Fine. The food is good." His smile faded. "When do I get to go home?"

Samuel looked down at his file. "Tomorrow, I think. They have nothing to hold you."

"Why 'tomorrow, you think'? Why don't you know?" Gregor asked gruffly.

"They should drop the charges tomorrow. It is complicated. Day after tomorrow at the latest."

"Tomorrow," Gregor said emphatically.

"Okay, tomorrow," Samuel replied. He didn't know what else to say in the face of Gregor's demand. He knew that the Feds were at this hour going over Gregor's tax records. It was a recent development, apparently Special Agent Dobkins's idea. Samuel had prepared all of it. If Gregor didn't get out tomorrow, it would fall into his lap. Those records had been his responsibility. He felt a shiver go down his spine.

"I have a message for dear Ivan. Make a note of this, please. It will comfort him in our time of trial. Tell him that I have faith that justice will prevail. He should look at Luke 4:2. The Good Book can tell us all."

Samuel scribbled down the note, looking curiously at Gregor. The man had never read the Bible or any other religious book. He had openly scoffed at every religious belief that he had ever come into contact with. The only religion in Gregor's life was written on his visa request form, where he had lied that he was a Baptist.

-106-   *August 29, 1994, Los Angeles, California*

JAKE CLIMBED THE STEPS to the concrete landing of the second floor. He strode up to the door of Apartment 22 and knocked solidly three times. There was no response. He knocked solidly again. He heard a tread of feet inside and the doorknob turn. The door came open three inches and Jake could see four chains at different levels go taut as the dark face of Federico Martínez peered out. His eyes were watery. Jake had obviously awakened him.

"Mr. Martínez?" Jake queried officially.

"Yeah, what's it to you?" Martínez replied testily.

Jake pulled the FBI identification from his back pocket and passed it through the opening in the door. "My name is Special Agent John Wren, Mr. Martínez. I would like to have a few words with you."

"What, you work with that Cassius guy?" Martínez's voice was a hoarse whisper.

"I'm sorry, sir. That is not a name known to me." Jake tried to sound like what he thought an FBI agent would sound like.

Martínez's eyes narrowed. "What office are you from, man?"

"Oakland regional," Jake replied. He was inwardly starting to worry. Why would it matter what office he was from?

"And you don't know the guys from San Fran, man? What's up with that, huh?" He shut the door and Jake heard the chains being unlatched inside. The door opened all the way and he let Jake in. "I guess you are okay, man. Are you in on the sting?" He motioned for Jake to sit down on the sleeper sofa.

"You mentioned a sting, Mr. Martínez. Could you please elaborate?"

"You don't know, man?" The actor's eyes narrowed again with suspicion. He looked once more at Jake's ID. "This is not like the other agent, man. You got another ID?" Jake reached into his back pocket as Martínez turned away from him and entered the efficiency apartment's kitchen. He opened an old Frigidaire and pulled out two cans of Coca-Cola. He walked back over to Jake and handed him the Coke in exchange for the driver's license. "Have one, man. Breakfast of champions, you know." He looked at the California driver's license and passed it back to Jake. He popped the lid of his cola with a hiss. "Okay," he said simply. "Why are you here?"

"Mr. Martínez, you were spotted outside the villa of Gregor Viktorovich two days ago. You dropped off two men. Why?"

"I don't know, man. It's supposed to be secret and compart-mentalized. Yeah, that's the word. Compartmentalized. It's your operation, man. Why don't you call San Fran and ask them?"

A bead of sweat formed on the back of Jake's neck and ran down his back. This was making him nervous, but he had no choice but to go forward with his ruse. From where he saw things the chain of events stopped with Martínez. If he couldn't get a lead from here, that was it. He would have to go home. Was it possible that Martínez was working for the FBI? No. They didn't recruit civilians, did they? *No, this isn't a dime-store novel,* Jake thought. He decided what to do and said, "So, you say that you were working for the FBI two days ago in south Oakland. Is that a true statement?"

"Yeah, man. Call Special Agent Cassius at the San Francisco Office. He'll tell you."

"You said that this other FBI agent's identification was differ-ent than mine. How was it different?"

Martínez's eyes rolled slightly up and to the left. "He had the picture, right? But it didn't have that little seal in the plastic over it. His badge was different, too. It just said 'Special Agent' on it. No little eagle, like yours."

Jake was thinking as fast as he could. Someone else had posed as an FBI agent for Martínez. There was some kind of plot afoot that was well beyond him. "Mr. Martínez, I assure you that my credentials are in order. The man who you talked to before was a fake."

"What?" The actor looked extremely doubtful. "He had this fancy office in San Francisco, and we got paid with government checks, man. Mine didn't bounce, if you know what I mean. Maybe you are the fake. I didn't know the Bureau let you have ponytails, man." He motioned toward Jake's hair.

"I assure you that I am quite real, Mr. Martínez. We have to blend in. Can't always do that with a crew cut any more." Jake's mind was racing. "Did this other agent have your record? What did he know about you?"

"He picked me out of a casting line, man. It was secret, you know."

Jake began a little recital. "Federico no-middle-name Martínez, born June 27, 1966, age twenty-eight. Parents both illegal aliens. You are an American citizen by virtue of your birth in this country. First arrested at age fifteen for burglary. Two months at juvenile hall. Next arrest at age sixteen for assault and battery. Four months in juvenile detention. Next arrest at age seventeen for burglary, again, four months in juvenile detention. Next arrest at age eighteen, armed robbery. Sentenced to five years at the state penitentiary. Served two years. Paroled in 1988. Flawless record while on parole. Since that time you have worked as an actor and a construction worker. You have received twelve speeding tickets in the last eight years, three in the last twelve months. In general, you appear to have thoroughly reformed yourself and have become a more or less useful member of society. Is that all correct?" Jake smiled. "It's from memory. I'd have to go back to the office to look at the file if I missed something." He had recited verbatim what Lieutenant Allen had told him on the phone the previous day. He had written it all down on yellow Post-it notes in the morning and had reviewed them last night.

Martínez's mouth dropped open. "Yeah, that's right, man! How do you know all that?"

Jake knew that he now had control of the situation. He took on a serious, condescending tone. "Mr. Martínez, the real FBI keeps records and has access to police files." He handed Federico a blank card with a telephone number on it. "Call this number."

Federico dialed 1-510 and the seven digits of the number. Jake could hear Lieutenant Allen's gruff voice on the phone, which was against the actor's ear. "Federal Bureau of Investigation, Oakland Field Office. May I help you?"

Federico hung up. "Okay, man. I believe you. You're legit."

"It appears that you are involved in some kind of illegal conspiracy. It is apparent to me that you are not aware of this. Things will go better for you if you cooperate. I am certain that I can help you, if you help me."

Martínez collapsed. "I don't want to go back to jail, man. I never want to go back there. I'll tell you everything." His face screwed up as if in agony. "Man, do you know what happens to little guys like me . . . you know . . . in the pen? Fuck, man, I'm not going back there! I'm not going to be nobody's bitch."

Jake nodded in understanding and watched as the actor stood up and walked past him. From behind the couch, he extracted a hand-held cellular phone and a black box with an on/off switch, a green light, and a probe which extended about a foot from the box. He set the two items on the coffee table in front of them. "This was how the sting was supposed to go down, man."

-107-   *August 29, 1994, San Francisco, California*

SPECIAL AGENT ROY DOBKINS sat morosely across from the special-agent-in-charge, making his report. "It doesn't make any sense. We know that those guys were there to broker a deal. We know that Gregor has something illegal to sell. The E-mail explicitly identifies the merchandise as weapons-grade plutonium. But we can't keep the bastard in jail."

"I know. It's frustrating. The Constitution is, at times, a very annoying document," Harry Trasker said in mock recrimination. "Has anyone contacted our terrorists?"

"No," Dobkins replied dejectedly. "They said that nobody would contact them if they were taken by either side. They looked all through the rogues' gallery downstairs and didn't spot their 'Special Agent Cassius.' The guy is a fucking ghost."

"Tap their phones?"

"Yes, we tapped their phones, hooked recorders to their cellular phones. Got them, their houses, their cars under surveillance. Making them wear wires. Direction finders on their cars and in their shoes. Those guys are walking, talking Circuit Cities,

Harry. Not a peep. Not a fucking peep. It's a dead end. It just burns my ass that we have to let that Russian hood go."

"Nothing in his tax records?"

"Nothing. That little bastard who does his accounting and lawyering is pretty good. He soaked his suit through with sweat while we were going over everything. He knows that Gregor will have his ass if there is anything on paper that is out of order."

"Nothing else that we can hold him on?"

"Nothing. If that little bastard lawyer was on his toes he would have realized that the seizure of the financial records was illegal. It isn't on the warrant."

"What?"

"We fucked up, Harry. We were in a hurry. We just got a free fishing expedition."

"Damn."

"Harry, you don't think that some terrorists would really set off a nuke, do you?" Dobkins looked nervous.

The special-agent-in-charge sighed. "Well, we've read all the profiles. Most of these guys are trying to get sympathy and support. You don't get that when you set off a nuke. You and your group and your group's grandmothers get hunted down like animals by all the civilized powers. It doesn't make sense to use a nuke for terrorism. It just doesn't make sense. But . . ."

"Yes, but. It's a big but, I know," Dobkins said.

"There just could be some wacko faction out there that doesn't care about the consequences. That's the 'but' that we have to concern ourselves with."

"Nobody hunted down Beta Cell."

"If they had used a nuke in the World Trade Center, I think that things would have been pretty ugly," Trasker said.

"One of two things needs to happen for us to nail Gregor and Cassius. One of them is that Arnold downstairs breaks the other half of the E-mail and we get a bead on where the stuff is. The other is that we can catch the exchange. Apparently, it has not happened yet."

-108-

SAMUEL AND GREGOR walked down the courthouse steps. Though in no way a throng, a group of about ten reporters waited for the men. They were mostly from local print and radio, but there was one mobile television crew. The small group ran up the steps toward Samuel and Gregor as they exited the building. The judge had dismissed the charges on insufficient evidence. As the first breathless reporter reached the pair, Samuel held out a restraining hand and said, "My client is innocent and has no comment."

The two continued their descent, and the reporters, not to be thwarted, followed. The cameraman ran ahead, filming the famous Russian mafia figure. One of the reporters shouted, "Isn't it true, Mr. Viktorovich, that you do not reside in Russia because you have spent time in jail there, under the old Soviet regime, and that you feel that it is easier to operate your criminal enterprises from this country?"

Gregor turned to face the microphones and camera. "I do have one statement to make. I am an honest businessman. I live in this country because your free enterprise system allows businessmen to prosper like no other system in the world. You have a great country. I was vindicated today. I was not found 'not guilty'—I was found innocent. Today, I go home a free man, in a free country, to resume my business. Thank you." He turned from the reporters and walked to a waiting Mercedes, driven by Constantine. He and his lawyer stepped in, sat, and closed their doors.

"Get me away from these idiots," Gregor muttered. Constantine smoothly eased the vehicle away from the curb and into the evening rush hour.

-109-

"MAN, THEY MUST NOT give you guys shit for travel allowance," Federico commented as they got into Jake's rented Ford Escort.

"True, true," Jake said by way of apology.

He started up the little car and they drove out of the parking lot. Federico began to navigate. "It's on Spence Avenue. It's number 4009. Security Do-It-Yourself Storage. I haven't been there to check the stuff out because I'm not supposed to know shit, you know? Anyway, the place must have a touchpad to get in because Cassius gave me this slip." He held it up for Jake to read. Penned in a childish block print was "#4009#1988*"

"Yes, you're right, Mr. Martínez. Looks like a touchpad code."

Thirty minutes later, the Escort pulled off Spence Avenue and Jake could see the rows of identical concrete sheds with roll-up metal doors through the gate. There was a touchpad on the driver's side before the gate and Jake tapped in what was written on the paper. The gate started to slide open. He drove through and it slid shut behind him. He turned left and drove down the first row of sheds. The numbers were in the hundreds, so at the end of the row he took a right and drove past the end of seven rows and took another right. Shed 4009 was the fifth on the left, and he pulled up beside it. He killed the engine and got out. Federico got out of the passenger side.

There was a combination lock on the latch for the rolling door. Federico turned to Jake and handed him another slip of paper with a combination on it. Jake looked at the paper, turned the dial of the master lock several times, and pulled at the base. It didn't open. He tried it again, and on the second attempt the lock snapped open. He removed it from the latch and rolled the door up.

Inside the shed was a crate covered with a tarp. Jake pulled the tarp off and saw that the crate was labeled, "Vacuum-packed Meals. No refrigeration required. Count 144." He walked back out to the car and popped the trunk. He returned with a jack handle that was pointed at one end like a crowbar for the bygone days when all cars had hubcaps. The Escort had none. He jammed the handle into the lid of the crate and heaved. It gave, and he moved to the other side and repeated the procedure. Then he loosened the other two sides, dropped the metal handle, and lifted the lid off. Inside were boxes that were labeled like the crate as vacuum-packed meals. He lifted out a box and put it on the concrete floor of the storage shed. He pulled open the top and removed a silver-wrapped package marked in English, French, German, and Spanish, "Vacuum-packed chicken meal. No refrigeration required."

Jake examined the package as Federico spoke. "Looks like I was gonna trade chicken dinners for something, man." He started to laugh.

Jake drew a knife from the sheath on his belt at his back and unfolded it. He stabbed the package and heard the small rush of air from breaking the vacuum. He pulled the foil apart slightly and saw another package inside. It was wrapped in a distinctive brown paper covered with red and yellow dots. He cut into the paper wrapping and saw white powder in the gap. Jake had never seen cocaine before. He didn't know what to expect, but he remembered that he was supposed to be an FBI agent, so he did what he had seen FBI agents do on television. He licked his pinkie finger and stuck it into the powder and touched it to his tongue. It wasn't sugar, salt, or flour. He knew what they tasted like. The spot on his tongue became numb.

Federico looked down at the package and exhaled loudly. "Holy shit, man! This must be a million dollars' worth of the shit! We'd better get outta here! The muchachos who move this stuff are not to be fucked with."

-110-

August 30, 1994, San Francisco, California

IVAN YURCHENKO had been in trouble with the law since he was nine years old. The son of an alcoholic father, he had first been arrested in Leningrad while breaking into a state-owned store. That had been in 1979. After that, his home had been a series of juvenile detention and training centers, Soviet-style. If he had been a little older, he would have made his way east in a train to a labor camp for extreme antisocial behavior and right deviation. But he had not been older. He had been a child. During one of his unauthorized outings from a training center on the outskirts of Moscow, he had first run into the Dark Path. He had seen a group of men breaking into a state-run pharmacy, and after they had left with several crates of morphine in the back of their Ladas, he had followed them. His résumé of crime had impressed the organization, and he was taken in.

Initially, he was not trusted. No one was trusted. He had to work his way up through the ranks. His career with the Dark Path had begun at Pavilion Four in the Exhibition of Economic Achievements complex in north Moscow, off the Mira Prospekt. There, he operated as a pickpocket, taking wallets and purses from unsuspecting tourists in the shadow of the world-famous statue of "The Worker and the Kolkhozina." From there he had moved into the ranks of what are currently called the *gopota*, or the young men who act as muscle for a low-level, street-corner mafia executive. Next, he ran the street corner, skimming 10 percent off the top from a city block and shaking down taxi drivers with the help of his boys. After that, he took control of several black-market *obmen valuta*, or currency exchanges. At this point, the Dark Path decided that he was the genuine article. They gave him control of the supply of hookers and drugs to foreigners in the upscale Hotel Metropol. By this time, communism had fallen and the battle for the banks had begun. The Dark Path needed to protect its money-laundering infrastructure, and Ivan had personally seen to the execution of three Moscow bankers. Ivan's last job before Gregor elected to whisk him away to the United States was the brutal murder of the bank manager of Novo Zigursk.

That odyssey left Ivan standing at the corner of Union and Hyde streets in the doorway of a grocery store, next to a phone booth. The trembling lawyer had delivered Gregor's message, and Ivan had known what to do. He had driven to a B. Dalton bookstore and looked at a Bible. He found that Luke was the third

book of the New Testament. That meant the third phone booth
on a predetermined list. "Four" meant Thursday, the fourth day of
the workweek. "Two" meant to be there at 2 P.M. It was 1:55 on
Thursday and Ivan was waiting for his phone call. He knew that
Gregor was out of prison, but he had not gone to the villa. Gregor
had always stressed that no deals could go down from the villa.
The terrorists had been an aberration planned by another party.
The results of that aberration were plain to see.

At 2 P.M. the pay telephone rang and Ivan picked it up. "Hello."

"This is Alberto," Federico Martínez said on the other end of
the line. When Gregor had told Martínez to pick up the men at
3:42, it had said the same thing to the "terrorist" that it had told
Ivan. Martínez continued. "You have an address for me?"

"Yes, and you have one for me?"

The prearranged code phrases exchanged, the two men talked.

"I'll see you in the morning," Ivan said, and hung up.

·111·

August 30, 1994, FBI Regional Office,
San Francisco, California

DEWITT ARNOLD ran his fingers through his hair and stared at the
computer. It was dutifully running a dictionary scan on the
passphrase for Cassius's secret key. Word after word automatically
zipped from the database and was rejected. After the dictionary
scan, he would run a phonetic misspelling check, then a check of
famous quotations. He had 600 megabytes of quotations. After
that, he would run a proper names check and a historical figures
check. Then he would run the data from several library CDs. It
was complicated.

If the passphrase was "the truth shall set you free," say, he would
probably find it. A simple change in this easily remembered phrase
would not give him the key. "The truth shall set you free" was not
the same as "THE TRUTH SHALL SET YOU FREE" or "The

Truth Shall Set You Free," or "thetruthshallsetyoufree." He would have to write three programs and go through his entire database three times before he hit the correct combination—if it was any of them.

"What if this guy chose a truly random passphrase?" Dewitt muttered to himself. He pictured something like "jJkd9fnjdsp))9." He would never find that. And if he never found it, they would never nail Gregor. More important, they wouldn't find the plutonium until the bad guys wanted them to. The computer expert sighed and began writing a program to push the text from *The Library of the Future* CD through the passphrase.

·112·   *September 1, 1994, Los Angeles, California*

AS LUCK WOULD HAVE IT, the two storage facilities were only three miles apart in the urban wasteland of Long Beach. Before one shed stood Federico Martínez, posing as Alberto, and a pasty-faced Russian named Andrei. Several miles away, in front of another rolling metal door, stood Roberto, one of the three terrorists remaining in the operation, and Ivan. Ivan and Federico were both holding hand-held Motorola cellular phones. They were speaking to one another in English, the international language of business, trade, and crime.

"The combination, please," Ivan said into his phone.

"0-2-32," Martínez told him. "The combination, please," he said in turn.

"0-22-04," Ivan mouthed into his phone. "Hand the phone to Andrei."

"Very well, hand the phone to Roberto."

Andrei and Roberto confirmed that the sheds were being unlocked. Both were armed to protect their merchandise in the event of a double cross. Federico noted with trepidation Andrei's black Heckler & Koch MP-5 slung carelessly under his arm. There was a certain amount of honor among thieves, but guns were the Lloyd's of London of the black market. Insurance. Both could hear the scraping of metal rollers in their tracks over the cellular link as the two sheds were opened almost simultaneously.

Ivan walked into his shed with a crowbar and tore the top off the crate. He saw the vacuum-packed dinners and removed four boxes at random. He returned to his car and retrieved a briefcase from the trunk. Roberto reached menacingly into his jacket, where the semiautomatic pistol rested. Ivan raised his hands in surrender. "It's just a little chemistry set, my friend. I must test my product before the trade is final."

Roberto motioned for him to take it into the shed. Ivan set the briefcase on the ground and opened it. Inside were a propane burner, several test tubes, a small measuring spoon, and two chemical bottles. He placed the test tubes in a rack and measured out a dry chemical with the spoon and dropped it into the bottom of each test tube. From the other bottle he transferred with a pipette 2 milliliters of clear liquid into the test tubes with the dry chemical. He opened four dinners from the boxes that he had chosen at random and spooned out a tiny amount of powder from each, dropping it into the test tubes. Then he ignited the burner and heated the test tubes one by one. Each turned bright orange, and he grunted with satisfaction. He cut off the gas, walked to the pavement outside the shed, and dumped the hot liquid. "Good," he said, "the deal is done at this end."

Federico's test was easier. He approached his crate, placed the black box on top, slid the probe into a hole, and flipped the ON switch. A few moments later, the green light came on, indicating that he had the correct box. He flipped the switch back to OFF and turned to Andrei: "The deal is done at this end." Andrei relayed the message and put the phone on the ground. "Enjoy," he said, and walked to his rented car to leave.

Two hours later, back at his apartment, Federico pulled aside the curtain and placed a Pepsi can on top of a 7-Up can on the window ledge. The pair of cans would be visible from the street and the apartment parking lot. They were the signal to Federico's controller that the swap had been made. He would receive a telephone call to turn over the location, and then he would be mailed his last paycheck. Jake sat in the bushes with his camera and a notepad. He would photograph every car and pedestrian that came within sight of the two cans until Federico's phone rang. Two hours later, he had exposed 113 frames on pedestrians and autos that could have received the message, and Federico's telephone rang.

After Federico passed on his message, he rushed out to the bushes to tell Jake. "John, he just called." They were on a first-name basis.

"Thank you, Federico." Jake stood out of his cramped position and rubbed his upper thighs, which had gone numb. He followed the actor back into the apartment and extended his hand. "Thank you, Federico. You have helped me a lot." Then he started to leave. As an afterthought he turned to the erstwhile terrorist and asked, "May I have that black box? I want our lab boys to take a look at it. We may be able to tell something from that radio receiver."

"Sure," Federico said, and bent behind the couch to retrieve it. He handed it to Jake. Then, the FBI agent who was not an FBI agent bid farewell to the terrorist who was not a terrorist.

On the way to the storage shed that contained his quarry's merchandise, Jake made two stops. The first was to a Mail Boxes Etc., where he FedExed the black box to Geery. The second was to a grocery store, where he picked up peanuts, Hershey bars, and Pepsi. Those tasks completed, he headed to Walker's Storage to see who picked up the box that had been exchanged for the cocaine. He wondered whether he should alert the authorities about the cocaine, but he didn't know what kind of web he had become entangled in and what strings were attached where. He just didn't know enough to reveal half of the deal to the authorities. He didn't know how it meshed with the other half and needed to find out more.

Jake was burning inside to go into that shed and see what the box contained. All the evidence that he had gathered suggested that the box was the one that had turned up in his town, had been sunk in his lake, and had gotten five people killed. He desperately wanted to know what was in it. Drugs? He didn't think so. A lot of people are killed over drugs, but mostly insiders: dealers, pushers, mules, law enforcement, and, of course, users. Not too many people who were outside the trade warranted much attention. What was in that box must be extraordinary.

·113·   *September 2, 1994, Los Angeles, California*

JAKE SAT IN HIS CAR sweating. He didn't know how long he was destined to wait for someone to show up at the storage facility and pick up the box, but he was equipped for the duration. He had purchased enough peanuts and Hershey bars so that he could sit outside the facility for days, if it was necessary. It was not.

A U-Haul truck with a picture of the Washington Monument and "AMERICA'S CAPITAL CITY" on its side drove up to the gate just as darkness started to fall. A small, dark-skinned man stepped out of the cab to reach the entry touchpad. When he reached the post, he removed a sheet of paper from his pocket and referred to it as he pressed the numbers. Jake could see him roughly punch the numbers with his stout index finger and then look expectantly at the gate. It began to slide open, and he stepped back up into the cab. When the gate was fully open, he gunned the engine and moved the truck down the line of sheds immediately before him. The driver eased halfway down the row, carefully noting the numbers on the doors, and came to a halt just past number 1957.

Jake's heart started to beat rapidly. This could be his man. He watched intently as the driver got out of the truck and walked to the back. The sliding door on the rear of the truck clanked up–

ward as the man lifted it. He leapt up onto the bed, lowered the loading ramp, and disappeared into the darkness inside. A few seconds later, he pushed out a two-wheeled dolly with straps and rolled it down the ramp. He was whistling "Objects in the Rear View Mirror are Closer than They Appear," a popular song from the previous summer by Meat Loaf. Jake recognized it. Diana had listened to it repeatedly on her radio.

The man rolled the dolly over to Shed 1957, still whistling, and pulled the paper from his shirt pocket again. He grasped the combination lock and started to turn the rotors.

Eight hours later, Jake was still behind the U-Haul truck as it took an exit off Route 880 and drove into a community in Hayward. The driver had pulled over once at a truck stop off Interstate 5 to buy gas and two Pepsis, taking no notice whatsoever of Jake. While he had been inside, Jake had quickly photographed the truck from behind, front, and both sides, ensuring that the license plate was in good focus.

The truck entered a housing development of small, single-family homes priced in the $150,000s, which was rock bottom for the entire San Francisco Bay area, each located on a quarter-acre lot. The driver stopped and backed up the driveway of one of the houses. From his car Jake noticed the "FOR SALE" sign, which had a "SOLD" sticker affixed diagonally across it. There were no lights on in the house. The driver got out of his truck and walked to the rear. A few minutes later, Jake could hear grating inside the truck as the crate was loaded on the dolly and the creak of the wheels as it was rolled down the ramp and into the driveway. The driver opened the garage door and rolled the crate inside. A few moments later he came back out and locked the door. Jake watched as he walked to the front door, lifted the doormat, dropped the key underneath, and then tossed the dolly and ramp into the back of the truck and returned to the cab. Starting the engine, he pulled out of the driveway. Jake did not follow him. He could only be in one place at a time, and it would be with the box. Having been awake for over twenty-four hours, Jake slid into the back seat and went to sleep, his head crooked in his arm. For the first time in many nights, he had no nightmares. He was too tired.

-114-

"I THINK WE MAY HAVE a composite of Cassius," Roy Dobkins said breathlessly as he entered Harry Trasker's office.

"Don't we already have one?" the special-agent-in-charge asked, genuinely mystified. "Do you know where he is?"

"No. But I know where he might have been." Dobkins looked self-satisfied. "Remember when I told you about the Agency's source in Vladivostok?"

"Yes."

"Well, another one of this guy's reports came across my desk three days ago, all blacked out so that it was essentially useless, but it did say one thing—that Special Agent John Wren had shown up unofficially and had snooped around." Dobkins cracked his knuckles. "Well, I wondered what Agent Wren was doing in Vladivostok, so I looked the guy up. Turns out the guy is dead. Killed on the job during a kidnapping investigation ten years ago. We never got his ID back, but you don't go pestering widows about IDs after they've buried their husbands. We forgot about it. The Walker case was rolling and it got lost in the wake."

"So what does this lost ID have to do with Cassius?" Trasker asked.

"Well, it could have a lot to do with Cassius. This guy could *be* Cassius. Cassius impersonated an FBI agent for those actors. Cassius found Gregor. Cassius may be checking out the operation in Vladivostok. He seems to be a very careful man." Dobkins paused to let that sink in. "Anyway, I called the Agency and got jerked around for a while until I got hold of one Jonathan Wentz, file clerk and agent runner. He owns the source in Vladivostok. He wouldn't tell me who the source is. I told him that I thought it might be Thomas Johnson and he clammed up, but eventually he agreed to send an Agency sketch artist around incognito. Wentz faxed me this today." He handed a sketch over the table to Trasker.

"Cassius has a ponytail, huh? This is different from the composite that we got from the actors. The notes say dark brown hair and blue eyes. The actors said stringy white-blond hair, short, and blue eyes. These are two different guys."

"Exactly, Harry. Cassius could be an organization. I think that this guy is involved." He tapped an index finger on Jake's forehead.

-115-

September 3, 1994, Hayward, California

JAKE AWAKENED TO SEE sunlight streaming through the eastward-facing windows of his car. He looked at his watch—7:20 A.M. He had slept only three hours, but he felt good. It had been a solid sleep, the sleep of the dead, without dreams. He sat up in his car to look at the house where the box had been dropped. In the daylight, it was a cheerful little A-frame with an attached garage painted light blue with white trim. The garage was large enough to accommodate two automobiles, but Jake didn't see any through its windows. There were no cars in the driveway, either. He noticed that there were no curtains or blinds in the front windows. He decided to take a closer look.

He walked to the front door and knocked. He hadn't thought of what he might say if someone opened it. His heart accelerated and he decided that he would tell the suburban housewife in her nightgown that he was looking for Clarence's house. No sleepy-eyed housewife answered the door, so he started to take a look around. He lifted the welcome mat and noticed a set of keys underneath. He replaced the mat and looked again at the picture windows in front of the house.

The paint that had spilled onto the glass had not been scraped off. When he looked through the window, he saw that there was no furniture in the house. The walls were unpainted, buff-white

Sheetrock and the empty floors were unfinished wood. As far as he could tell, no one lived here. He walked over to the garage and cupped his hand over his eyes as he peered inside. He could see the box in the middle of the concrete floor, beside a post that ran from the center of the floor up to the ceiling. Farther back in the garage there was a large object under a sheet about the size of a small automobile, but the shape was wrong. It jutted out and up and had slopes and curves in all of the wrong places. Jake was trying to figure out what it might be when he heard a car drive by the house. He turned rapidly and saw that it was one of the automobiles parked in a driveway three houses down. Someone was beginning her commute to work.

Jake figured that it would be worth the risk to leave the house for an hour and contact Lieutenant Allen. He needed to get some license plates traced and his film developed. He ambled back to the house and pocketed the keys. Then he drove to Southland Plaza, which was the nearest mall he saw from the freeway. He dropped off the four rolls at an Hour Photo and found a phone booth.

Allen answered the phone. "Oakland Police Department, Narcotics, Lieutenant Allen speaking."

"This is Jake."

"What can I do for you, Jake?"

"I've got 114 plates that I would like you to run. I just want name, address, vehicle description."

"Oh, is that all?" Allen said morosely. "Sure you don't want me to play the Oakland office of the CIA today?"

"Hey, it worked, okay?" Jake answered.

"Seriously, though. Need anything else?" Allen asked.

"Well, if any of their DMV records indicate that they are criminals and killers, you could pass that on."

"One hundred and fourteen? What have you been doing? You just going after a random guy now?"

"No, John. This is legit. One of those plates should be the customer. I'll explain it to you later. I've got to get back."

Allen pulled out a pen and a yellow legal pad from his desk drawer. "Okay, shoot."

Five minutes later he had recorded all 114 plate numbers on his pad. Allen sat at his desk, trying to think of which investigation to toss this plate ID under. He couldn't just say that it was for Clarence's friend, the vigilante. Thinking of no investigation under which he could reasonably explain the data search, he picked up the phone and made a call. It was to one of the technicians at the Department of Motor Vehicles.

The technician was a former Oakland PD street cop until he took eight rounds from an Uzi submachine gun in a shoot-out with a gang member on South 94th Street. Allen had helped to secure him the state job with a pension and OPD service time counting toward retirement. Confined to a wheelchair, the young man was grateful to Allen—the computer operator job at DMV had been a good thing

"DMV. System operator."

"Greg, this is John, over at Oakland PD," Allen said.

"John! How are you doing?" Greg asked enthusiastically.

"Greg, listen. This is confidential. I have an informant over on 75th. He gave me some plate numbers going in and out of a dealer's pad down there. Out-of-town people, you know? I'm afraid that I might have a leak in Narcotics, because some of my other informants have been tapped, if you know what I mean. This guy is real important to me, so I'm coming to you direct. Can you help me?"

"What do you need, John?"

"Name, address, make of car."

"Lay the perps' plates on me, baby," Greg said.

-116-   *September 3, 1994, San Francisco, California*

"OKAY. YOU CAN SEND in one minute." Dewitt Arnold hung up the phone and set up his computer to receive the latest intercept from the surveillance team. A few moments later, the screen of his computer filled with the sequential transmission of data. When it was done, he saved the file and called them back. "I got it. Thanks."

"No problem," the team leader said before he went off line.

Arnold brought up the decryption program and ran it on the latest E-mail that Gregor had received. When prompted, he typed in "Thou,too,Brutus?" and saw the message plaintext appear on the screen. When he saw the message, he didn't know what to feel. He picked up the telephone and touched four numbers, dialing the internal extension for Special Agent Dobkins.

"Dobkins," the agent answered.

"Roy, you'd better come down here. More E-mail."

"Okay, Dewitt. On my way."

Five minutes later, both men were staring at the short message.

```
Gregor. Good doing business with you. Your on-
ramp to the cocaine superhighway is Captain Eric
Rollins at Southport Yachts, San Diego. Your
representative should tell him that Cassius sent
him. Adios.

                    Cassius
```

"DEA is going to be happy," Dobkins said. "We can also probably take Gregor down on trafficking if we can tie his representative to him, which we won't be able to do." Arnold didn't say anything. He knew that Dobkins wasn't through. "What this message means is that the trade has gone down. The material has passed from a known player to an unknown player. This is bad, Dewitt. This is bad."

"Want me to forward the tip to the DEA?"

"Yeah, they deserve a floater every now and then. Tell them to knock Captain Cocaine out of the ballpark." Roy walked out of the computer room to return to contemplating the composite sketches of Jake Weichert and Andrew Oliver. It was all he had now.

-117-

THE *AUGUSTINA*, a fifty-thousand-ton freighter of the Maynard Johnson line, was tied to the pier by only two breast and two spring lines. It wasn't going to stay long. It lay beneath a crane which was lowering pallets full of crates into the forward cargo bay. On one of the pallets was a crate numbered 16344. It looked like all of the others.

The ship was being loaded with consumer goods for a starving Russian market. Its next stop, after a rhumb-line transit across the vast blue Pacific, was Vladivostok, where it would be unloaded at the piers of MJTT, which also handled the import/export business of the Johnson line.

On the bill of lading, crate number 16344 was listed as "Vacuum-packed Chicken Dinners," with a side note "no refrigeration required." The interesting thing about this crate was that it did not contain chicken dinners. It had not come from the factory with its cousins but had been delivered to the Johnson warehouse three hours previously by a rented U-Haul truck and placed among similar boxes. The U-Haul had picked up the crate from a storage shed in southern Los Angeles.

-118-

JAKE RETURNED TO THE BLUE AND WHITE HOUSE at about 10 A.M. and placed the key beneath the welcome mat. He walked around and looked into the garage. Everything was as it had been. He went back out to his car and sat down to wait. After an hour, he decided to move the car to a less conspicuous location down the street, where he stayed all day. At about 6:30 P.M. a blue Mercury Tracer pulled into the driveway. The sun was just beginning its descent into the western horizon.

A man got out of the car and looked around. Seemingly satisfied with his cursory inspection, he walked boldly to the front door and lifted the doormat. He bent down, picked up the keys, and stood on the darkening porch, looking around again in the twilight. His long ponytail moved from side to side along his back as he turned his head. Still satisfied, he walked off the porch and around to the garage door. He inserted the key, and Jake saw him lift the handle and go inside, closing the door behind him. A few moments later, Jake could see light streaming under the garage door and through the windows. Shortly afterward, the light was blotted out from each of the windows in rapid succession.

Jake swallowed hard and opened the car door. He had to figure out a way to see what was going on in that garage. He walked silently up the driveway to stand before the door. Roughly cut black poster board had been taped onto each of the windows, and Jake sidled from one to another looking for a crack. In the last pane on the right he found a small half-inch gap between the frame and the cardboard cover, which gave him a limited view of the garage. What he saw inside startled him.

The scene reminded him of the movie, *The Andromeda Strain*. The man wore a baggy white suit with a helmet over his head. The front of the helmet was a clear glass or plastic visor, which allowed the wearer an almost complete range of vision. Jake could see the sweat on the man's brow through his face shield. From the back of the helmet, a rubber line ran out to several air tanks. A regulator was affixed to one of the tanks through which the air feeder line ran.

The man, who looked like a deep-sea diver, walked over to the sheet which covered the oddly shaped object. He pulled it off, and again Jake was amazed. What he saw was a workbench with several bottles of chemicals, glassware, a mortar and pestle, and a machine which resembled a meat slicer. The entire workbench was enclosed in a yellow-tinted, clear plastic bag formed of several pieces joined together. At several points along the bench, sleeves with gloves at the end had been attached to the containment to allow access inside without any physical contact with the interior of the bag. He also noticed that the bag had a single breathing hole linked to a metal can with the letters "HEPA" on it.

Jake stood transfixed at his pinpoint of light, watching the proceedings. The diver (what Jake was calling him in his mind) went over to the crate in the center of the garage and pulled off the lid. From within, he removed a cylindrical container of dull gray metal and carried it over to the containment around the bench. He opened a flap and slid it inside onto the top of the bench. Closing the flap, he walked over to a small red toolbox and opened it, removing an instrument resembling a soldering iron. He walked back to the flap, held the two halves together, and closed the plastic into one piece with the heat sealer.

This done, he hurried to the bench, inserted his arms into the sleevettes, and began to work. Jake watched the whole operation with interest. From the cylindrical gray container, the diver removed a spherical object that was tinted yellow on the outside, about the size of a tennis ball. He placed it in the meat slicer, moved the apparatus gingerly, and removed a slice of the material. Jake could see that underneath the yellow outer coating, the material was silvery gray. The diver inserted this slice into a beaker. Uncapping a brown bottle, he poured a clear liquid into the glassware. The metal dissolved, and the liquid turned red. This process was repeated until the entire sphere of metal was liquefied. He removed a second sphere from the container and painstakingly dissolved it as well. The diver then proceeded to consolidate the liquid that he had generated into four bottles, which he corked. He threaded a cap over each cork.

With his task completed, the diver began to perform a number of odd jobs. He removed a device with some sort of probe and ran it around the outside of the containment. He paid particular attention to what the device indicated when he held it over the can marked "HEPA." Next, he took out a device that resembled a tiny vacuum cleaner, placed it on the floor, and ran it for one minute. He opened up the device and removed a small circle of paper that resembled a coffee filter and placed it under the probe of the device that he had used before. Apparently satisfied, he made a small cut in the plastic of the containment and inserted the tiny vacuum cleaner. After running it again, he removed another filter and put it against the probe. Next, he reached inside the slit that he had cut and ran a piece of filter paper over several surfaces inside the containment and placed it against the probe. He removed his helmet, and Jake could see that he was smiling. The hazel eyes of the nihilist chemist twinkled with delight.

-119-

CLARENCE SAT IN A CHAIR against the wall and observed Geery at work. He was taking apart the black box that Jake had sent them. Jake had said in the note that it was a radio receiver of some sort. He wondered if Geery could tell anything about who made it by breaking it down. Geery was obliging and Clarence was watching.

Geery loved to take things apart and put them back together. He loved to know how things worked. Consequently, he knew a lot about a lot of things. He was unscrewing the faceplate screws from the device. "Looks like this is some sort of homemade jobbie. This is your basic Heathkit put-it-together-yourself box."

"Do you think you'll be able to tell anything from it?"

"Don't know. Just have to see." He removed the last screw and tugged at the faceplate. It pulled to an inch above the box and stopped. Geery reached underneath with thumb and forefinger and turned the nut which held the on/off switch to the faceplate. It fell into the innards of the box and the faceplate came free. Geery could see the circuit board. "Looks like a little programmable read-only memory and a few other odds and ends. Nothing on the circuit board indicates that this is a radio receiver."

"What?" Clarence said. "Then what is it?"

"Dunno. Have to looksee a little more." Geery noted that a single screw held the circuit board in place and selected another jeweler's screwdriver to attack it. A few moments later he removed the circuit board and looked at the back. "Handmade." He pointed to the back of the board for Clarence. "Machines don't make those big solder marks."

"So what is it?"

Geery had already turned his mind again to the inside of the box. "My, my," he said. "What have we here?" He reached a nimble hand into the box and tugged on the wires that descended into the probe. When they came out, there were two cylindrical tubes taped together.

"What is it?"

Geery smiled but had a serious look in his eyes. "This, Clarence, is a Geiger-Müller tube. This other tube looks like some sort of enclosed scintillation detector."

"So what does that mean?"

"Well, it means that this is not a radio receiver, per se. It is a radiac. It detects radiation. I'll have to bench test the board to figure out what levels set off the green light, but this thing lights up in the presence of a certain amount of radiation."

"Holy shit," Clarence muttered.

"No. I would say *un*holy shit."

-120-

September 4, 1994, Hayward, California

JAKE SNOOZED in his car seat. The diver had left the previous evening without any of his equipment and without the bottles. Before he had departed, he had put the key beneath the welcome mat. Jake concluded that another party would be coming to pick up the bottles. He didn't have any sophisticated equipment to alert him if the garage door was raised again in the night, so he slept with his windows open directly across the street and had to hope that the combination of restless sleep in the chill autumn air, any engine noise, and the rumble of the door would wake him. A wave of cumulative exhaustion rolled over him as he closed his eyes, and he slept soundly. He was fortunate that the truck didn't come to pick up the bottles until ten the next morning.

Jake had been awake for two hours and was just beginning to wonder if he could sneak off for a few minutes and get a McDonald's breakfast when the U-Haul pulled into the driveway across from him. It was not the same truck that had delivered the box, although Jake could not tell from his angle what its license tags read. He could see the driver, who was also a different man, go up to the front porch and lift the welcome mat. He grabbed the key and walked to the garage door, where he inserted it and turned the lock. Jake could see him bend down and lift the door roughly. He went into the garage and looked around, allowing his eyes to adjust to the dim light within. He spotted the box into which the diver had placed the flasks the previous evening, bent to pick it up, and carried it to the back of his truck. He balanced the box and its liquid contents precariously on the bumper with his knee as he flung open the rear roller door. He gripped the box with both hands and slid it onto the bed of the truck. Then he hopped up inside, and Jake lost sight of him. A few moments later, he dropped back out of the rear of the truck with the same box. It was empty. He tossed it carelessly into the garage, shut the door, locked it, and walked to the front porch to replace the key under the mat.

As the driver started the engine of the U-Haul, Jake started his own engine. He followed the truck as it left the neighborhood and drove north on Interstate 880 in light midmorning traffic. The truck pulled off the freeway, taking the Martin Luther King exit and entering Berkeley. It turned right onto Shadduck Avenue and continued for a few miles until it took a second right into a suburban neighborhood, where it pulled up to a small, red-brick house surrounded by a white picket fence and came to a halt. The driver got out and disappeared into the back of the truck.

A moment later, he jumped down to the ground and reached into the truck. He emerged holding a two-foot-cube cardboard box and carried it in a bear hug to the front door of the house.

The driver rang the doorbell, and a dark-complexioned man who looked as though he might be Greek or Turkish answered the door. The driver handed him the box and apparently told him to wait as he ran back to the truck and retrieved a clipboard. The dark man signed some papers and closed the front door. As the driver started his truck, Jake flipped a coin. Heads, he would stake out the house. Tails, he would follow the truck. The quarter landed next to him on the seat of his rented car. It was heads, and he stayed. The truck drove off, and Jake waited for something to happen.

At 3 P.M. the man who had signed for the package walked out of his house. He was dressed in a blue pair of coveralls, with the letters SJWTP printed on the back. The man had not taken the box with him, so Jake did not follow him. He decided to add burglary to impersonating a federal officer on his list of misdeeds.

-121-   *September 4, 1994, FBI Headquarters, Washington, DC*

SPECIAL AGENT JENNER stood tall before the Director. The Director was not happy. Neither was Jenner, but she was just doing her job. Her department head stood behind her. He had brought Jenner and her file straight to the top as soon as he had finished reading it two hours previously.

The Director of the Federal Bureau of Investigation, Charles Briar, was staring at the single-page brief before him and again flipped through the rest of the file, examining in a cursory fashion the highlighted portions of telephone records and photocopies of several canceled checks.

"This is bad," Briar said. It was the understatement of the year, and he knew it. This little brief would be the biggest scandal to hit the White House since Watergate. It could quite possibly take down the President. He continued, "Let me see if I understand. Dawson. Senator Dawson. Personal adviser, aide, and confidant of the President of the United States. *That* Dawson?"

"Yes, sir," was all that Jenner could say at the moment.

"How did you happen across this bit of information, Special Agent Jenner?" Briar asked gruffly.

"Sir," Jenner said nervously, "an unsigned letter from a 'concerned citizen' came into the Miami Field Office. They thought that it was a prank, but everybody remembers how the Walker case started out, so people don't flush as many anonymous letters as before. Anyway, they forwarded it to me. I sent a few agents to check out this Jalopi Enterprises in Orlando. They've cleared out, but they left some records, including maps of the assassination sites and a few financial records. The financial records led us back to Dawson. We obtained his telephone records, including his calling card. It reflects ten calls to the offices of Jalopi Enterprises and one recorded call to Colombia. His home telephone records reflect return calls from Jalopi and one collect from Colombia. The canceled checks were obtained and show that he contributed $20,000 to Jalopi Enterprises. Sir, the man is involved."

"Why?" Briar asked.

"I do not know, sir," Jenner answered honestly.

"Arrest him," Briar barked. "No publicity. No cameras. Just go and get him. Get a warrant and arrest the son of a bitch. I have to take this to the President." He handed the file to the special agent and nodded a dismissal. Nobody moved. "Go and get the cocksucker! Now!" he shouted. Jenner and her department head literally ran out of the office. Then he picked up the telephone to call the White House.

-122-

September 4, 1994, Berkeley, California

JAKE FOUND A SUPER 8 MOTEL only a few blocks from the red-brick house and checked in, paying cash for two days and registering as Mr. McMurto, Amway salesman. The clerk barely looked at the signature, took the cash, and handed him the key to Room 208. A few moments later, Jake ascended the stairs to his plain little room with brown carpet, brown wallpaper, and brown bedspreads. He turned on the light and sat on the bed to examine what he had taken from the Greek man's house. He figured that the man was Greek from the name on his mail. He had taken all of the correspondence that he could find and two calendars from under magnets on the refrigerator.

From the mail and its contents, Jake discerned that Mr. Onasis owed Citibank Visa $2034.12. His bank statement showed a recurring deposit of $1,212.34 every two weeks, so he made about $35,000 a year. The recurring deposit was from San Jose Water Treatment Plant. Now he knew what SJWTP stood for. His wife had a separate bank account, which indicated that she made more money than her husband and didn't like to mix their money. He read through everything without determining much else of value until he came to the computer-generated calendars.

The calendars were work schedules. Apparently, both husband and wife worked shifts, and this was a way that they could keep track of one another. The man was on a swing shift today and so was his wife. They should both arrive home this evening around midnight. Jake breathed a sigh of relief and looked at his watch—5 P.M. He still had several hours if he needed to go back in. He already thought that he might have to. The calendar also indicated that the wife worked at Cedar View Hospital. *A nurse,* Jake thought.

He picked up the motel telephone and dialed 9 to get an outside line. Then he dialed Lieutenant Allen's office number.

"Lieutenant Allen," he answered.

"This is Jake."

"Yeah, Jake. I've got some info for ya."

"Can you come over and meet me tomorrow to hand it over?"

"Sure, Jake."

Jake gave him the address, thanked him, and hung up.

He replaced the receiver and picked up the phone again. He dialed 9 to get an outside line and dialed collect to the 803 area code.

"Sheriff," Clarence answered the phone.

"Clarence, this is Jake."

"I've been waiting for you to check in, Jake. Geery found out something really important."

"What?"

"Well, that radio you sent us. It's not a radio. It's a radiac."

"A what?"

"A radiac. Something to detect radiation. That little light comes on in the presence of radiation. You know, like nuclear stuff, Jake."

In his brown Super-8 Motel room, Jake's eyes dilated, and he felt the hairs stand up on the back of his neck. "Clarence," he said, "I've got to go. I'll call you back tomorrow." He hung up the phone and ran out of his room, slamming the door shut behind him. He had just "got it," and he was frightened.

-123- *September 4, 1994, Smithsonian Institution, Washington, DC*

"DR. PRUITT," the anthropologist answered the phone.

"Dr. Pruitt! Just who I wanted to talk to. My name is Sergeant Dyer. I work at the National Personnel Record Center in St. Louis."

"Yes," Pruitt's eyes brightened under his graying eyebrows. "What can I do for you?"

"Well, sir, you made a request recently for records. My turn-over log doesn't indicate exactly what you wanted." He paused. "I just took over this job. Anyway, a funny thing happened yesterday. We got a truck full of records from the Vietnam era."

"Interesting," Pruitt commented.

"Yes, sir. These records had been sitting in an outlying building at Clark Air Force Base since the end of the Vietnam War.

When Mount Pinatubo blew in '91, they got sent to Fort Lewis in Washington State. I don't know why. Probably the nearest base to Puget Sound, if the records came on Navy ships. Anyway, now I have a couple thousand more records. If you would let me know what it is that you are looking for, I'll forward anything else that I have."

"Gladly," Dr. Pruitt said. "Are you ready to take notes?"

"Yes, sir."

124   *September 4, 1994, Fox County, South Carolina*

THE TEMPERATURE HAD DROPPED into the lower forties and Geery decided to build a fire in the fireplace. He really didn't need the heat, but he always felt a certain calming action in the presence of fire. As he walked out to his woodpile to pick out a few logs, he thought about the Zen book he had read that had stated, *Before enlightenment, chop wood, carry water. After enlightenment, chop wood, carry water.* He was in a contemplative mood.

One hour later he was sitting in a rocking chair before the fire with the radiac in his lap. He was thinking about what it meant. Orange and red flames reflected off his eyes.

"So, it has finally happened," he said to the fire. "We stole nuclear fire from the gods and now we are going to be chained to the rocks, fifty years later." He had a mental image of Prometheus. He had discerned that the device in his lap was set to light at very low levels of alpha particle emission. That was disturbing to him. This was not a device for measuring gross levels of radiation. It was not made to be used around an operating nuclear reactor or a waste site. It was made to find little helium nuclei, shooting out from an emitter. It is a common myth that weapons-grade plutonium is highly radioactive. It is not. Geery knew this. It just emits tiny helium nuclei, alphas. A layer of aluminum foil would make it undetectable to even this radiac. That was when he decided that he was going to leave the woods and reenter the world, just for a little while.

-125-

September 4, 1994, Berkeley, California

JAKE NOTICED THE "NUCLEAR FREE ZONE" sign with the trefoil symbol as he entered Berkeley. He hadn't seen it the last time. The irony of it was not lost on him as he drove directly to the red-brick house and looked around. There were no lights in the windows and no cars in the drive or in front of the house. Apparently the calendars were accurate. He walked boldly to the front door and removed his Richland County Public Library card from his back pocket. He had already entered the house once, so this was almost a habit by now. There was a deadbolt lock above the doorknob, but Onasis had neglected to lock it as he rushed out of the house for work. Jake squeezed the gray plastic card behind the latch and pulled it forward. He pushed the door open and walked inside, closing it behind him. He felt rushed and decided not to concern himself with secrecy. He turned on the lights and looked around. The box that had been delivered earlier in the day sat in the middle of the living room, off to his right. He approached it and examined it. He reached to his belt and removed his folding Schrade knife, extending it and slicing the clear tape that bound the seam on the top of the box. Opening it, he saw four glass bottles with corks and screw tops lying in styrofoam packing peanuts. Onasis had obviously not opened the box. He had not seen it. The contents of the bottles were fire-engine red. *It looks like Hawaiian Punch*, Jake thought offhandedly.

Leaving the living room, Jake glanced down at his watch. It was 9 P.M. He gave himself two hours, to be conservative. He climbed the stairs and entered the first room on the right. When he flipped on the light, he saw that it was a bedroom. He walked to the closet and was happy to find a wool blanket neatly folded on the top shelf. Taking it, he turned off the light and went downstairs to the box. He removed the bottles carefully, wrapping them in different folds of the blanket to prevent them from coming into contact with one another and risking breakage. Holding his bundle as though it were a child, he walked out of the house and deposited it in the trunk of his car. He returned to turn off the lights and close the door.

He drove out of the neighborhood and looked for a convenience store. "Where is a 7-Eleven when you need one?" Jake muttered to himself. Finally, he noticed a Circle-K across the divider on the left. He made an illegal U-turn and pulled in. Inside the store he bought an emery board, clear packing tape, and four glass bottles of Hawaiian Punch. Several minutes later he had finished stripping the styrofoam labels off the sides of the bottles and had sanded the labels off the tops of the screw caps with the emery board. Uncapping the bottles, he removed the rubber gaskets and scraped off the "collect all four face cards and win a trip to Hawaii" phrases from inside the tops.

One hour later he drove out of the suburban neighborhood for the third time. Inside the living room, the box was resealed with four bottles of red liquid inside.

-126- *September 5, 1994, Smithsonian Institution, Washington, DC*

"DANIEL BROWN RUPERT. Sergeant. United States Army. Special Forces. Jump school at Fort Benning. Three tours in Vietnam, beginning in the early sixties as an adviser. In the late sixties he went in with a unit that was killing whatever they could find on the Ho Chi Min Trail north. In 1969 lost his eye and got his only Purple Heart. Processed out." Special Agent Ersoy looked at Dr. Pruitt. The anthropologist was superimposing two X-rays and squinting at them. Ersoy continued. "His prints were on file, so I ran them through AFIS, just out of curiosity. He came up with a

C flag. So I called Langley. Turns out that he worked in Laos for Civil Air Transport, an Agency proprietary company, hustling guns on the ground for them, but he was fired after only two months. Seems that he liked hemp and Langley frowns on that, so they let him go. Anyway, that may be how he got such a good look at the 727 and knew about that rear ramp."

"Yes, it is definitely the same man," Pruitt said distractedly, as if he had not been listening. "The dental charts are very close, and take a look at this." The anthropologist held the two X-rays up to the fluorescent ceiling light. "The left one is of the one in your crate. The right one is from the hospital in the Philippines. Look at the frontal sinus. See this indentation on the left?" Pruitt pointed above the brow ridge on the left X-ray. "Same thing over here. Sinuses are as individual as fingerprints. They aren't used as much because not everybody has had their skull X-rayed."

Ersoy stared at the negatives. "Well, my hat is off to St. Louis. They came through."

"Oh, it was just chance. If these files had not been lost for twenty years, the X-rays would have been destroyed. The Army destroys medical records and X-rays after six years. I think it cuts down on lawsuits," the anthropologist smiled.

·127·

September 5, 1994, San Francisco, California

THE TAPE SPUN BACKWARD after Andrew hit the button. The machine beeped and then the message came out of the speaker. "Mr. Cassius, uh, this is Mr. Onasis, with the treatment plant. Uh, the supplement has been added to the system." The machine beeped and Andrew placed it before a microphone that was attached to the back of his computer. He played it again, making a digital file of the message for his records. He encrypted it and saved it on-disk along with scanned .gif files of the photographs that he had used to compel Onasis to cooperate. He put the disk in a box on his desk and hit Speed Dial #1 on his phone.

The secretary at Itasco answered. "Itasco Construction, this is Millie. May I help you?"

"Yes, I would like to speak with Aaron, please. This is Mr. Oliver."

"Yes, sir. Please hold while I transfer you, Mr. Oliver," the secretary said brightly.

There was silence on the line for a moment and then the detective picked up. "Hello?"

"Hello, Aaron. It is time for you to clean up the Greek's house."

"Yes, sir," Aaron responded dully as he heard the line go dead. He wasn't certain that he wanted to cross the line that he was about to cross. He had done a lot of things that he would have agreed fell into gray areas, but there wasn't even a speck of gray in what he was about to do. It was squarely in the black, but, then again, so was Aaron's bank account lately. He rose to leave his office.

-128-   *September 5, 1994, The White House, Washington, DC*

THE PRESIDENT SAT in his patent-leather chair before his desk in the Oval Office. A forlorn Charles Briar, Director of the Federal Bureau of Investigation, stood before him. The President had not offered him a seat. Briar was wondering if J. Edgar had ever felt this way.

"So, Charles, what is all of this nonsense about Dawson's being arrested? He has been on board with me since the campaign! This is nonsense!"

"Sir, we have evidence which links him to the conspiracy to assassinate Judge Alvarez . . ."

"Poppycock!" the President interrupted. "You must be joking. Not only is the man not capable of such an act, he simply has not had time. What a bunch of bull! This is some kind of political ploy, Charles. You know that."

The Director bent down to pick up his briefcase. He popped it open and removed a folder. Showing the folder to the President, he walked up to the desk and laid it before the most powerful man in the world. He opened it and pointed to the first page. "This is Mr. Dawson's telephone record, Mr. President."

"Yes?"

"Well, sir, the highlighted entries are calls to and from Jalopi Enterprises and to and from a public telephone in Bogotá, Colombia."

"This proves nothing. Most of these calls are on a calling card. Anybody could have made those calls."

"Sir, the calls correspond to Dawson's movement. For example," Briar turned three pages, "this call was made from the Marriott Hotel in San Francisco. The date corresponds to Dawson's visit to that city for a mayors' conference on your behalf. But there is more, sir."

"Okay, I'm waiting." The President was showing thinly veiled alarm that was ever increasing.

Briar flipped a few more pages over in the folder. "These, sir, are photocopies of canceled checks which Mr. Dawson wrote from his personal account to Jalopi Enterprises. We raided the premises of Jalopi and uncovered detailed records for the assassination of Judge Alvarez and the federal prosecutor. There were also records of a transfer of $100,000 to an account in the Netherlands Antilles for Dawson from a bank in the Bahamas. This bank launders a majority of the cartel's money which comes out of New York. Sir, Dawson is involved, and up to the neck."

The President's face had grown hard and his jaw set. His mind was working in overdrive in an attempt to find a spin on this situation that would not be disastrous for himself and his party. He could not find one. He looked at the Director. "Okay, get to the bottom of it. Is there anything else?"

"Sir, I briefed you several days ago on a suspected plutonium shipment into the United States," Briar said.

"Yes, I recall. The Russian government denies it."

"Yes, sir. The law-enforcement side also has recanted the initial report. In fact, despite the kinder, gentler image that they are showing us, Yuri Gorodov has been removed and reposted. He was the station chief who alerted us to the problem."

"Sounds like the problem is solved, Charles." The President smiled a smile usually reserved for cameras.

Briar was nervous. "Sir, we believe that the initial report was correct. Something has gone missing over there. We believe that the principals involved are Gregor Viktorovich and the Cali cartel. Both of these are very much suppositions, and we have no idea of the intended use of the material."

"Maybe the Colombians want a nuclear narco navy," the President said, laughing.

"What?" Briar asked, and, remembering who he was addressing, added "sir."

"The cartel has subs. Fucking submarines. Got it in a brief this morning from Defense Intelligence. They found one in overhaul in a dry dock by satellite. My joke was that maybe they want to go to nuclear power. Then they could deliver anywhere in the world." The President fell silent.

"Anyway, sir," Briar cleared his throat nervously, "our investigation uncovered a cutout between an unknown party and Viktorovich which was to arrange the exchange of two unknown items. The cutout consisted of a group of Hispanic men trained by someone who impersonated an FBI agent. Several days before we arrested the cutouts, another man impersonating an FBI agent went to speak with the chief executive of Maynard Johnson Tackle and Toys Company. MJTT pays protection and allows shipping space to Viktorovich. The chief executive is a source for the Agency, or so one of my agents has concluded. He reports unusual shipments, particularly weapons, over there. He reported on the special agent. We believe that the two may be connected. The initial report out of Russia, before the denials, implicated Viktorovich's organization."

The President frowned. "So, what you are telling me is that the stuff is here. Is that correct?"

"Well, sir, what I am telling you is that we do not know, but that we have reason to believe that it arrived and was transferred successfully to an unknown party, perhaps the cartel. That is our working model. Drugs for nuclear material in the first transaction, more drugs to follow for a happiness-starved market in the former Soviet Union and Eastern Europe. It breaks the Italian monopoly on cocaine into Russia and Eastern Europe, if it is what we think it is."

"Well," the President breathed deeply, "I don't suppose that you have any good news to tell me."

Briar looked at his feet as if they were of considerable interest, encased in black, plain-toe Florsheim shoes. He replied, "No, sir."

"Thank you," the President said in dismissal.

-129-

September 8, 1994, Berkeley, California

JAKE SAT IN SILENCE outside Onasis's house. The man had rotated back to the day shift, and Jake expected him to be home within the hour. He planned to interview him about who had sent him the box. He was carrying a tiny black .22-caliber Beretta in his coat pocket, just in case he had to get rough. The gun looked like a toy or a gussied-up cigarette lighter, but, with one hollow point in the chamber and seven more in its clip, it had considerable knockdown power for its size. Jake knew that it didn't take a big gun or a big man to intimidate someone. A child could do it with a small gun if he wished. The thought made the long-ago healed exit wound in his back itch, and he reached around to scratch it.

He didn't want to use the gun. He just wanted answers, and he meant to have them tonight, before the man's wife came home.

All he needed to know was who had sent him that box. Once he had that one tiny piece of information, the Greek would never hear from him again. He wanted to get the Big Enchilada, as Federico would have said. If Onasis was the enchilada, he would also never hear from Jake again. He would die.

What Jake did not know was that someone else was already waiting for the Greek. Aaron was not nearly as courteous as Jake. He wasn't waiting outside. He was waiting inside on the sofa in a living room that was growing dark as the sun waned to the west on the opposite side of the house. Earlier in the day, he had made short work of the lock on the front door and entered, wearing white cotton gloves. He had hauled out the television, personal computer, VCR, and Onasis's wife's jewelry box. He had tossed the house in the hopes that the police would write it off to a burglary gone bad. That done, he had served himself several vodka tonics from Onasis's liquor cabinet. He had noticed Jake sitting in the car opposite the house but had thought nothing of it. The curtains were drawn in the living room, so Jake could not see Aaron.

Onasis's car approached and turned into the driveway. The headlights flashed across the front of the house, as he made the turn, and settled on the garage door before the glow dimmed as the man flipped them off. He stepped out and slammed the door shut on the aging blue Audi. For a moment, Jake considered confronting Onasis before he had gotten into his house but dismissed the thought. He would wait for a moment and knock on the front door as soon as some lights had come on inside. He sat and watched. A light came on in the front room, visible through the curtains, and then Jake saw the Greek's silhouette through the window. Another silhouette rose onto the backlit curtain. An arm was raised so that it was parallel with the ground and there was an object in the hand. Jake saw the muzzle flash and then heard the report.

He stepped out of his car and saw a man running out of the door. It was twilight, but Jake could see that he had dark hair. He was wearing a long gray coat and white gloves. It was all the detail that Jake could pick out from the fleeing blur. He gave chase, yelling, "Stop! FBI!"

The man did not stop. He reached the main thoroughfare and ran to the right. Jake turned the corner twenty yards behind him. There were no pedestrians except a wino sitting on the bus-stop bench. The two men raced past him, and the drunk stared at them in wonder. Jake yelled at the man again, "Stop! FBI!" The fleeing man did not even look back. Before he could consider the consequences, Jake drew his pistol from his pocket and quickly sighted down its short barrel, aiming for the middle of the man's back. He fired once and missed. He sighted again and fired. The man stumbled, grabbed his right shoulder, and then resumed running, but a little slower. Jake pocketed the pistol and renewed his chase.

Jake came around the next corner to see his quarry boarding a city bus. As the bus pulled away, he trotted alongside it, banging on the door. The driver stopped and opened it. "Well, git on, if you want it so much!" the large black female driver said with an irritated smile.

Jake stepped in and looked around at the passengers. The man was not there. Aaron had forced open the rear door and had jumped to the curb as Jake scanned the inside of the bus. Jake stepped back out onto the pavement as the driver slammed the door in his face with a sour look. He glanced across the street and saw the murderer getting into the back of a yellow taxi. He chased the cab, but the man just waved at him from the rear window.

Two hours later, the drunk was interviewed by the Berkeley police with regard to the murder of Minos Onasis. He had suffered from "temporary inliquidity," as he put it, and had not been able to purchase a bottle of anything all day. Consequently, he was able to describe the chase and the FBI man shooting the fleeing man with extraordinary clarity. The police officers gave each other several sideways glances as they listened but wrote nothing down.

When it was over, they gave the man two dollars each in payment for the entertainment and wished him well.

-130-

September 10, 1994, San Francisco, California

"GOOD EVENING. My name is Rebecca Holly. This is 'Headline News.' " Andrew watched the pretty brunette anchor with intense interest. He was not interested in her smile. He had been waiting and watching all day. They should have gotten his letter yesterday. They would have to tell the public. Every half hour he flipped on the television. He was waiting for his letter to be the lead story.

"Our top story at this hour: the Federal Bureau of Investigation has released the contents of a letter received this morning." A typewritten translation of the letter Andrew wrote filled the screen.

```
We have warned you. Valens must be released. We
have contaminated the water supply of a major
metropolitan area with radioactive plutonium.
When Valens is released, we will disclose the
location.
```

The screen returned to the anchor. A sketch of a masked terrorist appeared above her left shoulder. "The FBI believes that the organization responsible is the Revolutionary Armed Forces of Colombia, or the FARC. They also believe that this same organization was responsible for the assassination of Federal Judge Maria Alvarez and the attempt on the life of Federal Prosecutor James McAdams. The Environmental Protection Agency is working around the clock examining water samples from every major system in the nation but urges consumers to purchase bottled water distributed prior to August 30. The President, currently returning from Camp David, has issued an executive order directing all bottlers, distribution centers, and retailers to affix tamper-proof seals and date stamps to water in stock prior to August 30. Brian Spitz is on location with Dr. Avery Stewart at Livermore Laboratories." The image shifted to two men standing next to the Livermore front gate. One was holding the microphone.

"This is Brian Spitz. I am at the Lawrence Livermore Laboratories with Dr. Avery Stewart. Dr. Stewart, could you please describe the severity of this terrorist threat?"

Dr. Stewart looked nervously at the camera and then eyed the ground, showing a balding head to the lens while he spoke. "Plutonium is not an extremely radioactive element. It only emits alpha particles. Outside the body, a person could be protected by several sheets of paper or a wrap of aluminum. Inside the body is different. If ingested, the element is specifically absorbed by bone marrow in humans. Because it emits alpha particles at a high rate, it is a very dangerous radiological poison." The scientist stopped speaking.

"So, this threat should be taken seriously?" the reporter asked.

"Oh, yes. This is serious," the scientist added.

"At what levels is the poison likely to be fatal?"

Stewart coughed into a raised fist. "The effect is cumulative. A single ingestion at a low level may not cause irreparable harm, but several doses at a low level build up. It does not go away until it disintegrates by radioactive decay. The International Committee on Radiological Protection set the maximum allowable level of plutonium in the body at 0.04 microcuries."

"How long does it take to disintegrate?" the reporter asked.

"Twenty-three thousand years," Stewart replied.

Andrew switched off the television. "The President must react. He must," he said to the dark screen.

-131-

September 10, 1994, Berkeley, California

SINCE PONYTAILS ON MEN are not unusual in Berkeley, the Kinko's clerk barely noticed Jake as he sat, brows furrowed in thought, before the IBM computer in the corner and tapped at the keyboard cautiously. Jake didn't own a computer and was not familiar with word processing, so this letter was taking him a long time to write. He wasn't certain who to send it to but figured that the CIA would take care of it. He had found an address in the *World Almanac and Book of Facts* at the library. After about an hour at the machine, he consulted the reference manual on the word-processing program and pressed shift-F7 reluctantly, hoping that the obscure command would not erase the letter he had worked so long and hard to compose. It did not. The laser printer to his right hummed to life, and the letter appeared in the tray.

Jake slipped on the white cotton gloves that he had purchased at the Army-Navy Store down the street and lifted the letter gingerly out of the printer. He had gotten the idea from a "Scarecrow and Mrs. King" episode he had seen on the television in his motel room immediately prior to the ABC News flash about the plutonium. With the gloves on, he inserted the letter into the priority mailer that he had purchased for $2.90 at the post office. He had only handled this with the gloves on as well. He sealed it and walked to the counter. The computer time had cost him four dollars, and the printout, fifty cents. The clerk noticed the white gloves as Jake counted out the change but said nothing. It was Berkeley, and if a guy wanted to walk around with sissy white gloves, that was his business.

Jake posted the letter at the mailbox immediately outside the Kinko's store and stuffed the gloves in his back pocket as he walked back down the street to the Super 8.

·132·   *September 10, 1994, Federal Courthouse, Washington, DC*

THE CAMERAS WHIRRED, and flashes illuminated the courthouse steps like a bombardment as Ronald Dawson, former senator from

California and aide to the President of the United States, descended them. The steps seemed to be designed awkwardly for Dawson as he stumbled on his lawyer's arm. It was as if at each step he had to decide whether to take one or two. One and a half would seem to have been his preference.

Raymond Woolard was acting as his lawyer. A flawlessly groomed black man in a custom-tailored gray suit, he walked at Dawson's side, steadying him by the shoulder. He had managed to get Dawson released on a $500,000 bond while awaiting trial. It had been a hard sell, but he had done it. He had argued that Dawson's considerable family wealth and strong connections to the community ensured that he would not flee. Privately, Woolard was not so confident. He knew that the former senator's current disorientation was not solely the result of the trauma of imprisonment. Woolard also knew the signs of withdrawal when he saw them. Dawson had a problem, a chemical problem. It made his lawyer nervous.

The reporters approached in a throng, surrounding the two men. Woolard cleared out a space in front of him with a stiff arm like a fullback. He said only a few words as he hustled Dawson into the waiting Cadillac, but they were recorded on at least a hundred tape recorders and twenty television news cameras. "My client declines to comment on the charges, except to state that he is innocent. We will prove that in court." The lawyer straightened his tie, smiled, and got into the car.

Pulling away from the curb and dodging photographers attempting to get a good shot of Dawson from the street, Woolard turned to his client. "What are you on?"

Dawson didn't acknowledge the question.

Woolard grabbed his shoulder. "Dawson, look at me!" He shook the man. "We aren't going to win this case if you walk into court with a monkey on your back. You got that? This case isn't about conspiracy. It's really about drugs. If you use, you lose. Got that?"

·133·

JAKE SAT CROSS-LEGGED on the bed. By his right knee was a stack of photographs. By his left knee was the list of names, addresses, and models that Lieutenant Allen had given him. With the help of his FBI credentials, he had tracked down the two U-Haul drivers through rental records. They had nothing to do with anything. Both local men, they had been pulled out of the union hall at Mare Island and paid cash to pick up unspecified merchandise and deliver it. One had made the run to Los Angeles and had been paid $1000. The other had made the run from Hayward to Berkeley and had been paid $300. They rented the trucks themselves and pocketed the difference. They did not know who employed them. It was another dead end.

After losing the man who killed Onasis, Jake was beginning to feel that he was done. When the Greek died, the last thread was severed. He needed to find another clue. He had already gone through the photographs once, to verify that he hadn't missed a plate number. He hadn't. There was no way he could check the identity of the pedestrians. He had to assume that something lay in the plates. He began to flip through the photos, looking at the car models.

About halfway through the stack, he noticed that the car he had photographed with the California tag KSR756 was a black Ford Taurus SHO. Lieutenant Allen's list identified the car as a Mazda P/U. Odds were that the owner of the Mazda had bought a new car, but there was a chance, albeit a slim one, that the owner had taken a minor precaution. Before driving by to see the 7-Up and Pepsi cans in Federico Martínez's window, he may have switched his plates for a day. He may have done it with someone in his neighborhood. *It is possible*, Jake thought. With the resolve of a man with no other options, he took the address with him and walked out to his car.

-134-

September 13, 1994, San Francisco, California

ANDREW WATCHED the news report, mesmerized. "Good evening. I am Rebecca Holly. This is 'Headline News.' Our top story tonight: Ronald Dawson, the former senator from California, is dead."

Andrew leapt from his chair and threw his arms into the air. "Yes!" He began to clap and sat back down to listen, tapping his feet on the floor excitedly.

The screen had shifted to the image of Dawson being hustled into a car by his lawyer. Andrew caught up with the commentary midway. A male voice was relating the story. "$500,000 bond. Dawson was found hanging from an electrical cord in the basement of his Manassas, Virginia, home. It was apparently suicide."

A stately woman with shoulder-length brown hair, dressed severely in a charcoal full-length dress with a jewel neckline, appeared on the screen. She was artfully dabbing a tear from her left eye and looking at the camera. The caption at the bottom of the screen identified her as Mrs. Dawson. She spoke for the cameras. "The Senator was under a great deal of strain from the false accusations he was besieged with. The family will spare no expense to clear his name." She looked to her right, apparently hearing a comment from that direction that was not picked up by the CNN microphones. She lost her composure. Pointing a finger at the cameras and reporters, she screamed, "It was you that killed him! You! You people hounded him without mercy!" Tears began to stream down her face. She turned and walked away.

Andrew muted the sound on the television and began to laugh. "No, it was me," he said to the screen.

-135-

September 13, 1994, Columbia, South Carolina

THE CLOUDS ROILED the midday sky. It was as dark as night as Gary Geery headed down Route 378 in the rain. Water droplets pelted his clean-shaven head and ran down his face, dripping from his eyebrows to his cheeks as he marched. His aquamarine eyes seemed to glow with their own fire behind the falling liquid. He was wearing a dark olive canvas jacket and olive trousers. On his feet, he wore rust-colored, nylon-topped boots. A black knapsack was tossed over his left shoulder. He didn't seem to notice the puddles as he splashed through them. He had a lot on his mind. His thumb was out, but no cars stopped to pick him up. He didn't expect them to.

On the outskirts of town, he finally approached a convenience store. Entering, he exchanged a ten-dollar bill with a nervous cashier for a roll of quarters. He walked back out into the deluge and stood next to the pay telephone. He fed all of the coins into the phone and listened to them clink into the cash box as water coursed down his arm, soaking the paper wrapper. He dialed a long-distance number.

The call was received by an electronic exchange. The female monotone voice gave no indication of what number he had dialed and instructed him to enter the four-digit extension of the party he wished to reach. His tradecraft was dated and the computerized operator hung up on him before he had decided what to do. He redeposited the quarters into the phone after they fell out as a refund and dialed again. It took him eight attempts at dialing random four-number extensions and being hung up on before he reached the desk of a man named Robert Littlejohn. Littlejohn had fallen from grace quite suddenly in 1987 in the wake of Iran-Contra and was holding down a job in the Office of Training, denied even the privilege of a secretary. Ironically, he too had been stuffed down a hole, just like O'Connel, by his then-superior, James Barrow. The last seven years had embittered the formerly aggressive officer, who was now watching the clock, waiting for his pension. Littlejohn answered the phone lazily, "Extension 7712."

On the other end of the line, Geery began the recitation which had failed to gain any sympathy in the previous seven attempts.

"Yes, this is Gary, from Thompson's Heating and Cooling. I'm working on Mr. Michael O'Connel's heat pump. He told me to call and give him the estimate, but I lost the extension. I know that the State Department is big and all, but could you help me out and transfer me or something?"

Littlejohn thought this over for a moment. This approach was a typical internal security provocation, designed to see who would violate the rules and give information to an unknown party over the phone. *Fuck 'em!* he thought. "Extension 6225," he said, and hung up.

Geery dialed again. When asked for it, he punched in the extension and was transferred to O'Connel's secretary, a lissome brunette named Amy who taught aerobics classes at night. A few moments later she buzzed through on the librarian's intercom and said in a questioning voice, "Sir? There is a Beowulf on line 2? He says that he wants to talk with you?"

A chill ran down O'Connel's spine. The hairs stood up on the back of his neck. The big man's lower lip trembled and he felt a bead of sweat materialize on his brow. He had not heard that name since 1962. He picked up the telephone and hit line 2. "O'Connel."

"Surprised to hear from me, Mike?" Geery asked.

"Yes, Martin, I am. How have you been?" O'Connel could think of nothing else to say. For all he knew, Martin Gore had been rotting in a Cuban prison for thirty years, starved and tortured. What was he supposed to say? *How did you get away?*

"Well, Mike," he said casually, "I have been doing fine since I managed to get my butt off that wretched island."

O'Connel was silent for a moment. "Well, Martin, what can I do for you?" The big man noted the sound of rain in the background. He grabbed his memo pad, wrote "trace this call" on it, ripped off the sheet, and handed it out to Amy. She flew with it down the hall.

"Stop sweating, Mike," Geery said. "I'm not showing up to ask for a gold watch and a retirement check. I'm not even going to come and kill the whole sorry lot of you. I should, but I'm not going to." He paused, and the librarian heard the wind blowing and sheets of rain falling in the background. "Don't bother about tracing this, either. It won't tell you anything. If you are curious, I am in Columbia, South Carolina, and it is raining outside. I won't be here in twenty minutes, so don't bother."

"We aren't tracing this call, Martin," O'Connel lied, noting how easily he did it. The habit of deception dies hard.

"Sure, Mike," Geery said with obvious skepticism. "I'm calling because I am going to do you people a favor and I need some equipment. Have you got a pen?"

"Yes," the librarian answered, not lifting a finger, having already engaged in-line taping of the conversation.

"On the afternoon of the 15th, which is forty-eight hours from now, I am going to leave a rented car unattended at the scenic overlook on Interstate 80, at mile marker 83, Nevada. Don't put any dogs on me. I'll be watching. You won't want to by the time we're done. Got that?"

"Yes," O'Connel said, watching the tape roll.

"I need two ITT hand-held night-vision viewers. I need forty scopolamine-tipped darts on .22-caliber short cartridges and two scopolamine grenades, for use inside a car or van. Give Technical Services a day's work. There may be a few people I don't want to hurt—just night-night for a while," he said.

"Okay," the librarian said, inflecting the response to indicate that he was writing all of this down.

He continued, "I want one .44 magnum Smith & Wesson, because there is one guy at least whose head I'm gonna blow clean off." He paused. "I need two MR-35 punch guns. They are new, built by the frogs, but you guys have never balked at buying new toys before."

"Yes," O'Connel acknowledged.

"The last thing that I need is a Winchester Model 70 custom sharpshooter. Harris bipod. Supersonic silencer and flash suppresser.

Leupold 20x scope. Three hundred rounds of .308-caliber full metal jacket." He paused. "Is Fraser still at 'The Farm'?"

"Dead," O'Connel said.

"What about Barry Wilhelm?" Geery asked.

"Retired," the librarian said, wondering where this was leading. He was beginning to worry whether he had enough tape in the machine.

"Find Wilhelm. I want him to compile the firing data on the Winchester for me. Out to five hundred yards. Tape the ballistics data on the stock, right-hand side."

"Is that all?" O'Connel said. At this point he felt as if he were humoring a madman.

"Yes. I can get the rest."

"You said that you were going to do us a favor, Martin. What would that be?" the librarian asked, in the tone nurses reserve for the insane—soothing, not betraying his knowledge of the other man's madness.

"I'll put it this way, Mike. My bet is that you guys are trying to hunt down some plutonium. Now, you may have your heads up your collective ass, or I may be wrong, or both, but I think I know where it is. I'm going to go get it. If you want it, leave those presents in my trunk on Interstate 80. A few days afterward, you'll receive a telephone call to check the trunk of a car somewhere else, and you'll get your equipment back and the material."

"Please insert eighty-five cents for the next full minute," an operator's voice said. O'Connel heard him hang up the phone.

The librarian hadn't heard about the plutonium, but when you've been around for thirty-four years, you have friends. He began to make some discreet phone calls around the building. He found that while Martin might be crazy, there was a chance that he wasn't. The Agency wasn't quite what it used to be in many respects, and O'Connel was, after all, no longer in the operational side of the house. He ran the library. In Martin's day, the big man could have gotten him everything that he wanted, sent it on an Agency aircraft wherever he desired, and fudged the accounts later.

As things were now, O'Connel called some friends in the civilian sector who knew how to obtain dangerous big-boy toys. Barry Wilhelm and he paced out the range themselves on Wilhelm's farm. The librarian copied the ballistics data lovingly onto a three-by-five card and laminated it to the stock of the Winchester. He took two days off from work and paid for it all out of his own pocket, finally chartering a plane to fly him to Nevada where he personally put the items into Martin's mobile dead drop. It took a lot out of him to accomplish this in the limited time. It was the least he could do for the man he had given to the DGI over a quarter of a century before.

-136-

September 14, 1994, Walnut Creek, California

JAKE ROAMED the house. It was a tiny single-level, one-and-half-bath ranch with two bedrooms. One of the bedrooms contained a computer and a desk; the other bedroom, the bed and closet. In the closet, Jake found the damaged trench coat. *Yes, I have the right guy,* he thought. He walked across the hall and looked at the computer. He didn't want to become involved with another computer after the difficulties he had encountered typing a half-page note. He felt, however, that there might be evidence on that machine, so he carried it out to his car and placed it in the trunk. He entered the house again and brought out every disk that he could find. He remembered Geery and all the computers he had back in the woods. Geery would know how to read all of the stuff that was written in there.

It had taken Jake two days to locate his quarry. He found the Mazda pickup truck on the first evening and noted that it had the correct license plate affixed. This strengthened his belief that the switch had been intentional and that the other car and its owner might be nearby. He had roamed the subdivision for two days without locating the black Ford Taurus from the photograph.

He expanded his search area during the previous evening, moving to adjoining suburban developments and cruising the streets slowly, looking at parked cars. He had even been escorted out of a nearby community by a security service rent-a-cop. Jake was not deterred.

A little after midnight on the previous evening, he had found a black Ford Taurus. Jake didn't know how many similar cars existed, or he would not have felt so confident. The next morning, he sat across the street and watched the owner leave for work. He could not be certain, but he looked a lot like the man who had killed the Greek. That was when Jake decided to add another breaking-and-entering to his list of misdeeds. Finding the bloody trench coat, he elected to add a second burglary as well.

The theft of the computer complete, Jake closed the door and went to his car. He drove back to Berkeley and emptied out the motel room. Continuing on to Walnut Creek, he stopped at a Wal-Mart and purchased a solid wooden baseball bat and fifty feet of nylon rope. He returned to the rancher and re-entered.

Three hours later, standing beside the front door, Jake saw the Taurus pull up. He saw the driver get awkwardly out of the car and grimace as he stood, reaching his left hand over his chest to touch his right shoulder. He walked slowly to the door and Jake tensed as he heard the key inserted in the lock.

As the door turned inward and the man stepped forward, Jake swung the bat as though he were going to knock the man out of the ball park. *This is how it all began,* Jake thought as he struck. Aaron caught the blow in the stomach, below the rib cage, and bent double. Jake raised the bat from the kneeling figure and dealt him a milder blow on the back of the head. Aaron was out cold. Jake glanced out the door to ensure that no one had observed his batting practice and dragged the detective inside, closing the door on the world outside.

When Aaron came to, he was tied to one of the kitchen chairs. One foot was tied to each leg and his arms were bound behind his back. Jake was standing before him, holding the bat halfway up the shaft with his right hand and tapping the palm of his left hand with the tip. "Who are you?" the detective asked.

"Well, I'm more interested in who you are," Jake said, continuing to tap the bat in his hand.

"C'mon. What do you want, buddy? My car? My wallet? Just take it and go, okay?" Aaron tipped his head toward the pocket where his wallet lay. "What's this about?"

"Just think of this as one of those random acts of violence you see on TV."

To begin, Jake gagged him with a dishtowel and smashed both of his feet with the bat, shattering the metatarsals and phalanges in several crunching blows. Aaron's eyes bulged and watered. He strained against his bonds. When the detective had stopped howling into the dishtowel and his cries had subsided to a dull whimper, tears of pain streaking his cheeks, Jake removed the dishtowel and began the questions.

The questions came in rapid succession and Aaron cooperated completely. The detective did not know the full details but sketched around the periphery of a plot so vast that Jake did not fully understand it. It was the first time that Jake had heard of a senator named Dawson. The detective described finding Gregor, finding the cocaine connection, finding a hit man, finding the electronics technician, finding the chemist, finding and killing the Greek. He was the finder. He found what his boss asked for. His boss took it from there. He told Jake his every theory and conjecture about what his boss was doing. Finally, he told Jake who his boss was.

With the interrogation complete, Jake again gagged the detective with a dishtowel. He broke his fingers one at a time, whispering "Diana" into the detective's ear as he snapped one, and "Bud" as he snapped the next. He took the bat and broke the detective's lower legs one at a time. In breaking his left leg, he also broke the chair, and Aaron came crashing to the ground. Mercifully, the investigator passed out. Jake continued to beat the inert body until he grew tired. As his final act, he delivered a crushing blow to the skull and walked out of the house.

Afterward, Jake could not explain to himself what had happened in that house. He was, by nature, a gentle man. He would capture moths that were attempting suicide against the naked bulbs in his shop and ferry them outside into the night. He even swiftly ended the lives of fish that he had caught. In the house, it had been different. He had been cruel, almost demonic—possessed by a fury so great that it overwhelmed him and reached beyond him. With each blow he was holding Diana's limp body in his arms. Each broken bone was allowing Bud to rest easier on the bottom of the lake. He had dropped several notches on the evolutionary ladder, but he had become a god. Two hours later he was standing shoulder-deep in the waters of the bay off the island of Alameda. He was weeping like a child and washing himself with the certain knowledge that part of him would never be clean again.

·137·

September 14, 1994, Central Intelligence Agency,
Langley, Virginia

THE DIRECTOR OF THE Central Intelligence Agency, James Barrow, stared at the letter. He ran his hand nervously over the thinning brown hair which topped his head. His right cheek twitched. His hands trembled slightly as he lifted another cup of coffee to his lips and read it all again. He hit the intercom button. His secretary answered, "Yes, sir?"

"John, could you please have Archives bring up everything in the Sniffer files and call the Director of the FBI. Ask him if he would be willing to meet with me over here at his earliest convenience, but emphasize that . . ." The DCI paused, rethinking what he wanted to do.

"Sir?" his secretary asked.

"John, just get the Sniffer archive. I'll call the Director myself," Barrow said.

"Yes, sir," answered the secretary.

Barrow pulled out the top drawer of his desk and looked at the telephone numbers his predecessor had taped there. He dialed. "Office of the Director, Federal Bureau of Investigation. This is Jamie. How may I help you?"

"Yes, Jamie. My name is James Barrow. I am the Director of Central Intelligence. May I please speak with your boss?"

Jamie looked at the caller ID display and then down at a list of numbers taped on the corner of her desk. "Just one moment, sir," she said.

A moment later, Briar came on the line. "Hello, James, what can I do for you?"

"Well, Chuck, I've received a rather unusual report on my desk about plutonium. I think that we should get together and talk. I would meet you somewhere else, but I intend to show you material that is classified. I would rather that we talk here. It is possible that the big guy is making a mistake over in the war room."

"I will be there in under an hour," Briar said.

Fifty-five minutes later, Charles Briar was ushered into the DCI's office, a blue "No Escort Required" badge dangling from his lapel. Barrow motioned for the FBI chief to take a seat, and he did. Before any words were exchanged, the DCI handed Briar a copy of Jake's letter and said, "Before we start, read this, Chuck."

Briar began to read. His face reflected relief, then concern, then confusion:

Dear Sirs:

I am writing to inform you that terrorists have not poisoned the water supply. I have the material. I intercepted it and intend to turn it over to the U.S. government as soon as I have finished my investigation. I am just an ordinary citizen, but I fear that I cannot give you my identity because you would, no doubt, arrest me. This is what I know. It may help you to accept this letter as something other than a hoax. 1) I know that the plutonium was shipped out of Russia via the Pacific port of Vladivostok. 2) I know that the recipient was a man named

Gregor. 3) I know that Gregor exchanged the plutonium for a crate full of cocaine with persons who he believed were Colombian terrorists. 4) I know that these persons are not terrorists. They are actors. 5) I know that these actors were employed by another party who is, as yet, unknown to me. My only purpose in writing this letter is to allow you to tell the country that it is safe to drink the water.

The DCI watched as Briar read the letter. When the FBI man looked up, Barrow asked, "Well, Chuck, what do you think?"

Briar glanced at the piece of paper again before responding. "I'd like to send this to my special-agent-in-charge in San Francisco, if I might. It tallies in every respect with what our own investigation has unearthed, with the exception that we don't know where the material is. If we are to believe this letter, someone does."

The DCI looked at Briar with a careful, concerned expression on his face. "Chuck, you know what's going on across the river right now, don't you?" He motioned toward the Potomac.

Briar looked down at his feet. "Well, yes. The President of the United States is sitting in the war room with every hawk on the Hill trying to decide whether to invade Colombia and make it a protectorate or just bomb it into the Stone Age. I'm surprised that you aren't there."

"I sent the deputy DCI. I needed to read some of these reports again after I read this letter." He pushed a blue folder over toward Briar. It was stamped in black with the word BIGOT. Ten names were listed underneath the stamp. Briar was not on the list. "I'm going to go and get a cup of coffee, Chuck. I wouldn't know if you read what was in that file while I was gone, would I?"

The DCI left, locking his door behind him. When he came back twenty minutes later, Briar had returned the folder to its original position and was sitting thoughtfully in his chair. He had read every Sniffer report. He did not feel enlightened. In many ways, the information from inside the cartel confused the issue further. He realized, however, that the cartel and Colombia were innocent of any sin against the United States of America. Their guilt was only the complement of the greater guilt of their voracious northern neighbor. They simply provided what the United States demanded: drugs, lots of drugs.

Briar spoke. "So, they didn't do any of it. Not the judge. Not the prosecutor. Not the plutonium. Those are an inside job."

"That is what it looks like to me, but I haven't seen your investigation in San Francisco," the DCI said.

"Our investigation there points in the same direction, but this just adds further weight. Thank you, James," Briar replied.

"I think that we need to go to the other side of the river, Chuck. If we are wrong, they can always invade next month."

-138-

September 14, 1994, Cali, Colombia

EMILIO WALKED QUIETLY onto the concrete deck. Santiago was sipping his customary glass of red Chilean wine and regarding the sunset thoughtfully. Tonight was different from the other nights, however. Santiago had summoned him to come and see the sunset with him. Emilio was nervous. Santiago had not been happy over the last few weeks. He had been particularly displeased by the American strikes that had devastated 30 percent of his production capacity.

"Come and sit, Emilio." Santiago beckoned him to a chair that he had placed next to his. This, too, was new. His boss had never offered him a seat on the deck. Emilio sat down nervously. Santiago spoke again. "Emilio, Emilio, did you know that the American Drug Enforcement Agency arrested Captain Rollins and a Russian named Ivan, who was contacting him today?"

"No, Santiago, I did not."

"Look at the sunset, Emilio." Santiago gestured toward the west. "So beautiful. Red. Orange. Blue-tinted clouds as it descends. It is beautiful, is it not?"

Emilio looked toward the sunset. It *was* beautiful, although he rarely took the time to consider such things. "Yes, Santiago."

"Emilio, did you know that you were the only other person who knew about the arrangement with the Russians?" Santiago ran a finger around the rim of his glass and took a sip. "Did you know that? It was just me and Captain Rollins . . . ," he took another sip of his wine to add a meaningful pause, ". . . and you, Emilio."

Emilio began to sweat. He felt a tingle in his spine. "No, Santiago."

"Emilio, Emilio, I have known that you were working for the Americans ever since you came out of the prison in Nencoona. I have let you live because it is useful for the American Central Intelligence Agency to know certain things about us. It is useful for them to be able to find us to move drugs through Venezuela. It is particularly useful if they know that we are not killing their judges or poisoning their water. Don't you think that kind of knowledge in their hands would be useful, Emilio?"

He could not answer. Any answer would incriminate him. He was sitting before both judge and jury. Nothing could help him.

Santiago continued. "Emilio, the problem is that it seems that you are telling them all of the bad things about us and not the good. They have bombed us and shot missiles into our laboratories. They damaged my operations on the West Coast of the United States." He paused again, sipping his wine. "Emilio, I want you to sit and enjoy the sunset with me. It's your last."

-139-

September 15, 1994, Alameda, California

JAKE DIALED the phone slowly. He had not touched base with Clarence in two days. The last time that he had called, the sheriff had told him that Geery was heading out to help him with the disposal of the plutonium. And the last time he had talked to

Clarence, he had not been a murderer. He was still adjusting to the idea that he had killed a man. It seemed like a dream, something he would wake up from, something that hadn't happened. The whole previous month possessed that quality of the unreal. *Maybe it has all been a dream, all a dream since they hit me with the bat. Maybe I will wake up in a clean white hospital bed with Diana smiling at me*, he thought as he dialed the last three numbers.

"Sheriff," Clarence answered.

"Clarence, this is Jake."

"Jake! I was starting to worry about you. Geery called. He is driving across the Sierra Nevadas as we speak. He will meet you at Pier 91 on the San Francisco side of the bay at 10 P.M. He says that it is along the Embarcadero."

"Okay, Clarence. Got it. Pier 91."

"Jake, I am flying out to help. Pick me up at Oakland International at 10 A.M. tomorrow. I'll meet you at the luggage carousel."

"Okay, Clarence, 10 A.M. Got it."

"Jake? You okay?" Clarence asked.

"Yeah," Jake answered in an unemotional monotone. "Fine."

"You ready to take these greaseballs down, Jake?"

"Yeah," he said, and hung up.

-140-

September 16, 1994, San Francisco, California

DEWITT ARNOLD was a frustrated man. He had run a dictionary check. He had run a phonetic misspelling check. He had run a quotation check with almost every conceivable variation in capitalization, punctuation, or lack thereof. He had run a library check on what he had. He had run an acronym check based on the first letters of 300,000 quotations. It was done. No joy. He had decided that he would run a Spanish dictionary check and had a CD with the data. He just needed to write a program to throw the words into the mix. He decided to keep the random check going.

He logged into the San Jose *Mercury News* computer and down-loaded the Sunday newspaper as he began to write his program. After a few minutes, the download from the *News* was complete, and he logged the existing passphrase test program into that direc-tory. The Sunday edition was now being fed in as possible passphrases.

Thirty minutes later, he had completed the program for the new data and walked over to halt the search. He could not believe his eyes when he saw the words on the screen. PASSWORD AC-CEPTED: Alea iacta est. Dewitt dropped the disk in his hand on the floor and ran to the phone. He dialed the four-digit internal extension for Roy Dobkins.

"Special Agent Dobkins."

"Roy, get your pimply white butt down here! We've got it!" Arnold yelled into the telephone.

"On my way!"

Dobkins ran in three minutes later. Arnold was reading the article that had contained the password. "Look at this, Roy. You know how there's been a lot of hoopla about them finding out who D. B. Cooper was?"

"Yeah. Haven't had time to read much about it. They say that he was shot, right?" Dobkins said.

"Yeah," Arnold nodded, and then added offhandedly, "I should have been an anthropologist. Those guys get all the glory."

"Huh?"

"Never mind," Arnold said. "Anyway, read this real quick, then we'll look at the E-mail."

Associated Press, Manila, the Philippines—The recent discov-ery and identification of the body of D. B. Cooper has stirred some memories in at least one old soldier in the Philippines. Sgt. Edward Taylor, USA, Ret., worked in the machine shop of Clark AFB on loan from the Army from 1969 until 1971. He currently resides in Olongapo, where he owns and man-ages a disco. He distinctly remembers the wounded Green Be-ret, Daniel Brown Rupert (a.k.a. D. B. Cooper), requesting that he engrave the slogan "Alea iacta est" onto the glass eye that he had received in the hospital. The slogan means "the die is cast" and is reputedly what Julius Caesar said prior to crossing the Rubicon and starting a civil war against Pompey. Caesar ultimately became the emperor of the Roman Empire. Sgt. Taylor thought it a brave sentiment and did as the wounded man requested.

"Okay, that's very interesting, but let's read the mail. We may be able to bring in Gregor based on what he replies."

"Right," Arnold agreed, and began to decrypt the messages that Gregor had sent. It was a gold mine. Gregor was more wordy and specific than Cassius. His messages detailed the seizure of the two warheads, including type and mass of plutonium. They described the shipment date, container number, ship name, and port of entry. They gave the backup codes for the exchange, and then the messages stopped.

When Dobkins read the last message, he threw his hands in the air in disgust. "That's what 3:42 meant. Third number on the list, Thursday, 2 P.M. Fuck!" Dobkins looked at his watch. It was 6 P.M. "Well, no reason to get a judge out of bed. We'll get the warrant in the morning and nail the son of a bitch. I was hoping something would point us toward Cassius's identity."

Arnold looked distracted. Something was tickling the back of his mind, something lurking in the cobwebbed sections that housed the Ph.D. in ancient history. He looked up at Roy thoughtfully. "Roy, this is nuts, but here it is. The passphrases might have told us. Just a crazy idea."

"Well, Dewitt, spit it out."

"It's like this, Roy. Caesar said, 'Alea iacta est.' That was when he crossed the Rubicon, like the newspaper story. So, D. B. gets this put on his glass eye. D. B. was apparently shot to death. Well, the passphrase that Cassius assigned to Gregor was 'Thou, too, Brutus?' Caesar said that when he saw Brutus among the conspirators who were about to murder him. Caesar had treated him like a son. Cassius was the name of the leader of the conspiracy."

"Okay," Dobkins said. "So?"

"This is crazy, but there's nothing to lose in trying, right? Maybe Cassius is the guy who shot D. B., a fellow conspirator in the hijacking or something. This isn't the 1930s, Roy. They don't force everyone through a year of Latin. Most people don't even know what 'E pluribus unum' means."

"What?"

"Stick your hand in your pocket, Roy. Pull out a coin. Any coin."

Roy obeyed and withdrew his hand with a shiny 1994 nickel. The profile of Thomas Jefferson looked away from him. He turned it over. On the back it said E PLURIBUS UNUM, MONTICELLO, FIVE CENTS, UNITED STATES OF AMERICA and showed a picture of Monticello. "I'll be damned," Dobkins said.

"What does it mean, Roy?"

"Never thought about it. Never noticed it," the agent confessed.

"I rest my case, Roy. Forty years ago, almost any high-school graduate would have recognized the words 'Alea iacta est,' or 'Veni, vidi, vici' or 'Et tu Brute.' They may not have known what they meant, but they would have recognized them. Remember *Ghostbusters*? When they said, 'We came, we saw, we kicked its ass,' or something along those lines?"

"Yeah, that was funny," the agent said, smiling.

"Well, the people who laughed the hardest at that were the older people, the people who understood the classical reference. 'Veni, vidi, vici.' Caesar said it a long time before Bill Murray."

"So Cassius is old. Is that what you're saying?"

"Well, he could be. Today, a very select group of people understand what that Latin phrase means. It doesn't come up in everyday life. He could be older. He could be a Latin scholar turned to evil ways." Arnold grinned mischievously. "Or, it is just a one-in-a-million chance that he happened upon that eye and built passwords that he could remember around it."

"One in a million," Roy said to himself.

"Anyway, if this is the kind of guy who shoots people in the Cascade Mountains, he may have his prints on file in some out-of-the-way place that isn't on the national computer. Send the print to all the small police departments and sheriff's offices in Oregon and Washington. It's a dumb idea, but why not?" Arnold held his arms apart apologetically.

"Why not?" Dobkins grinned. "You're right. It's a dumb idea, Dewitt, but I can fax the print tonight after I write up a new warrant for Gregor's arrest."

·141·   *September 16, 1994, Oakland California*

GEERY, JAKE, AND CLARENCE lay on the hill overlooking Gregor's Spanish-style house and compound. They had discussed the plan in Jake's motel room all afternoon. Geery and Clarence had been excited, Jake subdued, quiet. He had described what he had observed at Gregor's house and on his reconnaissance of Andrew Oliver's estate without emotion. They had examined Jake's photographs of the compound from two weeks ago. Geery had looked at it all as a commander, Clarence as a soldier, and Jake as a passive observer, a passenger on a through train. Finally, toward the end of the evening, shortly before they were about to leave, Jake had gone to the tiny bathroom to wash his face. When he emerged, Clarence and Geery were sitting on the bed facing him.

"What's wrong, Jake?" Clarence asked.

"Nothing," he replied.

"It seems to me that you don't want to go through with this, Jake," Clarence said, testing the double action of his MR-35.

"Well, I have misgivings. What about the police? Can't the police get them now? We know who all the players are, Clarence," Jake remarked as he looked at his hands, considering what they had done. He told his friends about the man he had murdered in Walnut Creek.

Clarence looked at Geery. Geery looked back at Clarence, who spoke. "Forget it, Jake. He deserved what he got. Jake, listen to me. The way the legal system works is this: Gregor and Oliver have money, lots of money. They have lawyers. When everything has gone through the wash, what would happen is that you would go to jail. The cops or the FBI aren't going to buy an anonymous tip. You saw the FBI pick the Russian up. Where is he now, Jake? Sound asleep in his waterbed, no doubt. They would get off on a technicality. They killed Diana. They killed Bud. Who knows how many other people they've killed? They conspired to poison a city and you have misgivings?" Clarence's anger and disgust were evident.

Geery considered what he had heard. He had killed hundreds of people for less reason, although he had never tortured anyone as Jake had done. He didn't have any qualms about torture, but the need had never arisen. Geery thought of most men as upright animals that were either harmful or not. The harmful ones should be weeded out. He was attempting to empathize with Jake's reluctance, but he could not. So, Geery said what he felt he needed to say to make the operation go through. "Jake," he paused, thinking again. "Tonight, we are the authorities. I am working for the government, just for tonight. Maybe at some time in the future, I can explain it to you. You have thwarted these men. I have been sent to punish them. There are other bad men. New ones are born every day. But these particular bad men will never do this again. That is all. You will not be asked to kill anyone tonight. You just tell me who they are and do what I tell you. Just like the plan." The real authorities, of course, knew nothing about this.

So there they were, lying on the hilltop. Clarence was examining the MR-35 punch gun that Geery had handed him. It was light, apparently made of polymers and aluminum. Clarence tested the action. It was smooth. The shells resembled 12-gauge shotgun shells, but instead of 00 shot, they would propel tear-gas capsules or a 35-mm split hollow rubber ball with the knockdown power of a .38 special at ranges up to twenty-five yards. Clarence had five tear-gas capsule cartridges loaded and five ball shots in his pocket. He was ready.

Geery and Jake were looking through two pairs of $3,000 ITT hand-held night-vision viewers, examining the scene below. The night was bright enough, the lights of the nearby city reflecting off the sky and the moon, so that they could see fairly well without them. With the viewers, they saw the scene as if in broad daylight. The two men were looking at the dirty white van parked across the street from Gregor's house.

"That would be the good guys," Geery observed.

"Just looks like a van to me," Jake said. "When they raided the compound, it was a black one."

"Oh, I think that they may have more than one van in the inventory, Jake." Geery reached over and adjusted a knob on Jake's viewer. "Look now. See the little bit of red light peeping out the door there?"

"Yes."

"Well, that allows them to keep their night vision while still being able to see the dials and meters on their electronic gizmos," Geery said. "Well, we have to take them out, for a little while." He scanned the street once more. "They are all in the van. Good." He reached into his knapsack and handed Jake a scopolamine grenade. "Just like the plan, Jake. Go!" He turned to Clarence and nodded for the sheriff to go with him.

As Clarence and Jake descended the hill toward the FBI surveillance van, Geery removed his sniping rifle from its case and set it up. He flipped up the covers on the scope and sighted into the courtyard of Gregor's house, adjusting the rifle on its bipod. He consulted the ballistics data on the stock and adjusted the rear sight. Satisfied, he slid back the bolt of the Winchester, inserted a long, wicked-looking .308 round, and slid the bolt home. He spread a cloth on the ground to the right of the rifle and laid out five additional rounds. He settled into a prone position, allowing his eyes to adjust completely to the available light. It would be a 300-yard shot. Simple. Now, the waiting.

Down on the street, Jake and Clarence approached the van cautiously, slithering on their stomachs across the asphalt. When they reached the door, they both stood. Clarence withdrew a tube from his pocket and laid three one-foot lines of superglue on either side of the door. Jake pulled sections of bicycle tubing out of his back pocket and held them against the glue for thirty seconds. Quietly, they crouched and repeated the procedure on the two front doors. It had been Geery's idea. They only needed to slow the FBI men's exit from the van for a few moments. Clarence looked at Jake, who nodded. The sheriff stood and crashed the butt of his rifle through the passenger window. Jake heard the click of the latch and saw the side doors swing open against the rubber bonds and rebound. He pulled the pin and tossed the scopolamine grenade through the broken window. In a matter of moments, the three agents in the van were unconscious.

Clarence ran to the wall of the compound. Jake followed him. As Geery had instructed them, Jake knelt at the base of the wall, lacing his fingers for the sheriff's foot and boosted him up. On top, Clarence sighted the three windows facing front and fired tear-gas capsules in rapid succession through each of them. He sighted over the house and lobbed two behind the compound. The intended result was to force the occupant of the house into the interior courtyard. Clarence turned the gun over and began stuffing the ball rounds into the weapon.

From the hill, Geery stared through the scope. A gray-haired man in silk pajamas ran into the courtyard, looking disoriented and confused, coughing. Geery sighted at the junction of his neck and head and squeezed the trigger slowly, a conscious effort to allow the discharge of the gun to surprise him. In this way, he knew that the aim was true, that he had not pulled in anticipation. His rifle spat. A .308 with full metal jacket caught Gregor in the windpipe above the Adam's apple and tumbled through him, severing his spine. He fell. "You can always count on Barry Wilhelm," Geery said as he worked the bolt, ejecting the casing and inserting a second round. He scanned the compound outside of the courtyard. Three spotlights clicked on, illuminating two men running toward the front gate. They both had pistols in their hands.

Clarence saw the two armed men approaching the gate and dropped off the wall, back to the outside. He flattened himself along the wall and aimed at the entrance, but he remembered that his weapon was nonlethal and dropped it on the ground. It was intended for the FBI or any other innocent parties that they might encounter. As he reached for his service revolver, he heard the impact of two bullets as they hit the other side of the wall and the sound of bodies falling. There were no more approaching footsteps. He had not heard the shots.

Clarence motioned for Jake to give him a hand up. The sheriff peeked over the top and then pulled himself up the rest of the way. There were two men lying dead on the ground, blood pooling around their heads and necks. They were sprawling, outstretched almost comically, with their pistols lying next to them like toys. They would be nothing but chalk outlines within twenty-four hours. The sheriff would never know that their names were Andrei Borovoy and Constantine Zharkov. They had once posed as tourists in Clarence's county. The sheriff dropped back down outside the compound. Geery appeared with his knapsack and rifle case. "Let's go!" he said, pointing toward the car. The three men walked briskly to Jake's rented Ford Escort.

It was so easy, so easy, Jake was thinking. *Is it supposed to be this easy?*

"Even real live Mafia don't really know shit about physical security," Geery observed, as if reading his mind. "I bet that the inside of that house was packed with motion sensors. There are motion sensors on the lights that pointed out the two fleeing banditos for me." Geery tapped his head. "Don't ever go inside if you can get them from the outside."

Jake nodded.

·142·

September 16, 1994, FBI Regional Office,
San Francisco, California

IT WAS CLOSE to midnight. Dewitt Arnold remained at his computer. It seemed anticlimactic. He had solved the riddle, found the passphrase. They had read the unreadable. The Russian was in the bag. They now had the evidence to make the indictment stick through to a conviction. But that was not the point. Cassius was the point. Cassius had done this, and they still did not know who he was. Arnold read all of the decrypted messages again, scrolling the screen. All he could come up with was that crazy theory he had given to Roy. He could look at these messages until he received an engraved invitation to an ice-skating party in Hell and they wouldn't tell him anything new. He flipped off the monitor. His phone rang.

"Arnold," he answered in a subdued voice.

"Dewitt, you are a genius and a guru! I fall humbly on my knees at your feet!" Dobkins's voice sang through the line.

"What did I do?" Arnold asked, genuinely mystified.

"We got an ID, Dewitt! We got an ID! I'm calling in a team right now and waking up Judge Erwin to get the warrant. We are driving over to nail Cassius!"

"You mean that I was right . . . you know, about the Latin?"

"I don't know, Dewitt, but it doesn't matter. A deputy in Cowlitz County, Washington, called me back. They aren't on AFIS. He pulled night shift at the drunk tank and decided to start looking at thumbs since he didn't have anything else to do. He faxed me the print and the arrest photo. It's the guy the actors described. Dead on, but younger. His name is Andrew Lloyd Oliver."

·143·

September 16, 1994, San Francisco, California

GEERY, CLARENCE, AND JAKE sat outside Andrew Oliver's two-story, Tudor-style house. Set back from the street in a nice suburban neighborhood, it was located near the rear of a four-acre stretch of well-manicured lawn. In security terms, Gregor's estate was a "hard" target, physically secure. Walls. Guns. Guards. Andrew's estate was what would be termed a "soft" target. It had no walls to scale or guards to eliminate. Andrew's security was based on safe information. His walls were encryption algorithms. His guns were information. His guards were passphrases. The three men outside could not know this.

Geery surveyed the house through the night-vision binoculars. Jake had described it for him, but the information had not been as complete as that on Gregor's. There had been no photos of this house, for example. Also, it did not reveal many secrets about its interior from the outside. There was a chimney, the only landmark. Gregor's sprawling Spanish home had told all to a viewer from the hills. Looking up at the Tudor house revealed nothing.

Geery stood and began to pace back and forth on the sidewalk, muttering. "Not good, not good. Not good to go in. We don't even know how many people are in there." He looked at Jake accusingly.

"I told you all I know, Gary."

"What do you think, Clarence?" Geery asked.

Clarence put down the ITT viewer. "Don't see any movement in the house at all. There are a couple of lights on poles. They've got motion sensors. I can't see a way to a door or window that won't turn on a light. Nothing else. Probably a standard burglar alarm inside. House that big probably has auto dial on the alarm to the local PD."

"I think that we should watch it for a day. Maybe get the guy when he goes to work," Geery said.

"How about I go and ring the doorbell?" Jake suggested. Both men looked at him as if he were mad. "We don't want to kill this guy." The other men's expressions turned hostile, and Jake hastened to add, "Well, at least not right off. We don't know why he did it. Don't you want to know why he did it?" Geery and Clarence exchanged glances and looked back at Jake. "What if I just go up to the door and ring the bell? I'll tell him that I was a business associate of Aaron's. I'll tell him that I have Aaron's files and that I need to talk to him. I don't know what's in the detective's files, but Oliver doesn't either, I expect. He won't call the cops on me, not when he's basically gotten away with this. I'll find out why, and then you can get him in the morning when he backs out of the driveway."

Geery began to shake his head. "Foolish, foolish!"

"I want to talk to him, Gary," Jake said urgently.

"Jacob in the lion's den. I'm against it," Geery argued, but motioned with his hand for Jake to go if he insisted.

Jake walked alone across what seemed to be several football fields of manicured grass. Four spotlights automatically lit his path when he reached a point twenty yards from the house. Clarence had been correct. He strode determinedly up the three brick steps onto the landing for the front door. As he stepped onto the landing, the front door was lit as well. It was solid oak, checkered with indented squares. Narrow stained-glass windows of a random pattern framed the door on either side. Jake pressed the doorbell. It rang like a clock tower inside, deep and reverberating. Dong. Dong. Dong. Dong.

He stood there nervously for a few minutes, hearing nothing. Finally, a voice came through the glass on the right. "What do you want?"

"Mr. Oliver, I am a friend of Aaron's. We need to talk."

"Aaron is dead. We have nothing to talk about."

"I have his files, Mr. Oliver. We need to talk."

"Wait there," the voice said.

Jake heard nothing. Clarence and Geery saw what was happening clearly, however. A man vaulted quietly over the railing of a ground-level porch on the left side of the house. He was carrying a pistol in his hand. Geery flipped up the caps on his scope and sighted. Clarence gently placed a hand over the end of the scope. "Gary, I know that you can take him. Jake's a little different kind of man than me or you. He attaches meaning to things, you know. For us, this is over when you take him down. For Jake, it's over when he knows why. Okay?" Geery sighed and shrugged his shoulders, indicating his disinclination to delay action, and relaxed.

The next thing that Jake heard was a voice from behind him: "Hands in the air. Turn around slowly." He obeyed. A pale man with thin whitish-blond hair approached him, a snub-nosed .38 in his right hand. "Turn back around. Against the wall. There." Andrew pointed. Jake stood facing the wall as the man patted him down with one hand while the other held the barrel in the small of Jake's back. "Okay, keep your hands in the air and walk off the porch. Turn right." He marched Jake around to the back of the house to a terrace that led onto two sliding-glass rear doors. The man directed Jake to open one of them. They entered into a sunken living room with a stately fireplace set off to the right. An overstuffed black leather couch sat directly across the room from the fireplace. The farthest wall was lined with oak built-in bookshelves. A rectangular glass-inlaid cocktail table occupied the space between the couch and the hearth. A black leather recliner was next to the fireplace. A brass lamp standing on an oak end table lit the room.

"Sit on the couch," Andrew ordered. Jake obeyed. When he was seated, Andrew backed into the recliner and sat, training the gun on Jake. "So, what do we have to talk about, Mr. . . . ? I'm afraid I missed your name."

"Jake."

"Mr. Jake, what do we have to talk about?"

"Mr. Oliver, I know about the plutonium. In fact, I have it. Onasis never put it in the water system."

Oliver said nothing. He gave Jake a poker face, showing no surprise, but his clear blue eyes scrutinized the other man, searching for a motive. "What in the world would I have to do with plutonium?" Oliver finally asked. He had decided that denial was the best approach.

Jake sighed and looked at his hands. "Mr. Oliver, I'll tell you what I know. I know that three guys hit me with a baseball bat and tied me to a concrete block and dropped me in 150 feet of water. I know that one or more men killed those three and killed my fiancée." He paused. *Fiancée. I never called you that before.* "And one of my friends. They were all killed over a box, or what was in it. I know that this box came from Vladivostok. I know that it went to a Russian guy in Oakland. I know that he traded it with some actors who were told to impersonate terrorists. I know that the trade went down. I know that a man in Hayward dissolved the little metal ball into liquid. I saw it delivered to Onasis, who works in the water treatment plant. I stole it from there. I watched your man kill Onasis. I killed your man." He fell silent. His gaze dropped again to his hands.

Andrew's expression became wary. He simply stared at the other man for almost a full minute before speaking. "What do you want? Money? A job?"

"No, nothing like that," Jake said, not meeting the other man's eyes.

"What, then? What do you want?"

"I just want to know *why*, Mr. Oliver. I just want to know why." He said it slowly, with a palpable sadness, finally lifting his face to meet the other man's gaze.

Andrew had rarely seen such an open-faced, ingenuous man. He appeared to be bereft of any ulterior motive. "What would I get in return for the 'why,' Mr. Jake?"

"I will walk out of here and you will never see or hear from me again. I will destroy the records that your detective kept. I will turn over the plutonium to the government." He looked up at Oliver and said candidly, "I will take away with me the two men sitting across the street with a sniper rifle. We came here to kill you. We already killed the Russian."

Jake said these words with such sincerity and directness that it was impossible for Andrew to confuse them with a threat. They were only the facts. *The man wants to know why,* Oliver thought.

He ran his scarred left hand through his hair, composing his answer. "Mr. Jake, I am a wealthy man. My annual income is seven figures. My liquid assets, eight figures. My material assets, eight figures." Andrew paused and looked down at the gun. He stood and gave Jake a world-weary look before he turned his back and placed the weapon on the mantel beside a framed picture. "I am filthy stinkin' rich!" he screamed into the chimney stones while pounding out the rhythm of these words on the rocks. His sudden outburst startled Jake. Then Oliver's voice became hushed, quite abruptly, and he said, "And it didn't make any difference at all." When he turned around, he appeared unruffled again, but Jake could see that his eyes were now covered with a thin film of tears. He sat down again in his chair, leaving the gun where it lay. "No point in that," Andrew said, motioning with his head toward the .38, "if your friends are outside waiting to kill me as you say." He rubbed both of his eyes with the palms of his hands as if suddenly fatigued, and leaned back in his chair. "Even if they're not," he muttered indifferently. He exhaled heavily and returned his hands to his lap, turning a probing gaze to Jake. His expression became circumspect. "You are not a rich man, are you, Mr. Jake?"

"No."

"But you are not poor, either. I mean, you have never been, in your life, a poor man, have you? I mean, not able to pay your bills, buy food, give your mother a Christmas present?"

"No, not really," Jake replied honestly.

"Let me tell you something, Mr. Jake. When you are a poor man, really and truly penniless, you look at the rich and think that if you had their money you could do anything." His tone was subdued, but he placed a gravelly emphasis on the last word. Andrew's voice became more forceful. "You wonder at their petty concerns and cannot understand why they are not happy." He reflected for a moment before continuing. "But, if you work hard and are single-minded, you, too, can become wealthy." He pointed a finger at Jake for emphasis and then his voice became strident.

"Then you begin to realize that there are some things, Mr. Jake, that money cannot buy."

Jake only nodded his head in assent. This seemed to irritate Andrew, who stood up abruptly and walked back over to the hearth. He picked up the picture frame and examined its contents before continuing in a sharp tone. "I am not talking about some bullshit trite little saying like 'money can't buy you love.' Plenty more people love you when you have money. You just don't love any more of them." This comment seemed to sadden him and he fell silent, gently replacing the photograph on the mantel. His voice dropped again. "No, I am talking about more concrete things. Do you understand, Mr. Jake?"

"I think so."

"Well, I needed them. The things that I could not buy. There was only one thing in this world that I cared about." Andrew picked up the frame from the mantelpiece and handed it to Jake. It contained a color photograph of a lovely, smiling young woman. She was wearing a tight-fitting riding habit and standing beside a bay gelding. She held a helmet in one hand and a riding crop in the other. Unruly blonde hair tumbled over her shoulders as if she had just shaken it out of the helmet.

"She is beautiful," Jake commented, looking at her exquisite face for a few moments.

"That is, or was, Corinne, my only daughter. A powerful man in Washington gave her cocaine. She died in his bed." Andrew paused. Jake tried to reconcile the beauty in the photograph with death. Diana was the same. He could not see the memories and the coffin at the same time. "I wanted to hurt the men who had done this to my baby, Mr. Jake. I wanted them to pay, but there are things that even ten million dollars cannot buy. They cannot buy missiles and ships and aircraft to strike at the heart of the production of the poison. They can buy the death of a man, but they cannot unveil his deceit and secure his humiliation and degradation before the public. You can pay a man to kill another man. You can rarely pay a man to commit suicide."

Jake listened carefully, trying to make sense of the rambling, disjointed sentences presented to him. Andrew continued. "To do all those things, Mr. Jake, it takes more than money. It takes brains. It takes will. Then, it takes money. It cost me $1.5 million and some change. Do you know what I got for that money?"

"No," Jake said, finally feeling a red tide of anger building within him. "Except for four bottles of red liquid."

"I got peace of mind, Mr. Jake. Peace. For $1.5 million I brought down a powerful and corrupt man. I brought him to his knees, publicly humiliated and dead by his own hand. I got two military strikes against the narcotics cartels. Each one of the Tomahawk missiles sent into the laboratories and fields cost over a million dollars, Mr. Jake. If I do not miss my mark, I have secured an invasion of Colombia. Thousands of American soldiers will hunt down the traffickers like animals. Even without any more retaliation by the government, my return on my investment has been phenomenal." Andrew shook a fist in the air for emphasis.

"What about all the people who would have died from the poison?" Jake asked, struggling now to keep his voice calm.

"Stalin killed twenty million. Hitler killed almost as many. Their ends were evil. My end was good. A couple of thousand people is a small price to pay. No great end has ever been achieved without the shedding of blood, Mr. Jake. Not one. Read your history."

Jake stared at Andrew for several long moments, trying to memorize his face. He looked into his eyes, hunting for a spark of insanity, searching for any justification to betray his promise. He hoped to detect the aura of a rabid animal that needed to be killed. He wanted to see an element in the man that would justify shooting him when he walked out for the morning paper or drove to the grocery store. He saw none of that. What he saw was nothing more than an ordinary middle-aged man with stringy blond hair, a man who was average, common, typical, and mundane to the extreme. *He did it all out of love,* Jake thought, *just like I crushed a man's skull for love.*

Jake shifted on the couch and took out his wallet. He opened it and pulled out a ragged-edged color photograph. He looked at it, and a sad, nostalgic half-smile crept onto his face. It was of Diana, red hair loose and streaming down her back. She was wearing slacks and a bright green blouse, holding a green beer in her hand. Her green eyes twinkled underneath a green party hat. Two years ago they had gone to Five Points for St. Patrick's Day. Jake stood up and walked over to Oliver. He handed him the picture. "What about me?" he asked, stumbling awkwardly over the words, his throat tight and tongue heavy from the effort to keep the tears at bay. "What about her, Mr. Oliver?" Jake said, "This is Diana. I loved her. You killed her. I want you to look at her and tell me that the end justifies the means."

Oliver said nothing. He looked at the red-haired woman and then glanced up at Corinne on the mantelpiece. He grasped the bridge of his nose between thumb and forefinger, lowering his head and closing his eyes. Jake heard him inhale two quick breaths through his nostrils. Andrew sat motionless for a long time before he coughed, raised his head, and opened misty eyes. After a few moments, he handed the picture back to Jake.

Jake would never know if Oliver felt any lasting remorse, but at that moment he saw a change in the man. Confronted with a real and innocent victim, Andrew seemed to shrink. The abstract righteousness of his actions could not sustain him. His face had the look of an evangelical preacher who, in midsentence from the pulpit, realizes that he does not believe in God and is immediately brought to his knees by the shame of his hypocrisy. "But what about *her*?" Jake repeated hoarsely as he replaced the picture in his wallet. "What about her?" Oliver said nothing. Jake turned to walk out the glass doors. Andrew made no move to stop him.

The three men did not speak as they drove out of the neighborhood. Geery had obviously been reluctant to pack his gear, but Jake had insisted. "Three is enough for tonight, Gary," he had said. "I made a promise." Three separate sets of thoughts filled the silence in the car as it rolled down suburban streets. Geery was

considering dropping the other two off at the airport and returning to finish the job. Clarence was thinking about his former wife.
Jake was putting the story together, attempting to fathom cause
and effect and purpose, incorporating what he had learned in the
sunken living room before the cold hearth.

They had not traveled far when they were passed by three
vehicles going in the other direction. A panel van and two large,
four-door cars sped down the lane. They were all painted black.
Jake turned his head to watch and thought that he might have
seen men urgently talking to one another on hand-held radios. It
could have been his imagination.

144   *October 1, 1994, Fox County, South Carolina*

JAKE SLOWLY DROVE into town. He was returning from a big tackle
store on Assembly Street. He had stopped at Cromer's to pick up
some peanuts for Joe. He also had stopped to buy flowers. Passing
by the enormous sign that announced the birthplace of Leroy
Johnson, he noticed that the mockingbird sign had been taken
down. Diana's shop had been boarded over with plywood. Instead
of continuing straight to the tackle store, however, Jake took a left
and drove up into the hills, toward the Baptist church. Next to the
church was a graveyard, Diana's resting place. He had not yet been
to the gravesite. His only glimpse of the burial ceremony had
been from the woods when her casket had been lowered. He had
not yet acknowledged her death. Being here now was his concession, his assent. He would place the flowers on her grave and nod
his head at death, knowing that she was gone forever. He would
say good-bye. He pulled his pickup into the red clay and gravel
parking lot of the church and came to a halt. As he got out, he
noticed that the sky was clear blue and beautiful. It was cool outside. He smelled the pungent sweetness of fallen leaves and pine-
wood smoke in the air. It was a day that Diana would have liked.

Autumn leaves and brown pine needles crunched underfoot as he made his way to her grave. He stepped carefully in the poorly marked, jumbled country cemetery. It was over two hundred years old. He finally found Diana's headstone. Her name and the years of her life were engraved above a generic flourish in the light gray granite. Below it were engraved words that seemed familiar to Jake. He felt that she somehow had reached out from beyond the grave to give him her simple answer to his complex question. He never went to the cemetery again, but he never forgot the words on her headstone. Jake found in them the meaning for his life:

And you learn and you learn,
With every goodbye, you learn.

-145-

MICHAEL O'CONNEL was feeling old and tired as he left work that evening. He stopped on his way out and gazed for several minutes at the stars carved into the marble of the lobby wall. Each represented a CIA officer who had died in the line of duty. This secret memorial was a somber place. No names were displayed, for a clandestine life also requires a veil in death. O'Connel knew a few of the men who were on that wall. He now knew that one of those stars was still walking around.

Martin Gore had hung up the phone before Amy managed to get Technical Services to run the trace. Consequently, the only evidence of Martin's existence was the tape from the librarian's on-line recorder. He did what he thought was the only decent thing. He told Technical Services that the trace had been a mistake, someone playing a hoax, and then he destroyed the recording. Martin's star would remain where it was.

Odd, he thought, *to have my first operational assignment end this way, three decades after it started. Things were so different back then, weren't they, Martin?* Gore was the first agent that the big man had run. O'Connel touched his nose and chuckled inwardly. *For one thing, the old schnoz was only broken in one place when I met you.* His mind wandered back. He was a young man then, barely out of college and fresh from "The Farm," ready to set the world on fire. Controlling SOD operations in those days was as close to the front lines as he could get in the actual shooting war with communism. Korea was over, and no one had yet tossed the gasoline on the Vietnamese tinderbox. A boxer in college, big and pugnacious, O'Connel had been pegged early in his training to go to Covert Action Staff. He was glad to be there.

Back then, his obedience had been absolute. He viewed his seniors and the DCI as if they possessed a godlike aura and infinite intelligence. It was only later that he learned that most of them were just tired old men viewing an insane world in the framework of a worn-out paradigm. In their time, they had been authentic heroes, the genuine article, OSS-era men, schooled by the acknowledged spymasters of the world—the British, of course— and veterans of a war against the greatest evil that man had yet seen. A still greater evil reared its head, and these same old men were still ordering operations into the late 1960s that were tired retreads of midnight jumps into Nazi Germany. The amazing thing was not that so many of these ill-conceived plans had failed, but that so many had succeeded. It was a testament to the human will to make a square peg fit in a round hole. *It was people like you, Martin,* O'Connel thought.

With age and seniority, his own limitations had begun to dawn on him. One morning he woke up and realized that *he* was the men who had ordered him to sacrifice Martin Gore. They had not been wise. They were just like him. When he had been told to order his agent into the hands of the DGI for violating his visibility parameters, he did it and assumed that it was right. He assumed that it was necessary to advance the cause. He later learned that it was necessary to spare John F. Kennedy an embarrassment. *Martin, I wish you knew that I regretted what we did to you long before you called my office. I never again broke faith with another operator. I wish that you knew that, too.* O'Connel turned to walk out into the night.

Martin had kept faith with O'Connel. He delivered the liquid plutonium in a box to the lobby of the San Francisco Office of the Federal Bureau of Investigation, 450 First Street, and called the librarian. O'Connel called the FBI. He would like to have seen the chaos in the lobby when the contents of the box were made known. Gore left the weapons in three lockers at the Greyhound bus station in Oakland and mailed O'Connel the keys. No one could ever recall seeing the bald man with aquamarine eyes in either place. *You were always like that, weren't you, Martin? So noticeable, individual, and distinct, but invisible, transparent, part of the surroundings. A walking, talking paradox.*

As O'Connel left the building, he looked up at the night sky. Langley's location, away from the lights of the city, afforded him a magnificent view of the stars. He inhaled deeply, feeling the crisp, clean evening air in his nostrils. Revived by the cool air, he began the trek to the parking lot. He stopped by the statue of Nathan Hale and gazed at his face for a moment. "You know, Nate," he said, "if you were half as good as Martin, you might have gotten away with it." He paused long enough for the bronze man to reply. Hearing nothing, he continued, "Well, I've read that you were an honest and honorable man. I guess we need at least one around here to remind us."

·EPILOGUE·

Sergeant Daniel Brown Rupert was laid to rest at Arlington National Cemetery with full military honors. The President, who had been a Special Forces adviser in Vietnam prior to the war, quietly granted Rupert amnesty for air piracy charges to allow the honors. Although there had never been a trial, this was necessary due to a rumble from regulation-thumping pinheads officed in a five-sided building nearby.

Dewitt Arnold was into Andrew Oliver's computer files within minutes after the raid. All of his encryption had been protected by the password engraved on the glass eye in his desk drawer. Oliver had recorded the details of the murder of his brother Todd and D. B. Cooper in great detail in his computerized encrypted journal. On the federal charges stemming from the transportation and possession of a controlled substance with intent to poison a public water supply, Oliver received seven consecutive life terms. He would be eligible for parole after fifteen years, but he still must stand trial in the state of Washington for two counts of first-degree murder. The evidence against him is overwhelming. In all of the proceedings and interrogations thus far, Andrew Oliver has never mentioned the man with the ponytail who came to visit him the night of the arrest. Roy Dobkins showed him the sketch of Jake during one session, and Oliver gave no hint of recognition. Otherwise, he has cooperated fully with the authorities.

The FBI caught up with Chamber in Houston. He had been arrested by the Texas Rangers in connection with several hits in Austin. Hair and Fiber identified one of his turtleneck pullovers as matching the fibers found on the rooftop across from the Miami federal courthouse. If the state of Texas can hold its horses on executing him for crimes committed there, Eddie Smith will face federal charges.

Captain Kukchinko was shot in the Lubyanka Prison outside Moscow. His execution, a single gunshot to the back of the neck, followed immediately after the execution of Viktor Avdoshin and

Yosef Golovkin. The Russians have fallen back into their old ways, demonstrating their paranoiac aversion to airing their dirty laundry in public. There was no public trial, and they deny that they are missing any nuclear material. The ultimate irony for Kukchinko was that after imprisonment for two months, his body had recovered from the delirium of withdrawal and the ravages of abuse. The week preceding his execution was his first period of lucidity in a number of years.

Anne Dawson, widow of the late Senator Dawson, is running for his old seat. Unofficial polls indicate that she may become the next senator from California. Of course, her campaign will have to keep her gallivanting with a thirty-three-year-old dentist tightly under wraps for the bid to succeed.

Following the demise of Gregor, Yuri has taken over as *vory v zakone* of the Dark Path. He is currently enjoying the *dikaya zhizn*, or "high life," in Moscow's Hotel Metropol. He is determined to exact retribution but, as yet, has nothing that would lead Russians into Fox County again. Sources say that he is extending his long arm toward Cali once more.

Domingo Valens was defended ably by the so-called white powder bar in Miami. The federal prosecutor was able to convict him on only one count of possession. He will be returning to Colombia in eleven months. Emilio Sampar was executed, as Santiago Valens promised. The irony is that Sniffer was killed largely due to the Agency's failure to share his product. It is likely that he was doomed either way, however, and no one at Langley has lost much sleep over it. Santiago has not rebuilt the laboratories that were destroyed in the Cauca Valley. He has been busily moving the processing plants to Brazil as quickly as possible. He is currently considering turning himself in to Colombian authorities under a generous plea bargain that would protect his existing wealth.

Thomas Johnson was arrested by the Russian Federal Tax Service on charges of willful evasion. He is imprisoned in Vladivostok. Maynard Johnson's pleas to the State Department have succeeded in drawing the IRS's attention to certain accounts in the Netherlands Antilles. Like son, like father. Langley has denied all contact with Thomas Johnson.

Roy Dobkins received a promotion and will be taking over as special-agent-in-charge in New Orleans. Dewitt Arnold will go with him, as soon as the computer technician finishes testifying at Andrew Oliver's murder trial in Washington State. Roy will have quite a territory in New Orleans. People who think that the nation's captial is corrupt should spend a month in the Big Easy. Roy has kept the sketch of Jake from the Cassius case file and considers that portion of the case still open. He continues to believe that the fake Special Agent Wren was involved in the importation of plutonium.

John Allen attended his retirement party and parted amicably with the OPD. That same afternoon, he called to ask Clarence if Fox County could use a deputy. He will be moving to South Carolina next month.

Clarence is getting back together with Joyce. Before returning to Fox County, he spent two days in Oakland extolling the virtues of the quiet life in South Carolina. She relented, after securing a promise from him that he would quit smoking. All that she had ever wanted was for him to ask her back. It took ten years, but he has done it.

Jake has picked up where he left off: fishing, swimming, learning. For those who might be curious about his gunshot wound and former occupation, his bachelor's degree from Yale was in philosophy. There aren't many positions at major corporations for even a Yale-trained philosopher, so he became a junior-high school-teacher in Washington, DC. He was shot by a drug-dealing eighth-grader whose beeper he had confiscated prior to the beginning of class.

The liquid plutonium was transported to the Barnwell Low-Level Nuclear Processing Facility in South Carolina, where it remains in storage sixty-five miles south of Joe's Bait and Tackle Shoppe.